PRAISE FOR JUDGES

"Lays the foundations [of the *Judge Dredd* universe] perfectly. Each story is quickly devoured, packed with twists and brutal political analogy... it's the rise of fascism, eerily familiar and terrifyingly plausible.

"This is the Justice Department as *The Wire*, and it really works for the stories being told here. Essential reading for fans of Judge Dredd and the Big Meg."

Starburst Magazine

"I found this a hard read... the Judges are so calculated and arrogant, and there's no compassion for the police—who are considered part of the problem.

"And yet I did enjoy it; because it made me feel something, even if it was unpleasant. There were times I had to put it down to process what had happened and what I thought about it. I loved the conflict it caused in me. It's fast-paced and uncompromising, keeping true to the essence of the Judges."

British Fantasy Society

"By the end of the book I was left wanting more: more of this world, more of the political and social changes surrounding the Judge system, more of what was going on outside of this one little town...

"I know Carroll has written other *JUDGES* books and am looking forward to seeing the story continue."

Set the Tape

"After decades of seeing Dredd blow away 'creeps' with little to no regret, it is interesting to see this first generation of Judges dealing with their role as executioners...

"This is mature storytelling, both in terms of narrative structure and themes, and pulls out twists that are both shockingly brutal and grin-inducingly effective. Accessible and rewarding, this deserves to sit on the shelf (virtual or otherwise) of every *2000 AD* reader out there!"

Pop Culture Bandit

"A story that gets a lot done. Strong characterisations, and a gradual reveal of the history of Dredd's world."

James Green

JUDGES

Dedicated to
John Wagner

An Abaddon Books™ Publication
www.abaddonbooks.com
abaddon@rebellion.co.uk

First published in 2020 by Abaddon Books™,
Rebellion Publishing Limited, Riverside House,
Osney Mead, Oxford, OX2 0ES, UK.

10 9 8 7 6 5 4 3 2 1

Creative Director and CEO: Jason Kingsley
Chief Technical Officer: Chris Kingsley
Head of Books and Comics Publishing: Ben Smith
Commissioning Editor: David Thomas Moore
Series Editor: Michael Carroll
Marketing and PR: Hanna Waigh
Design: Sam Gretton, Oz Osborne and Gemma Sheldrake
Cover: Neil Roberts

Based on characters created by John Wagner and Carlos Ezquerra.

ISBN: 978-1-78108-793-0

Printed in Denmark

MICHAEL CARROLL • MAURA MCHUGH •
JOSEPH ELLIOTT-COLEMAN

EDITED BY MICHAEL CARROLL

ABADDON
BOOKS

INTRODUCTION

I'VE BEEN ASKED by my editor David Thomas Moore to pen this introduction to the second omnibus of *Judges* novellas, and I'm more than happy to do so, especially since the bulk of today's work so far has involved scanning old magazine articles for my comics blog and writing an irate diatribe about how narrative is *not* the same thing as exposition, *actually*.

If you've read the first *Judges* omnibus you'll have seen some of the effects of the introduction of Special Prosecutor Eustace Fargo's new, hard-line Department of Justice to the United States of America in the early 2030s.

It all began with *Judge Dredd: Origins* by Dredd's creators John Wagner and Carlos Ezquerra, which—almost thirty years after the character's debut in the British anthology comic *2000 AD*—finally showed us how Dredd's world evolved from our own.

But the stories of the first Judges on the streets are only barely touched upon in *Origins*, so that's where we come in. When designing this series David and I made a conscious decision to focus on the Judges whose names didn't necessarily go down in history. They're not saving the world at every single turn: most of the time they're just doing their jobs, trying to keep the citizens alive and put the perps behind bars.

Or put them in the ground, that's another option. The Judges have the power to dispense instant justice. Someone commits a crime and you as the arresting Judge decide their punishment there and then. No trial. No getting off on a technicality. No appeals. You decide they're getting ten years, they're gonna *serve* ten years, and it starts right now. No, they don't get a phone call.

But in a decaying society punishing the perps isn't always so straightforward, because first you've got to determine the difference between the real criminals and the desperate citizens just trying to survive.

My novella *The Avalanche* kicked off the *Judges* series, with the first batch of Judges arriving in a small Connecticut town—and their first case is the murder of one of their own. George Mann's *Lone Wolf* is a tense procedural thriller in which the Judges have—legally—executed a serial killer on the street only to discover that there's another victim out there somewhere, possibly still alive. And in *When the Light Lay Still* by Charles J. Eskew a cop who has testified against his former partner for the avoidable killing of an innocent signs up to become a Judge.

Response to the series has been amazing, I'm happy to report. And a little bit divisive, too, which is even better. Readers familiar with Judge Dredd and his world will know that there's a huge variety of different types of stories that can be told, so it was important to us not to produce cookie-cutter adventures: all three are very different books.

The positive reaction to *Judges* has also led to a comic-strip spin-off, *Dreadnoughts*, debuting soon (as I write this) in the *Judge Dredd Megazine*, with a script by me and sumptuous art by John Higgins and Sally Jane Hurst.

With this second set of three novellas, we've moved on to the 2040s. The Judges have been established throughout the nation but the old guard are still there, the remnants of the old ways that the Judge system was designed to supplant.

But any citizen of a nation that's been forcibly occupied by another will tell you that the introduction of a new policing system does not—*can* not—ever run smoothly. Same thing applies when a nation's own government decides to tackle crime with a new, uncompromising police force. Those who will suffer most aren't the criminals but the ordinary people. In the short term, at least. But give it time and things *will* get better, that's the promise. It'll be worth it in the end! No pain, no gain, amiright?

In *Psyche*, Maura McHugh introduces a new and very powerful sub-division to the Department of Justice: Psi-Div. If you think the ordinary Judges are tough, wait until you encounter those who can judge you for your crimes before you've even committed them. It's an ingenious and memorable science fiction/horror tale that skips between the 2040s and Dredd's era, a hundred years on.

Joseph Elliott-Coleman's novella *The Patriots* is a tense, often frenetic thriller in which two Judges find themselves facing overwhelming odds in a city that's clearly only hanging on by its splintering fingernails—and the discovery that the Department of Justice isn't the only organisation attempting to rise to power.

My own contribution to this omnibus, *Golgotha*, presents the story of Errol Quon. All she ever wanted was to be a cop, but now the era of ordinary police officers is coming to an end, and she has to learn to cope with being one of the last of their number.

I'm sure you're eager to get stuck in, dear readers, so I won't keep you much longer. But before we part, I'd like to thank Maura and Joseph for their excellent contributions to the world of the Judges, David Thomas Moore for his oversight (that's the *good* kind of oversight, not the negligent kind), the cuddly crew of adorable editorial geniuses at Abaddon and Rebellion, and as always Judge Dredd's wonderful parents John and Carlos.

Next stop... the 2050s!

Michael Carroll
Dublin, January 2020

GOLGOTHA

MICHAEL CARROLL

For the faculty of St. Laurence College,
Loughlinstown, and especially

Mr. Gerry Murtagh

who taught me that every book
needs good characters, an even gooder story,
and the very goodest of writing.

PROLOGUE

St. Christopher, Connecticut
Tuesday, January 4th 2033
17:52

"NIÑO'S GONNA *FLAKE*," Gabriel Drake Nyby told his boss. "He's *not* built for this kind of pressure."

The passenger seat of Romley's Tesla was warm and comfortable, and much as Gabe was afraid of Romley, part of him wanted the conversation to go on longer. It was cold out there and the cops were pissed that one of their own had been shot by a Judge. They were liable to take it out on anyone who crossed them.

A block ahead, the four cop cars parked at awkward angles in front of the main entrance to Mercy South Hospital were tinted orange by the setting winter sun.

Romley pursed his lips. "All Niño has to do is put an end to Officer Chaplin. Once that's done, Chaplin's colleagues will rebel against the Judges. That'll give us time to recover our stock."

Gabe's phone buzzed in his pocket and he dug it out and flipped open the cover. "Aw man... That's not going to happen now." He glanced to the side: Romley was still staring straight ahead, towards the hospital, and as usual wasn't showing any emotion. "Nodge says the Judges've already destroyed the stock. Piled it in the empty lot across from the factory and just torched it. Damn Judges work *fast.*"

"Yes. They do." Romley tapped a rapid beat against the steering wheel with his thumbs. "All right... So in *your* judgement, Niño is not going to be able to go through with it?"

"I doubt it. He's no killer, Mister Romley. I mean, not in cold blood like that."

"Is he still using?"

Gabe hesitated long enough that there was no need to answer.

"I see. I thought so. My own fault for relying on an addict. I should have dealt with him sooner, but he had such good contacts..." More tapping on the steering wheel. "But he's out of our reach now, and out of our control."

Gabe's phone buzzed again. "Aw hell no... Now the senior Judge is on the scene, along with Captain Witcombe. Niño's got no chance now." Another sidelong glance at Romley. "He'll talk, or he'll run. He's not going to be able to stand up to them."

"Okay." Romley continued to stare towards the hospital for a moment, then turned to Gabe. "Mister Nyby... Consider yourself promoted, on the grounds that you do me two small favours. You're unlikely to be able to get to Niño, so forget about him. There are only three others in the organisation who know who I am. You, Francie Hamilton and Merrick Bergin."

Gabe almost flinched at that last name. "Bergin's one of *yours*? We've been in a low-level turf war with him for years!"

"I know."

"Jesus. All the trouble that guy caused us. You know he offed three of—"

"You'll *drop* that subject, Gabriel. You're going to take Hamilton and Bergin out of the picture, permanently. And immediately. Then you'll go west. Chicago at least, preferably further. One way or another Niño Aukins is going to talk to the Judges and we can't stop that. He doesn't know you're working for me, but he'll name you as a friend and that might be all the Judges need to come looking for you. Do you understand?"

"Yeah, but, look, Niño's built a network of contacts over the years. If they can get that out of him—"

"None of them know anything that could lead back to me. So we'll let the Judges have Niño as their prize."

"If you're sure. But I can't just take off and—"

"You're either an asset or a liability. Choose *now*, Gabriel."

"Asset."

"Good. I want Bergin and Hamilton dead tonight. Get to them before the Judges do, and then leave town. I'll find you when I need you."

"Look, I can't just take off. I'm gonna need—"

"Glovebox. Forty thousand. Take it. And if you squander it, or draw the wrong sort of attention with it, I'll find you that much sooner."

"I understand." Gabe popped open the glovebox and pulled out the thick envelope. "Hamilton and Bergin. Two in the head, two in the heart. Not a problem."

"One last thing." Romley reached over and rested his hand lightly on Gabe's arm. "I know you have a four-year-old son you've avoided telling me about. His name is Raphael, chosen to please his mother who has a thing for angels. Which is also one of the reasons she chose *you* as her partner. You're embarrassed about that, so you've told your friends that your son is named after a turtle."

Gabe stopped breathing.

"You didn't tell me because you were scared I'd use him against you." Romley patted Gabe's arm, and smiled. "I was right about you from the start. You *are* a good judge of character. You only see the boy once every couple of weeks anyway. He barely knows you. A clean break really is the best way. And it won't be forever, I'm sure. A few years and things will have settled down enough for you to come back."

"What about my—?" Gabe cut himself off. There was no arguing with Romley. When you went to work for him, he learned everything there was to know about you. Treated you like you were the only one he really trusted just so that you'd trust him in return, until the day you realised that he was doing the same thing with all of his *other* seconds-in-command. Gabe had known about Niño and Hamilton, but that was all. He'd never even suspected that Merrick Bergin was in *anyone's* pocket, let alone Romley's.

"Go," Romley said. "I know I can rely on you to do the right thing, Gabriel. Your son is also relying on you."

Clutching his envelope full of fifty-dollar bills, Gabe climbed out of the car and clicked the door closed behind him.

The Tesla moved away gracefully, the only noise being the hiss of its tyres on the asphalt.

Gabe zipped up his jacket, then stuffed his hands deep into his pockets as he quickly crossed the road. His old Lexus was three blocks down. He knew it had a little over half a tank—enough gas to get him out of the state, but first he had to make two stops.

Hamilton would be easy enough: Gabe and Francie had known each other for nearly thirty years. Not exactly friends, but close enough that he knew she'd open the door to him.

Gabe unlocked his car and climbed in. It started first go, which he took to be a good omen, and he let it idle for a while in the hope that it would warm up.

Francie Hamilton fronted as a respectable woman, in a nice neighbourhood, the sort where the houses still put Christmas wreaths on the door and the local kids loved the winter because they'd make fifteen or twenty bucks for every drive they shovelled.

Gonna have to leave the engine running... a gunshot on that street will bring every neighbour to their windows.

He hoped that it would be Francie herself who answered the door, and not one of her kids.

Getting to Merrick Bergin was going to be a lot tougher. Gabe didn't even know exactly where the man lived—but he knew enough people who did. A couple of them owed him favours. He'd start with them first, then move on up the chain. But it had to be done fast, and without alerting Bergin. Simple rule: if you're gunning for a guy, don't tell him.

Before the night was out, a lot of fingers and teeth would be broken. And families.

Gabe reached under the passenger seat and groped around until his fingertips brushed against his old reliable Sauer Mosquito. The Lexus had been sitting there for so long that the gun was almost too cold to touch.

But it would warm up soon enough.

CHAPTER ONE

Merrion, Mississippi
Thursday, May 5th 2039
14:01

ERROL QUON HAD daydreamed about the graduation ceremony for most of her life. She'd always pictured a bright sunny day. A pool-table-flat lawn covered with perfect rows of wooden chairs occupied by the cadets' proud family members. The cadets in their dress uniforms, crisp creases, polished brass, everything a perfect fit. Beaming smiles as they accepted their certificates. A rousing cheer as they tossed their caps into the air.

That's how they did it in the movies. A ceremony to mark not the end of their training, but the beginning of a new life.

Whenever some friend or relative had been boasting about their kid's wedding costing a fortune, Quon's mother Sharlene always commented, "A wedding is not a marriage." Likewise, a graduation ceremony was not a career. It didn't matter that there was no band, no press photographer, no flags or ribbons. What mattered was the intent.

Eighteen of them started together at the Police Academy in Merrion, a much lower number than in previous years, but that was no surprise. Almost no one wanted to be a police officer any more. Quon's one remaining friend from high school, Jess, had begged her not to join the academy: "What's the *point* of trainin' to be a cop? They're already obsolete. You wanna be a *Judge*, that's the future."

Her own parents agreed. "I know you had your heart set on it, punkin," her father, Nicholas, said, "but you have to face up to the fact that life won't always work out the way you want."

But she'd signed up anyway. She'd always known that being a police officer—especially one of mixed race here in the south—was going to be tough. Old prejudices often ran deep, and with the rise of the Judges, she felt that ordinary cops would be needed more than ever.

On the first day, at orientation, the academy's lecture hall echoed as the tutor read out each cadet's name and details, then he said, "This day ten years ago, this hall was full. One-forty cadets. Now... eighteen." He looked at the students in turn, and to Quon it seemed that he settled on her. "A lot of you aren't going to make it."

He was right. Of the eighteen cadets in her class, four quit in the second week. Three more before the end of the first month.

The others stuck with it, though. At first. But one-by-one, they'd fallen away until only Quon and Milo Visconti remained.

Visconti was exactly a year older than Quon, which they'd discovered during that orientation class. It had given them a reason to talk to each other, and to bond.

Their relationship was intensely physical at first. Frenzied nights of dorm-sneaking and perspiration and giggling and stifled cries of ecstasy, but that aspect quickly faded as appetites and curiosity were slaked. They remained friends, no hard feelings, no recriminations.

Quon thought of it as her first grown-up relationship. Jess had once told her, "You know you're grown up when you can break up with someone and not hide when you see them coming. Though I suppose that might mean maybe you weren't so interested in the first place."

Aside from Jess, Quon had never managed to cultivate any close friends; just people she knew. She was okay with that. People were complicated and didn't stay inside the lines. Jess was a good example. If you wanted her to do something, you just had to tell her that she wasn't allowed to do it. Or that she wasn't *able* to do it.

Opposites attracted; Jess was spontaneous and reckless and dangerous, and Quon was careful and considerate and respectful.

But it was only when she left home for the academy, and no longer had her parents and Jess to act as landmarks, that Errol Quon realised who she really was.

Three months into their training, she told Milo, "Some people live to bend the rules... I like to *straighten* them. Neat rows. Order over chaos. If everyone obeyed the law, we would all be much happier. It's that simple."

He laughed at that, "Yeah, good luck surviving in the real world with *that* attitude, Quon. They're gonna grind you into paste on the first day. I'm not saying we should totally go with the flow, though. I figure we should make the flow go with *us*. You know what I mean?"

"Be the pace-setter, not the follower."

"That's it."

But a month after that, Visconti told her, "I'm done. This job is a dead end, Quon. The Judges are running the show now."

"They made you an offer," Quon said. A statement, not a question.

"Sure did. I'm surprised they haven't talked to you yet."

Her only response was a shrug. Representatives from the Department of Justice had approached her twice, and both times she'd immediately turned them down. She'd never told Visconti about that: much as she liked him, she knew his ego wouldn't respond well to learning that the Judges had favoured her over him.

Visconti was gone within the hour.

The following morning, Captain Deitch called Quon to his office.

She knew what he going to say: it was obvious from the cleared shelves, the packing crates piled up against the wall, and the stack of folders on his desk that he was steadily sorting into two smaller stacks.

"Cadet Errol Quon. With your friend gone you're the last one standing." He gestured towards the packing crates. "Told you last month they were gonna shut us down, and now they have. As of tomorrow morning, the contractors are moving in. Gonna strip the place, remodel it for the Judges. The first Academy of Law in the Magnolia State. Guess we should be kinda proud of that, in a way."

The captain regarded her in silence for about five seconds, then said, "Sorry, kid. We've all been retired or sidelined, so..."

Quon didn't move, didn't change her expression. She'd always been good at keeping her emotions under wraps. But inside she felt like she was standing on the edge of a cliff. "Sir... I request a transfer. To another academy. I think that's within my rights and—"

"Yeah, it's within your rights. But it's not gonna happen. *All* the academies are winding down. They're trying to shed their cadets, not take on more. The Department of Justice cut every goddamn state's police training budget down to near *zero*." The captain picked up the final folder and moved it over the stack on his left, hesitated, seemed to come to a decision, then dropped it onto the other stack. "We have no staff, no money, no academy. Quon, if you don't want to be a Judge, go get yourself a job in a library or something. That'd suit you: they like to keep everything neat and tidy, same as you people."

She raised an eyebrow. "You people?"

He nodded. "Yeah. Well, no, I don't mean you people like... you know I don't give a damn what race someone is, or who they—I mean..."

She knew what he meant. What they always dance around. If you're female and tall, with a strong build and short-cropped hair, the average person will assume you're a lesbian. It suits them to categorise people. Makes things easy. She understood that.

She let him off the hook. "What about you, Captain? You're only, what? Fifty? That's young to retire."

"Not as young as some." He dropped into his chair, leaned back with his fingers interlocked and resting on his chest as he looked around the office. "Nineteen years I've been here. I've seen it *all*, Quon. Good cops, bad cops, clock-watchers and thugs and those goddamn ghouls who want to become a cop because they got a thing for seeing dead bodies. Every kinda weirdo and freak came through those doors and it was my job to knock the rough edges off them, mould them into a shape that'd fit neatly into society. So I can tell when someone's *got* it, and when they haven't. Quon, you've got it. Ten years ago, you would have passed with honours. You'd have made a great cop. Now..." He shrugged. "You seriously never gave any real consideration to joining the Judges? Just say the word and I'll contact Judge Leverett. Give you my highest recommendation."

"I don't want to be a Judge, sir. Just a cop."

He smiled. "That's because you're an idealist, Quon. Your biggest flaw."

She decided to cut him off before he embarked on his 'You want everything to be sunshine and roses' speech. "Yes, sir. You've told me that before. Sir, what do I do now? Are you telling me that I have no choice but to quit?"

"Well, no academy, so, yeah. You kinda *do* have to quit."

She nodded slowly. She'd seen this coming. They all had. When Fargo introduced the Judges, everyone knew that it wouldn't be long before there were no more ordinary police officers. That day was some ways off—there were still a lot of cities where the Judges barely had a presence—but no academies meant no new officers coming down the pipe. That had been one of Visconti's strongest arguments: "You'll be signing on to a ship that's already sinking, Quon."

She still had five weeks to go. If the Judges would just hold off that long, then she'd be a police officer. Sure, in time the Judges would take that away, too, but it would be better to be an obsolete officer than an obsolete cadet.

Captain Deitch gestured towards the door. "Take off, Quon. You're just making this harder on yourself. Clear out your locker and... I was gonna say if you hurry you'll catch the next bus home, but what the hell, it's not like *I've* got anything else to do. I'll drive you."

"Or you could not."

"Meaning?"

"Meaning that the contractors might be coming tomorrow but they won't be doing all the work at once, right? So we'll stay on. You train me. It'll go faster with just one student. We'll work around the builders and decorators, not give them any reason to complain about us still being here. And when we're done—if I pass—you'll give me my commendation and find an assignment for me, just like you would if none of this had happened."

She had more prepared, but the captain jumped to his feet almost immediately.

"All right. Yeah. Let's *do* that. Screw Fargo and his dead-eyed dreadnoughts, pushing us around like we're no better than cold broccoli on a kid's dinner plate." He began rummaging through one of the crates piled against the wall. "Your records are here somewhere... We're gonna finish your training, Quon. You're gonna graduate and become a damn good cop and we'll show those pushy bastards that they've got a long way to go before they can control *us*."

QUON KNEW THAT a lot of other people would have smoothed the path for her, but Captain Deitch had a point to prove to the Judges. He push her hard, personally supervising every minute of her training even as the physical building was being noisily stripped and rebuilt around them.

On the day of her unarmed combat final she was already on the mat in the academy's gymnasium, waiting for her opponent to finish warming up, when the doors were pulled open and Senior Judge Leverett strode in.

Leverett stopped in front of the captain and glared at him. "The hell is this, Deitch? You know you're trespassing?"

"No, we're not. This precinct was absorbed by the Department of Justice, and I haven't quit yet." Deitch stepped to the side to see past the Judge. "Cadet Quon is about to take her finals in U.C. You're interfering with that."

Leverett pulled off his helmet and looked towards Quon. "My offer won't remain open forever, cadet."

She shook her head. "Thank you, sir, but I don't want to be a Judge. I believe that the law should work for the people, not the state."

"Then I'm shutting this down. All of it."

Captain Deitch said, "We're not costing the department anything—I've been paying the instructors from my own pocket—and the country's still going to need cops for a few more years. You should be *thanking* us, Judge."

Leverett smirked. "All right, then. Quon, let's see what you're made of." He called out to Quon's instructor, Blake, a former Marine who was charging them a hundred bucks an hour. "Unarmed combat. Right?"

"Yes, sir." Blake approached the mat wearing his usual smug grin and cracking his knuckles—he knew Quon hated that.

"She any good?" Leverett asked.

"She's fast. Got a strong right, a little weak with her left. And she's hesitant. She pulls her punches." Blake's grin spread wider as he stared straight into Quon's eyes. "Because she's too *dainty*. The little princess doesn't want to *hurt* anyone."

"Then I'm giving you both permission to let go," Leverett said. "Three minutes, no rules, no consequences. Anything goes."

Captain Deitch grabbed the Judge's arm. "That's not how this is done."

Leverett shrugged him off. "It is today." He nodded to Quon. "If this man is not unconscious or begging for mercy by the end of your three minutes, I'll consider this—whatever this is... Captain Deitch's *experiment*—to have failed, and you're both out of here."

"We don't agree to that!"

"I don't care what you agree to, Deitch. I'm a Judge. I make the rules, I give the orders. Quon, your three minutes starts... now."

Blake lunged at Quon and she immediately raised her arms as she shifted her weight back on to her left foot.

He was only a little taller than her, but at least twenty kilos heavier, and with two decades' more experience. And strong, too. Tendons like steel cables, skin like leather.

She pulled her head back and to the left as Blake's clawed fingers slashed her face, close enough that the hairs on the back of his hand brushed her cheek.

He'd been aiming for her throat. If he'd connected...

She'd known he was dangerous, but a killing blow, in front of a *Judge*?

You have *been holding back*, she told herself. *Blake and Captain Deitch have both told you that.*

It wasn't that she was afraid to hurt someone: when it came to physical force, there was no point in using more force than was necessary. Keep things neat. Stay inside the lines.

Blake faked a jab with his left, but she'd seen him do that before, and easily blocked his right fist.

She ducked back and to the side, shot her left leg out at the same time. Slammed her heel straight into his groin.

The impact told her he was wearing a protective cup, which she'd expected: he was a thug, not an idiot. But he flinched all the same, pitching his top half forward and dropping his hands to protect himself.

An elbow to the side of his head, hard. He stumbled, and

she body-slammed him, crashing into him with her shoulder.

His feet skidded, lost their grip, and as he hit the mat butt-first, he tried to grab onto her. He was too slow. Her knee cracked into his chin and sent his head crashing backwards, then two sharp punches to the solar plexus and a final jab to the throat stole his breath.

Clutching his neck as he gasped and shuddered, Blake stared up at Quon, eyes wide from shock more than pain.

She straightened up. "My advice... Lie there for another two minutes, fifty seconds and then beg for mercy."

Quon stepped back, and looked towards Judge Leverett.

He was silent for a moment, then turned to the captain. "All right. Point made. Carry on."

THE GRADUATION CEREMONY took place indoors, in what was once Deitch's office. Instead of a crowd, the only onlookers were Quon's parents and two contractors who agreed to cease hammering for five minutes.

Captain Deitch shook Quon's hand. "Congratulations. The only graduate of the class of 2039. I am... very proud of you, Officer Quon."

Quon's mother began to applaud, and was quickly joined by her father and one of the contractors. The other one cheered and tossed his hard-hat into the air. It clunked loudly off the freshly-plastered ceiling before hitting the floor and rolling away.

As they watched the contractor chase after his hat, Captain Deitch said, "I'm sorry there's no certificate or... well, anything else." He lifted an envelope from his desk, handed it to her. "Your assignment."

Quon opened the envelope. "Golgotha, Alabama."

Deitch nodded. "Best I can do. No other force is taking on anyone else. And even this one had closed its ranks, but Captain Bonacki owed me a favour. The Judges are making it very clear that the old ways are gone." He shrugged. "You realise what this means, Officer Quon?"

"Sir?"

"You have graduated so now *this* place..." He glanced around the room. "As of now, this academy is officially defunct. The last police academy in the country has just passed out its last officer. That's you, Quon. You are the last person to become a police officer in the United States of America."

CHAPTER TWO

Golgotha, Alabama
Sunday, May 11th 2041
10:22

OFFICER ERROL QUON took the stairs three at a time, gun in her left hand, her right on the rail to haul herself that little bit faster. She was nine floors up already: the elevators were broken as usual. The sweat raced down her back, but the day was so hot it evaporated before it reached her belt.

She hit the tenth floor and heard Judge Kurzweil chasing after her at least three floors below, and officers Huck and Astley a floor or two further down, and panting so loud she could hear them over the thunder of their boots.

Their target was 1208, a large one-room apartment, temporary home of Deborah Rozek. And currently the only occupied apartment on the floor—that simplified things. Rozek would certainly know by now that they were coming, and she'd be frantically flushing her little paper packages down the toilet. There was a time when that trick would have worked, too, but not now. The Judge was just going to arrest her anyway, evidence or not.

The race wasn't to reach Rozek before she'd flushed the

stash of TT. It was to get to her *while* she was flushing it, and before she had time to bolster her defences.

Outside, on the street, six more officers were covering the exits. Rozek had eluded the cops for years, but the Judges had taken less than a week to track her down. They had someone on the inside, Quon was certain, but they only confided in cops when it was absolutely unavoidable.

Twelfth floor. Rozek's apartment was at the end of the corridor, past several overflowing garbage bags swarming with flies the size of grapes, and a full roll of carpet that had been lying there so long it had sprouted a substantial collection of mould and fungi.

Quon knew that this was not the time for subtlety. Forcing a deep voice, she roared out, "Police! Get clear of the door!"

A volley of shots instantly shredded the door to apartment 1208, and much of the wall beside it, and Quon suppressed a smile. The Judges would have them burst in without warning or provocation, and a lot of her fellow officers were happy to go along with that, especially in a situation like this. But so far Quon had managed to avoid overstepping that particular mark.

If things ever reverted back to the way they were before Fargo, before the Judges... She wanted to be certain that her arrests would stick. Now, Deborah Rozek had given her ample reason to enter the apartment. Probable cause: that was the main difference between the cops and the Judges.

Not that she was dumb enough to enter right now. As silently and smoothly as she could, she approached the doorway, keeping her back to the wall and her gun ahead of her. In her normal voice she said, "The cop's down—but there's more on the way!"

She was two metres away from the perforated door when a man leaned out, "That you, Kresha? How did..."

The old man froze, very much aware of the muzzle of a Heckler and Koch 45 a hand's breadth away from his face.

The sound of a toilet flushing in the apartment was followed by a woman's voice: "Dad—what the hell? Get back here!"

The old man dry-swallowed. "It's... uh..."

Quon pulled the old man's gun from his hand—she recognised it as a modified Scorpion VZ61, fully-automatic yet smaller than some handguns—and tossed it back onto the roll of carpet, then grabbed him by the collar. "It's safe," she whispered.

"Dad!"

The old man's expression collapsed as he realised he was betraying his daughter. "Yeah, it's safe."

Quon whispered, "There's more coming. We have to go."

He nervously wet his lips. "C'mon, honey. Kresha says we gotta book."

She pulled the man close, her forearm around his neck, then stepped into the doorway, keeping him in front of her, and her gun-arm over his shoulder aimed into the apartment.

Deborah Rozek had a habit of using people as shields, so Quon thought it was only fitting that she do the same.

Past the trembling old man's head, she could see Rozek staring at her open-mouthed, slowly raising a lowered gun. Another Scorpion.

"Drop it," Quon said. "Opening fire at an officer is an automatic twenty."

"*Already* opened fire," Rozek said, her gun now levelled and steady, aimed square at her father's head. "You might have noticed the door and wall."

"I don't want the extra paperwork so I won't count that if you don't. Trust me. There's a Judge with the rest of my crew and you know what that means, Deborah. She's gonna sentence you on the spot. Maybe even execute you. Surrender to me and you get to live—and you'll get a *lawyer*. She's not going to give you that option."

Her teeth clenched, Rozek said, "You take your goddamn hands off my father or I swear I'll start killing you so slowly that old age'll probably get you first."

Still standing in the doorway, Quon was aware of Astley, Huck and Judge Kurzweil cautiously advancing along the corridor. "Time's melting away, Deborah. What's it going to be? There's four of us. You can't win. Dealing in Trance is a class-A felony. You're not stupid. You knew that when you started, so don't blame *us* for doing our job. No one *forced* you to be a dealer, so whatever happens is on you. Drop the gun. Last time I'm gonna tell you."

"I want a guarantee that—"

A sharp crack, and Deborah Rozek dropped to the ground.

The old man screamed, and began to thrash in Quon's grip, struggling to get to his daughter. She pulled him back out into the corridor and slammed him against the wall. Officer Huck was already rushing towards him, handcuffs ready.

"You *have* to do that?" Quon yelled back at Judge Kurzweil as she ran into the apartment. "She would have surrendered!"

Quon dropped to her knees next to Rozek. The woman was lying on her back, alive, but only just. Quon slapped one hand over the dime-sized entry wound in her left shoulder, then rolled her up a little to cover the exit wound. It was almost as large as her fist. She felt warm, wet, sharp fragments of bone grinding together with every twitch and convulsion. Kurzweil's shot had hit the top of the humerus, shattering it. Whatever happened, Deborah Rozek was never going to have full use of her left arm again.

"Paramedics are on the way," Kurzweil said, and as she was tucking her gun back into its holster, Quon noticed that it was still coated with plaster dust from the wall.

"I count at least thirty fresh bullet holes in the wall and door," Kurzweil said. "Perp already gave up her right to surrender. She's lucky I didn't take a head-shot. Life in an iso-cube, all assets seized." Kurzweil glanced back towards the old man out in the corridor. "The father, right? Same sentence."

Kurzweil hunkered down on the other side of Rozek and handed Quon a steri-patch. "We're gonna assume all other family members are involved and share equal responsibility until they can prove otherwise. And *you* are going to tell us everything you know about your supplier."

"She's unconscious," Quon said, pressing the steri-patch over the entry wound. "Can't hear you."

"Maybe she can't hear me right now, but she *will*. And she'll talk."

The sirens of an approaching ambulance echoed through the streets as Quon said, "That's optimistic. These people are a lot more afraid of their supplier than they are of a prison sentence."

"Yeah? Then Rozek here is about to undergo a revelation."

CHAPTER THREE

Brendan "Dallas" Hawker had been a day-shift supervisor in Folkson Fabrications for exactly twenty years when word came down the pipe that things were looking bad. Orders were down. They'd never really picked up after the bad summer nine years back, when the new import regs just about crippled the home-grown market and turned the government's "Buy the Best—Buy American!" campaign into little more than joke fodder for the late-night talk-show hosts, but this was supposed to be the factory's busy season, yet they were barely working any harder than they had been in winter.

And two months ago Kerwick over in packaging had retired and there was still no word from management on who might be replacing her. Not a good sign.

As he walked his standard route through the factory thirty minutes before shift's end—just in case anything needed to be sorted before the night shift came on—he couldn't stop thinking about how much he'd given to this place. Twenty years. If his career here in Folkson had been a kid, it'd be nearly old enough to have graduated from college by now.

Most of the Sunday afternoon shift looked up long enough to give Dallas a nod as he passed, his presence a welcome reminder that quitting time was at last approaching. That was the other reason for his regular patrol at this time of the day: the workers had learned to associate him with good news.

He let his fingers run along the rail surrounding the conveyor as he walked, feeling the steady, comforting thrum of the machinery. Eight metres per minute, this weaver could do, if you pushed it. A constant feed of brightly-coloured nylon, cotton and latex-blend threads streamed into the machine to be tightly woven into specifically shaped cloth pieces. Not an inch of thread was lost, Betty Folkson used to tell everyone back when she still ran the place. Most clothing factories bought in rolls of fabric and then cut them as required, leaving a lot of waste material. These machines wove the threads directly into the required shapes, and did it so neatly that the pieces didn't even require hems and the patterns always matched at every seam.

Dallas had his eye on the next generation of machines: they were faster, more flexible, and could even contour the fabric as they constructed it: that was going to be a game-changer for the lingerie market.

But not if the rumours were true. If Folkson had indeed sold out to that Chinese company, they were screwed. Didn't matter one iota how many supermodels or internet influencers you could pay to recommend your products if the customers couldn't actually buy the damn things.

Man, twenty years, he said to himself. He'd been single when he started here, sharing an apartment with Brendan Reisert. That was how he'd acquired the nickname "Dallas"—Reisert had been there first, therefore Brendan Hawker had to have a new name. He'd always wanted people to call him 'Hawk,' but he'd grown up in Dallas so that's what stuck.

He smiled when he remembered how angry he used to get whenever Reisert introduced him to someone new: "This is Dallas. He's in women's underwear."

He'd go into a mild panic about that. "No, I work in the factory where they make Honeyroll Lingerie!"

After a few months, when he noticed that some people were

very keen on finding out more—Honeyroll was an expensive, quality brand—Dallas started making the joke himself. That was how he'd met Gwen.

As he made his way down the packing line, old Otis Conner saw him coming and beckoned him over. Otis was the plant's longest-serving employee: he claimed that on the very first day of operations, Mrs Folkson had arrived to open up and he was already waiting for her. She'd been so impressed with his 'moxy' that she offered him a job on the spot. Dallas knew that the truth was a little different: Otis had served six years for burglary and he was one of a number of parolees Folkson had agreed to take on in exchange for favourable tax breaks. But Otis was a nice old guy and nobody took much heed of his tales anyway.

When they were close enough, both Dallas and Otis removed their ear mufflers. "What's the story?" Dallas asked.

"All good, Dallas. Just... we've been hearing things, you know?" Otis shrugged. "I've only got four years until retirement. You get what I'm saying?"

"I do, sure." Dallas glanced around, and the nearest workers suddenly returned their attention to their job. "But outside of people telling me that they've heard something, I've not heard *anything*, if you see what I mean. They're just stories. There's *always* stories. You remember when the rumour was we were getting bought out by Pepsi-cola? All because a woman from Pepsi came to talk about a tie-in promotion."

Otis nodded. "I guess. But when you've been here as long as I have, you can smell it in the air."

"Things're gonna work out okay, Otis. They always do."

"Yeah, maybe." Otis stepped closer just in case any of the other workers was listening. "Tonight's still on?"

"That's the plan."

Another nod. "See you then."

Dallas moved on. Four years and Otis would be retiring from the factory. That'd be a great time to dump him from the group—a sort of natural end to the more active part of his life—but it was too long to wait. He was just too damn slow, and he'd started second-guessing everything. That was him masking the effects of his age, Dallas knew. He'd watched his own father doing that for years. The others wanted Otis gone now, and they expected Dallas to tell him.

Twenty minutes later, on the freeway home, Dallas's phone rang.

"It's me," Patience Belaire said. "Have you spoken with Otis yet?"

"Not yet. Tonight, if I get the chance. I want to do it when there's no one else around. I think he suspects, anyway."

"All right. I've just got word that the cops hit Deborah Rozek's place. With a Judge. They took her in. Wounded, but walking. Took her father, too."

"Damn... *That's* gonna throw a spanner into the ointment."

"We'll talk tonight," Patience said. "See what the play is before we make any decisions, okay?"

"All right." Dallas ended the call. Patience was usually good at keeping everyone calm and rational, but he was sure that his gut feeling was on the money this time: something was going down. Something big.

"Do you remember the Judges who came to St. Christopher?"

Propped up with his elbow on the pillow, Gabe Nyby nodded, then remembered that he was on the phone. "Sure, yeah."

Romley said, "Two of those Judges are now here in Golgotha. Hayden Santana and Unity Kurzweil. That's no coincidence."

"Unity? That's her real name?"

"I neither know nor care, Gabriel. I wasn't the one who named her. But I found out she was here, which is more than you did. And shielding me is your job."

Gabe sat up and swung his legs off the bed. "How could they have found out *you're* here, if they even know at all? You've changed your name and identity three times since then." He reached out with his free hand and pulled back the blinds, even though he could tell from his bedside clock that it was early evening already. He'd successfully napped through the hottest part of the day, and once again thanked his younger self for not being remotely interested in taking on a nine-to-five career.

But it wasn't the time of day that informed Gabe that this was an urgent call: when it came to Mister Romley, *every* call was urgent.

"I don't *know* how they found out. Yet. You're my only link to those days."

"Well, it wasn't me. Even if I *was* the sort to sell you out, I'm just as deep into all this as you are. And aside from me the only people you've had direct contact with are Sully, Leila and Winston. No way they'd talk either."

"Then if it wasn't deliberate, we're left with someone screwing up, or the presence of Judges Kurzweil and Santana being purely coincidental. If you were me, Gabriel, which of those options would you be more inclined to believe?"

Gabe stood up and began searching through the piles of clothes on the floor for items that were reasonably fresh. "The former. But they're good people, sir. You know that. They don't make mistakes."

"Deborah Rozek worked for Sullivan Reidt, and Reidt works for you. If Rozek names him, he'll point to you."

"Sully is never going to talk. He'll put a round in his own skull first. He's even told his people that: 'The Judges come for me, you don't let them take me alive.'"

Romley paused for so long that Gabe was sure the call had dropped, then he said, "Stay on top of this, Gabriel. Watch those Judges. They have created a void in our operation in the shape of Deborah Rozek. Any further upset to the balance will require some drastic action."

"We can make *sure* she doesn't talk. I have contacts in the precinct who can get to her."

"If she were *in* the precinct, those contacts might be useful. The Judges have her elsewhere."

* * *

Quon was so used to seeing Judges in the police station that she barely registered the man's presence as she walked through the office towards the coffee nook. It was only as she was loading a fresh cartridge into the espresso machine that she became aware of him watching her.

She turned around and looked directly at him, but he didn't turn away as she'd expected. Perhaps he wasn't actually looking in her direction: it was hard to tell with the almost opaque visor on his helmet.

The thought occurred to her, as it had occasionally in the past, that for all she knew he might not be a Judge. Could be anybody. The uniform lent authority, and the helmet lent anonymity.

As her coffee brewed, she returned her attention to the box of espresso cartridges, giving each one a little twist to the left or right so that their labels lined up, then glanced back at the Judge.

He was definitely watching her, she concluded.

He tracked her as she carried her cup back across the room to the temporary desk she'd been using for the past five months. Captain Bonacki refused to assign Quon to a permanent post, or even give her a partner. Two years on the beat and she was still on foot-patrol.

The other officers in the station were generally pleasant enough to her, but they didn't interact any more than the job dictated, and sometimes not even that much. It could be a struggle to keep up with her cases when the duty sergeant often omitted her from relevant briefings and e-mails.

A plain-clothes officer dropped a stack of thin folders on the corner of her desk and passed on without slowing down or speaking to her. As she was straightening them up, the Judge approached.

"Quon. With me. Captain's office. Now."

He didn't wait for her to respond, just assumed that she'd follow.

She hated that. The Judges treated everyone else as a subordinate. She left her espresso on its coaster and followed him anyway, ten paces behind as he strode out of the main office, through the public lobby and towards the Captain's office. He opened the door and walked in, and Quon heard him say, "Need the room, Captain."

As she reached the door, Captain Bonacki barged out, almost barrelling into her. He had a face like thunder and was muttering under his breath.

The Judge pulled out the small office's second chair and said, "Sit."

As she lowered herself into the chair, he silently pushed the door closed, then pulled off his helmet and placed it on the captain's desk.

Quon felt like she was about to be shot or fired. Or arrested. You never knew with the Judges exactly what you were going to get, except that it wasn't likely to be good. They don't haul you into the office and close the door if they're going to give you chocolate.

The Judge was in his forties, she guessed. His grey hair was cut so tight it was almost shorn, but that didn't disguise the fact that nature was thinning it for him. Two-day stubble grew like grey and black moss on his weather-beaten face.

"Name's Hayden Santana. Senior Judge. My colleague Judge Kurzweil tells me you objected to her methods this morning."

She wondered where he was going with this. "That's true. She almost killed a perp who was about to surrender."

"Had you given the perp clear and sufficient instructions to lower her weapon?"

"Yes."

"Had the perp begun to lower that weapon when Judge Kurzweil opened fire?"

"No, but—"

Judge Santana shrugged. "Then I don't see what the problem is, other than *your* lack of follow-through."

"We needed her alive."

"She *is* alive. And when she's recovered, she'll talk."

"Why should she?" Quon asked. "She's already received the maximum sentence. What's her *incentive?*"

Santana picked up an ornate fountain pen from the captain's desk and peered at it. "I *like* fountain pens. They're a relic, but there's something more... tactile about them compared to ballpoints." He held it closer to Quon. "Look. See that inscription? 'To Captain Jameson Bonacki, with gratitude.' Hand-carved, and hand-engraved. He told me he was given this by the members of his yacht club. He can't sail, doesn't own a boat, and we're three hundred kilometres inland, and yet he's a member of a yacht club. What does that tell you about the captain?"

"Not my place to say, sir." Whatever the Judge was building up to, Quon wished he would just get to it.

"Of course it's not." Santana dropped the pen back onto the desk beside its holder, and Quon fought the urge to reach over and put it back properly.

"I've been watching you for weeks, Quon. Looking into your background."

She started to rise. "I'm not interested."

"I say you could leave? Sit. We're not going to ask you to join us, Quon. You've made your feelings on that very clear. Now... Judge Kurzweil told me about *your* performance today. You had a chance to take down the perp, but instead you put yourself at risk. Explain that."

"I'm not an executioner."

Santana looked at her steadily for a moment. "Not an executioner. All right." He drew his gun from his holster and held it down by his side. "So she's got her gun in her hand, like this, and she's raising it..." He began to slowly lift his arm, aiming the gun towards her. "Stop me when we get to the point where you'd actually shoot her, Quon."

She said nothing, just watched his arm rise until his gun was pointing directly at her face.

"Really?" Santana asked. "You're *that* slow? Or that *stupid?*

You'd let the perp live even though she was preparing to open fire at you?"

"I was certain I could talk her down, sir."

"But you didn't." Santana slid his gun back into its holster.

"Only because Judge Kurzweil shot her through a hole in the wall."

"A hole that Deborah Rozek herself had created only moments before. Quon, she was a known manufacturer of high-volume street-grade narcotics who'd already served eight for assault, and she was a pretty solid suspect in eight killings and countless other assaults, and that's not including all the people her products have put in the infirmary or the morgue. What *more* does it take for you to reach the conclusion that the world is better off without her? A bullet costs a buck fifty. A lifetime in prison will cost the state *millions*. And that's millions that could otherwise be spent on healthcare or education. So execution would have been the preferred option."

"I'll agree with you the day you show me how to *undo* an execution."

Santana raised an eyebrow. "Smart mouth, Quon. Look where that's got you. Two years on the job and still on the beat. None of your colleagues want to work with you because you refuse to step outside your comfort zone. In your first month you reported Officer Littman for excessive force when apprehending a known felon. Protocol demanded an investigation, so Littman was put on leave. How many crimes could he have stopped if you hadn't got him shelved?"

"Sir, that man was armed with a stick, and Littman shot him in the *face*. It was a miracle he survived. He's never going to be able to talk properly again."

"Quon, times change, and attitudes have to change with them. Your colleagues are using a heavier hand than before because they know it's necessary."

"Some of them are doing it because they know they can get away with it. Judge, if we wrongfully *arrest* someone, we can apologise and let them go, but execution is a pot we're never going to be able to un-break. When we start down that road, there's no easy way back."

"We're already *on* that road, so those who refuse to keep up are liable to get dragged away by the tide."

"Great. Mixed metaphors *and* mixed messages." Quon inhaled deeply, and let it out slowly. "What do you *want*, Judge Santana?"

"We have reason to believe that a Trance-Trance manufacturer who went to ground back in '33 has resurfaced here in Golgotha. He's avoided capture this long by having a support network that's so vague most of the people involved don't even know they're part of it. He's willing to sacrifice anyone and everyone to ensure his own safety. If this guy has a set of morals at all, it's only because he stole it from someone else."

"You think he supplied Deborah Rozek?"

"We *know* he did. Quon, our analysts figure this S-O-B is responsible for seventy-one per cent of all Trance in the USA. He creates the base product and sells it in bulk to other manufacturers. They cut it themselves, tweak it a little to give it their own slant... their own... what's a good word?"

"Spice?"

"Yeah, that'll do. Some of the samples we found in Rozek's apartment are untainted. The chances are high they came directly from our guy. Plus we have another very strong lead that puts him here."

Quon nodded. "So if Judge Kurzweil hadn't almost killed Rozek, you'd be able to question her already."

"That's not the point."

"It's *my* point."

"Whatever. Kurzweil knows the case, but you know this city. I want you to work alongside her until this is through."

He's kidding, she thought. *He has to be.* "Sir... I don't have the qualifications or the experience to do that."

"You do if I say that you do."

"Why me?"

"Two reasons. First, because it's a certainty that some of your fellow officers are in this guy's pocket. You're the only one I'm one hundred per cent sure is clean. And the other reason is that near as I can see, you're not scared of anyone." He smiled. "Not even *us*."

"I don't have any reason to be scared of Judges. I've never broken the law."

Santana snorted. "Yeah, well, most people don't see us that way."

"Do I have a choice?"

"Of course. You could quit and all the people you might have saved from Trance addiction will die slowly and painfully."

Quon rolled her eyes. "Right. Okay, I'm in, but I need to know everything. What's the nature of your lead?"

"I trust you, but I won't say more than that unless it becomes necessary." Santana absently stroked the stubble on his chin as he regarded Quon. "I do understand that you don't like the way things are right now... I don't like it myself. I was a lawyer before I joined up. Made it my job to protect the people regardless of their status. But I came to see that I wasn't a part of the solution. I was part of the problem. And the root of that problem is that people commit crimes because they believe they have a better-than-even chance of getting away with those crimes, that the potential reward is worth the risk. So the Judges are necessary to keep the peace."

Quon said, "And now we have a society in which the people are more afraid of the law-makers than they are of the law-*breakers*. That's not a democratic solution."

"I never claimed that it was democratic. Or even fair. But it *is* a solution."

CHAPTER FOUR

OVER DINNER, GWEN Hawker asked her husband, "Oh, did they give you anything for your twentieth anniversary?"

Dallas snorted. "Take a guess. Nah, I mentioned it to Jonas this morning, but all that did was give him an excuse to remind me he'd been there longer." He reached to his left, pulled Jason's fork from his hand and turned it the other way up. "We don't *stab* our food in this house. It's pasta, not your mortal enemy."

Jason said, "Yeah, but the pasta's in league with the beans and they *are* my mortal enemy." He speared a forkful and shoved it across the table towards his sister. "Look! That's not sauce—that's pasta-blood!"

Evie rolled her eyes and resumed texting with one hand while holding her fork in her other hand. Dallas had watched her slowly moving her food around the plate for the past ten minutes. Her usual trick of trying to make it look as though most of it had been eaten.

Dallas occasionally wondered where these kids had come from, and he was sure that Gwen wondered the same thing. They were so flaky. He and Gwen had always been practical. If there was a problem, you dealt with it. Something broken? Fix it. But Jason and Evie would ignore a squeaky hinge or a dripping tap forever, they never turned off a light—or anything else with a switch—and they'd leave the doors and windows wide open in the middle of summer, and then have the temerity to complain about all the bugs.

Someone else will come along and sort it out, that was their way of thinking. *Probably my own fault*, Dallas told himself. *Spent too long showing them how to do stuff over and over, not realising that they were smarter than me and just getting me to do everything for them.*

He glanced along the table towards Gwen, who was watching the TV in the other room off to the side. The kids couldn't see it from this angle and still didn't know that when they thought she was listening to their stories about school she was really reading the subtitles on the TV. He didn't want to be around on the day they found out after years of putting up with her 'No television at the dinner table' rule.

She saw him looking, and asked, "So, are you going to the club tonight?"

Dallas nodded. "Uh-huh."

"Well, just make sure you drive safe."

"Will do." They'd never spoken about it, but she knew. She'd known right from the beginning.

She didn't know all the details, but she knew that he wasn't really going to the golf club. But it *was* a club, in a way. The same people meeting in the basement of Patience Belaire's enormous house at least twice a month, that was a club.

The news about Deborah Rozek's arrest still bothered him. The Judges would interrogate her and before long the city would be flooded with Justice Department trucks and bikes. No one would be safe then.

Dallas looked around at his family again. Evie had successfully hidden a large portion of her meal under her knife and fork and was only minutes away from declaring herself done. She'd eaten maybe three mouthfuls. That didn't bother Dallas too much. So many parents micro-managed their kids. When he was Evie's age, his diet had consisted of cereal and pizza, with the occasional burger every now and then for variety.

Jason had lined up twelve spiralled pieces of pasta on the left and right side of his plate and now appeared to be conducting manoeuvres.

The boy was a lost cause, probably, Dallas decided. Too mired in his own imagination. But Evie, to be fair, showed promise. She still had no idea about the real world, still didn't seem to be able to comprehend the concept of emptying the dishwasher, but Dallas had tapped into her phone and regularly read the messages she exchanged with her friends. She was the one they all came to first when they needed help or advice.

Gwen didn't know that Dallas had tapped the kids' phones, and he wasn't about to tell her. And if she ever discovered that he'd tapped *her* phone too, there'd be absolute hell to pay.

For some time now he'd been thinking that Evie might be ready. She wasn't really a kid any more. Sure, fifteen was very young, but she knew her mind, and though she'd quit the gymnastics team a year ago, she still trained. She was small, fast, strong and agile. With a little guidance, she might make a good candidate to replace Otis Conner.

He might drop her name at tonight's meeting. Just casually mention that she had her own way of solving problems and didn't necessarily go by the book. Let Patience and the others draw their own conclusions.

THE JUSTICE DEPARTMENT had booked Judge Santana a small apartment in an old tenement building on Golgotha's South Street, a three-minute ride from the precinct.

This was his fifth day staying in the apartment and by now everyone on the street knew his name, and they knew to stay out of his way. Crime in the area had dropped to almost nothing, and Santana hadn't even had to do anything other than just be there.

As Santana climbed off his Lawranger outside the building, the junkie who lived on the third floor opened the door and walked out. He stood at the top of the steps for a few moments, watching awkwardly as Santana locked up the bike.

Buddy McKinty, twenty-eight years old, unemployed, handsome but with thinning hair and a too-thick beard, a little overweight and seriously underwashed. The man's body odour permeated the building.

Despite the warmth of the evening, Buddy was trembling slightly, and not from fear.

"It's got to be tough, huh?" Santana said. "Riding it out."

"Don't know what you mean, Judge."

"You want some advice, citizen? Clean yourself up."

"Hey, I never touch the stuff."

"That's a lie, McKinty. You're a serial pothead who also dabbles in meth and Trance. For special occasions, right?" Santana took a step closer. "And right now, you're *aching*. You've got that hunger, that void inside your soul that's just crying out for a hit." Another step. He knew that it was almost impossible to drag an addict away from their drug of choice: it was easier and more effective to *lead* them away.

"No, Judge, I swear you've got me wrong. I wouldn't..." He faltered, and looked down at his feet.

"When I say you ought to clean yourself up, I'm not just talking about the narcotics. Take a *shower*, McKinty. A long one. With soap. Excessive body odour caused by negligence is anti-social. There are laws, and penalties."

"Yeah, but the, uh, the body cleans *itself* after, like, a coupla months. Natural oils and stuff."

"That's *hair* you're thinking of, and it's a myth. You want people to respect you, don't you? First, they've got to see that you have respect for *yourself*. Wash. Clean your teeth. Eat some damn fruit and vegetables now and then. Stop stuffing yourself with poisons. Go out and make a positive mark in the world so that when you're gone, people will miss you, not celebrate, or just shrug."

McKinty was still trembling as he vigorously nodded his head. "God, yeah, absolutely. I'm gonna do that. Straighten myself out and just, y'know, get a grip on things. I'm gonna do it. Get a job and get my girl back and... y'know... just be the *best* me that I can be. You got it."

Jesus, he's so far over the edge. "Buddy... That's the *Trance* talking." Santana tapped his own forehead with a knuckle. "Screws up the chemical balances in here. Supercharges your sense of empathy which gives you a boost if you think you've made someone else happy, sickens you if you think you've let them down. How long have you been using? Be honest."

"Uh... a long time. Since, uh, '34. Six years."

"That's *seven* years. You want to get clean?"

"Absolutely, man. And sorry about lying earlier. I'm gonna turn this around."

"Who's your supplier, Buddy?"

McKinty began to back away, towards the door. "Hey, no, I can't tell you that! They would... Well, it would be bad. They already know you live here. That makes them *real* antsy."

"Don't worry, I'm not about to turn you into a snitch. But I had to ask, right? I just want you to get clean. In *every* sense." He pulled off his gloves, then popped open one of the pouches on his belt.

McKinty flinched and took a step back towards the door.

"Relax, will you? I'm gonna give you *this*," Santana said, holding up a folded fifty-dollar bill. "The store on the corner is still open. Buy yourself some soap and shampoo and toothpaste. Shower when you get back. Do it properly—scrub every inch. Then tomorrow morning you go to the Goodwill on Wilkes, they've got some nice clothes there. They're used, but they're very cheap. You want a good pair of jeans—no rips in them—and two or three shirts. Nothing with a slogan, got that? Just plain T-shirts. You got any change left over, get your hair cut and your beard trimmed. Then in the afternoon, when you've had *another* shower, you'll hit the streets again and every store that's open, you'll go in and ask for a job application. Be polite and respectful. If they tell you to take a hike, you apologise, thank them for their time, and you'll leave. Doesn't matter how rude or dismissive they are to you, always treat them with respect and never raise your voice."

McKinty nodded. "Absolutely." His gaze still hadn't left the fifty no matter how much Santana had waved his hand around while issuing his instructions.

"Buddy, do you understand what I'm trying to do for you?"

"Sure do, Judge. Helping me get back on the right path."

"That's right. If you need help filling out the applications, you ask me. Now, I'm putting my ass on the line here for you, Buddy, because Judges are *not* supposed to do this. Don't let me down." He placed the fifty into McKinty's grubby hand.

McKinty tucked it into the back pocket of his jeans. "Cool, thanks. I appreciate this, I really do. You Judges are..." he hesitated, still trembling a little. "I'm gonna say... not popular."

"We know that, Buddy. But we're not here to be popular. We're here to make sure that everyone is safe. That's what it comes down to. I mean, you know how much a Judge earns in a month?"

The trembling man shrugged.

"Nothing. We don't get paid. The Department supplies us with food vouchers so we can eat, and they cover the rent. And they pay for our equipment, of course, and we get a small stipend for emergency situations, which is where that fifty came from. But we don't get a salary, or even a pension. See what I mean? We're here for the people. Sure, we come down *hard* on the citizens if they break the law, I won't deny that. But we also pick them up when they fall." He playfully slapped McKinty on the shoulder. "I can see that you've... well, I won't say you've fallen. But you're in danger of losing your grip. I want to help you keep climbing, to continue the metaphor. To help you to rise to your full potential."

Buddy McKinty nodded once again, and straightened up. "Yeah. I see where you're coming from, Judge Santana. Lot of people say the Judges are just fascists. Like, totalitarians? That you created a crisis, then used that crisis as an excuse to seize power. But it's not about you guys taking the power from the people, right? You're taking it from the billionaires who keep us down."

Santana grinned. "That's it exactly."

Buddy copied Santana's smile. "We all gotta do our part, right?"

"Right again." Santana retrieved his helmet. "I gotta get a couple hours' sleep." He backed towards the door. "You mind what I said, Buddy—get clean and stay. The soap kind and the *sober* kind."

"I'll do that, Judge, I promise."

Still smiling, Santana threw him a casual salute, and pushed the door open with his shoulder. Inside, he took his first deep breath since he'd climbed off the bike. The building reeked of dry rot and marijuana and stagnant water and old, warm garbage, but it was nectar compared to Buddy McKinty's stench. Of all the pieces of advice Santana had given him, he hoped Buddy would at least take heed of the one about showering.

PATIENCE BELAIRE'S ORIGINAL name, which she'd legally changed twenty-four years ago, was Pauline Belmont.

Dallas had known this for years, but had never brought it up. People don't like to know that you've run a background check on them. And he was sure she'd done the same to him and the others.

Patience was forty-six, average height, a slender frame, large eyes, and Dallas supposed that in another life he might have been attracted to her. But she was the sort of woman Grandma Hawker described as "flouncy," with "airs and graces," and he didn't care for that. One time, Patience delayed a job because she couldn't find the right kind of scarf.

Anyone else, Dallas would have told them where to get off, but this club was her creation, the meetings took place in the basement of her house. And she was good at the job, plus she'd bankrolled the group for the first few years. Besides, arguing with her wasn't like arguing with Gwen, who had the decency to actually listen to the other person instead of just waiting for them to finish talking.

The basement was comfortable—padded cane chairs, thick carpet, cool wafts of air from the vents—and the only thing Dallas didn't like was the low ceiling and its criss-crossed clusters of cables, light-fittings and pipes. Even though the lowest light-fitting was several centimetres above his head, he could never shake the feeling that one of these days he was going to crack his skull open.

At exactly nine p.m. Graham Mealing entered through the storm doors at the rear of the house—Patience didn't like them using the front door, where someone might see them—and nodded to Dallas as he removed his night-vision glasses from around his neck.

"Just you?" Mealing asked. "Where's herself?"

"Upstairs." Dallas dropped into the most comfortable chair before Mealing could get to it.

Mealing was about thirty, tanned and healthy, and carried himself with a swagger that Dallas found irksome. Even when he was supposed to be keeping a low profile, he looked as though he wanted people to notice him. "A braggart," Grandma Hawker would have called him.

Patience came down a few minutes later. "We're it, tonight. The Draughtons are working tonight, and Shelby and Otis can't make it. So where are we?"

Dallas said, "I'm on Weitzner tonight."

"Everything's checked out?"

"Yeah, we're clear with this one. As clear as we've ever been."

"Okay," Patience said. "Best of luck with it." She turned to Mealing with an expectant look. "Graham?"

He reached into his jacket's inside pocket and produced a tightly-rolled sandwich bag, then tossed it to Patience. "Today's spoils."

Patience unrolled the bag and held it up to the light, revealing about fifty small paper-wrapped bundles.

"TranceTrance," Mealing said, grinning. "And it's uncut."

"Nice work," Dallas said. "So where'd you get it?"

"A dealer who hangs at the junction of Fifth and Harper." Mealing's smile grew wider. "This white car pulled up to the kerb—an old Toyota, I think—and a guy got out and put something in a trash can, then drove off. Didn't get the licence plate, though. I didn't even really register it until my guy—who I *was* watching—walked over to the trash can and took out the package."

"Okay, a standard drop, then," Patience said.

"Right. My guy disappeared into a doorway for a few minutes. I figure he was unwrapping it. He comes back, talking on his cell, and a couple minutes after that, his underlings start approaching. Same shtick as always with these guys. The underlings talk to the money guy half a block away to arrange the deal and hand over the cash, then he signals the one who's holding to give the dealer whatever's been paid for."

Dallas knew that this was how the deals were usually done on the streets, but he'd only witnessed it himself a couple of times. It was like he suffered from drug-dealer blindness. Same thing with hookers and pimps: he almost never seemed to spot them until someone else pointed them out. Undercover cops were a different thing, though. He could almost always tell.

The first time Dallas and Mealing met had been here in Patience Belaire's basement. They shook hands, and it was almost an hour before Dallas realised his watch and wallet were missing.

Mealing could walk past a dealer and lift the contents of their pockets without slowing down or even seeming to touch them.

Patience unlocked the old safe under the basement steps and removed a small electronic weighing scales. "One-ninety-four grams. Take off thirty for the wraps... At the current street rate of forty a gram, that's over six and a half thousand dollars' worth."

Dallas whistled. "Good haul. Someone's going to get kneecapped for this."

"If not worse," Mealing said.

By now, all the dealers in Golgotha had heard of the phantom pickpocket, and about once a month one of them experienced it directly, but Mealing was so good at his job that he could do it right in front of them and they still wouldn't see it. He claimed to have once removed a man's necktie and replaced it with a bright pink one without the man even noticing.

"You're still an idiot, though," Dallas said. "If you steal someone's entire stash, they'll spot it pretty quickly and then warn all their colleagues. Then the person being kneecapped might be *you*. But if you—"

"I know. If I take only three or four packages out of a stash of twenty or thirty, they might not notice for hours. You've been singing that same tune for a long time now, and I've still never been caught."

Patience said, "I agree with Dallas. You could take a few units from a dozen dealers and greatly lower the risk. By the end of the night, the net haul would be greater. But it's your own life you're risking." She locked the baggie and the scales back in the safe. "I didn't want to do this without the others here, but we have things we need to talk about."

Mealing said, "Right. Otis. Dallas, you tell the old fart yet that he's becoming a liability?"

"Not yet."

"You'd want to pull your finger out, then, before he gets caught and rats us all out."

Patience stepped between them. "I'm not talking about Otis. But, yes, we do need to deal with him. Right now, we have the Judges to worry about. There are more showing up each week, and a contact of mine who's close to the president's office has told me that Golgotha might be one of the cities chosen for a new buy-out scheme."

Dallas shrugged. "What's that?"

"That's where they target an entire precinct and offer everyone a very generous retirement package. We're talking almost a million dollars to each officer. But it's contingent on *everyone* signing the deal, and there's a time limit. If everyone signs before the time runs out, then everyone gets their full deal. But if there's even *one* person unsigned, everyone who's signed gets only a quarter of their deal."

"So all the cops in Golgotha are going to be rich?" Mealing asked.

"*If* everyone signs," Patience said.

"Ah, who wouldn't take a deal like that? They'd need to be crazy to hold out against *that* sort of pressure."

"There's always one," Dallas said.

As Quon took the eraser to the duty roster on the office's giant whiteboard, a shadow fell across it, and she turned to see Judge Kurzweil standing behind her with her arms folded.

"So what now, Officer Quon?"

"You tell me. You outrank me."

"Not for this task."

Quon resumed her self-appointed task of updating the roster. If she didn't do it, no one else would. Or they might, but it wouldn't be neat. They'd do a sloppy job of erasing the old entries, or they'd mix capitals and cursive, or put entries in the wrong column.

Kurzweil said, "You're wondering whether one of your colleagues informed Deborah Rozek that we were coming, right? Whoever it was didn't give her enough time to flee—you take that into consideration?"

Quon looked around the room. The day shift had ended fifteen minutes ago and the office was now in that quiet lull before the night shift really got started. "Judge Santana still hasn't told me who we're looking for."

"That's down to me. But not here."

"Because if some of the officers here *are* working for him, they'll know you're after him. And I'm putting myself in the cross-hairs by working with you. It's not like I'm Ms Popular as it is."

"True. They call you The Little Princess behind your back. There's a pool on how long it's going to be before your blind adherence to the letter of the law gets you maimed or killed. Or gets someone *else* maimed or killed."

Quon glared at the Judge. "You think that's funny?"

"It's ironic. Out of all the cops in this precinct you're the one who's most suited to being a Judge, but you're the one who least wants it." Kurzweil leaned a little closer. "You know... We have the power to draft you if we can demonstrate that it would be in the interests of the Department of Justice."

"That's press-ganging. It's basically *slavery*."

Kurzweil shrugged, and stepped back. "I've never heard of it being used, but the option is there. It's a logical approach. We serve the people as a whole, and sometimes that means restricting the freedom of a small number of individuals."

"And you wonder why I don't want to be a Judge? You say we can't talk about the case here, so let's go somewhere we *can* talk. The sooner we get this done, the sooner I can stop feeling sick about the way you people work."

Quon began to walk away, but Kurzweil grabbed her arm and held her back. "Then you'd want to toughen *up*, Princess, because this is not a job for the delicate of constitution or the faint of heart. We're dealing with people who would torch a packed orphanage if they could see a profit in it. Back when our guy realised we were getting too close, he ordered his lieutenants to pull the plug on the whole operation. Each of them believed that they were one of only three or four, and they just had to eliminate the others. But the next morning we were looking at forty-six fresh bodies. Eight of those were children of the lieutenants who'd had to be eliminated because they were witnesses."

Quon pulled her arm free of Kurzweil's grip. "You think I

don't know that this is serious? I'll do the job, Kurzweil, but we'll do it *my* way, not yours."

"So we have to play by your rules even though the enemy doesn't?"

"No. We have to play by the rules *because* the enemy doesn't."

"Nicely put," Kurzweil said. "That'll be a great inspirational quote they can put on our headstones."

CHAPTER FIVE

Gabe Nyby had been sitting in his old Lexus in the alley behind Stuckey's Bar for eleven minutes when the passenger door opened and Officer Astley eased himself in. "It was The Princess who took her down," Astley said. "Officer Quon, I mean. Her and Judge Kurzweil."

"You were there too," Gabe said.

"Yeah, me and Huck. But we kept back."

"Like the gallant heroes you are. Catch me if I swoon."

"What else should we have done? There was no way we could keep Rozek off their radar any longer. It was her own fault. She didn't keep her head down."

Gabe glanced towards Officer Manfred Astley. He was in his late thirties, greying, married to a beautiful woman who had subsequently borne three very plain daughters. The income supplements that Gabe provided were almost enough to pay off the family's debts and get them out of the loan-sharks' cross-hairs. Almost. Romley had a rule about that: "If you want to keep someone in your pocket, do not afford them the opportunity to fly free." Astley still owed the sharks around sixty-five grand, with an extra thousand added in interest each month. Gabe's money paid off the interest, but not much more than that. Kept the sharks happy, and Astley under control. "Where are the Judges holding Rozek?"

Astley shrugged. "There's no way we can find out, unless we tail them. And even then, getting to her would be impossible. The Judges tell us nothing. Don't you have any of *them* on your books?"

"Do you honestly think I'd tell you if I did?"

"Guess not. But they're human, right? Everyone has a weakness. Everyone has needs. Problems that need to be sorted. You find a crack in their armour and that's your way in. You read the lefty press, they present the Judges like they're robots or something. They call them Dreadnoughts. Means they're afraid of nothing. They just march over the country and do whatever they want." Another shrug. "Well, they're stone-cold bastards, that's for sure, but deep down they're still just *people*. People can be bought. That's your area, Gabe, not mine. You find out what they want most of all, then dangle it before them."

"So you're telling me you've got nothing?"

"I can tell you where they're staying, if that helps. But you don't wanna go taking one of them out. You kill a Judge, they'll turn the whole damn country upside-down and inside-out trying to find you."

Gabe didn't respond to that. He had his own memories of St. Christopher, and a sense of the life he could have had if that young Judge hadn't been killed on her first day there.

"And now the Judges have taken The Princess under their wing," Astley said.

"What do you mean?"

"Santana pulled Quon off regular duty and paired her with Kurzweil. Could be symbolic, you know? If the last police officer to be recruited signs up to the Department of Justice, then that shows everyone that the old ways really are over. I mean, I'd nearly think about signing up myself except—"

"Except that you know I wouldn't like that," Gabe said.

Astley nodded slightly. "Sure, yeah. I know that." A pause. "Look, I'm sorry about Rozek. There really was nothing else we could have done. I mean, I sent her a warning that we were on the way. She had about seven minutes. Not my fault if she wasn't prepared to run. In that business you should always have a getaway bag ready."

"Uh huh." Gabe knew that Astley had done only what they'd expected of him, but it never hurt to make him sweat a little.

"Seriously. What else *could* I have done?"

"Take a hike, Astley. But keep your ears and eyes open. We are close to the tipping point here. If I decide that it's all getting too much, I might have to leave town. You know what that means? I will no longer need your services. And that means you won't get paid."

Astley said, "Understood," and opened the car door.

In the rear-view mirror, Gabe watched Astley make his way along the alley, and half expected him to turn and shoot at any moment. Always a potential hazard in this line of work.

Though Deborah Rozek knew who Gabe was, she didn't know about Romley: she had every reason to believe that Gabe was at the top of the tree. And regardless of whether she talked, someone was going to have to take her place.

He ran through the hierarchy in his head. Gabe got the raw product in bulk from Romley, and sold it to Sully Reidt, Leila Bronson and Wynne Winston. They were the only ones who knew Romley even existed, and they didn't know his name.

Every member of the hierarchy above street-level had no more than four people working under them. That was the rule: don't get greedy. "Greed is the seed of failure," Gabe told his subordinates, with instructions for them to pass it on. "We can all become rich if we play by the rules. But if one of us tries to grab too big a share, then we'll all suffer."

Deborah Rozek had been one of Sully Reidt's underlings. She'd cut the product down, then supply it to Philip Hollins, Noelle Vetter and Father Milton. They passed it on to their dealers, and some of them had sub-dealers of their own. Leila Bronson once described the hierarchy as, "the only pyramid scheme in the world that actually works."

Everyone knew the names of those working under them, but that didn't hold true for the other direction. Though Deborah Rozek knew Gabe, her own people had never heard of him.

With Deborah gone, her suppliers would soon run dry. He could promote one of them, but that was a risk. None of them had the skills or temperament required. Plus promoting someone meant that everyone below them was automatically raised up a level. Better to keep them on their current level and match them with a new up-line. Philip Hollins was a plumber who did call-outs, so that gave him access to a huge range of potential clients. Gabe figured it was best to pass him on to Veena Danese, another of Sully's underlings. Danese was a twenty-six-year-old motorcycle courier who supplied Golgotha Technical College.

But Noelle Vetter and Father Milton were harder to match. Vetter had cultivated a very prim and proper exterior that he knew she wouldn't want to abandon—plus she wore a permanent 'butter wouldn't melt' expression; there was no way anyone else would take her seriously—and Father Milton was already walking a fine line between his duties to his congregation and his customers. Until they found a replacement for Deborah, he could temporarily assign them to Danese, but that would stretch her too far.

For now, it would be better for them to deal directly with Sully Reidt, and let *him* choose Deborah's replacement.

Gabe started up the Lexus and drove on through the alley, slowing down and carefully steering around what might have been a dead or sleeping junkie.

AT NINE P.M. Dallas Hawker and Graham Mealing left Patience Belaire's home via the storm doors in the basement. They quickly and quietly darted to the rear of the garden and through the thick, two-metre-high hedge, emerging in the woods that backed onto the Conley Golf Club.

In silence, they crossed the golf course towards the lights of the club members' parking lot. In the unlikely event of meeting someone, Mealing was carrying his night-vision glasses, and Dallas had his owl-spotting notebook tucked into his pocket.

When they reached their cars, Mealing asked, "You sure you don't want company? Two heads, and all that? Or at least someone to keep watch?" He held up the glasses. "These can come in handy."

"I'm more comfortable working alone," Dallas said.

"Yeah, me too. I've got my eye on a nice little prize that should shake things up, but it's one of those things that you don't want to talk about until it's done."

"I get that. Just... don't do anything stupid, all right?"

Mealing grinned again, threw him a casual salute, and said, "Fight the good fight, man."

"You too."

On the road back to Golgotha, Dallas automatically started to key his destination into the satnav but caught himself just in time. As Shelby Demps once told him, "You'd be an idiot to think that the Department of Justice isn't tapped into the satnav system, logging everyone's destinations."

He didn't even need the satnav to tell him the way: he'd been planning this long enough to know the route by heart. Pender Buildings, twenty-fourth street. Basement apartment. He knew the street well, but for safety at least one drive-past would be required. Not in his current car—he wasn't that dumb. He kept the spare in the low-rate twenty-four-hour lot over in South Lorraine. It wasn't even registered to him.

The seven members of the group each had their own way of getting the job done, except for the Draughtons; they were a married couple and worked as a team. But where the others played it relatively safe, the Draughtons got a sexual thrill from taking a hooker off the streets, and Dallas didn't like that. They should be doing it for the good of the community, not to get their rocks off. And in his view their search for a bigger kick was causing them to become careless.

At first, all Cindy and Billy Draughton did was drive the

woman to the far side of the county, empty her pockets and leave her stranded there with little more than the clothes she was wearing and a religious pamphlet that bullet-pointed all the different ways she was going to Hell. No easy way home meant that was a night the woman wasn't plying her trade on the streets. As Billy had put it, "Not spreading her diseased juices."

Shelby had once asked them, "What about dudes? There are just as many male hookers as there are women." That had not gone down well, and it was clear to the others that the Draughtons had never considered that. Eventually, they awkwardly clawed their way around to the viewpoint that a woman on the game was in more danger than a man, therefore they were saving her.

But lately you could see it in their eyes that they were just getting off on the risk. They'd picked up their most recent victim from outside a busy roadside bar, not a quiet street corner.

Dallas didn't like that at all. That was too close to straying over the line. A week ago he'd asked Cindy, "What happens when you're out some night looking for a target but you can't find one? You pick some girl who looks like she *might* be a hooker?"

"We would never do that!" Cindy protested. "We always make sure. Always."

Billy had said, "Sure the danger *is* kinda a thrill, but that's not why we do it."

Hell it isn't, Dallas thought.

"And even if it was, what difference does it make? We don't touch the girls in a sexual way, so they don't know about it."

"What if you pick up an undercover cop?"

"That won't happen," Cindy said.

Shelby asked, "It won't happen because you have something in place, or because you just wish very hard?"

Billy said, "If it does happen, then she'll flash her badge long before she realises what's really going down. And then we'll show her our pamphlets about how Jesus can save her soul."

"We know what we're doing," Cindy reassured Dallas.

"Yeah, Jesus would be real proud of that. You'll get caught, and bring the heat down on *all* of us."

The argument was cut off there: Patience would only tolerate a certain amount of what she called "infighting."

Her own approach to the team's self-appointed task was a lot simpler, and very effective. She posed as mugger-bait. With her hand-made camel-hair coat pulled loosely closed over a too-short dress, and her three-inch Louboutins clicking down the sidewalk, she could do an excellent impersonation of a high-society woman who taken a wrong turning on the way home from a party and ended up in a seedy part of the city.

She told Dallas at their first meeting: "Three nights out of five, some guy'll approach me asking if I need help. And just about every time that happens, he then tries to snatch my purse out of my hand, or sometimes he'll produce a knife and demand I had it over, along with my watch and jewellery."

"What'll you do when someone pulls out a gun?"

She'd smiled at that. "That's happened a few times. I know how to disarm a man with a gun. My mom wanted me to be safe. From the age of ten I trained four days a week with a former instructor for the IDF." She handed him a table-knife. "Pretend that's a real knife. Try to stab me with it."

A few minutes later, when Dallas could breathe again and the pain in his arm had subsided to a dull ache, he conceded that she probably did know how to take care of herself.

The following week Dallas had got to watch her in action. That had been a gun-in-face situation, on a quiet, mostly-derelict street on the north side of the city where even the squatters refused to stay in the vacant apartments. And it wasn't just a lone mugger. The first had walked straight up to Patience with the gun already in his hand, and the other approached her from behind, also armed.

Dallas had been watching from a block away, in his beat-up second car, and he was sure that he'd be driving back alone.

Patience nervously handed her purse to the first man, then

pulled off her earrings, and her necklace, handed them to the second man. And then one of them demanded her bracelet on her left wrist, too. She reached for it, and grabbed the tiny handgun she kept in her left sleeve.

She shot the first man point-blank in the chest, instantly spun and shot his friend in the shoulder before he had time to react.

He started to back away, and she shot him again, this time in the throat.

Two minutes later, she was back in the car and telling Dallas to floor the accelerator.

His heart raced, his pulse pounding so loud that he had driven a further ten blocks before he realised that she was talking to him.

"... because there's no way we can *trust* them."

"I'm sorry, what?" He glanced down at Patience's lap, where she was going through the muggers' wallets.

"The cops. We can't give it to them because we can't trust them."

"You took their guns too?"

"Of course. I wasn't about to leave two loaded handguns on the streets where some kid might find them. Same with their drugs." Patience held up two baggies, each containing small, square paper wraps and what looked like pot. "A bunch of drugs, two low-lifes *and* two guns off the streets. That's not a bad night."

That had been five years ago, and by Dallas's count Patience had terminated at least eighteen such scumbags here in Golgotha, and maybe the same number in Demopolis and Montgomery, where she also had homes.

She was careful, always, to make sure that there were no witnesses, either human or electronic. The last thing she wanted was for word to get out about what she was doing. She once told Dallas, "If I ever see even a *rumour* along the lines of 'wealthy socialite vigilante' then I'll change my methods immediately."

He didn't want to know what other methods Patience might decide to use.

Of the rest of the group, Otis Conner was a cat burglar—no longer top of his game, but still good for jobs that didn't require much climbing. And Shelby Demps was their inside man. He wasn't a junkie, but he sure looked like one. An adolescent case of Hodgkins Lymphoma had left Shelby underdeveloped, and though he'd now been in full remission for two decades, he was thin almost to the point of emaciation. Extra-loose clothing and walking with a deliberate stoop and a distracted look helped sell the effect.

Dallas estimated that between them, the group did more good for the community than three dozen police officers. And for free, too. Sure, Otis and Shelby had been known to pocket a few bucks here and there from their targets, but that was okay. Neither of them earned a lot of money and saving the city wasn't cheap.

Dallas parked at the multi-storey lot in South Lorraine, and walked up a level to get his old car, a beat-up Hyundai that looked like it'd struggle to do more than thirty with a tail-wind.

He reached Twenty-Fourth Street a half hour later, at a little after ten: Pender Buildings, a six-floor stone-clad apartment block with grand steps leading up to the main entrance, and a gate at the side, past which were smaller, narrower steps down to the basement apartment.

He drove past twice, slowly, peering out at the buildings as he held a crude hand-drawn map of the wrong street in one hand. Just in case a cop—or a Judge—stopped him. If that happened, he even had an alibi: followed correctly, the map would lead him to Otis's place. Otis knew how to react if Dallas were to show up at the door looking sheepish and with a cop watching from the street.

The light behind basement's windows ebbed and flowed, and occasionally flickered gently: the occupant was watching TV.

Dallas parked the car on the next block, and walked back.

Dark clothes, woollen hat pulled down low, black leather gloves, small backpack, and dark, rubber-soled boots. It was a quiet area and he didn't want anyone to remember hearing footsteps.

Four days ago he had walked past the gate leading to the basement steps and quickly sprayed the hinges and bolt with penetrating oil.

Now, the gate opened silently. He darted down the steps and into the shadowed alcove that sheltered the apartment's front door.

People have habits, routines—rituals, almost—that make them predictable. The occupant of the basement apartment always went to bed around ten-thirty, and part of his night-time routine was to put the chain on the front door, slide the top and bottom bolts, and activate the alarm.

It wasn't yet ten-thirty, which meant that the chain was not on, the bolts were open, and the alarm was off.

The door's lock was a simple pin-tumbler, the work of a few seconds with his half-diamond pick and tension-wrench. Otis Conner had taught him how to pick locks, and it occurred to Dallas that it might be best to get the old guy to teach Evie a few tricks *before* the group informed him that his services were no longer required.

As he pushed open the front door, he was hit by the faint smell of scorched oregano and roast lamb, and from behind the closed-over door to the sitting room came the sound of a cop show on TV. The latest episode of *Street Judge*, Dallas realised, and for a moment he considered abandoning his plan: he hadn't seen the new episode yet and didn't want to spoil it.

The target was Gregorz Sabin Weitzner, Greg to his friends. Fifty-one years old, in reasonable shape, no major health issues. Lived alone, no pets.

Dallas took a moment to reassure himself that Weitzner had this coming.

He silently closed the front door. From his backpack he removed his home-made cosh: a hand-stitched leather sheath as long as his arm that was filled with a kilogram of ball bearings suspended in silicon rubber sealant. He hefted it in his hands, gently swung it around to test it.

Satisfied that he could get a good swing, Dallas reached up to the fusebox over the front door and flipped the main breaker.

The apartment dropped into darkness and silence, then came Weitzner's muttered voice: "Aw, what the *hell*?"

It was followed by the grunts of a fifty-one-year-old body pushing itself out of an easy chair, then the sitting-room door opened. There was just enough light coming from outside for Dallas to see Weitzner stepping into the hall.

He lashed out with the cosh, a prefect shot into the man's stomach. The weapon was heavy enough to wind him, but soft enough to not break the skin or leave much of a mark.

Gasping, clutching his stomach, Weitzner began to pitch forward. Dallas was already raising his arm high. He brought the cosh down again, hard on the back of Weitzner's head.

The man hit the floor face-first, the sharp crack of his forehead on the hardwood planks echoing through the hallway.

Dallas reached back up to the fusebox and reset the main breaker.

The hall lights flickered back to life as he knelt down next to Weitzner. He was still breathing, moaning softly. Conscious, but only barely.

Dallas leaned close and whispered, "You *deserve* this. If there's even a speck of a conscience in there, you know that."

He straightened up, got to his feet. In the sitting room, on the floor next to the sofa, he found a slim drinking glass that still contained a few millimetres of light beer.

Back out into the hall. Weitzner, still face down and groaning, was weakly flailing his arms—feeble attempts to summon enough strength to get up.

Dallas knelt down beside him again, used his free hand to grab the man's hair and pull his head back. "You've had this coming for a *long* time." He pulled back further, almost lifting the top half of Weitzner's body up.

"Wh—what..." Weitzner's eyes were rolling, his lids twitching. A string of red-traced drool spilled from his burst lower lip.

"What did you *do* to deserve this? Is *that* what you're trying to ask?" Dallas pulled back even further, thankful that he kept himself in shape: Weitzner wasn't a big man, but he was heavy enough. "You *know* what you did. Elizabeth Chamberlaine. Lizzie to her friends. Eight years old."

"Nnnnooo... no... j-jury said not guilty!"

"Because you or your lawyers bribed someone to destroy the traffic camera footage that proved you were there." Dallas cracked the rim of the drinking glass against the floor. "Driving forty-one in a school zone."

"W... was accident. She ran *out*. I couldn't stop..."

"*Didn't* stop." Dallas's arm was trembling with the effort now, but he tightened his grip on Weitzner's hair. His teeth clenched, he said, "I believe that you hitting Lizzie Chamberlaine with your car *was* an accident. That's not why I'm here. Driving away and leaving her there... that's shameful, despicable, but maybe just about understandable: an act of panic and desperation. But destroying the evidence was *deliberate*. That was cold. That was unforgivable."

Dallas placed the cracked drinking glass on the floor in front of Weitzner. Looked down at it for a second, then nudged it a little into a better position.

He leaned closer still, so that his lips were almost brushing Weitzner's ear. "And *this*... this is *justice*."

The tension in Weitzner's body and his own weight was all it took. Dallas didn't even need to push.

All he had to do was let go.

The glass's jagged edge sliced into Weitzner's carotid artery.

Dallas straightened up, then quickly stepped back to keep his feet clear of the rapidly-spreading pool of blood.

He opened the front door again, stepped out and closed it behind him.

CHAPTER SIX

KURZWEIL WAITED UNTIL the waitress had taken their order before she quietly said, "His name is Irvine Desmond Romley. Or it *was*, back then. We've no idea what name he's using now. He's Caucasian, mid-fifties by now. Slick and smart, and absolutely ice-cold. Exceptionally dangerous."

Quon watched the Judge from across the diner's chipped and scratched table and couldn't help wondering whether the Department of Justice would be covering the bill. In a place like this it wasn't going to be more than about forty bucks, even with a tip, but still. They'd drafted her onto this taskforce, so she shouldn't have to be out of pocket.

It was late, and Quon had insisted on getting something to eat. The diner wasn't the best in town, but it was near, and it was open, and it wasn't too busy: they'd managed to get a booth by the window.

As Kurzweil pulled off her gloves, she said, "Other than that, we really don't know very much about him." She tucked the gloves inside her helmet, then set it down on the seat next to her. "No background, no social security number, no family history. We've never managed to get a clear photo of him, let alone fingerprints or a DNA sample. The man's a cypher."

Quon leaned back and absently chewed on her thumbnail.

"How is that even possible? My cousin Paul said you Judges have comprehensive files on *everyone*."

Kurzweil frowned. "You don't *have* a cousin called Paul."

"That's exactly my point. Romley's a supposed drugs kingpin who's got his tentacles all over the country, and not *one* of his people has ratted him out?"

"Oh, they have, but *they* don't actually know anything about him either. They *think* that they do, just like they think that he's a relatively small-time operator. The first time we ever heard of him was back in Connecticut. One of his people—Niño Aukins, a dealer, junkie and a sort of go-between guy—told my boss about him. We went after Romley... but there wasn't a trace of him. He was in the wind, but had left absolute carnage behind. And every one of his people we've managed to track down believes different things about him. He's married, single, gay, straight, American, foreign, old, young. One of his subordinates is absolutely convinced that Romley is just a facilitator and the real power behind the throne are his twin sisters, but no one else has ever mentioned a sister *or* a brother. Fact is, we're still not even certain that Romley was ever his real name."

The waitress approached the table and Quon saw that her hands were trembling as she set down two sets of cutlery wrapped in paper napkins.

"We, uh, we're *out* of curly fries, sorry. Is non-curly fries okay instead?" She was very clearly avoiding the Judge's gaze.

"You have tater tots?" Quon asked. The girl looked like she was seventeen at most. High school during the day, worked the diner at night. A clean but old uniform, scuffed shoes, a modest promise ring on her engagement finger.

The waitress nodded far too enthusiastically. "Tots? Sure."

Quon glanced at Kurzweil, and saw the Judge looking back at her. "What's wrong?" Quon asked the waitress.

Her voice barely a whisper, she said, "Please don't shut us down! I *need* this job!"

Kurzweil asked, "Why would we shut you down?"

She nervously cleared her throat. "Because... you know. You're a Judge. You can *do* that."

"I can. Doesn't mean I *will*, unless I have a reason. *Is* there a reason..." She looked at the waitress's name tag. "... Monique?"

Monique shook her head. "No. No, we keep everything clean and there's no rats and even though we have a little trouble sometimes on Friday and Saturday nights that's not *our* fault."

She glanced over her shoulder, and Quon turned to see the manager, two cooks and four other serving staff hurriedly looking away.

"Far as I can see, you have nothing to worry about," Kurzweil said. Then corrected herself. "But that cracked pane in the door, the one with the tape over it? How long has that been broken?"

"Since St. Patty's Day last year. A guy came in wasted and cracked his head against the door so hard it needed sixteen stitches. Um... His *head*, not the door."

"The glass has been broken for seventeen months? Tell the owner I said they have three days to get it fixed—that's a serious safety violation."

"Maybe you could tell her yourself, directly? If one of us tells her, she'll blame us and take the cost of the repairs out of our tips."

Kurzweil pursed her lips. "No, *you* tell her. And if she *does* try to use your tips to pay for it, you also tell her that the Department of Justice considers that to be theft. She'll be looking at four months in an isolation block. And remind her that the Department frowns on the idea of someone shooting the messenger. If she still gives you a hard time, report her. We don't punish the innocent for doing the right thing."

After the waitress thanked her and walked away, Quon said, "Well, *that's* a lie. You lock people up all the time for the flimsiest of reasons."

"No, we *don't*. And I wish people wouldn't keep spreading stories that we do."

Quon adjusted her cutlery so that her knife and fork were parallel with the edge of the table. "A friend of mine is serving three years for tax evasion."

"That's hardly a flimsy reason," Kurzweil said. "That's a serious crime."

"She owed four thousand dollars. You could have just garnished her salary to get that back. Now she's lost her job *and* she's in prison. How does that help anyone?"

Kurzweil nodded slowly, and it seemed to Quon that she was suppressing a smile. "You're talking about Sasha Mansell, from Bayram Park. Hardly a close friend. You barely know her. Yes, we do keep detailed files on everyone. Mansell *deliberately* avoided paying her income tax, and went to considerable effort to hide that. And the reason she's serving three years instead of a few months is because she assaulted the Judge who arrested her. We Judges are not the enemies of the people, but we're also not going to let ourselves be victims."

"The way I see it, this country is a leaking boat and the Judge system is like trying to plug the holes with papier-mâché made out of the bill of rights."

"Yeah, that's *very* clever." Kurzweil leaned forward, resting her elbows on the table. "To get close to Romley we need to first get to his people, and to do that, we need to peel away the layers of the hierarchy. Deborah Rozek is the first major step in that direction. The fact that uncut product was found in her apartment tells us that she's close to the top. We uncover as much of the hierarchy as possible and then we strike. Hit the upper levels at the same time."

"So they don't have a chance to warn each other."

The Judge nodded. "There's a balance... the longer we wait, the more names we'll uncover. But more time also means it's more likely that Romley will realise what we're doing and then he'll shut everything down again. That's why arresting Rozek was a risk."

"They'll know you're interrogating her."

"Right. I expect they're paying very close attention to us. Could even be spying on you and me right now."

Quon was suddenly aware of everyone else in the diner. She glanced around quickly, but the novelty of having a Judge in the diner had worn off and no one seemed to be looking in their direction, not that that meant anything.

Kurzweil said, "Even if the plan fails, we should be able to shut down a large section of his empire."

"So why me? Why not just bring in more Judges?"

"Judge Santana believes in you, and I trust him."

"I won't break any laws."

"Quon, Judges *make* the law. That's how it works these days."

"I know, but when everyone starts to see sense again and the old ways are reinstated, I want to still be able to stand by my convictions. In both senses of the word."

Kurzweil was about to respond, but sat back when she saw the waitress, Monique, approaching with their order.

As she put the burgers and fries down in front of the Judge, Monique said, "Manager says there'll be no charge."

"There *will* be a charge," Kurzweil snapped. "Judges don't accept gifts. And nor do regular police officers. When we're done, bring us the tab like you would for any other customer."

Eyes wide and trembling once more, Monique backed away.

"Bit harsh," Quon said.

"If we want the citizens to trust us, we have to be absolutely spotless. There should never be *any* doubt that a Judge is clean and above reproach."

"Jesus... One day, that's going to come crashing down on you so *hard*. You're still people, and people are *always* potentially corruptible."

"Except you, Officer Quon? You set yourself apart from your fellow officers because you know that they will often bend or break the law, and at the same time you criticise us Judges for being too rigid. How the hell does *that* work?"

Quon didn't have an answer for that, and they ate in silence until Monique brought the bill.

CHAPTER SEVEN

Monday, August 12th 2041
02:15

Officer Quon climbed off the back of Judge Kurzweil's Lawranger motorcycle and took a moment to look around because she wasn't sure she had the strength to do much more than stand up. It wasn't so much the effect of the unsettlingly fast ride across town, more the long day and the late hour.

Or the *early* hour. She'd started her shift at the precinct at eight the previous morning.

She should be at home in bed, not in the middle of an unfinished strip-mall that had been abandoned nine years earlier when the contractor absconded with all the developers' money.

Kurzweil gestured towards the only store with four completed walls. "After you."

Quon hesitated. As she was asking "What's in there?" she spotted two more Lawrangers parked nearby.

"Temporary base of operations. Go ahead."

There's a strong chance she didn't *bring me here to execute me*, Quon thought. But you heard a lot of stories about the Judges and how they rose to power. Some people said—quietly, and off the record—that Chief Judge Fargo had a secret army of spies and agents who were given complete autonomy and answered to no one but him. And there were rumours that Fargo's people had infiltrated every level of the government and were the real power behind the throne. You'd see it on the propaganda flyers littering the ground after every public gathering: "We were so busy trying to stop the country from falling to fascism we failed to realise that it already happened decades ago. Back when we were all focussed on the elephant—and the donkey—in the room, we failed to notice the snake in the grass."

With a loud creak of unoiled metal on metal, the makeshift door—a sheet of corrugated aluminium normally used for roofing—was pushed open from the inside, casting a growing triangle of light across the cracked concrete ground. Then a shadow appeared in the light, and Judge Santana emerged.

"Quon." He beckoned her closer. "You ready for the night shift?"

She approached him. "Sir, I've been on for eighteen hours straight."

He gave her a blank look. "So is that yes or no?"

"If anything it's a cry for caffeine. But you Judges don't indulge, do you?"

"We do not. And nor should you. No caffeine, no refined sugars, no alcohol. All a well-honed body should need is a balanced diet and regular sleep."

"I'd settle for the latter."

Santana moved to the side. "After you." To Kurzweil, he said, "I figure she's about ready."

Quon had started to step forward, but now paused. "Ready for what?"

"Not you." Santana pulled the door open a little wider. "Take a look inside."

In the centre of the bare-walled store, between two other Judges Quon didn't recognise, a crumpled shape lay on the floor, half in deep shadow from the single temporary light fixed close to the ceiling. For a moment Quon couldn't make out what she was looking at, but then it moved and she saw that it was a person wrapped in frayed blankets and old cloth sacks.

Kurzweil pushed past Quon and reached down to pull a blanket from the figure's face. It was an old man, completely bald, covered in bruises, scratches and dirt.

And then Quon moved closer, and saw that this was no old man. It was Deborah Rozek. Beaten, bruised, stripped, her head crudely shaved, her face covered in blood and tear-streaked dirt. "God... What the hell have you *done* to her?"

Still standing in the doorway, Santana said, "She's been refusing to cooperate, to reveal her suppliers."

"So you *beat* it out of her? Jesus, Santana! This is *America*, not some third-world dictatorship!"

"Correction," Santana said. "We *tried* to beat it out of her, but she still wasn't talking. She's tough. But so are we. She's close to breaking now." He addressed one of other Judges. "Lavigne, stand her up."

Judge Lavigne reached down and grabbed Rozek's right arm, hauled her to her feet—and had to hold her up. Rozek was weak to the point of exhaustion, unable to even lift her head, and Quon was sure she was quietly whimpering.

Santana stepped up to the woman and took hold of her chin, raised her head and looked into her vacant, flickering, bloodshot eyes. "Deborah... can you hear me?"

A slight nod, then a weak whisper, "I hear you, Judge."

"I want you to tell me the name of your supplier. Now, I know you don't *want* to give anything away, but the sooner you do, the sooner you can sleep. You'd like that, wouldn't you? A soft, warm bed. Clean sheets. In a place where no one can get to you. You'll be *safe* there. Maybe a little pain-relief for your shoulder, too. You could sleep then. A nice long rest, then breakfast in the morning. I know you must be hungry. Thirsty, too, judging by your chapped lips. A long, chilled glass of ice-water is just waiting for you, Deborah. Ice-cubes clinking, condensation beading on the outside of the glass—doesn't that sound good? But first, you have to give me the name I'm looking for."

Deborah Rozek weakly shook her head. "N... no." She inhaled slowly, deeply, then shuddered. "No snitch."

Santana said, "Right... she's close. Another dose should do it."

Lavigne handed Kurzweil a filled hypodermic syringe, then pulled back Rozek's sleeve. Rozek saw the syringe and immediately winced, feebly tried to shrink back from it.

Quon grabbed Kurzweil's arm, dragged her away from the barely-conscious woman. "What the hell?" She slapped the syringe out of from the Judge's hand and it clattered across the floor. "No! No, you're *not* doing this, Santana! Doesn't matter what she's done, you don't get to *torture* her! She has the right to—"

Santana snarled at Quon. "She has *no* rights! For *years* she's been a major distributor of heroin, meth-amphetamines, TranceTrance and Grud knows *what* else. Dozens of people have died because of her. Hundreds more are addicted. People like Rozek destroy entire *neighbourhoods!* And she was able to do that because the old regime protects the guilty. Well now that regime is dying and it's up to us to save the innocent. *We* get to make the rules because without us, there's nothing but chaos!" He pulled a cell phone from his pocket, and tossed it to Quon.

She caught it before it hit the ground; it was already connecting to a call.

"Talk to her!" Santana snapped.

Quon raised the phone to her ear, and before she could speak a woman's voice said, "Listen to me, Officer Errol Susan Quon. Judge Santana is right. The old ways are dying... But they're not gone. Not yet. This transition period is... difficult, we all understand that. But the transition is inevitable, so it's in everyone's best interest that we all work to make things easier, not harder."

"Who are you?"

"I'm not important," the woman said, "but my *message* is. We can't go back. At least, not yet. We're on a journey that we *must* see through to the end, because to abandon it would leave us in a much worse position than before. To extend your analogy from the diner... America's a slowly-sinking boat, but it's on a river of lava. We might not like the destination, but we sure as hell can't get out now."

"You were *spying* on me? You *bugged* me?"

"Nothing so clandestine. I was sitting in the booth behind you."

Quon had vague memories of a well-dressed woman sitting alone in the booth, but she didn't recall seeing the woman's face.

"Officer Quon, you were chosen to assist in this case because you have the strongest moral compass of all the officers in your precinct. You will not break the rules, for any reason. Never let a friend off with a fine. Never cut through the gas station to avoid the lights. You would never use any more force than is absolutely necessary to get the job done. And you have never once abused your position. We respect that. Truly, we do. Judge Fargo himself knows your name."

She didn't know what she was supposed to do with that information. "Why are you telling me this?"

"Because that strong moral compass of yours was pointing you in a direction we would all regret. You've already unfastened the clasp on your holster, haven't you?"

Quon glanced down at her hip: she had automatically thumbed open the clasp when she'd grabbed Kurzweil's arm.

The woman continued: "You were about to take action against a Judge, and that would be a *crime*. We can't have our most upstanding officer—the nation's youngest and last police officer—breaking the law, can we?"

Quon felt her strength dissipate. *She's right. I've painted myself into a corner. What they're doing is legal.* Anything *they want to do is legal.*

Judge Kurzweil picked up the syringe and again approached the prisoner, and again Deborah Rozek tried to pull herself free of Judge Lavigne's grip.

Kurzweil balled up her fist and slammed it into Rozek's face. Rozek fell limp once more, and her head lolled as Kurzweil injected the syringe's contents into her arm.

The woman on the other end of the call said, "*Now* do you understand the situation, Officer Quon?"

"I do. I can't fix all this with the laws as they are. And an ordinary police officer can't change the law. But a *Judge* can." She lowered the phone, then tapped the End Call button and handed the phone back to Judge Santana. "All right. I want you to understand that I *despise* this, but you do what you think you have to do. And when we're done... I'll do what *I* have to do."

Santana nodded as he tucked the phone back into his pocket. "Good to hear it. The Department will be lucky to have you."

CHAPTER EIGHT

WHATEVER HAD BEEN in the syringe had made Deborah Rozek talkative, almost giddy, but very unfocussed. Her words slurred, and she drooled almost constantly as her head lolled and bobbed.

After a few minutes Quon couldn't watch any more. She stepped back out onto the parking lot, sat down on the kerb, and waited.

She's always known that her time as a cop would come to an end long before she reached retirement age, but hoped it wouldn't be like this.

She had to become the thing she hated in order to defeat it. And even then... there were no guarantees. Not even close.

At the academy back in Mississippi, Captain Deitch had told her, "The Judges are a band-aid solution to a problem that requires major surgery and a lot of recovery time. Trouble is, some of them don't understand that. They think that this is the destination, not the journey."

Quon could see that attitude in Kurzweil, but less so in Santana. There was some hope there—though not much—that she might be able to help him to shift his point of view. Or if not, then maybe she'd have a chance to make a difference to others once she was a Judge.

The most recent reports she'd seen on the Academy of Law stated that the training period for incoming Judges had been increased to three years, and as a consequence many first-wave Judges were being pulled off the streets for retraining.

Three years, Quon thought. *I can do that. Then once I'm back on the streets, I can start making laws for the people, not the state.* Unless their indoctrination involved some sort of brainwashing—and given the way they were currently treating a prisoner, she couldn't rule that out.

She flinched when the door screeched open behind her.

"That was tough going, but we've got a name," Santana said. "Her up-line is Sullivan Reidt. He's not on the system. Mean anything to you?" He extended his hand down to Quon.

Quon hesitated before grabbing the Judge's hand and allowing him to pull her to her feet. "Sully Reidt's a drunk. I don't know where he lives, but he spends a lot of his time in the Air Heart. Most of it passed out in the lavatories."

Kurzweil was checking her gun's magazine as she emerged from the store. "The Air Heart... That's a biker's bar, right? Gonna be interesting."

Santana said, "It's almost zero-four-hundred. No point in even approaching the place until about twenty-one hundred tomorrow. You two knock off, get some rest."

Quon said to Santana, "Judge, I doubt Sully is even involved. I told you, he's a *drunk*."

Kurzweil looked at Quon like she was an idiot. "If we were allowed to gamble, I'd tell you that ten bucks says that he's *not*. He'll be as sober as, well, me. I've seen that before. Dealer hangs out in a bar and does his expert impression of being passed-out drunk whenever a cop approaches. You're not inclined to suspect that the guy who's got his own puke drying to a crust on his shirt and his own piss squelching in his shoes is a high-level dealer." She nodded towards her Lawranger. "I'll give you a ride home, Quon."

Quon remained standing next to Judge Santana as they watched Kurzweil stride towards her Lawranger.

"Feet getting cold?" Santana asked.

"No. But sending a Judge into the Air Heart is reckless. We don't even know for sure that Sully will be there."

"If he's not, one of his friends will tell us where to find him. Judge Kurzweil is good at persuading people to cooperate."

"So I've seen." Quon glanced back at the store for a moment, then followed Kurzweil to her bike.

DALLAS HAWKER WAS already awake when his alarm clock ticked over to five-thirty and began to beep. He reached out and tapped it into silence, then lay there for a moment listening to the standard, comforting sounds of Gwen's slow, steady breathing, the gentle hum of the air conditioner, and Evie's snoring in the next room.

Fifteen years old and she snores like a steam train struggling to get up a hill. Pity the poor bastard who ends up having to sleep next to that. Dallas shook his head briskly, trying to cast out the idea that one day his daughter would be regularly sleeping with someone.

How the hell can she be fifteen already? Fifteen years ago was yesterday. *Where does the time go?* In the fridge there was still half a jar of mustard he'd bought the first time he and Gwen had gone grocery shopping together.

In the bathroom he sat down to pee while he was brushing his teeth. He knew Gwen hated that but what was she going to do? Dictate the way he urinated? He liked to think that they were equal partners in their marriage, but there were some areas where each left the other to their own devices.

Dallas's hobby was the main area into which Gwen knew it was best not to stray. They'd never talked about it, but they'd talked *around* it. An item on the local TV news might spark a comment from Gwen like, "Someone ought to do something about that," and Dallas would say, "I reckon someone will."

He was sure she didn't know *exactly* what he did when he

went out at night, but she knew that he'd always come back. And she knew that he was careful, that was what mattered most. There was some comfort in knowing that Gwen wasn't going to have the experience of the cops knocking on the door in the middle of the night to tell her that her husband had been shot dead while trying to ambush a serial burglar.

The day shift at the factory started at eight, and the drive took an hour at most. Half an hour to have breakfast and take a shower meant Dallas had the remaining hour to work out on the equipment in the garage.

He wasn't trying to build muscle, just stay in shape—three of his friends from high school had already had heart attacks, one of them fatally—so he always took it fairly easy. A hundred sit-ups or crunches, alternating day to day, a hundred push-ups, fifty reps on the bench with the free weights set to forty kilograms, followed by thirty minutes on the treadmill. In the winter he'd sometimes take a run around the neighbourhood instead, but in the height of summer, even this early, it was hot out there.

Dallas stretched and flexed a little as he approached the weights bench, then stepped up onto it. He reached up to a white-painted pipe that passed directly overhead and used a small pencil to make a mark on it. There was a neat line of fourteen marks now: they'd be unnoticed by anyone else, he was sure, but he could see them when he was lying on his back, using the bench. See them, and focus on them.

FIVE YEARS EARLIER, Patience Belaire welcomed Dallas and the others into her home for the first time.

As they all worked to clear some space in the semi-dark basement—except Otis, who was on a step-ladder holding a flashlight between his teeth as he attached a new light-fitting—she told them, "I'm not going to be the leader. Like I said in the chat room, I don't think we *need* a leader. But this is my house so I have a few rules."

Cindy Draughton said, "Right. Like, no smoking, no spilling stuff on the rugs, that kind of thing."

"I was thinking more along the lines of there should be no *vendettas*. If you've been personally wronged by a criminal, then that criminal is off limits to you. Not just because your anger might make you sloppy, but also because you don't want a trail leading back to you."

Everyone flinched as the light above Otis flickered on. He said, "Sorry. But Ms Belaire is right. We have to be cold, and detached. If you take down someone, you have to be the *last* person the law would suspect."

Patience said, "Exactly. And the second rule is that we operate in secrecy. No one must know. *Ever.* We don't do this for glory. No posts online, however opaque they might be." She looked at Billy Draughton. "That's directed primarily at *you*, William. Twice last month you posted, 'Feeling great tonight, wish I could tell you why!'"

"Yeah, but there's no *way* anyone—"

Dallas cut in, "As my grandma would have put it, 'Being a feckin' eejit is free, but that doesn't mean you should grab the opportunity with both hands.'"

Billy shrugged. "What does *that* mean?"

Graham Mealing said, "It means you don't want people to wonder what it is you're boasting *about*." Addressing the rest of them, he added, "And, your honour, I'd like the court to take into consideration the fact that if this guy can't comprehend something as simple as that without the rest of us having to spell it out for him over and over, then maybe he's just too damn stupid for this game." He glanced back at Billy. "No offence."

Billy Draughton laughed at that, a genuine, warm laugh, and that endeared him to Dallas: he didn't have much time for people who were easily upset.

Patience, true to her chosen name, waited until they were done before continuing: "The third thing is that this must always be a non-profit organisation: all cash, weapons or narcotics—or anything else—recovered from a job are to be given to me for later disposal. Cash and other non-illegal goods will be donated to charity. Guns and narcotics will be destroyed."

"What about a stipend?" Otis asked, lowering himself into a beat-up old armchair. "I don't have a very high income—as Dallas will testify—and as an ex-con I'm fairly closely monitored. The IRS has audited me four times already. So if I'm seen to be spending too much on, say, gas, that'll raise a few flags."

Mealing said, "Yeah, that's a point. I don't want to be out of pocket." He grinned. "Heh, that's appropriate considering what I do. But even so, *you* might be loaded, Patience, but the rest of us aren't."

It was Shelby Demps, always the quietest of the group and sitting in the corner, who said, "This is a hobby. Hobbies cost money."

"I know: if you haven't got the money, you don't do the hobby," Mealing said. "But I'm not asking for much, just enough to cover the costs."

Patience nodded at that. "I understand that... but we have to be careful. Suppose it all backfires and we get arrested? We'd need to be able to prove that we're not criminals." She paused for a moment. "Okay, yes, vigilantism is against the law, but we're stopping *worse* criminals. So if it all falls apart, our strongest defence will be that we believe we're providing a public service. Taking a cut would disprove that."

Dallas said to Otis, "*I'll* cover the cost of your gas. And whatever else you need, within reason. Tools, batteries for your flashlight, that kind of thing."

"I appreciate that, but you shouldn't have to. I could skim, say, five per cent off the top. Only of the cash I take, nothing else."

Dallas saw Patience's shoulders sag at that, so, firmly, he said, "No cuts. Simple as that. If we take a thousand bucks off a target, then we hand in that thousand bucks. That's the rule."

Patience nodded. "Right. And we hand in *those* thousand dollars."

"I just said that."

"No, I mean, we hand in the exact cash we take. The very same notes. Don't go making change because the target happened to have a bunch of five-dollar bills and all you have is a twenty and you need to stop at the Seven-Eleven on the way home. For all we know, the cash could be marked in some way."

They spent the next hour exchanging ideas, with Shelby continuing his trend of contributing the least and Mealing being the most argumentative. Otis's suggestion that they all learn basic car maintenance was well received—you can't call out triple-A if your ride breaks down when you're fifty miles away from your alibi—as was Patience's demonstration of the most effective garotting technique, performed on a dress-maker's mannequin that Dallas couldn't help noticing was already almost shredded from dozens of deep, vicious stab-wounds to the abdomen.

As they were winding down the meeting, Patience remembered one last rule that she'd almost forgotten: "Don't take *anything* as a keepsake. We only take weapons, narcotics and cash from the targets. Nothing else. No trophies."

HIS REPS COMPLETED, Dallas lay back on his bench and stared up at the pipe across the ceiling. These marks were reminders, that was all. Not trophies.

Fourteen reminders of fourteen kills.

It bothered him a little that he couldn't remember which way around the sixth and seventh kills had been. One of them was a seventeen-year-old joyrider who'd caused a fatal accident on the freeway—Dallas had rigged that one to look like a self-administered hanging—and the other was a young mother who'd left her kids home alone for a week while she went on a Trance binge with a group of friends, and despite the media circus she'd somehow managed to retain custody of the youngest two. Dallas had simply lured her out of her home and put a screwdriver through her temple. Someday, a developer would dig up her remains and people would finally realise she hadn't fled Golgotha of her own accord.

But which had been sixth and which seventh? He sighed and sat up. No point sweating about it. Some element of the kills that put them in context would come to mind later, when he was thinking about something else. Probably in the middle of the afternoon production meeting when Ed the sales manager was once again awkwardly trying to shoehorn a football metaphor into an anecdote about selling underwear.

CHAPTER NINE

Errol Quon emerged from her bathroom wrapped in only a towel to find her mother sitting on the end of her bed and looking both disappointed and angry at the same time.

Quon had long since given up on the idea of attempting to persuade her mother that she couldn't just walk into someone else's apartment unannounced, that the key was for emergencies only.

"What is it now, Mom?"

"You're still not up! At this hour!" Sharlene Quon said. "I didn't raise my only child to be a slug-a-bed slob. What must your friend think of me?"

Even as Quon was asking, "What friend?" she realised she'd forgotten that Judge Kurzweil had chosen to sleep on the sofa instead of going back across town to her boarding house. Quon hadn't offered the sofa or any other form of accommodation: the Judge had just declared her intention in a tone that implied it would be pointless to resist.

"Is she still here?"

Sharlene's lips thinned. "Oh, she's here. She's *here*, all right. Woke up when I let myself in and pointed her gun at me and demanded to know who I was. She even asked me for identification! And now she's out there sitting at your bar eating toast."

"It's a counter, not a bar."

"I've a mind to report her."

"To who?"

"To *whom*, Errol. *Ob*jective case, not *sub*jective. And I'll report her to the person or institution to whom one reports bad Judge behaviour."

Quon rolled her eyes. "Mom, I was on duty all weekend and working most of the night. What do you want? Or are you just here because one of your spies phoned to say there's a Judge's motorbike outside and you drove a hundred and sixty kilometres to see for yourself? That's it, isn't it?"

Before her mother could answer, the bedroom door was pushed open. Judge Kurzweil was stripped down to a t-shirt and a pair of shorts. It was the first time that Quon had seen her without her uniform. She seemed smaller, but no less dangerous.

"Clock's ticking, Quon. You've had almost six hours' sleep. I'm giving you fifteen minutes to eat and do whatever else you need to do. And I recommend you change your locks." She looked towards Mrs Quon. "You're clearly not shy about telling everyone that your daughter is a police officer, nor that you have a key to her apartment. That's not just reckless endangerment: it's remarkably stupid, short-sighted and selfish."

"You can't speak to me like that!"

"Of course I can." Kurzweil stepped back, pulling the door closed behind her. "Fourteen minutes, Quon."

SENIOR JUDGE HAYDEN Santana had been a Judge for over eight years, so long that it was only on the rare occasions that he was wearing civilian clothes that he remembered what it was like not to have people automatically shy away from him.

At zero-two-hundred hours he was sitting on a bench in Varley Square in the heart of Golgotha and looking around as he slowly ate a sandwich, occasionally checking his cell phone.

No one was staring. It felt strange. And a little unsafe, too. He'd grown used to the cocoon of the uniform and helmet and without them he felt like an egg without its shell. Maybe that was something to bring up at his next evaluation: suggest that all Judges should spend a couple of days per month out of uniform. It might help bring them a little closer to the people they were duty-bound to protect.

That had been one of his fears since the day he signed up: the Judges need to be elevated so that the people can see, fear and respect them, but separation works in both directions... If the Judges start to believe that they're better than ordinary citizens, that's a one-way trip to corruption, and hearty protein for the ravenous anti-Judge movement.

His old courtroom sparring-partner Spender Gant was still making waves in that regard, still railing against the system, trying to bring others around to his cause. He might as well try to catch umbrage in a bottle for all the good it would do. Sure, people were scared of the Judges' brutality, but they were always damn glad to hear the rumble of an approaching Lawranger when they were in trouble.

Santana checked his cell phone again. The screen showed a map of the city with a single flashing dot. He zoomed in on the map, confirming again that the dot hadn't moved much in almost an hour. It was directly behind him, forty metres away.

The range on the tracker was pretty good, and it was accurate down to two metres, which was more than adequate. It was the refresh rate that was the problem. The tracker emitted a brief burst every four minutes. Anything more frequent would require a larger power-cell, which would be harder to hide.

A voice off to his left said, "Spare change?" and Santana turned to see a shabby, weather-beaten old woman holding a battered paper cup out to a fresh young couple sitting on the next bench. They ignored her as though she were totally invisible, and she moved away, on to the next bench.

Any other day he might have arrested the woman for panhandling, or at least moved her on.

He didn't know how he felt about that. People can fall into poverty through no fault of their own. Any fool knew that. And poverty was a deep pit with slippery sides. Sometimes, the only way out was if someone above threw you a rope. Society provided plenty of ropes, but most of them came with strings attached. We will give you free food and accommodation and all you have to do is worship our god. Or move to another town. Or deliver this package without the cops finding out. Or agree to take part in this clinical trial.

In one of his recent public speeches, Spender Gant had said, "No one's denying that this country is in trouble, but the solution is not the sledgehammer approach of the Judges. It is the velvet glove. We have billionaires making decisions that affect the lives of people who won't be able to afford to eat tomorrow. That's where the Judges and I agree: people who have never been hungry or cold should not have the power to shut down food banks. If you want to learn how to build a wooden table, who do you talk to? The man who owns the multinational furniture company he inherited from his parents, or the woman who earns a living by making tables from scavenged shipping pallets?"

Santana could see where Gant was coming from, but he wanted to reformat the nation's infrastructure without tackling the underlying problems. That was like changing a flat tyre without stopping the car.

The Judges weren't the ideal all-round solution either—even Fargo himself would probably admit that—but they were a solution to the problem of rampant crime.

He checked his cell phone again. Still no sign of movement. Could be hours yet... And those hours would be better spent in uniform. Someone else could watch the perp.

He crumpled up the paper sandwich bag and stuffed it into his jacket pocket as he stood up. Stretched a little as he turned around to look towards the perp.

Noelle Vetter, thirty years old, female, neatly-dressed. Carried a clipboard and stopped random strangers, asked them if they were interested in participating in a survey about local zoning ordnance laws. Santana and some of his Judges had been taking turns watching Vetter all morning and not one person had agreed to contribute to Vetter's survey. But she did get a lot of people *pretending* to be interested. Regular customers. She wasn't carrying, though. She just took the money and signalled to the crew further down the block when someone made a purchase.

Buddy McKinty's friend Sergi Nieto had been one of Vetter's regulars.

Judge Groom had followed McKinty to Nieto last night, watched him buy fifty bucks worth of Trance. Stayed on Nieto until he'd handed his elastic-wrapped roll of bills to Vetter this morning.

Santana desperately wanted to march over to Vetter and take her down, but what good would that do? Someone else would take her place. "You get better fruit by climbing higher," Marisa Pellegrino used to tell him.

If Kurzweil had no luck with Sullivan Reidt, then maybe Vetter would lead them to someone, who would in turn lead them—eventually—to Irvine Romley.

It *could* be done, but Romley was, to use Judge Boyd's description, "One deviously slippery drokker." Getting close to him wouldn't be enough. Even killing him wouldn't do it. He had to be *broken*. They would take him alive and the festering sack of scum would split open and spill everything he knew. His entire operation, all the names and dates. And that would be enough to shatter the entire network of Trance distribution throughout the USA, because there had never been a drug lord who didn't have their own cadre of bitter rivals, and sure as the seabed is moist, they knew *everything* about those rivals. Crack one, and the rest would be revealed.

Forty metres away, Vetter approached a man in his thirties and he dodged past her at the last second, barely acknowledging her. Santana figured that if her fake survey had been about sex or cookies, just about everyone would stop.

Santana turned away and called Judge Lavigne on his cell. "Lunchbreak's over. Heading back to base. Eyes on the target at all times."

"Will do, sir."

After another glance back at Vetter—still nothing happening—he started to head back across the square in the direction of bus that would take him back to the precinct, and almost absently pulled his cell phone out of his pocket one more time.

The dot had moved. It was no longer centred on Noelle Vetter, but was now seventy metres down the street.

He fought the urge to spin around back towards Vetter. Instead, he slowed to a stop as he made a call. "Tracker's on the move. Anyone see the handover?"

"No, sir," Judge Lavigne said. "And I haven't taken my eyes off her."

Judge Steinmetz said, "Same. But that cit who brushed past her a couple minutes ago—he's the only one she could have handed it to."

Santana swore. "Who's got him? At least tell me one of you got a clear look at his face!"

"Negative," Lavigne said. "I'll poll the street cam footage."

"All right." Santana began to walk towards the signal's most recent position. "Dispatch a shadow team to trail this creep. With Rozek out of the picture he'll have to deliver to someone else. I'll keep on him until the team can take over. And I want an ID on him ASAP."

"Sir, you're unarmed and out of uniform. Protocol recommends against that."

"If I were in uniform, he'd spot me. And don't quote the book to me, Lavigne—I *wrote* most of the drokkin' thing."

"Yes, sir."

Santana spotted the man about fifty metres in front of him. "Got him. Causasian male, thirties. Short dark hair, shades, blue denim jeans, pale yellow t-shirt, grey windbreaker jacket slung over his right shoulder, black boots. Walking at a steady pace… He's just turned left onto Beech Street. Didn't look: he knows exactly where he is and where he's going."

"No clear facial on the street cams, sir," Lavigne said. "But we've got him on the satellite view. And just received another blip from the tracker. Positions match—he's definitely the pickup guy."

"Good. What's our situation with the others from Rozek's list?"

"The priest has been tending the chrysanthemums in his garden for the past two hours. Hollins is on the road, coming back from a genuine plumbing job. Judge Mayall hasn't been able to get close to him, but she did lock a tracer onto his truck. An hour ago Hollins delivered a package to two of his people and picked up a bundle of cash. We had Groom watching one of them—so far identified only as Bovey, possibly a nickname—but I had to reassign him: cops found a deceased in South Lorraine."

Ahead, Santana's target was thumbing through his cell phone as he waited at a traffic crossing.

"Why'd they need a Judge?"

"The deceased, Gregorz Weitzner, was charged last year in a hit-and-run case. A little girl died. The prosecutors had an airtight case against him until their strongest piece of evidence got wiped. Traffic camera footage. The backups were wiped, too. And around the same time Weitzner's brother transferred fifty thousand dollars to an offshore account."

"Hackers," Santana said.

"That's what the cops figure. After that, the case disintegrated and Weitzner walked free. Then last night he slipped in his hallway and landed throat-first on a drinking glass. He lived alone. Guy from the cleaning service found him. He reported that the apartment was locked, but the alarm hadn't been activated. That's all they've got. But suspicion isn't—"

"Suspicion isn't evidence. So the cops are looking into the little girl's family?"

"Yes, sir. After the trial collapsed, her father and uncle were picked up twice for stalking Weitzner, and once for threatening behaviour. The uncle in particular is flagged as dangerous. Cops're talking to him today—wanted a Judge present for the intimidation factor."

"All right. Keep me posted. But don't let Groom linger too long on that. What about Vetter's other people?"

"Near as we can tell, Sergi Nieto only supplies to others when he's got a surplus, which isn't often. Rozek's also mentioned several other customers—all at about Nieto's level—and a subordinate dealer named Maroth or Meroth, something like that, but that's all we've managed to get out of her about that. She's pretty far gone now."

"And Rozek's father?"

"Still insists he never met anyone she dealt with, or heard her mention any names. We're inclined to believe him. He helped Rozek cut and package the Trance in the apartment, but her dealers never visited."

"All right," Santana said. "Keep the pressure on him. Give him water, but don't let him eat or sleep. When Rozek recovers enough, I want her to see him. The shock might jog a few more names loose."

"Shadow team coming up on your left, sir," Steinmetz said.

A battered pickup truck trundled past Santana and pulled in to the kerb. By the time he reached it, the driver and passenger had climbed out. Judges Cade and Martucci were dressed in casual civilian clothes, though it was clear to Santana that Cade was carrying her gun in her backpack. As Cade passed him, she muttered, "We're on him, sir."

"No action until you get the word."

Santana saw both Cade and Martucci nod in response, then allowed his attention to be snagged by the display in a bookstore's window. He lingered for a few seconds, then turned away, heading back towards Varley Square.

His Judges would get the job done. They were a good team, though he could do with a few more of them. Every week he put in a request for twenty new Judges, and about once a month he was assigned a single rookie fresh out of the academy.

He checked the map on his cell phone again. The target was continuing along Beech Street at a leisurely pace, still in possession of the tagged fifty-dollar bill Santana had given to Buddy McKinty the previous evening. The banknote was old, crumpled, and it would take an expert to detect that it was fake: its stitched-in strip of silver foil was a GPS transponder with a minute power-cell.

For decades conspiracy theorists had believed that their banknotes were secretly tagged and now it was finally true, at least in this case.

Santana knew that it was unlikely that the bill would get into the hands of Romley himself, but it might get close. At the very least, it should reach whichever creep Romley had appointed to be Deborah Rozek's replacement.

CHAPTER TEN

The Air Heart bar was a converted small aircraft hangar located eleven kilometres south-east of Golgotha, on the edge of what had once been Spin Ridge airfield. It was a meeting place for both aviation enthusiasts and bikers, and Quon knew that it was one of those dives where a cop shouldn't set foot alone, especially not after sunset. It bothered her that it was the sort of place that people pointed to when they wanted to prove that the new Department of Justice was necessary.

Low music thumped from the dark building almost in synch with its flickering neon sign—a slowly revolving propeller—and even from a hundred metres away, Quon was sure she could smell beer and whiskey.

They had stopped in the middle of a grove of trees, and as Quon climbed off the back of Judge Kurzweil's Lawranger, the Judge said, "Satellite shows seventeen motorcycles and eight cars. So we're looking at a minimum of twenty-five customers and staff."

"What if someone recognises me?" Quon asked.

Kurzweil looked her up and down in the moonlight. "They won't. In your shirt and jeans you look just like a normal person. Just order a drink at the bar, and look around as though you're expecting to see someone. If Sullivan Reidt is there, send me a text. And keep watching him." She nodded towards the bar. "Go ahead, Quon. You get into trouble, make some noise and I'll come running."

Quon hesitated, and the Judge said, "Nothing to be scared about. You think Judge Santana would have chosen you if he didn't think you could handle yourself?"

"That's scant comfort," Quon said. "And I'm not scared, just not sure that this is the right approach."

"If *I* go in first, Reidt's people will cause a distraction long enough for him to slip away."

"All right." Quon gave the Judge a nod, and set off towards the bar.

She remembered her one previous visit to the Air Heart, about eight months into her career, helping to mop up after a brawl that had started when one biker urinated on another's Harley. Fourteen fractured or broken limbs, six head wounds and one stabbing. No fatalities, and even the stabbing victim had been back in the bar the following night.

Sully Reidt had been there, Quon recalled. Half-slumped in a corner, unconscious next to an upturned table and a broken chair. Her colleague David Huck had tended to him.

Reidt was in his early forties, but looked and moved like he was seventy, at least. The prize for a lifetime of hard drinking.

A cluster of smokers and vapers were gathered outside the bar's entrance—their thick exhalations disturbing the cluster of moths that orbited the single bright light over the doors—so Quon waited in the shadows at the loose-gravelled entrance to the bar's parking lot until a car passed by at a relatively slow speed, waited another minute, then stepped out into the moonlight and gave a slight wave back to the imaginary driver who'd dropped her off.

She kept her head down and her pace steady, but was sure that they were watching every step she made. *They can see I don't belong here!*

But the only acknowledgement they made of her presence

was when one of them—a woman about her own age—pulled open the door for her as she approached.

"Thanks."

"De nada."

Quon stepped into the bar, half expecting the music to instantly cease and all the patrons to stop talking and stare at her. She was almost disappointed that no one seemed to even glance in her direction.

The bar's split-level design didn't disguise its origins as an aircraft hangar. A wide room with a floor made from old and slightly warped planks, decorated with wooden propellers and faded photos of biplanes and aviators wearing flying helmets and goggles. Off to the left a huge wooden staircase led up to the second level, which right now was closed off with a length of rope. On the right side of the ground floor a bald, thick-bearded barman was pouring a beer behind a long wooden bar. It was illuminated by a neat grid of orange and white LED strips overhead, and was by far the brightest part of the entire place, throwing everything else in shadow. The back and left-side walls were lined with semi-circular booths, about half of them occupied. She couldn't be sure with the poor light, but it looked like the clientele was split just about evenly between men and women, almost all of them bedecked in the timeless biker style: blue denims, boots, long hair. The only one who wasn't, as far as she could see, was a woman wearing a red shirt, red jeans and pure white sneakers who was getting up from a corner booth.

The rest of the ground floor held a dozen wooden tables of assorted sizes and shapes and twice as many chairs, all currently unoccupied, and Quon felt very conspicuous as she crossed it towards the bar.

The barman looked up at her and said something she couldn't hear over the music.

Frowning, she shuffled further along the bar, closer to him. "What?"

"I said, nice night."

"Oh, yeah, sure. If you like *weather*," Quon said. She saw that the man was missing his left ear, and tried not to stare at the scar-edged hole.

He smirked. "What can I getcha?"

In that moment, Quon couldn't conjure up the name of a single brand of beer. She didn't drink alcohol, never had—another reason her fellow cops didn't want to hang out with her—but she knew that outside of the movies no one ever just asked the bartender for "a beer." She glanced at the wall behind him, but couldn't read the labels on any of the bottles.

Then she realised she had hesitated for too long. She shook her head slowly and said, "Just... water."

The barman regarded her for a second. "On the wagon, huh?" Without looking around, he reached out to the shelf behind him for a half-litre bottle of water. "Good for you." He placed it unopened on the bar in front of her. "Eight-fifty."

Quon gave him a brief look that was meant to say, "Eight-fifty? Really? For a bottle of water? In *this* place?" then handed him a ten-dollar bill.

When she didn't say "Keep the change," he slid a dollar and two quarters back to her.

"So what brings you out, if you're not drinking?"

"I'm looking for someone." She leaned on the bar with one elbow as she opened the bottle of water, turning to look around the room at the same time. The booths were deep in shadow: Sully Reidt could be in any of them, if he was here at all.

"What's your friend's name?" the bartender asked. "I might know her."

Quon turned back. "What makes you assume it's a *her*?"

"Hey, I'm not judging. Making no assumptions here."

Clearly you are, Quon said to herself. "He's more... a friend of a friend. Of a friend. You know what I mean? Someone recommended him to me, but..." She looked down at her hands. *Please let this work!* "I'm thinking that maybe this is a bad idea."

The barman placed his hand on her arm and gently said, "Hey... Often the best things spring out of bad ideas. You're off the booze and I can see that you're hurting. I know what that's like. It comes in waves. Peaks and valleys. And right now you're in a valley and you're looking for something to ease the path, right? Get you through." He pulled his hand away, and nodded towards the back corner of the room. "The guy you want is in the corner." He leaned a little closer, and lowered his voice. "But that doesn't mean he's a *corner-boy*, you understand? He's no low-level street-dealer passing out little packets of dope or tabs or E or ten-buck bags of crawbies. We're talking bulk quantities. And we're talking *Trance*. Is that what you want?"

Quon rubbed her upper arms as though she were cold—she'd seen junkies do that a lot—then briefly glanced at the corner. The man in silhouette could be Sully Reidt, but it was hard to be sure. To the bartender, she said, "I've gotta be honest with you... I don't know *what* I want. I just know that I need *something*."

He nodded at that. "All right. But if you've not touched T.T. before, well, the first time it can be..." He put his closed fists on either side of his head and mimed an explosion. "You know what I'm saying? This isn't like getting drunk or high."

"Sure, yeah."

"It's gonna make you want everyone to love you, you know? That can be dangerous if you're not prepared."

"Maybe I'll just hold off for a bit." She recalled the behaviour of a drunk she'd run in five times in one month, and suddenly tensed her upper body and shuddered. "I'm gonna sit for a while, that okay?"

"Sure, yeah."

Quon stepped away from the bar, then turned back. "Thanks. And... if I ask for a drink later on, don't give me one?"

The barman gave her a thin-lipped smile, and nodded. "You got it. I mean, you *won't* get it."

She found an empty booth where she could nurse her bottle

of water and watch the corner booth without it being too obvious, then pulled her phone from her jeans and composed a text message for Judge Kurzweil: "Target possibly here. Hold tight."

Before she could hit Send, the man in the corner booth pulled out his own cell phone, and the light from its screen revealed his face.

She was certain now. It was him. Sullivan Reidt.

GABE NYBY PAUSED in the process of pulling off his shirt and looked from his bedside table with his buzzing phone to his bed and the naked woman occupying it, and back.

It was the ringtone he'd assigned to Romley's number. For a moment he genuinely considered ignoring the call. For over eight years he'd been Romley's right-hand man, always on call, never able to settle down. Didn't even have a regular girlfriend. These days, a quick tryst once every couple of weeks with Leila Bronson was all he permitted himself.

And he could tell from the look on Leila's face that she understood there was no contest: as hungry as he might be for human contact and sexual gratification, he was going to answer the phone.

"I'm sorry," he told Leila as he pulled his pants back up. "You know how it is."

"I do. Better than anyone." She shrugged. "Go ahead." She rolled onto her side, facing away from him, and Gabe sat down on the edge of the bed as he picked up the cell phone.

Romley said, "Gabriel... So many little things add up to one big thing. Increased Judge presence, the arrest of Ms Rozek... I put a watch on her people."

Of course you did, Gabe told himself, and glanced at the smooth contours of Leila's back. *You watch all of us. You know everything we do.*

Romley continued, "It took them some time, but my agents

concluded that someone *else* was watching her. And the fact that it took time meant...?"

Gabe said, "They were good at staying hidden. Professionals. Judges. So they got Deborah to talk."

"Exactly. And she knows Sullivan Reidt. She's certainly named him. Possibly named you, too."

"Right. Well, I have a way to get out of *that*. I can—"

"*Stop*, Gabriel. I'm not done."

"Sorry. Go ahead."

"You handed Ms Rozek's people over to Sullivan Reidt. Among them is a woman, Noelle Vetter. Eleven minutes ago Reidt's pickup man approached Vetter to collect her bank. She was in a state of panic: had been for hours, but she didn't know to whom she should turn. Some of her money disappeared earlier today. The figure itself is not important—only a couple of thousand—but it's the act."

"That's that goddamn pickpocket again! I swear I'll wring that bastard's neck so *tight* he'll be able to lick his own eyeballs!"

"No." There was another of Romley's unsettlingly long pauses, and Gabe knew what was coming next: "We're compromised, Gabriel. I want you to shut down all the lines of operation in Golgotha. You will eliminate *everyone* who knows me, or who might lead back to you. And do it personally—don't take the risk of hiring someone else. Fast and clean, Gabriel. And immediate."

Gabe again turned to look at Leila Bronson. *Aw hell.*

Eight years ago, he'd been relatively new to the business when he'd had to break away from his old life. He hadn't had the experience or courage to stand up to Romley.

Now a veteran, he had a much better idea of how firmly he could plant his feet if he felt sure that Romley was wrong.

But experience had also given him the understanding that Romley's intuition was very finely honed. If he thought that something was too risky, that didn't mean he had cold feet. It meant it was too risky.

Deep in the woods south of Golgotha, a buried fridge contained a thick canvas holdall. Gabe's getaway bag: cash, new identity, a few changes of clothes. Everything he would need to disappear forever.

I could do it. I could run and he'd never find me. He'd need someone like me to find *me, and I'm the only me he's got.*

Unless I'm not.

Unless I'm just one small cog in the machine. A cog who believes he's just about running the whole engine.

Jesus, of course *that's how it is. That's how he works. How he's* always *worked. He rewards us with a sense of self-importance. We're all obedient little soldiers who believe they're close friends with a general who only sees them as cannon-fodder.*

I could *run. And maybe he'd never find me... but he* would *find everyone else I know. Mom and Dad, and Raphael.*

Ten minutes later, he left his apartment with his Sauer Mosquito tucked into the back of his jeans, his old butterfly knife strapped to his left shin and his tazer in his jacket pocket.

He didn't have a cleaner, no friends who might call, didn't know the neighbours, and he was up-to-date with his rent. It could be weeks or even months before Leila Bronson's body was discovered.

CHAPTER ELEVEN

DALLAS HAWKER KNOCKED on his daughter's closed bedroom door, and waited for her response. His own parents had never shown him that level of respect. As far as they'd been concerned, it was their house and the kids were tenants with practically no rights.

Evie called out, "Yeah?"

"Got a minute? I just want to bounce something off you."

"Sure. Come in."

He opened the door and stepped into Evie's room, now a memorial to the almost manic obsession she'd had with unicorns and the colour lilac only a couple of years ago. She was sitting on the bed in the lotus position with her laptop open in front of her.

"Homework?"

"Would you believe me if I said yes?"

Dallas grinned. "Sure."

"Then, yeah, homework. We have to do an essay on shopping for boots."

"I hope you get full marks." He sat on the edge of the bed and turned to her. It felt like only a few weeks—a couple of months at most—since he'd last sat in that same spot and read to her stories about courageous pirates and vicious dragons that never seemed to kill anyone. "One of the guys in work has a son about your age, and—"

"No!"

"No what?"

Evie scowled at him, and for a moment he saw her mother in that scowl. "You're *not* setting me up with someone! God, that would be so *embarrassing*!"

"No, that's not where this is going. At lunch today he said that his son got into trouble at school for saying that the Judges are too lenient and that execution is the only way to deal with rapists and child abusers and murderers."

"Oh. Okay..."

"A couple of the younger people in work agreed with that. So is that a common belief among people of your age?"

Evie closed over the laptop and pushed it aside. "I don't know..."

"What do *you* think?"

"There's no easy answer, Dad."

"Suppose you know that someone did something like that, but there's no way to prove it. You're absolutely *certain* that they did it, okay? But for whatever reason, they're getting away with it. What should you do?"

"Go to the cops. Or the Judges."

"Suppose you know that's not going to make a difference."

"You could create a fake account online and post about it. Get the truth out into the world."

"What if that's not enough? Or what if you know you can't do that because fake accounts can always be traced back to their source." He paused for a second. "Always. And you should remember that, just in case. But back to the hypothetical question... You can't report them or out them in public. What do you do?"

She shrugged. "Mask and cape, that's your only option. Take the law into your own hands."

"That's a crime."

"It's *less* of a crime than raping or murdering someone or

abusing a child."

"So you'd punish them yourself... How?"

"They can't rape someone if they haven't got a di... uh, the right *equipment.*"

Dallas suppressed a laugh. "I've heard the word before, honey. I'm not going to be shocked. But even without the equipment, they actually can still do a lot of damage. Don't underestimate the depravity loose in this world. So what about *murderers*, then? How would you punish a murderer?"

"I suppose..." Evie frowned. "It wasn't an accident or an act of rage... I mean, if they knew *exactly* what they were doing when it happened, and they're not sorry, and they're likely to do it again... you'd have no option but to kill them."

"That's also murder."

"But it's not murder when a Judge does it. That's execution. The only *real* difference is that, like, society has agreed the Judge has *permission* to do it. Even though the Judges are the ones who decided that they were in charge."

Dallas had started to nod before she was finished. *She's got it. She understands.* This was a seed, really, that was all. It might take years for it to germinate, but eventually Evie would be ready to join the group. However, there was one more question. Possibly the most important one. He pushed himself to his feet. "Interesting... I'll let you get back to your pretend homework." He stopped at the door, and looked back. "Even the Judges can make mistakes. Suppose the *wrong* person gets punished, no matter how careful you were?"

Evie paused in the process of opening her laptop. "I guess that'll happen eventually. But then you have to balance the risk. Is it better to kill an innocent person or leave a murderer free to potentially kill, like, *loads* of people?"

"What do you think?"

"I think... if you *are* careful—really, *really* careful—and do all the research, the chance of getting the wrong person would be very low. If it was, say, one in a million, then... yeah. It'd be worth the risk."

"Yeah, that's just about what I said to the guys. No judicial system is ever going to be perfect. We have to accept that mistakes will be made." He nodded towards the laptop. "How much are they? The boots?"

"Six hundred dollars."

Dallas allowed his shoulders to sag in an exaggerated manner. "Good grief... Six hundred bucks. That's more than it cost me to bribe your mother into marrying me. Have you *got* six hundred to spare?"

Evie gave him a wide smile. "Have *you*?"

He pulled open the door. "We'll see."

"Is that 'we'll see' as in, 'No.' Or 'we'll see' as in, 'Yes.'"

He didn't respond to that, but he returned her smile as he stepped out of the room.

LYING ON HIS belly on the neatly-trimmed damp grass, the upper half of his body propped up on his elbows, Judge Santana adjusted the gain on his light-enhancing glasses and the orange outline of the large house came into focus.

"A children's entertainer?" he said softly. "You're joking."

"No, sir," Judge Cade said. She was back in uniform, crouched next to him, peering at her data-pad and using her left hand to block the light from the screen in case anyone was watching. "Two years in an actual clown college. I didn't even know they were real places."

"Well, they are. Any previous?"

"Aside from the usual parking and speeding fines... Drunken affray when he was seventeen. Then back in twenty-three he was hit with nine charges of theft of personal property all in one go. Watches, wallets and cell phones. Found guilty, got eight months suspended sentence. Nothing since."

Santana lowered the glasses and pushed himself up to his knees. "No connections with Romley or any of his people?"

"Absolutely nothing that we can find," Cade said. "Could be he's just a cash-mule, nothing else."

"Maybe. But he's a long way from home and he's got no legitimate reason to be out here right now, so he's definitely delivering. It's who he's delivering *to* that interests me. Rozek named Levi Briar and Veena Danese as her peers in the hierarchy, so why's he not delivering to either of them?"

"Sir, are you thinking we moved on Rozek too early?"

Santana glanced at Judge Cade. "Unsure. But we do have to consider that possibility." He knew that no operation ever ran one hundred per cent smoothly. There were always glitches and hiccups no matter how fastidious you were. Same was true for the bad guys.

Seven months ago one of Romley's people—their identity was still a mystery—had been using his cell phone to speak to the man himself. That had been on a crowded cross-town tram, during the morning rush hour. The call had been protected—that damned Martyrdomino data-laundering app: the sooner the tech labs cracked that one, the better—but the phone's volume had been high enough that snippets of both sides of the conversation were picked up by an unencrypted phone being used by the passenger standing next to him.

The Justice Department's scanning software had flagged Romley's voice, and that had kick-started the investigation in Golgotha.

"Full moon," Cade said. "And we're spread thin. Not ideal."

"If the world was ideal," Santana said, once again watching the house, "then it wouldn't need us and we could be home in bed instead of hiding on a golf course and spying on perps."

QUON SAT SLUMPED against the side wall of her booth doing her best to look despondent and not like she was spying on Sullivan Reidt. Occasionally, she poked at her cell phone in a half-hearted manner that she hoped no one could see through.

She'd texted Kurzweil that Reidt was present, and the Judge had responded, "Hold tight. Keep watching him as long as you're sure you're safe."

In the past hour fifteen people had visited Sully, all of them walking straight towards him, each one staying only a minute or two. No drinks, no chit-chat. This was purely business.

It wasn't until the fourth visitor that Quon noticed the woman in red jeans whose hand drifted down by her side every time the door opened, her eyes following the newcomer as they walked straight up to Sully.

After that, Quon became aware of other patrons guarding Sully. Two men in the booth next to him, three more in the opposite corner, a barely-moving drunk at the bar who was watching everything reflected in the mirror.

She couldn't help wondering what they'd thought of her when she walked in. Had any of them tagged her as "plain-clothes cop" or "Judges' stoolie"?

Now, the main door was pulled open again, and Quon glanced up to see a tall man silhouetted in the doorway. He strode straight towards Sully, his heavy boots thudding on the floorboards, oblivious or indifferent to the attention he might be drawing.

Quon almost flinched when the man came into the light from the bar and she saw his face. Manfred Astley. Manny to his friends. Officer Astley to the public.

She picked up her almost-empty water bottle and held it in front of her face as she slunk deeper into her seat.

Astley stopped in front of Sully. "I know, I know. There are *channels* and there are *ways*... I should always go to Nyby first. But he's not answering his cell and this is important."

Sully paused for a second, then kicked a stool out towards Astley.

As the officer sat down, he said, "The Dreads are all on assignment, and no one's talking. I've got a feeling they're making a move tonight. Now, I took a *big* risk coming here and—"

Sully whispered something and Astley immediately lowered his voice.

Quon knew she had to go. If Astley saw her here... He'd know she was working with Kurzweil.

Moving carefully and casually, she got to her feet and started heading for the door, pretending to be typing on her cell phone so she could keep her head down.

She was ten steps from the door when the barman called out, "So you changed your mind?"

Customers sitting at the bar and nearby tables looked up, and Quon felt her stomach clench. She fought the urge to check whether Astley was also looking. Without slowing down, she flashed the barman a quick smile and a nod. "Thanks, though."

"You're welcome."

Outside, she wove her way through the vapers and smokers—who seemed to be still the same people who'd been there when she arrived—and forced herself to remain at a steady pace as she walked towards the shadowed road turning where Kurzweil was waiting on her Lawranger.

GABE HAD WORKED out his 'cleaning-up' plan years ago, and kept it up-to-date, amending it to reflect every change in personnel. Anyone who knew Romley had to be dealt with decisively. And preferably immediately, though that wasn't always possible.

Every organisation had its hierarchy tree, and in most cases every member knew their own position on the tree as well as everyone else's.

But with Romley's tree it was different. Just about everyone who worked for him believed that they were only one or two levels removed from the top. Only Gabe, Leila Bronson, Wynne Winston and Sully Reidt had known that Romley was the boss.

Gabe's own underlings believed that *he* was in charge, and no doubt the same was true for Sully, Winston and Leila's people. All the way down to the lowest-level dealer, the instruction was clear: you never, *ever* tell those under you the name of the person above you. There was even a good, solid reason aside from protecting the higher levels: if you tell an underling the name of your boss, that underling might decide to bypass you.

The shadowed hierarchy—as Romley called it—was tricky to maintain, and the profits it yielded weren't as bountiful as they would be in an organisation with more transparency, but it had one huge advantage: the entire tree could be dismantled with only a few cuts.

Leila was gone. Two more branches to slice through.

Gabe steered his old Lexus onto East River Drive, a long, dark, barely-used road leading north out of town. Four hundred metres from Wynne Winston's house, in the road's darkest spot, he pulled the car in to the side.

All right. Let's get this done. Gabe checked again that his gun was loaded, then opened the car door and as he climbed out, his sweat-drenched shirt briefly stuck to the leather. Back in '33, the last time Romley had told Gabe to pull the plug on an operation, the night had been freezing, his breath misting in the air. But that had been Connecticut in the winter. Alabama in the summer was a whole different world. The night was alive, not silent. Buzzing with insects on the slow-moving river, the rich scents of night-blooming flowers, the constant low rumble of traffic on the distant freeway.

It wasn't just the heat that brought on the sweat. Gabe usually considered himself to be pretty stoic and unflappable, able to deal with just about anything, but *this*... this had him clenching and unclenching his fists as he walked towards Winston's house.

You have to do whatever Romley says, he told himself. *That's the simple rule of life, if you want to* have *a life. You have to do what he says because you don't know who else he's got working for him.*

Wynne Winston was in his late fifties, a big man who always wore shirts at least one size too small, and always buttoned right up to the collar even on the hottest days. He looked like the sort of guy who was carefully living off the proceeds of a long-finished football career, and that was exactly the impression he wanted people to have. In this business you don't want to come across as too wealthy, no matter how many millions you have stashed away. His house was rented, built by Hogan Eillers on his own farmland some ten years ago. The plan had been that his daughter Kendall would raise her family there, but Eillers had never actually discussed that plan with Kendall. It had only occurred to him that she might have a mind of her own after she announced she was moving to New Mexico.

So Eillers had been more than happy to rent the house to Wynne Winston: at least it meant that the place was occupied and he could pretend to his friends and neighbours that had always been the plan.

Winston had three former wives and one kid with each of them, none of whom he spoke to. At the moment, Gabe knew he was involved with a woman who called herself Orchid and dressed like a Vietnamese housemaid she'd seen on a rerun of *China Beach*.

Gabe didn't care about Winston one way or the other, but he liked Orchid—he couldn't remember her real name right now—and was glad she never spent the night.

Winston had to go next, because Sully Reidt worked nights. Winston was much more likely to be alone.

He knew that the gates to Winston's home were watched by a security camera, but the Eillers' farmhouse next door wasn't: it paid to keep on top of things like that. Gabe pulled on his gloves, hauled himself up onto the stone wall, and dropped down on the other side. Winston's lawn was on the far side of a dense strip of twenty-year-old spruce pine trees.

If there had been more time, Gabe would have lured Winston out of the house—he had a dozen good stories that he was sure would do the job without arousing his suspicions—but that was too risky now.

He ducked under a low branch and crept as quietly as possible through the undergrowth. There was no way anyone in the house would be able to hear him from here, but if he disturbed a fox or something, then *that* might make a lot more noise.

A soft voice ahead of him said, "Sit rep."

Gabe froze.

The voice came again. "Acknowledged. I.R. shows that target is present. Alone. Asleep. Upstairs, rear bedroom."

Without moving his feet, Gabe tilted his body to the left, then right, trying to get a glimpse of the source of the voice.

Then he saw him, close to the edge of Winston's wide, immaculate lawn. A Judge, hunkered down, watching the house through high-tech binoculars.

His first instinct was to shoot: at this range, the Judge's body armour wouldn't be enough to stop the bullet. But he resisted that. Where there was one, there could be another. Or several. But if there were more than one, would they be watching the house from different locations? He wasn't sure about that.

Gabe realised he was holding his breath, and allowed himself to relax a little. *If there* is *more than one, they're not right here. If there were, there's no way I'd get this close without being spotted.*

He shifted his weight back onto his left foot and used his right to gently prod the undergrowth ahead. Nothing but a thick, soft bed of decaying pine-needles.

A tentative step forward: the ground silently accepted his weight.

His gun was no use here. Even if he attached its suppressor to muffle the sound, the gunshot would still be recognisable to anyone with firearms experience.

Five metres from the Judge, Gabe crouched, pulled up the left leg of his jeans, and removed the butterfly knife from its clip. He opened it silently.

Another three steps. Close enough now to be able to smell stale sweat, leather polish and gun-oil: the distinctive odour of a Judge.

Another step, with the blade of the butterfly knife level with the crouching Judge's neck.

At the last second the Judge heard him, or maybe just sensed him: he turned, his hand already on his gun.

But he was too late. Gabe buried the blade into the Judge's neck right to the hilt.

With his free hand he grabbed the Judge's shoulder and lowered him gently to the ground.

He knew there was no going back now, no matter how this night turned out. *You just killed a Judge. They are going to hound you to the edge of the world for this!*

He shook himself: this wasn't the time to catch that particular train of thought. It wouldn't be long before they checked on this Judge, and when he didn't answer their comms, they'd dispatch someone.

He used the Judge's infra-red glasses to scan the area: if there were any other Judges out there, then they weren't emitting any heat.

He moved on, sticking to the cover of the trees until he reached the point where Winston's gravel-covered drive began to curve towards the house.

Then he stepped out of the shadows. The cameras would pick him up if he approached the front door, but there was an easier way. Winston's bedroom was at the south-facing rear of the house.

Gabe scooped up a handful of gravel from the drive and tossed one of the stones at the bedroom window, then waited a few seconds. Another stone, thrown a little harder this time.

The bedroom light flicked on, and then Wynne Winston's face appeared at the window, peering down.

Gabe saw the man's expression of annoyance turn to recognition, and he put his finger to his lips and motioned for Winston to come to the door.

A minute later, Winston slid open the back door and stepped out. He was holding a small, snub-nosed pistol down by his side, and hadn't bothered to close over his dressing gown. "What the hell time do you call this, Nyby?"

"We've got trouble," Gabe said, forcing himself to sound

breathless and a little panicky, which wasn't hard considering what he'd just done. He leaned to the side, peering past Winston into the dark house. "Are you alone?"

"Yeah. What kinda trouble?"

Gabe widened his eyes and pointed inside. "Alone? Then who's *that*?"

When Winston turned to look, Gabe shot him in the back of the head.

Winston's body collapsed face-first into the house, and Gabe shot him four more times to be sure, two in the head, two in the heart.

He was back among the trees before the echo of the last gunshot had faded, darting past the body of the Judge without even glancing at it.

CHAPTER TWELVE

"Astley," Judge Kurzweil said. "So why didn't he rat us out to Deborah Rozek yesterday morning? He had plenty of time to warn her."

"But not much opportunity." Quon looked back in the direction of the Air Heart bar, part of her still convinced that at any moment someone would come rushing out to find her. "You ordered me, Huck and Astley to accompany you on the raid. I rode with them..." She turned back to the Judge. "Huck drove, and Astley told me to sit up front. He sat in the back. Just before we caught up with you, I turned around and saw him texting on his phone."

"So he *did* warn her."

"Looks like it. She'd already flushed most of her stash before we got there. Don't know why she didn't run, though."

"More scared of her employers than she was of us." The Judge unclipped her radio from her belt. "Kurzweil to central control."

"Go ahead, Judge."

"Patch me through to Judge Santana."

"Stand by..."

With her free hand Kurzweil released the catch that opened the storage area under her Lawranger's seat, then pulled out a spare gun. "You ever fire one of these?"

Quon took the gun and examined it under the moonlight. It felt heavy and solid, exactly the sort of gun she'd expect a Judge to carry. "Only fired my own gun twice outside the range. Warning shots both times."

"Well, we Judges do things a little more permanently. You—"

The radio buzzed in her hand. "Santana. Go ahead, Kurzweil."

"Quon reports that one of her colleagues is meeting with the target. Has suspicions that we're about to make a move on them. He also mentioned another name: Nyby. That's new to me."

"Same here," Santana replied. "All right. The sand's running low on this... We need to move soon. Kurzweil, you're going to want to take Quon's pal alive. Could be he's at least as important as the target. You know how to play this. Santana out."

Kurzweil tapped on the barrel of the gun in Quon's hands as she put away her radio. "That's got a stronger kick than any handgun you've used before, so hold it two-handed until you've got the feel for it. You've got a thirty-four round mag there. I recommend against setting it to automatic because that'll empty the clip in one-point-three seconds and absolutely shred whatever you're aiming at." Kurzweil slapped two more magazines into Quon's empty hand. "Don't have a spare helmet for you, so when it all goes down, you find cover and *stay* there. Don't open fire until they fire first. Or I tell you. We want Sullivan Reidt and Manfred Astley alive and conscious, that's the priority. Anything else is secondary to that. Understand?"

Quon nodded. "Sure."

Kurzweil stepped closer and put her hand on Quon's shoulder. "No, I don't think you do. If we can get them to talk, we're that much closer to Romley. You know how many people die each year directly because of a Trance overdose? About six hundred. Add in the *indirect* deaths—gang wars, robberies, muggings, all the rest—and we can double that number. Then there're the serial users who don't die but are left in a semi-vegetative state and require constant medical supervision so they don't drown in their own saliva or starve because their digestive system is shot. The tens of thousands of casual users so out of their minds they can barely function. All they want to do is chase that high that Trance gives them when they think they've made someone happy. And we can't forget the people on the edges: their families and friends who also suffer because of the addiction."

"Okay," Quon said, shrugging the Judge's hand away. "I understand. Reidt and Astley are the path to Romley, and when we have *him,* that all ends."

Kurzweil was silent for a few moments. "That's not what I mean, Quon. Not *just* that. Apprehending these people will save countless lives that would otherwise be lost or ruined, so that means we have to think of the greater good. If our targets take an innocent person hostage and that's the only thing stopping us from apprehending them, then there's no contest. No question. The hostage's life is of secondary importance."

"That's *not* the way I work. That's a sick, twisted approach to the law!"

"And *that* attitude is why people like Romley are able to do what they do. They know how to play the system, to get everyone else to carry them." She stepped closer to Quon. "If we don't stop Romley, hundreds more will die. Maybe *thousands.* You don't leave a malignant tumour to grow just because cutting it out might damage a few healthy cells. So you are going to set aside your saccharine, twinkly, Pollyanna ideals about fairness and equality and justice for all because that way of thinking has shielded bastards like Romley from justice a lot more than it's protected their victims. You don't have to *like* this, Princess. But you're damned well going to find a way to live with it."

* * *

SANTANA LOOKED TOWARDS Judge Cade, watched her taking her usual series of deep, quick breaths. She always did that to psych herself up before going into action, but he didn't think she was aware of it. He imagined he could almost hear her heart beating from here.

"Weapons," Santana said softly, and Cade nodded and began to silently check through her equipment. Megan Cade was the newest member of his team, assigned only six weeks ago. Still green, still wet... but she was good. Efficient, smart, insightful and fast. And she understood the point and purpose of the Judges: on her second day as part of his team, Cade argued a point of law with Judge Enger and then told him, "We're not here to *rule* the citizens. We're here to *protect* them."

Now, crouched in a sand bunker close to the tenth hole of the golf course, Santana took one last look around. Five hundred metres behind them there was a brief flash of headlights as a car made a tight turn in the parking lot, but no other signs of movement.

"Weapons clear," Cade said.

Into his radio, Santana said, "All units, I want a green or red, down the chain. Judge Lavigne."

Judge Lavigne's voice crackled over the radio. "Target's in sight. Path clear. Green. Steinmetz?"

"My target's not alone," Steinmetz said, "but there's no immediate danger. It's green. Bruno?"

"Good to go. All green. Kurzweil, you're up."

Judge Kurzweil said, "Stand by. Our deputy's moving into position now. Get back to me at the end of the chain. Mayall and Enger?"

"Enger here. All green. Martucci."

Silence.

Judge Santana said, "Martucci, what's your status?"

Again, no response.

"Central control, this is Judge Santana. Need you to ping Judge Callum Martucci's comms ASAP."

"Stand by, Santana... okay, Judge Martucci's comms read as fully functioning."

The knot in Santana's stomach tightened. "Cade, call his cell phone." Martucci had been assigned to Wynne Winston, named by Deborah Rozek as one of Sully Reidt's colleagues. Santana had judged Winston to be a low-risk capture: he was relatively stable, lived alone, no bodyguards, and wasn't known to have any particular combat skills.

The younger Judge already had her cell phone out and was tapping in a number. "On it... it's ringing..." She held the phone to her ear, and after a few seconds she looked up at Santana. "He's not picking up."

"Damn..." *Can't do anything about that right now*, Santana thought. "All units, continue with green or red. Carrera?"

"Full green. Melendez?"

"Green. Judge Groom?"

"All green here," Judge Groom said. "Back to you, Kurzweil."

"Deputy's in place—we are green."

Crouched next to Santana, Cade said, "Eight to one."

"Not so old that I've forgotten how to *count*, Judge Cade." *We don't have a choice. Can't abort now.* Aloud, he said, "Central, I want you to point a satellite at Judge Martucci's position and have a team on standby to go to his aid if necessary."

"That's going to take a few minutes, Judge."

"Just do it."

"Wilco."

"All units, prepare to go on my signal." Santana picked up the light-enhancing glasses again, but that was just to mask his concern. Martucci was a good Judge. He knew the protocol. If his comms equipment was fully operational, the only reason he wouldn't respond to a call was if he'd been compromised.

And if one of them had been compromised, then they were *all* at risk.

Judge Cade was clearly thinking the same thing. "What do we do, sir? Abort?"

"No. We've never been this close." Santana lowered the glasses and put them away. "We execute as planned."

CHAPTER THIRTEEN

THIS TIME THERE were no vapers clustered outside the Air Heart bar, but that didn't lessen Quon's awareness of her footsteps crunching across the gravel towards the entrance.

She was also very much aware of Judge Kurzweil's spare gun tucked into the back of her jeans, only barely hidden by the pulled-out tail of her shirt.

Officer Astley had warned Sully Reidt that the Judges were up to something. That meant they'd be hyper-alert inside. As soon as she pushed open the door, everyone would turn to look at her, including Astley.

But she'd be in silhouette for a few moments, that was something. He wouldn't recognise her immediately.

Could have said no, she told herself. *Should have just told Santana to do his own dirty work. They didn't need me.*

But he didn't draft me in because they needed my skills. This is part of the indoctrination. They wanted me to join the Department of Justice, and their plan worked. I've already told them that I'll sign up.

She pulled open the door and stepped through, and as before the music kept playing, but this time everyone did turn to look at her. Even Astley.

She walked over to the bar and as she was about to move

into its light, she raised her hand to give the barman a friendly wave—and managed to place her hand where it blocked the line of sight between her face and Astley.

"Welcome back," the barman said. "That didn't take long."

"My ride got delayed," Quon said. A glance in the bar's mirror told her that Astley had turned back towards Sully. "Figured it's better to wait in here."

"Another water?"

She nodded as she fished another ten-dollar bill from her pocket. "What the hell, you only live once. Hit me."

Right now, she knew, Kurzweil would be somewhere around the back of the bar preparing to go into action.

"All you've got to do is stop Reidt or Astley from leaving," the Judge had told her. "Anyone else gets in your way, you deal with them hard and fast. No exceptions."

Quon still hadn't agreed to that. Still didn't believe that the Judges' brutal approach was right. But she also knew that this was important. Catching Romley would greatly slow the flood of Trance; maybe even stop it completely. Save a lot of innocent lives.

The Judge's last words before their paths diverged had been, "One of the lives you save might be your own."

Now she just had to wait for the signal.

DALLAS HAD WALKED about ten metres from his car when he saw the blue-white light of a cell phone almost directly ahead. *Someone else on the golf course.* It wasn't likely to be anyone in the group: one of their strictest rules was to be as subtle as possible when crossing the green in the direction of Patience's house: you do not draw any attention to yourself.

Probably just teenagers, he figured, but he decided to go the long way around anyway. He was already a little later than usual tonight, partly because of the time he'd spent talking with Evie, mostly because that conversation had been running through his mind on the drive over, and he'd taken his time.

Evie was the future. He was as sure of that now as he was that Jason was a lost cause. A great kid, everyone said so, but he was too flighty. To do the job well you had to be grounded. Even the Draughtons were grounded, to a degree.

God, we're going to have to do something about them, Dallas thought. *They're allowing their genitals to do the thinking.* He had a mental image of Cindy and Billy attempting to have sex in their car after they'd robbed and dumped another hooker, and shuddered. Pretty soon they'd need to go further, take a greater risk. When sex is part of the equation, all the other variables eventually get demoted.

Otis got a thrill from what he did, too. They all did. But that thrill was based on adrenaline, not testosterone. That was understandable. Necessary, even. Adrenaline kept you on your toes, kept you alert. *Can't be alert if all the blood has deserted your brain in favour of your pants.*

He'd have to talk to Patience about them. And about Graham Mealing, too. He was also taking a lot of risks.

Maybe we need to put a pin in everything *for a while. Regroup. Take a few weeks off to sort out exactly what it is we're doing, and why we're doing it. Take the opportunity to sort out Otis, too. He's just getting too old. If you're no longer sharp enough to operate an autoloom without supervision, you definitely shouldn't be breaking into junkies' drug-dens and stealing their stashes.*

Dallas had almost reached the trees when he heard the first gunshots.

FOR ABOUT THE twentieth time that day, Judge Hayden Santana silently cursed the Department of Justice for not sending him more Judges. They knew how important this task was—they were the ones who'd assigned him to it.

The I.R. glasses had shown him that the six people in the house were gathered in the basement: he instructed Cade to head around to the left and approach the front door while he moved to the right.

The house was on its own grounds, almost a square kilometre of prime real estate owned by Pauline Belmont. According to the Department's records, she was a forty-four-year-old engineering consultant who charged her clients a minimum of ten thousand dollars per week.

Santana still didn't know for sure how Belmont was involved with Romley's Trance business, but the pick-up guy, Mealing, had brought Vetter's money here. That itself was more than sufficient grounds for suspicion even if all six of the current occupants hadn't been gathered in the basement in a clandestine manner.

The plans of the house showed five exits: the front door, French windows at the left, attached garage on the right, and the back door and the cellar's storm doors at the rear of the house. Not to mention the ground-floor windows. He hoped it wouldn't come to that.

Over the radio, Cade said, "Hitting the front door... now!"

A burst of gunfire ripped through the house, and though he couldn't see it, Santana knew she'd shoot at the hinges first, then the lock. He trained his own weapon on the storm doors.

Inside the cellar, they'd already be panicking. The most unstable would probably be going for their weapons. Belmont seemed smart: she'd stay put. The wary but dumb would try to escape.

The storm doors crashed open, and a thirty-year-old man rushed out, his eyes wide. From the cellar came another short burst of gunfire and a shout of, "Billy! No!"

Santana roared, "You: Hands where I can see them!"

The man immediately raised his hands. "Don't shoot! We never touched any of them, I swear!"

Santana tossed a set of cuffs at the man's feet. "Put them on!"

"W-what? I don't..."

"Won't tell you again!"

"No, but—"

Santana cracked the butt of his gun against the man's temple, and he crumpled to the ground. "Cade?"

"Caught one trying to run. Old guy. He's down. Non-lethal wound."

Four more, Santana thought. He strode up next to the cellar doors and shouted, "You have one chance to come out of this intact. Surrender immediately. You have five seconds, otherwise I'll consider that to be resisting arrest. That'll be five years added to whatever sentence you get. Four. Three. T—"

A young man's voice from the cellar called back, "We surrender!"

"I'm coming in," Santana said. "I see anything but empty hands, I'll consider *that* to be an act of direct aggression against a Judge, the sentence for which is a *lot* shorter than five years."

ERROL QUON WAS the only patron of the Air Heart bar who didn't look up when the rear door was kicked open. Instead, she immediately moved back closer to the front door, hopefully out of anyone's line of fire. At the same time, she reached around behind her and grabbed the hilt of the bulky gun.

At the far side of the bar, Judge Kurzweil already had her gun drawn and down by her side. In a loud, clear voice she called out, "Music off. Lights up. Now!"

Quon saw the one-eared barman reach for a remote control, and moments later the bar was flooded with silence and light.

Kurzweil stepped into the centre of room and turned around slowly. "Don't let the helmet fool you—I have excellent peripheral vision. That allows me to see a lot of hands subtly moving towards what might be concealed weapons. Right now, those weapons are only hypothetical. If they get any more real than that, my own gun will come into play." She looked towards the corner where Reidt and Astley were watching her, then turned back to face the rest of the bar.

The moment Kurzweil turned away from Reidt, Quon saw him quietly pour a small glass of bourbon down the front of his shirt. He allowed himself to sag, like an inflated mannequin with a puncture, and in seconds he'd become the Sully Reidt she recalled. Drunk, confused, trembling, limp. The sort of drunkard that no one would suspect was a high-level dealer.

The Judge said, "Don't test me. I'm here for Sullivan Reidt and Manfred Astley. Anyone else, you sit tight and this evening will go relatively smoothly. And the smoother it goes, the less likely I'll be to investigate *all* of you." Without looking, she pointed towards a woman on the opposite side of her to Sully. "Don't bother trying to make a call. The local cell network had been temporarily shut down."

In a thin voice, the woman said, "I have *kids* at home..."

"Irrelevant." Still turning, Kurzweil said, "Reidt and Astley. You're coming with me. Anyone who stands in the way will—"

A man in the booth next to Reidt's shouted, "Jesus! Will someone just *shoot* this mouthy bitch?"

Kurzweil spun and her gun cracked, and the man twitched as blood sprayed from his right shoulder.

Even before he had slumped to the side, Kurzweil was moving towards Reidt with her gun aimed directly at Astley. "Incitement to commit violence against a Judge. Eight years. Anyone else even *breathes* funny, and this night's gonna be one the survivors will talk about for a *very* long time."

Something hit the back of Quon's legs and she realised it was the edge of one of the wooden tables. She still had her hand on the hilt of the gun tucked into her jeans, but a quick look around showed that no one else seemed to have noticed: they were all looking towards Judge Kurzweil.

But as she was turning back, she saw that one woman *was* watching her—the woman in red clothes and white sneakers.

The woman frowned at Quon and mouthed, "No!" as she shook her head.

She sees I've got a gun and thinks I'm going to draw on

Kurzweil... Quon nodded back, and released her grip on the gun.

At the far side of the room, Kurzweil had forced Astley to his knees. "Arms behind your back."

"This won't stick!" Astley said. "I'm allowed to be in a bar—no law against that!"

"It's *already* stuck." Kurzweil slapped handcuffs on his wrists. "Stay put."

She turned to Sully Reidt, who was now staring blearily at her and looking like he had no clue what was happening.

A voice to Quon's right softly said, "She's got her *back* to us! They ain't got eyes in the back of their heads, right?"

The booth second from the door. Three occupants, one female, two male. Bikers, definitely, but more than that: they were some of Reidt's people. Quon had seen them earlier watching everyone who entered the bar, shifting uncomfortably whenever someone approached Reidt.

They have a good angle, she realised. From here, they could open fire at Kurzweil with only minimal risk of hitting Reidt.

Something moved to her left: a man slowly reaching under the seat and withdrawing something large and metallic.

Judge Kurzweil said, "On your feet, Reidt!"

The woman who had claimed to have children at home said, "Look at him—he can barely *stand!* What's he supposed to have done?"

"Don't interfere," Kurzweil snapped. She grabbed hold of Reidt's upper arm and tried to haul him out of his seat, but the man just collapsed limply to the floor, lying on his back.

The Judge stood over him, aiming her gun directly at his face. "Playtime's over, Reidt. I know you're faking. You want to discover how long you can keep this up under interrogation?"

With her free hand she grabbed his left wrist and wrenched it to the side.

Quon couldn't see exactly what the Judge did, or how, but somehow the movement forced Reidt over onto his stomach.

How'd she do *that?* Quon wondered. *That's a trick I've got to learn.*

Kurzweil unclipped a set cuffs from her belt and reached out to slap them over Reidt's wrists.

The man suddenly spasmed and twist around, lashing out with his foot to knock her gun-arm away from him. At the same time, he screamed, "Open fire!"

BRENDAN "DALLAS" HAWKER didn't realise he was crying as he watched the Judges in action at Patience Belaire's house.

He crouched in the undergrowth on the edge of her property, close to the patch in the hedge where he and the others would often emerge from the woods after crossing the golf course. But not *always*: just as Patience had made it clear that she didn't want them to visit the house in the normal way, she had stressed the importance of not creating a trail through the woods.

Patience was smart like that. Always a step or two ahead of everyone else, even Dallas. It had been her idea that he and Graham would take up an interest in owls: a good reason to be out at night. Neither of them had cared much about any birds—nocturnal or otherwise—but Patience had insisted. So they'd studied, and bought guide books, and occasionally took time to visit relevant exhibitions. "A strong foundation for your alibis," Patience had called it. She'd even quizzed them a few times, just to be sure.

But now, having watched the male Judge haul Patience out of her home through the storm-cellar doors, Dallas knew that all her knowledge and careful planning had been pointless. You can construct the world's strongest, most fool-proof alibi and it won't matter a damn if some Judge just decides that you're guilty. They don't need evidence, just suspicion. And then there's no going back, no chance to appeal the sentence. A Judge's word is final. Once the Judge decides something, it's a done deal.

Another Judge—smaller, younger, female—pushed Otis Conner ahead of her as she came around from the side of the house. She didn't seem to care that the old man was limping, that blood was seeping from a bullet-wound in his right thigh.

When they reached the others, the young Judge shoved Otis roughly to the ground.

The male Judge stared at them in silence as he walked from Otis to Patience, then back. Then he pointed at Patience. "Who do you work for?"

She shrugged as well as she could. "I don't know what you mean."

"Mealing collected from Noelle Vetter. Delivered to you. To whom are *you* delivering?"

"Judge, I don't know who Noelle Vetter is, I assure you. I've never *heard* that name."

"By my reckoning, you've got in excess of seventeen thousand dollars in that safe, along with enough methamphetamines, heroin, cocaine and Trance-Trance to start your own criminal empire. You are all looking at life in an Isolation Block. Nothing's going to change that now. But *which* block and how well you're treated depends on the names you give me. You don't know Vetter? Fine. I guess that's possible that you know her by another name. But you must know the name of *your* supplier. Talk."

Cindy Draughton said, "We're not criminals! All that money and the drugs and the guns, we took all that from *real* criminals! That's what we *do*!"

The two Judges stared at her for a moment, then the male one said, "Cade?"

The younger Judge placed the muzzle of her gun against Cindy's head.

Oh God no, Dallas thought. Moving slowly, barely breathing, he started to back away.

Judge Cade said, "Explain. And make your explanation *very* clear. I don't like to be confused."

"We *help*. The cops can't... Sometimes, they *know* that someone is wrong but the *law*... We're vigilantes."

Shelby Demps said, "We don't steal from the innocent. We donate the money to charity, destroy the drugs and weapons. And we can prove it."

The older Judge turned to Graham Mealing. "Noelle Vetter is the woman in Varley Square with the clipboard."

Graham nodded vigorously. "Right. Yes, I know her. Didn't know her name. She's a dealer. Pretends to be doing surveys. I took her money." He looked away. "I'm good at that. That's what we *do*. Like Cindy said, we help."

"You *help*?" The Judge continued to stare at them all for a few seconds, then turned away. "Shit." He unclipped his radio. "Central control, this is Judge Santana. Six to pick up at my location, ASAP. Three wounded, nothing serious. Twenty years apiece, vigilantism." As he put away the radio, he turned back. "That twenty is your *minimum* sentence. You will all be thoroughly investigated. Not only have you taken the law into your own hands, your actions have disrupted a major investigation. You will all be held responsible for any negative consequences arising from that investigation." He shook his head slowly. "God*damn* it! Eight *years* we've been looking for..." He cut himself off, then turned away again. "Cade, take over. Right now I'm not sure I can trust myself."

Judge Cade addressed Patience Belaire. "Any crimes you or your fellow vigilantes have committed in the pursuit of your actions—no matter the circumstances—will be punished to the fullest extent of the law. Do you understand?"

Patience nodded.

"All of your assets will be seized and used to help cover the cost of this and other operations carried out by the Department of Justice." Cade looked down the line. "I'm not dumb enough to assume that we have every member of your group. I want to know who's not here but should be. Names and details of all of your associates, enablers and collaborators. Start talking."

Dallas didn't wait around to hear which of his friends would sell him out. Maybe all of them would. But he didn't blame them. He couldn't. He knew that in the same situation he would talk too.

He ran, and hoped that he was going in the right direction, just as he hoped that Judge Santana wouldn't hear him running.

Within a minute, they'd know his name. Two minutes later, at most, they'd have his address. Probably by the time he reached the golf-course, they'd have pinpointed his car: they'd know he was here.

He couldn't take his own car, then, but that was okay. Shelby had taught him how to break into older-model cars and hot-wire them. And there were plenty of vintage cars in the golf-course's parking lot.

Within ten minutes, the police would arrive at his house.

Gwen would have to admit that she knew, or at least suspected, what he was up to.

But maybe not. Maybe she never realised. If that was the case, then she might come out of this okay. Either way, he couldn't go back home. Not ever.

As he ran, he couldn't help but remember the first words he'd said to Gregorz Sabin Weitzner, moments before he sliced open the man's throat on a drinking glass: "You *deserve* this."

CHAPTER FOURTEEN

EVEN AS THE first gun was being fired at Judge Kurzweil, Errol Quon was dropping to the ground and flipping the table next to her. It was heavy, old wood. Thick, too. Oak or something equally dense, she hoped. A recently constructed replica might not be strong enough to stop a bullet.

As she ducked behind the table, she caught a glimpse of Kurzweil throwing herself forward, deliberately colliding with Manfred Astley, locking her arms around him as she hit the ground.

For a second, Quon thought that the Judge was using him as a human shield, but then realised that she was taking Astley out of the line of fire—Santana had instructed that he and Reidt were to be captured alive.

The three bikers in the booth on Quon's right were going for their weapons, but it was the one on her left—the man who'd pulled out the large gun hidden under his seat—who was the more immediate threat. He was standing now, almost calmly shooting at the Judge.

Still crouching, Quon shot him in the chest, the oversized gun's kickback almost enough to break her grip. She spun and opened fire at the three on her right. Six rounds, four hits: the first shot struck the woman in the chest, knocking her against the shorter of her companions. The impact threw off his aim—from the far side of the room came a deep, low scream that almost certainly wasn't from Judge Kurzweil. Her next two shots struck the third man in the wrist and stomach.

A sixth shot took care of the shorter man before he could recover his balance.

A peek over the edge of the table: Kurzweil was in a low crouch, blasting at two of Reidt's guards who were shielded by the wall of their booth. At least four others were moving into position.

She knew she had seconds at most before they realised what had happened to their colleagues closer to the door.

Near Kurzweil, Sully Reidt had squirmed around onto his side and was attempting to get to his feet.

The Judge raised herself up long enough to shoot him twice, once in each leg, then threw herself backwards a moment before something boomed and the chair she'd been crouching behind shattered into splinters.

The red-jeans woman screamed, "Joey!" and Quon saw her point in her direction. "She's with the Judge!"

"I saw her!" The barman was already swinging his shotgun around.

Half-crouched, Quon scrambled for the booth on her right, reached it just as the shotgun blast tore the top off the next booth.

The first man she'd shot was slumped forward over the blood-soaked table, his oversized gun still held in his limp fingers. Quon squeezed in behind him, pulled his gun free and loosed a volley of shots over the top of the booth aimed in the direction of the barman: she knew she wouldn't hit him at this angle, but the shots might put him off long enough for Kurzweil to get to him.

Sporadic gunfire continued to erupt from the far side of the room, punctuating the now-constant screams and moans of the wounded, but from this angle Quon couldn't see much.

Movement to her left: the red-jeans woman had squirmed

over the top of the booth to where the three bikers lay dying and was now grabbing for one of their fallen guns. Quon took aim at her, but the woman was faster than she'd expected—and more accurate.

The gun boomed and Quon felt something tap against her left shoulder, then her left hand dropped, all control lost.

But she still had her own gun in her right hand: two shots, and the back of the red-jeans woman's head was now spread across the wall.

Then there was silence, except for the moans and whimpers of the wounded and dying.

Kurzweil called out, "Quon! Hope that was you showing me you're still with us!" Her voice started strong, but cracked a little towards the end.

"I'm here," Quon said. She looked down at her left shoulder, at the blood seeping through her shirt. *Looks just like the wound that brought Deborah Rozek down.* "I'm hit, but it... doesn't *hurt*."

"Yeah, that's not always a *good* sign." Louder, but with noticeably more effort, the Judge said, "Anyone else doesn't want to spend the rest of their lives in an isolation block—or the rest of their lives dying in this room tonight—throw out your weapons. Now."

Quon heard the heavy thud of a gun hitting the floor, then another.

A man's voice said, "Wasn't us! Swear to *God*, we just came here for a drink!"

Still holding onto her gun, Quon cautiously slid out of the booth.

No sign of the barman—but there was a lot of blood and grey matter splattered all over the mirror.

At the back of the room, Kurzweil was on the ground, on her side, with her helmet off and her face painted with blood. She still had her gun-arm raised, but it was trembling from the effort.

Quon began to step carefully through the room, swinging

her gun towards every sound, every movement. Halfway along the left-side wall, a terrified young man and woman had their hands raised.

"Just stay put," Quon told them.

"We just came out for a drink!" the man repeated. "I can't *believe*—"

"Counsellors and paramedics will be provided if necessary. But right now, don't move."

The woman said, "But my *kids*..."

"You move, you'll be guilty of contaminating a crime scene," Quon said, uncomfortably aware that she was starting to sound like a Judge.

She found Sullivan Reidt back in his corner booth, crouched down so small that she would have missed him if not for the twin trails of blood from the wounds in his legs.

Officer Manfred Astley was dead, the lower half of his face spread across the floor. A shotgun blast, direct hit.

An unexpected wave of relief hit her then: Astley's family would be able to tell themselves that he probably died defending the Judge. That must have been what happened, since it was only the bad guys who'd had the shotgun.

Kurzweil said, "Quon... You gotta talk to Santana. I can barely..." As she reached to take her radio from her belt, her tunic shifted and fresh blood seeped out. "Gut-shot. It's bad." She smiled. "My own damn fault... You told me Sully was a drunk, and I said he was probably faking. I was right, but he still managed to fool me." She held the radio out to Quon. "Don't you go making the same mistake. Now you talk to Santana, I'll keep my gun on this drokker."

With her left arm useless, Quon had to put her gun down—but didn't take the radio. Instead, she pulled a pack of steri-patches from a pouch on Kurzweil's belt.

"Forget me! Just call Santana!"

Quon had to use her teeth to tear open the pack, and opening Kurzweil's tunic one-handed was awkward, the material slick with warm blood.

"She's not gonna make it," Sullivan Reidt snarled. "Neither are you."

Quon said, "Judge, if he moves, shoot him again." She pressed a steri-patch down over the wound in Kurzweil's stomach, sealed it around the edges, then awkwardly shifted around to her back.

The wound there was larger than a steri-patch. "Damn."

Kurzweil asked, "I know. It's bad. Stick four patches together, overlapped edges. That'll work."

"You're *dead*," Reidt said. "Both of you. And your families and friends had wanna prepare themselves because we'll get to them, too. Not gonna *kill* them, though." He smirked at Quon. "We've got the contacts and the means to *ruin* them. Bank accounts? Wiped. House? Repossessed. Jobs? Gone. Reputations destroyed. All the people you love are gonna suffer. We're talking dust-bowl trash, so low and reviled that even Mother Teresa herself wouldn't piss on them if they were on fire and she was already in mid-flow."

"Kurzweil, I don't know how long that's going to hold."

The Judge was still aiming her gun at Reidt. "Long enough. Now call it *in*—my arm is getting tired."

Quon watched Reidt as she spoke into the radio. "This is Officer Errol Quon, Golgotha, Alabama, for Judge Santana."

A woman's voice said, "Stand by."

Then: "Santana here. What's your status, Quon?"

"We need backup. Now. Kurzweil's been wounded. It's serious. Primary target's in custody, secondary target deceased. But the location is far from secure."

"I'm already en route. ETA nine minutes. Hold the fort, Quon."

The front doors slammed behind her and Quon spun around—the movement wrenching her wounded left arm and launching white-hot stabbing pains through her shoulder and chest—to see that the young man and woman had disobeyed her orders and fled the scene.

Can't blame them... Jesus, is this *what it's like being shot?*

She looked towards Kurzweil and Reidt. *Nine minutes until Santana gets here. Sully's wounds are minor. He'll make it.*

She was less certain about the Judge.

GABE'S CELL PHONE died a kilometre from the Air Heart bar, but that didn't mean anything. Coverage was always patchy out this way.

But as he pulled into the bar's parking lot, he knew that something had gone down. Something bad.

There was no music.

Run, he told himself. *Just run. Leila and Winston are gone, so that leaves only Sully. He's too stubborn to talk. He...*

Gabe knew he was lying to himself. The Judges could make *anyone* talk. And he knew how, too. Didn't always work unless you got the dosage exactly right, and it wasn't one hundred per cent reliable, but when it *did* work, their serum could loosen anyone's lips.

He slowly turned the car around so that it was pointing back towards the entrance, in case he needed to make a quick getaway.

Not that he'd committed to actually going in. Not yet.

If I run, Romley will hunt me down. Doesn't matter where I go, he'll find me.

I could surrender to the Judges, but he'd find a way to get to me because he knows *they'd be able to make me talk. He knows better than* anyone *how the serum works and he wouldn't take the chance.*

Just a couple of shots, then I'd be singing my heart out like a drunk canary doing karaoke.

In the rear-view mirror he saw the bar's door open and a young couple come running out, hand in hand. They darted past him and out onto the street.

That's a good sign, he decided. *Means whoever's in there doesn't have full control of the situation.*

He counted to twenty, then opened the car door and got out,

pushed the door most of the way closed—he didn't want to take the risk that someone inside might hear the telltale *Ka-chunk*.

Up to the bar door. He could hear a voice inside, a woman, but couldn't make out what she was saying.

He hunkered down low, pulled the door open a little—any jumpy, trigger-happy person inside would be more inclined to aim high—and peered in.

The bar's lights were on full, the air thick with gunsmoke and the metallic tang of blood.

A young woman with blood streaming from her left shoulder was aiming a gun down at someone crouched in the corner booth. Nearby, a Judge—obviously badly wounded—was also pointing her gun in the same direction.

Sully's corner, Gabe realised. *Got to be him. And you don't hold a gun on someone who's dead. They've got him. They'll take him in, he's gonna talk, and he'll name me.*

As he watched, the Judge collapsed onto her back, her gun falling to the floor.

Now that evens the odds. Still keeping the door slightly open, he straightened up.

Could shoot the woman, but then if that's not *Sully at the other end of her gun, she might know where he is. No way I can leave this situation without being sure he's dead.*

He cleared his throat and said, "Don't shoot! I'm coming in!"

QUON STIFFENED. SHE didn't want to look away from Sully Reidt, but the door was behind her. Without turning around, she called, "Who are you?"

"Special Agent August McCallion, FBI. Heard reports of... Hell."

"That's about right." Quon risked a quick glance back. A tall man stood in the doorway, hands down by his sides. "Come around to the left. Slowly. Keep your distance. You armed, McCallion?"

"Always."

"I see your side-arm before I expect to, there's going to be trouble."

"Understood," the man said. His careful footsteps scuffed on the wooden floor as he approached. "So what happened here?"

"Not for me to say."

This is wrong, Quon told herself. She wasn't sure why, but something about this felt sour. *Reidt's not going anywhere. But this guy... he could be anyone.*

And he didn't ask me who I *am.*

She turned, aiming the gun at the stranger's face. "Show me those hands."

McCallion was about four metres away. He stopped, and raised his hands. "You want to see my ID? It's in my inside pocket, on the left."

"I'm not in a position to hold the gun on you and check at the same time."

"This is true." The man slowly looked around. "What's also true is that you've lost a lot of blood. I figure over a litre, judging by the stains on your clothing. Your right arm's wavering. And a gun *that* size... I doubt you even have the strength to squeeze that trigger." He smiled. "So... you want to know who I really am? No dice. But I'll tell you why I'm here." He pointed down at Sullivan Reidt. "I'm here to make sure that Mister Reidt never sees the inside of a jail cell. Can't have him talking to the cops or the Judges."

From his position on the floor, Sully said, "Figured this wasn't a rescue. Officer Quon, this man's name is Gabriel Nyby. My up-line. *He's* the one you want, not me. There, Gabe. You were going to kill me anyway, now you've got to kill the cop, too. And do it fast: they've got backup coming. And... Officer? You might wanna look back this way a second."

Quon dry-swallowed. She hadn't take her eyes off the newcomer—McCallion or Nyby or whatever her name was—but she just knew, now, that Sully had a gun.

As though reading her mind, Nyby nodded and said, "Yeah, he's armed. This is his place—got guns stashed everywhere." He moved a metre to the right. "And now *you're* blocking his shot. You kill me, Sully kills you. But I've got no beef with you. I just want him gone." Moving slowly, Nyby reached around to the back of his pants and pulled out his own gun, held it down by his side. "I can't risk the Judges forcing him to talk. Sully *thinks* he can take their interrogation, but he can't. No one can. Deborah Rozek was way tougher than *this* jerk and *she* couldn't fight it."

"I know," Quon said. "I was there. They injected her with something and she—"

"Trance," Nyby said. "That's what they use in interrogations to break their subjects. It lowers the inhibitions, makes the user want to please everyone around them. The hard part is determining whether they're telling you the truth or what they think you *want* to hear." He briefly frowned at her expression. "You didn't know, of course. The Department of Justice don't like *that* one getting out, that the drug they're desperate to stop is one that *they* developed. Now... the clock's ticking, Quon, and wheels are in motion. You lower your gun, let me deal with Sully, and I'll walk away. Otherwise, you and he are *both* going to die. Make the right choice. The smart choice."

Quon's right arm felt like lead, her left was on fire, and she knew that Nyby had been right when he said that she lacked the strength to pull the trigger. It was all she could do now to keep the gun in the air.

Forcing herself to keep her voice steady, she said, "I'm not a Judge... but they *deputised* me, so I do have authority here. My word *is* the law. Sullivan Reidt, how'd you like a full pardon?"

"Suits me."

Quon gave in to her exhaustion, allowed herself to drop to the ground, opening up a direct line of sight between Sully and Nyby. As she fell, she saw Nyby's arm whip up and his gun flare.

Then he toppled forward, collapsed to the floor.

Quon turned back to see Sully slumped again, a large hole in his chest, smoke wafting from the gun held limply in his hand.

As she kicked the gun away, he spasmed, for real this time, and said, "Shoulda just shot *both* of you..."

Gabe Nyby coughed weakly. "You... you son of a *bitch*, Sully..."

Sully laughed, a bubble of blood forming on his lips. "You were here to kill *me*. Guess you got the word from himself, huh? Told you to clean house. I... I got the same message."

Quon looked back to Nyby.

He was face down, barely moving, eyes wide, his breathing ragged and weak. "He... shit. Thought I was Romley's *knight*... didn't... didn't know I was just a pawn..."

She picked up Gabriel Nyby's gun, and dragged over a low chair.

"Is... uh... is he... still alive, Quon?" Sully asked.

"Fading fast."

"Gabe... Hey, Gabe! *None* of us were knights... and... you only believed Romley was the king because... because *he* told you that he was. He..."

Sully Reidt stopped breathing, stopped moving, and for the first time that night, Errol Quon allowed herself to relax a little.

From outside came the familiar roar of a Judge's Lawranger.

SITTING ON A stool at the bar—and trying not to look at the barman's widely scattered remains—Quon winced as the paramedic tightened the bandage on her shoulder, and didn't feel remotely as lucky that it was a through-and-through shot as Judge Santana seemed to think she should.

"Small calibre, too," Santana said. "Didn't even clip the bone."

"Fantastic."

"No sudden movements," the paramedic said, packing away her things. "And that's only a temporary dressing. They'll treat you at Saint Luke's E.D., all right?"

"Sure, thanks." Quon winced again as she tucked away a loose thread on the bandage.

"That better? Happier now that it's all neat? Maybe if you squirm and twist in just the right way, the blood might soak through in symmetrical pattern."

They watched as two more paramedics lifted Kurzweil onto a stretcher.

"You saved her life."

"I disobeyed her order. She told me to contact you first."

"I forgive you. I'm sure she will too."

"And I shouldn't have had my back to the door. Dumb mistake."

"Yes, it was. So... what we talked about last night, Quon. About your future...?"

He offered his arm, and Quon took it as she carefully slid down from the stool.

"Yes, I'll stand by what I said. I'll sign up to the Department of Justice, train to be a Judge. But I'm never going to forget that we work for *them*, for the ordinary citizens, not the other way around."

Santana smiled at that. "You're going to make a good Judge, Quon. I had the same idea when I signed up: you can't swim against the tide if you don't get into the water, right? We *are* making a difference. Maybe we didn't get Romley this time, but we have seriously hurt him. Almost fifty arrests so far, with a lot more on the way. We've already seized at least twenty million dollars' worth of narcotics, and the same again in cash, and we've only just begun."

"Last thing Sully did before he died was imply that Romley's not the one in charge. He could have been just trying to rattle Nyby."

"Maybe. We've never encountered any other evidence that points to anyone above Romley."

"And Nyby said that Trance was created by the Department of Justice."

Santana shrugged. "That's the first I've heard of that."

"You use it in interrogations."

"At times, yes. It's not as effective as we'd hoped. You have to get the balance exactly right, which is tricky because long-term users build up a tolerance, plus there's a high risk of adverse reactions. But even if the Department *did* create Trance, that has no impact on the need to stop its spread." He nodded towards her bandaged shoulder. "You'll be out of action for a while... I'll have the Department send you some books. Might as well use your recovery time to get a head start before your training begins."

"I'm never going to stop fighting the system, Judge Santana."

"And I wouldn't *want* you to, Cadet Quon." He stepped back, and gave her a friendly wink. "See you on the streets."

CHAPTER FIFTEEN

Merrion, Mississippi
Monday, September 2nd 2041
13:02

THREE WEEKS LATER, Quon broke the news to her parents. She wanted to do it in person, not over the phone, so waited until she had recovered enough to travel.

"But you *hate* the Judges, Errol," Sharlene said. "They were the reason you wanted to be a police officer!"

"Not the *only* reason, Mom." She looked around the sitting room and wondered how it could have shrunk in the two years since she moved out.

Her father, Nicholas, appeared from the kitchen with a tray containing a teapot, three cups, and cookies on a matching plate. The good china.

I'm a visitor, she realised. *This isn't my home any more.*

"How's your friend doing?" her mother asked.

"She's still in recovery. We don't know yet if she's going to be able to walk again."

Her father sat down next to her and patted her knee. "You need to stop blaming yourself for that."

Here we go, she thought. *Here comes the advice on things they don't know anything about.*

"You could go into *private* security," Sharlene said. "There's a lot of money there and it's not nearly as dangerous."

"It's not about the money—Judges don't get paid, anyway—it's about doing what's right. I still hate the idea of Judges, but now I can see that they're necessary. For now." She lifted the lid of the teapot to check that the tea had sufficiently brewed, then poured an equal amount into each cup.

Nicholas Quon rolled his eyes. "Right. Until they get the current mess sorted out and then willingly relinquish the power we've handed them. Because that's always worked out so well in the past."

"It's easier to change the system from the inside, Dad."

He looked at her for a moment, then slowly shook his head. "Errol, in three years' time, when you've finished your training, you won't be thinking like that. They'll have that ideology beaten out of you within the first few months. You'll be as committed to the Judge system as Fargo and all the rest of his Dreadnoughts."

"Not me. Judge Santana told me that one of the reasons he wanted to recruit me was because I know my own mind."

"You're doing it again," her mother said.

Errol Quon pulled her hand away from the tray. It was a little habit, something she'd been doing for as long as she could remember. The handles of the teacups should be pointing towards the person for whom the cup is intended. That made sense. And it followed that if one of those people moved, then the cup might no longer be pointing at them, so it must be readjusted.

It's not a bad *habit, Quon*, she told herself. *Just a quirk.*

Three years in the Academy of Law will knock that out of you.

EPILOGUE

Indianapolis, Indiana
Thursday, September 17th 2043
21:14

THOUGH THE LOBBY of the Splendor Unlimited Hotel bustled with tourists and business people, Irvine Romley didn't raise his voice as he said, "*My* name is not important. But yours is. You've gone to great lengths to conceal it, but you can't hide anything from me. You *owe* me, Mister Hawker."

Dallas involuntarily wet his lips as he leaned a little closer to the well-dressed man. "I don't know *who* you think I—"

"Your former friends named you. All of them. You were charged *in absentia* with fourteen separate murders and countless other infractions of various degrees. Your wife broke under interrogation and admitted that she knew about your pastime: she is now serving life in an Isolation Block in Mississippi. Your children have been made wards of the state. I believe that the Judges are indoctrinating your daughter into joining their ranks. She's seventeen now... By the time she's an adult, she'll be more than ready. As for your son..." Romley shrugged. "He's not settling in well with his foster family."

"Jesus..." Dallas started to rub his temples, then stopped.

Two years on the run had taught him to be extra careful to avoid body language that might attract attention. "How did you find me?"

"It took a lot of money, Mister Hawker. Which you now also owe me. As of this point, you're working for me. In return, I can provide you with a good degree of protection. You won't have to keep running. So why don't we save some time and assume I've made the usual threats against your family?"

"Why me?"

"Because you're very, very good at what you do. You saw yourself as a hero, a champion, fighting the good fight for the downtrodden. But the truth is you're a thief and a serial murderer with quite remarkable skills. Those skills just need to be honed." Romley smiled. "So this intervention... this meeting we're having now... you're thinking of it as the end of the road. I saw that on your face the moment I used your real name. But this is *not* the end. It's the start of a whole new career for you. A lucrative one, for both of us. The Judges are tearing this country apart in their attempt to rebuild the American society, and that's where people like us are going to thrive."

Romley reached out and clapped his hand onto Dallas's shoulder. "And along the way, we'll have plenty of opportunities to give the Judges the payback that they deserve. *Smile*, Mister Hawker. For the right people with the right skills, the future is just as bright as we choose to make it."

ABOUT THE AUTHOR

Irish Author **Michael Carroll** is a former chairperson of the Irish Science Fiction Association and has previously worked as a postman and a computer programmer/ systems analyst. A reader of *2000 AD* right from the very beginning, Michael is the creator of the acclaimed *Quantum Prophecy/Super Human* series of superhero novels for the Young Adult market.

His current comic work includes *Judge Dredd* for *2000 AD* and *Judge Dredd Megazine* (Rebellion), and *Jennifer Blood* (Dynamite Entertainment).

www.michaelowencarroll.com

PSYCHE

MAURA MCHUGH

For Michael Carroll,
thrill-powered inspiration.

PART ONE

PAM REED

CHAPTER ONE

Psi-Division, Mega-City One
Tuesday, September 19th 2141
03:38

JUDGE PAM REED dreamed.

As one of Psi-Div's most dependable and senior pre-cogs (current rating: 81% accuracy), she trained her dreaming mind as hard as she trained her body. She viewed her talent as a virtual Lawgiver, which required skill and discipline to wield effectively. The intel about future potentials she fished out of the entropic currents of time and probability were vital to the preparedness of the Justice Department and the safety of Mega-City One. This was how she uniquely served the citizenry, and she prized her contribution to their welfare.

A scene began to swim into view, one different from the mundane information her unconscious mind sifted through and ordered during sleep. It was overlaid with the indefinable *zing* of an important vision.

Distantly aware of lying in bed, she brought the thumb and forefinger of her left hand together, which connected a circuit—thanks to embedded nanites—and activated a recording of her vitals as well as video and audio output of her experience. Sometimes, she said words or phrases aloud she didn't remember afterwards. All data could be useful in trying to piece together a better understanding of a prescient dream, which were often jumbled and symbolic.

First, a symbol. Ψ, rotating, followed by the word *Psyche*, which reverberated with a myriad of associations: secrecy, doubt, power, and fear. She forced the word past her slack lips so it could be noted.

A girl's face appeared, as if through rippling water. Young, with an engrossed expression. Pam knew that face as well as she knew her own. As if this woman *was her*—despite her being white, wiry and black-haired, and Pam being black and tall with a fauxhawk. The jolt of *recognition* startled her enough it nearly knocked her out of the dream, but she was used to tugging on slippery dream-strands; she pulled them back into focus with gentle determination.

The woman was sitting, very still, in the woods.

Woods! Where are there woods any more?

Pam's sense of self slipped in and merged with the younger woman's, and the whole scene snapped into being: she could smell the damp mulch under her boots. A slight breeze stirred the branches and leaves into casting shifting puzzles of light and shadow across the forest floor. Birds called to each other sweetly. It had rained earlier in the day; light droplets of water fell on her from above. She was perched on a moss-covered rock, and its cold, hard surface numbed her ass through her water-resistant camo combat trousers. She held a hunting rifle, but mostly she was enjoying the isolation, practising extending her senses as far as she could through the area, seeking light tendrils of thought.

Pam probed slightly, and snagged the woman's name: Phoebe, or Fee to her friends. But this jostled the woman's awareness and alerted her to the presence of an alien observer. She stood up and placed her hand upon the rough bark of a large beech tree beside her, reflexively using it to ground and steady herself.

Who're you, lady?

And Pam sensed a surprisingly hard push against her defences and an attempt to scoop information from her mind. She slammed up her shields, but she was no telepath.

Pam, eh?

Phoebe was looking around the forest, casting a mental mesh that unfurled rapidly out from her, seeking Pam's physical location.

Didn't your Mama teach you it was rude to enter a mind without her say-so?

Pam made no reply. The strength of the woman's focus was unnerving, if a bit raw. Pam began to recoil from the dream: it didn't feel like prescience. It had the tone of... memory.

Phoebe had narrowed her eyes, and her curiosity transformed into irritation.

Shoo!

And Pam was booted out, unspooling back to her bed, and the darkness of her quiet apartment.

She sat up, and pressed her hands against her heart, which felt like it was going to burst from joy.

She had been in a healthy forest. She'd heard birdsong. She had touched a tree! She inhaled the recycled air in her small bedroom, but the richness of fertile earth and healthy trees lingered.

There had been many times she had hated her talent, especially when Psi-Div separated her from her mother when she was five years old. In this moment, as tears slid down her cheeks, she praised her talent, thanking it for giving her a doorway into an impossible moment.

A beep indicated that Psi-Div Monitor wanted to speak to her.

She quickly wiped away the tears and pressed the sensor on the wall by her bed. A light screen shimmered into view before her, displaying one of the on-duty officers. Behind him other officers sat in front of arrays of screens, listening and noting streams of information from the psis working throughout

Mega-City One. They'd been alerted once she started recording her dream.

The man had a neutral expression and an efficient tone. They were trained to deal with agitated psis trying to explain their visions.

"Judge Reed, do you wish to log a warning?"

She shook her head, settling back into the familiar, calm demeanour she worked to maintain. Many of her dreams were bloody visions of death and destruction that lingered with her for weeks or years. It took a great deal of effort—and some meds—not to keep hearing the screams and the cries for help.

"No, nothing like that."

He looked down and a slight flicker of surprise registered. He'd read something on a feed. "There's been an alert raised about your voice recording." He raised his gaze and his tone slid into something more official. "Report to Judge Shenker for debriefing at oh-seven-hundred hours. He will take your verbal report in person."

"Roger that," she said. There was no point questioning why the head of Psi-Division wanted to meet her. She'd find out at the meeting.

She rewound and replayed the recording, and watched an IR image of her relaxed face on the pillow, her eyes moving behind their lids.

She only whispered one word: "Psyche."

CHAPTER TWO

Sector 06, Mega-City One
Tuesday, September 19th 2141
13:50

JUDGE REED BLESSED the audio dampeners in her helmet, but her thick-soled boots did nothing to cushion the bone-rattling vibration from the H-Wagon. A constant reminder that she was in the air, racing to Sector 06.

She hated flying. It was one of the most vulnerable spaces in Mega-City One: cruising past the city blocks, a target for bazookas, rail-guns or rockets. Taking out H-Wagons was a sport among some gangs. 'Eagle Shooting' they called it, and they maintained a leader board of the gangs that could shoot down the most ships in a year.

Plus, everyone knew the Pilot Judges were crazy. She'd take riding her trusty Lawmaster on the roads over this airborne target any day.

Sure enough, she heard the pilot on the comms in her helmet, "We've got a bogey!"

Her co-pilot let loose a howl of appreciation. "The drokking Army of Destructive Anachronism has a trebuchet on the roof of Genghis Khan Block!"

The H-Wagon veered sickeningly and its auto minigun shot a deafening burst, obliterating the primitive missile—shattered pieces rained down on the streets below.

The co-pilot added, as if teaching a class of cadets, "It's an extra 1,000 points if they even graze us with one of those. You'd almost admire their dedication."

The pilot snorted. "Drop a couple of Cry-Baby smoke-bombs on the roof and call it in. Let's see them weep and scramble. No detours today."

Reed gripped the harness straps across her chest and breathed deeply as she was bounced around, glad no one could witness her discomfort. She was the lone passenger on this trip, a special request by Judge Shenker. Yesterday, a gang war in Sector 06 resulted in the partial collapse of Hildegard of Bingen Block, which revealed an underground complex from when Washington DC was the centre of power, prior to the establishment of Mega-City One and the devastation of the Atomic War.

After the Judges took back control of the area and bounced the perps into iso-cubes, the clean-up crews were dispatched and Tek Div had sent drones in. The footage had shown an intact set of rooms among the rubble, and one of them had a door with the word *PSYCHE* on it.

Nothing that would normally involve her division, except for her dream the night before. But Psi-Div knew there were no coincidences, only synchronicities you haven't figured out yet.

"Get down there and see if it triggers something," Shenker had said to her in his office that morning. "That name has particular interest for Psi-Div."

He was looking drawn and more grizzled than usual. The other pre-cogs were spooked. There had been multiple, chaotic visions reported that night, and a palpable tension lay across the Div. Medication requests were up. The combination of 'wigged out' and 'doozy' was not a good mix among a group that had a reputation for being highly-strung.

Before she could ask any questions, he added, "No need to explain unless you get a hit. And if there's any data that can be retrieved, I want it brought back *here* intact for our analysts to examine."

"Yes sir," she said.

"Psi-Div has priority and jurisdiction. Don't let anyone tell you otherwise."

She paused. He'd made no comment when she described what she'd experienced that night. "What about the dream?"

He leaned back in his chair. "It's not typical for you, Reed. And the other pre-cogs are currently melting down. You're the only anomalous report." He paused, dragging a hand over his bald head. The rumour was that no Psi-Div Chief could maintain a full head of hair. "Figure it out and report back."

She saluted and headed for the door, but of course he needed a last word. "And Reed—that building is unstable. They're going to blast it in two days."

The H-Wagon landing jarred Reed out of her reverie. She had the straps off and was at the exit in seconds. The door squealed its protest as it lowered to become a ramp, and the tint on her visor adjusted to the glare of the afternoon sun filtered through the maelstrom of filth thrown up by the vehicle's arrival.

"I appreciate the ride," she said into her comm.

"You were lucky," the pilot replied. "Smooth sailing today."

"I think I'll drive back."

"Suit yourself. The annual BYOB Riot we flew you over will be subdued by tonight. Probably."

She signed off and muttered, "I'll take my chances."

The crippled Hildegard of Bingen Block left the H-Wagon extra manoeuvring space, allowing it to land close to her destination. One half of the block had sheared off and punched a gigantic hole in the street. Med Wagons whipped by constantly, fire trucks were pumping water over flames, and cries from those still trapped rang out here and there from the upper floors—along with occasional gunfire. A massive column of smoke rose from the site. Teks scrambled with huge cables from portable power generators to supply electricity for lights and power to help with search and rescue. Robot sniffer dogs and drones buzzed about.

Senior Judge Hardwick waited for her, tall and lanky and coated in layers of dust and muck. He was in charge of the excavation, and she could tell by the set of his shoulders and the sour look on his mouth that he wasn't too enamoured of Psi-Div taking over his sandbox.

"Good afternoon, Judge Hardwick—"

"I'm reporting this to the Chief Judge," he interjected with no preamble. His nasal tone was instantly irritating. "Psi-Div has no reason to be here. This is Archaeology's purview."

She could play the protocol game too. "The Council of Five signed it off to Judge Shenker. And I can think of better things I'd like to do than crawl into an unstable structure and provoke visions in a location where citizens are dying and looters are trying to break in."

She paused to see if he showed any ability to rein in his outrage. She'd checked his file before departure. They were similar in rank and seniority, but remaining sane and useful in her line of work was far more difficult than spending your days combing through the past.

She opted for conciliatory. "I know we don't have much time—"

"Twenty-four hours," he snapped.

"Judge Shenker told me two days."

He crossed his arms over his chest. "You get one day, I get one day. Then Demolition move in. And they'll blow us *both* up if we're not out on schedule."

She grimaced. He wasn't wrong. She glanced up at the gaping layers of the building: girders and cables poked out, and water poured in muddy streams down into a hole that smelled like an opening to hell. The creaks, groans and cracking noises made it sound like the building was crying out in pain.

"How am I getting in?"

Hardwick pointed over at an orange mini-crane being positioned close to the edge of the opening. From it dangled a small metal platform with a guide rail around it. "We winch you down. There's room for you, one Tek and gear. We'll monitor you on comms and with drones." He looked Reed up and down. "Do you have claustrophobia or vertigo?"

She shook her head so she wouldn't have to speak and betray any anxiety, but Hardwick carried on anyway, keen to deliver his lecture.

"This is dangerous work, best tackled by skilled staff. My teams are trained for this. If you can't handle it, then we can get whatever you need and deliver it back to Psi-Div..."

Reed compartmentalised. She was a master of putting fear, discomfort and entire memory chains into separate places in her mind so she could function as a Judge. And her pre-cog sense wasn't registering a warning; in fact, it was suspiciously quiet. She took this to mean her current path was the best possible action.

She gave him a tight-lipped smile. "I'm good."

He nodded and spoke into his comms. "Yoon, get over here."

A young Tek Judge standing by the crane put down a reinforced metal toolbox and jogged over. She was of medium height and had a bouncing, eager step. Reed figured she must be a recent graduate of the Academy, since the streets hadn't crushed her enthusiasm yet.

She arrived in a miasma of dust. "Hey, boss," she said, choking a bit at the end.

It was impossible to see Hardwick's eyes, but Reed imagined he was rolling them at Yoon's informal tone and eagerness. Psi-Div was the poster child for nonchalance, so it didn't bother her. She stuck out her gloved hand. "Judge Reed. Pleased to meet you."

Yoon's grip was strong and confident. "Judge Yoon. Can't wait to examine what's down there, Judge! There are so many secrets from the pre-Atomic War era that have been lost to us."

Reed fervently hoped she didn't have a jabber on her hands—the kind of person that didn't require a psi to know what was in her head, because she spoke every thought as it occurred.

"Hey, what kind of psi are you?" Yoon stepped back and touched her hands to her helmet. "What screwdriver am I thinking of?"

"I'm pre-cog, Yoon. If it's scrambled visions of the future you want, I'm your Judge."

Hardwick cut in. "Honestly, Yoon, how many Psis have you met? They don't scan Judges without permission."

"I haven't really met any—"

He ignored her and focused on Reed. "Demolition could change their schedule if the building destabilises further. They're already crawling through the structure setting charges, and they'll check in with me regularly. If I give you the order to pull out, you comply, fast. I don't want to explain to Shenker why his top pre-cog was flattened by a city block."

She got the message: he didn't understand why Psi-Div had been given authority or why a pre-cog had been sent to this job, and Archaeology liked solving puzzles.

Well, so did Reed.

"Let's get moving."

CHAPTER THREE

Hildegard of Bingen Block, Mega-City One
Tuesday, September 19th 2141
15:05

IT TOOK OVER an hour to examine the building's plans, watch the footage from the drones, slap glo-stickers on her armour, add the respirator module to her helmet, go through the supply kit with Tek, and get on the crane platform.

Close up, it didn't seem sturdy. It was a tight squeeze with Yoon and her stack of maglev cases. Yoon had also hooked a cable to the guide rail so she could pull it down and provide them with lights and power once they set up a base.

The crane whirred and lifted the platform, swung it slowly out and dangled it over the hole. Reed risked a look at the jagged chasm. They had to go down three levels. She initiated the breathing exercises she used to keep anxiety damped under control and raised her eyes—a drone flew beside her, watching and recording their descent.

Keep it together, Reed. Tek would love to have footage of a psi freaking out. You'd be on loop forever in the feeds.

The crane, operated by a robot, precisely positioned the platform and began lowering them at a safe rate into the darkness, through the mist of water and fire-suppressant pouring onto the building above them.

As soon as their heads passed the ground level, their lights clicked on. The heat increased as they glided downwards past the outlines of the broken corridors and rooms, and she broke out in a sweat—her uniform's fibres wicked it away. An inky blackness surrounded them except for the white maw above, their lights, and the beams cast by the drones. The chaos faded, but the further they sank, the more it sounded like they were moving through the innards of a patient on wheezing life support.

This is the second time I'm flying today. Better be the last.

Yoon had been monitoring their progress on the screen inside her helmet; excitement and curiosity suffused her voice as she said, "We're here!"

The platform juddered to a halt. Before them lay an intact hallway. Dust and particles floated in their lights. Yoon flipped up the rail and gingerly tested the floor with one foot before stepping carefully on it. "Here goes," she said, and moved slowly into the hallway. The platform swayed after she left, but the crane operator above them corrected for it. "Judge Yoon in Hallway Delta 5," she added. A drone floated before her, guiding her way.

Reed shuffled to where Yoon had stood. The Tek was silhouetted in the hallway against the drone's light, using a screen on her forearm to guide the hovering cases into the hallway.

She raised her leg to cross over and for one paralysing moment the weight of the building and the layers of *history* pressed into her mind. She lost any sense of herself under a barrage of impressions—ghost people walking right through her, some carrying mugs of coffee and chatting about baseball games and TV shows, others scheming and plotting the downfall of regimes, or detailing manoeuvres and missions from the time of her great-grandparents and beyond. Layers and layers of people who had inhabited this space.

Focus, Reed! Find your centre.

It was the cutting voice of her long-ago psi tutor, Judge Mishka Wallace.

Reed huffed in an energising breath and punched herself in her thigh. The scene before her swam back into view. She clenched her teeth and stepped into the hallway.

Sometimes, in stressful encounters, latent abilities surfaced in psis. Reed didn't know what had happened; some kind of psychometry, perhaps.

Shenker must have suspected something. *Or known information and withheld it.*

"Reed in Hallway Delta 5."

Behind her another drone whirred down over her head and took up a position just above and in front of her. This one was also conducting a variety of tests, including checking radiation levels and air quality. A thick layer of dust had been disturbed by Yoon's passage, and now swirled around Reed's boots.

Ahead of her Yoon waited by a nondescript white door. A simple black plaque with white writing declared it *PSYCHE.* Underneath it, another plaque: *DR. HELEN MURRAY.*

On the ground before the door, a faded piece of paper spun in a current of grime. Yoon bent down and picked it up, and Reed moved closer to examine it.

The image was bleached by time: a girl wearing a dress, looking up at a giant grinning cat in a tree. There was a quote beside it:

> *"But I don't want to go among mad people," Alice remarked.*
>
> *"Oh, you can't help that," said the Cat: "we're all mad here. I'm mad. You're mad."*
>
> *"How do you know I'm mad?" said Alice.*
>
> *"You must be," said the Cat, "or you wouldn't have come here."*

Yoon turned it over and noticed an ancient stain. "I think it was stuck on the door."

"Someone had a sense of humour," Reed said. She hated the association between madness and being a psi, even though they were often unhappy bedfellows.

Yoon tried the handle, but it didn't open. She pointed at a panel embedded in the wall beside it. "There's a device here, probably a card or hand-print scanner. Nothing's been powered on for generations."

Reed raised her boot. "I'll get us in—"

Yoon stepped in front of her, one arm held out. "For Grud's sake, is that your only solution?"

"In less than two days, these rooms will be pounded under the remains of a city block."

"Good point." Yoon stepped aside.

With great satisfaction Reed directed her boot at the lock. It snapped, along with the top hinge, and the door gaped open, askew.

As she pushed it back upright, the door popped off its final hinge, so she hefted it inside and left it propped against the wall.

They came into a large area with a series of cubicles, desks and chairs, many of them collapsed into parts. Yoon sent her drone ahead to survey the space. At the far end were three offices and another, larger meeting room.

BOOM!

The room shuddered and Yoon and Reed were thrown off balance. Somewhere glass shattered and metal screeched a protest. A huge crack zigzagged across the ceiling and dust poured into the room.

Immediately on their comms: "Standby, a floor collapsed up here."

"It's going to be fine," Yoon whispered as if to herself, and Reed could hear her breathing picking up.

"Keep going," said Reed. "Get as much footage as possible. We may have to exit early."

The drone flew by the office doors. One was assigned to Dr. Murray. The plaque on the next one read *Judge Earl Stone*.

"Bingo!"

Yoon turned to her. "What the drokk?"

"It's something my mother used to say."

The drone flew by the next room and the sign read *Network Operations Centre*.

Yoon almost purred. "Precious, precious data."

Across their comms came Hardwick's voice. "Demolitions are reassessing the building. I'll have an update in an hour. Yoon, get power on in that NOC—if we have any compatible interfaces. I want a report in forty-five minutes."

"Yes sir," she said, u-turned, and jogged back to the platform to retrieve the power cable.

Reed spoke, "Control," and was immediately patched through. She was already walking towards the Judge's office. "I need all files on a Judge Earl Stone. Go back to the earliest records." She stopped and looked around the dimly-lit cubicles. "Maybe Judge Fargo's era?" It felt strange saying the great Father of Law's name out loud. A little thrill passed through her.

Maybe he had walked through this room?

The door to Judge Stone's office was open, so the drone had slipped in easily and begun recording the space and its contents. By the time she had arrived, the drone darted off to survey Dr Murray's office.

She almost felt like knocking on the door. The office had a Spartan quality, from what she could see in the gloom. Another desk and chair, and three chairs opposite. A tall black box stood in a corner. A memory tickled. She'd seen something like this in antique films.

She walked over to assess it better. Three drawers. She tried the top one, and it resisted. Locked. She leaned into it and the old metal gave away to her strength, screeching in protest as it opened.

"Reed?" It was Control on her comms. The connection was poor, crackling and popping with noise.

"Acknowledged, Control. I don't have time to read the files. Give me the highlights."

"There's not much on Judge Earl Stone. He served as a United States District Judge, was thirty-nine when he entered the first Academy of Law class in 2031, and graduated top of his class. Must have been tough. He was a personal friend of Judge Fargo." The voice paused. "He was assigned to a team... that's redacted. Then the only record is his death in 2067. Most of his file is classified above our rank."

Reed pondered for a moment. "Send a message to Judge Shenker asking to release the file to my personal drive."

There was a burst of noise and Reed winced.

"Say again, Control, the connection is breaking down."

Through the static she heard the response: "Will relay the request, Reed. Stay safe."

She checked in on Yoon's drone feed: she was lugging the cable through the corridor and was entering the main room.

"Need an assist, Yoon?"

The Tek shook her head and continued straining to the NOC, dragging the cable behind her. She was breathing heavily. "You do whatever you're here for. I'm gonna raise machines from the dead. Psi-Div isn't the only division that does magic."

She stopped herself from saying, *We don't do magic*. There was no point and little time to get caught up with Division pride. Besides, there were some departments in Psi-Div that delved into... peculiar areas.

The drones had finished mapping this set of rooms, so she ordered one into Stone's office and directed its light into the metal drawer in front of her.

It was full of folders. Actual paper files.

"Grud on a greenie!" she said out loud.

She reached in and touched one carefully. As soon as her glove made contact, a section of the folder crumbled. She paused and called up the findings from the drone's analysis. The air quality was hardly breathable, but there wasn't anything to prevent her from removing her gloves.

She took them off and laid them on top of the cabinet.

This time, she looked carefully at their labels before

touching them. The first section seemed entirely taken up with requisition forms, budgets, and other administrative stomm. Several folders had handwritten notes such as *Garbage*, *Waste of Time*, and *Do Not Answer*.

A massive vibration rumbled through the building, and she held onto the cabinet for reassurance. Reed banished anxious thoughts about the building collapsing upon her. At least it would be a quick death, which was the best most Judges could hope for.

She regarded the paperwork, documenting the lives and habits of people long dead. This was all that remained of their existence. She was struck by the fragile nature of the material. It had sat in this darkened room for over a hundred years, surviving wars and conflagration, waiting to be found. She realised this constituted a treasure trove to Hardwick, and reflected at how frustrated he must be that she was the one opening it.

She decided to throw him a bone. She switched her comm to the team link. "Judge Hardwick," she said. "I've discovered paper files."

He answered instantly. She imagined him feverishly watching the drone feeds. "Yoon! Bring Judge Reed cotton inspection gloves ASAP."

Yoon replied, "I'm just—"

"This takes priority."

Yoon grumbled a little, but a few moments later she entered the room with a pair of white gloves. She was coated in dust and streaks of dirt, and with her respirator covering the bottom of her face under her helmet she looked like someone in a space suit. Reed must look the same. But instead of exploring space they were moving through time.

"Wow, a filing cabinet!" Yoon exclaimed, and handed Reed the gloves. "Look at those beauties!" she gasped, staring at the folders. "Bingo!"

Reed smiled under her respirator and slipped the gloves on.

Yoon's voice shifted into a lecturing tone. "Lift everything gently. Take your time. Support documents properly as you turn them. Always record fragile documents in case they break down during examination."

The building shivered again, and this time the floor beneath their feet groaned.

Hardwick broke in. "Demolitions are moving up their schedule." His voice shook with anger. "You have to be out in eight hours, and I can't send anyone else in. For Grud's sake! This is the best find we've had in years."

"We'll do our best, boss," Yoon said.

"Bring something back. Anything."

"Understood," Reed said. The comms clicked off. "Yoon, do what you can in the NOC. I'll see what I can discover here. Keep in contact."

Yoon saluted and bolted out of the room.

Reed took a moment to reassess. A strange shiver lingered on the fringes of her senses, but it was tantalisingly out of reach. If she had more time, she would have requested another expert from Psi-Div, but no one else was getting in here soon enough. Shenker had been clear about needing results... It was time to consider a more unconventional route. She thumbed open her med-pouch and lifted out the tiny set of cases that sat inside.

Reed opened the case containing two pills: psi amplifiers, or *psi-flyers* as her Div called them. Their usage had unpredictable side effects, and when taken too often could push talents into hyperactivity or burnout—none of which suited Psi-Div's purposes. The med was heavily controlled: psis were only issued with *one* at a time, and its use would be logged and would require a report justifying its consumption. Yet every Psi-Judge was adept at hoarding pills on the sly, and while Reed was a straight arrow, she wasn't above ensuring she always carried a backup amplifier that could be used without a compulsory review. And Reed figured if there was any occasion where she would get latitude for its use, it would be now.

She inhaled a breath and unsnapped one side of her respirator. The polluted air tickled her nose immediately.

She held up the pill, and just before she popped it into her mouth she noticed, for the first time, that it was stamped with a symbol.

Ψ

CHAPTER FOUR

18:17
05:45 hours to extraction

Finally, in the bottom drawer, Reed found something useful.

The first in a series of fat folders with a label written in Stone's all-caps scrawl: *REPORTS: 2044*.

She carried the first folder to the desk using both hands and laid it down carefully.

Reed flipped open the heavy card folder—half of it broke, and the piece in her hand disintegrated.

The top page was legible.

Transcript of voice recording of Judge Earl Stone's Report, September 18, 2044

Eustace knows I hate reports, damn him. I wasted enough of my life behind the bench writing opinions and issuing briefs, and he promised me those days were over. Judges are on the streets, dealing with crime as it happened, and punishing perpetrators immediately. No high-priced lawyers, no backlogged cases, no intimidation of witnesses. We're serving Justice, not wasting time.

But paperwork is the only constant of every regime.

He asked for a personal, frank record of my observations, so that's what he's getting. No fancy language or legalese. I don't know where he'll file this anyway. This isn't the kind of information the winning side keeps around once they're in charge.

Just bad luck I banged up my leg when the Mazers Gang shot out my Lawranger from under me during a drugs bust in Wyoming.

It was either back behind the desk until I was declared fit for active duty or take up this command and see some limited action.

PSYCHE. Some smart-ass classics major came up with that stupid name, you know it.

When Eustace was named Government Special Prosecutor for Street Crime by President Thomas Gurney in 2027, he made it his business to sniff out what all the Bureaus were doing on the downlow. That fixer of his, Marisa Pellegrino, was a big help. She can spot a black ops group before even *they* know they're being set up.

He was looking for it, though. He knew there were people out there who were *different*. People we needed on our side at this pivotal time.

Eustace summoned me to the DC Academy of Law, and I limped into his office using a cane, but I could still snap off a smart salute. Marisa was there, looking like she'd had a breakfast of hot intel covered in cream. He handed me a file with *PSYCHE* stamped across the front with the symbol Ψ.

"That's the Greek letter Psi," Marisa offered, with a cheeky grin.

Since my mother was Greek, I guessed Marisa was teasing. I gave her a long stare and nodded.

Then Eustace told me why they'd called me in. I almost laughed in his face, except Eustace Fargo never claims anything he can't prove.

And then he called her into the room. *Phoebe Wise.* Wiry, clearly ex-military, and the most direct, assessing stare I've ever seen in someone under thirty.

She told me the name of my toy giraffe when I was five.

I hadn't thought of Sebastian in at least four decades.

I warned her if she ever did that again, I'd punch her so hard she wouldn't know her own name, never mind what I called a soft toy as a kid.

She looked me right in the eyes and said, "You'd have to hit me first, sir."

The whippersnapper's got some attitude, but I'll find out if there's any guts behind that sass. Pellegrino told the girl to show some respect, but I swear she was smirking as she said it.

So maybe there's something to it. Eustace believes so, and he said he needs a hard-headed pragmatist to lead up a small team of *Psykes*, as they call them. Someone who can assess them in the field and see if they can serve the Law and be useful in tricky situations.

And if they can't... well, it will be as if this team never existed. Because technically it doesn't. We report directly to Eustace's office. To everyone else we're just a team of Judges doing our duty. No sensitive data logged on computers or in the cloud. Just paper. People don't even look for it any more.

Because if we have Judges with these... peculiarities, then there's got to be others like them out in the world, and they're bound to cause mischief. And Marisa hinted that there are even stranger situations happening that we need to investigate.

Eustace says a big change is coming, and we need every tool in our arsenal to be prepared for it.

And I thought everything was going to be simpler.

I never considered myself naive, but this time, goddamnit, I was an idiot.

Transcript of voice recording of Judge Earl Stone's Report, September 19, 2044

THE PSYCHE LAB is squirrelled away inside a maze of pencil-pusher offices in the DC politico-hive. I almost came out in a rash walking through the front door of an ugly two-story building clearly masquerading as a spook front-house. Places like this have a distinctive smell: intrigue mixed with corruption. These people specialise in bending the law, or evading it completely. It's a house of snakes.

My uniform drew attention, but Pellegrino was with me, wearing a power suit, sunglasses, and a don't-mess-with-me attitude.

She flashed a badge at the grey man sitting behind a desk wired up with alarms, and handed him an authorisation form. It had the Commander-in-Chief's John Hancock scrawled at the bottom. I used the time while they squabbled—Pellegrino out-talked him in the end—to take a good gander at my surroundings, noting all the surveillance.

The gatekeeper tried to hand me a plastic visitor's pass. I tapped my badge on my chest. "Don't bother, son, I've got a better one."

"Your helmet..." he stammered.

"Nope," I said. "Stays on."

I saw him cast a despairing look at Pellegrino for support.

"Judges, eh?" she said and shrugged, walking briskly to the elevators. As I joined her, she entered a code and pressed -3. The doors closed and the elevator lurched into life.

"Let me guess, that code changes daily."

"It'll be sent to your personal drive. There's another one you can enter if you're being forced to grant access to a terrorist."

She must have heard my snort of disbelief.

"I get it, Earl, you think you wouldn't cave. But we all have our breaking points."

"The way I see it, Marisa, just one of your Psykes can yank those numbers out of anyone's noodle. That's the real threat."

"I'm glad you appreciate the severity of the problem. Fargo thinks we need to get ahead of this as soon as we can."

The doors opened on another bland hallway. It was a giant grey warren, and I could feel my restlessness stirring. I didn't realise how much I'd come to enjoy riding my Lawranger until the threat of a desk job loomed. How'd I put up with being a regular Judge for so long? That life was impossible now.

The Psyche lab didn't advertise itself as anything else but another pointless project in a palace of bureaucracy. Pellegrino led me through a room of cubicles to Dr. Helen Murray's office. She let herself in without knocking. But of course the doc knew we were coming.

Murray's room was low on personal touches, but all the wall space was stacked with shelves and stuffed with books and binders. She didn't bother hanging her qualifications—she had nothing to prove, except her love of plants: they occupied any remaining space.

She stood up as we entered. Murray was a petite woman with her hair pulled back into a braided rope. She wore a white coat over trousers and a striped shirt. I figured she used the coat to lend her authority. A small Star of David gleamed on a chain around her neck.

Pellegrino introduced us and I was satisfied with the squeeze Murray put into her handshake. Not a pushover, then.

We remained standing. Murray had a cool, collected demeanour and was not afraid to scrutinise me. Another rat for the experiment, I guessed.

Pellegrino interrupted our eyeballing. "No need to pretend we haven't scoped each other out prior to this meeting. Helen, Earl here is team lead for the Judges. He makes all command decisions. You're in charge of the physical and mental health of the Psykes. Please play well together; don't turn this opportunity into a pointless pissing match. Our priority is to test the viability of Psyke Judges in the field. It could be a disaster, it could be a tremendous asset. We need the research."

Murray smiled. "I'm amenable to cooperation for the sake of progress. This division has been sadly overlooked and underfunded for decades. I appreciate Judge Fargo taking an interest. I'll do what it takes to advance our understanding of people with extraordinary gifts."

She had a pragmatic tone. For this one, it was all about the science.

"Glad to hear it, doc," I said. "But your *subjects* have to operate as Judges first, and wizards second. The country needs law and order more than it needs palm readers."

A heat rose in Murray's cheeks. She knew she was being baited, but she didn't rise to it.

"The parameters are clear, Judge Stone. But don't worry about my cooperation. I've been requesting a test group for years, and this is my first opportunity to observe psychically endowed subjects using their talents. This is my life's work, not a temporary assignment."

She was right. I didn't want this job. She clearly did. Pellegrino looked both of us over. "Fargo has finagled funding for a limited time. We need to prove that the Psyche project is a useful resource. Get results, and we'll extend your existence. And remember: your division doesn't officially exist in the Justice Department. Follow all ultra-classified protocols."

Marisa's phone chirped and she checked its screen. "Another day, another crisis." She grinned as if this was her relish on the hotdog of life. "Make history, not infamy."

With that parting shot, Marisa Pellegrino left the room with a bounce in her step.

A long moment passed as we watched her leave.

"She has a flair for the dramatic," Murray stated.

"That's a kind way of saying she loves trouble too much."

Murray gave me a hard look. "A common quality among law enforcement."

I nodded. "We run towards gunfire."

She extended her hand to the door. "Do you wish to meet your team? I've asked them to assemble in the briefing room. I assume you've read their files."

"Yep. Interesting bunch. Decent Judges, too."

She walked to the door and paused. "To alleviate any of your concerns, the first rule of Psyche is that the Judges are not allowed to use their talents to affect anyone here without permission."

"I know the score, doc. But how do we even realise if they monkey with our minds?"

Her response was swift. "Honour. The rule of law. These individuals respect the need for boundaries more than most." She led me towards the briefing room. "Of course, with the right trigger, anyone can go rogue."

With that cheery codicil, she opened the door.

It was a medium-sized room with an oval table and eight chairs, and a projector screen was pulled down at the far end.

The three judges stood to attention when we entered the room. They were in uniform, but their helmets sat on the table beside them.

Murray indicated me and said, "Good morning, everyone. I'd like to introduce your team leader, Judge Earl Stone. He will be making all mission decisions and is here to assess your ability to function as Judges while utilising your special skill set to enhance the work of the Justice Department."

The first one I noticed was Judge Wise. Her head was shaved on both sides with a strip of black hair down the middle. Medium build and attentive. I nodded at her and stopped myself from clenching my jaw. The memory of her plucking Sebastian out of my head like a toy in a claw machine still irked, but I wasn't going to let that ruffle me.

She stood beside Priya Dhar, who was barely regulation height. At least the boots gave her another inch. She had a sharp, short haircut, and a wide, muscular frame. She used to work in bomb disposal until she signed up for the Judges programme. She could create flames—or reduce them: a talent she'd used effectively in her last line of work. I wouldn't have believed it except I'd watched the video footage included with her file. Seeing her set a mannequin on fire, smother the flames and then reignite them had given me chills.

Finally, standing opposite them, Maddox Madden. African-American, tall, bald and graceful. He'd been a gymnast as a kid, and became a paramedic before he was accepted into the Academy of Law. This guy was an empath. Apparently, he could feel what other people felt. This sounded like a garbage talent for a Judge until I watched footage of him stopping a berserk gangbanger, bristling with weapons and high on TranceTrance, just by talking to him for a moment. The teen became a docile lamb and was led away by Madden. This ability, I was led to believe by Murray's notes, had a large emotional cost for Madden, and he was the one who required the most assistance via meds.

Normally, Judges aren't allowed any medication except for appropriate doses of painkillers, especially not anti-psychotics, but Fargo himself made an exception for this division. I wasn't convinced it was the smart call, but allowed that I should observe first and see how it played out. Fargo knew I'd raise a fuss if it impinged upon their ability to do their duty.

"Morning, Judges. Be seated."

They sat but watched me cagily. They weren't used to people knowing their secrets, and I reckoned the experience of being open to another Judge about what they could do was not going to come easy. They had hidden their abilities their whole lives, and it was only because of Murray's programme that they'd been sniffed out.

"I've reviewed your files, and I'm sure you've looked me up, so I'm not going to waste time with small talk. Our primary job as Judges is to enforce the rule of law in a country that until we came along was falling apart under systemic mismanagement, corruption and avarice. This little task force must always fulfil that primary function. We're going to test if you being able to do..."—I paused and made air quotes with my fingers—"'special stuff'... will enhance our ability to bring law to the lawless.

"People with your abilities are walking around with the equivalent of rifles, flamethrowers, and grenades when everyone else is empty-handed and whistling 'Dixie.' Your abilities can only be used to serve the Law or you will be jailed in one of those new isolation cells that Fargo's tech people are developing."

I paused and looked each of them dead in the eyes. None of them evaded my gaze.

"I'll watch your back and defend you like I would any other Judge, but if you break regs, I'll personally ensure you never see the sun again."

I glanced at Murray. "Over to you, doc."

I sat down by the top of the table and remained quiet, observing them. Murray had been working with them for a couple of months, so they relaxed once she began speaking. She discussed their rota of exercises and tests, and the prospect of a field mission very soon. They perked up at that. None of them had been on the streets since Murray's algorithms served up their names as potential candidates for this programme.

It was time to stop wasting this resource.

I stood up, and Murray stopped speaking.

"Assemble tomorrow at oh-eight-hundred outside the Justice Department. I'll pick a mission from Dispatch and we'll monitor your progress. By tomorrow afternoon I'll know if it's worth going any further with this experiment."

I guessed by Murray's flared nostrils that she wasn't too happy with my decision, but the Judges were sitting upright and had a spark in them.

"Doc, can you show me my office now?"

"With pleasure," she said with tight lips. I got the impression she relished the opportunity to tell me what she thought of my plan behind closed doors.

My office was a simple affair, situated next to Murray's, which suited me fine. I hoped not to use it too often. If I'm being tasked with leading a team, then I'm getting them out in the world, doing some good.

I closed the door and waited for the white coat to have her outburst.

But instead her body language changed and she grinned. "Our first field test. I never expected it so soon."

"You're happy?"

"They're well-trained Judges who have been cooped up and engaged with repetitive exercises for months. They need to affirm their purpose. They've proved they can deal with stressors and *control* their talent, but mostly that involved inhibiting it. Now, we need to observe if they are capable to releasing their abilities correctly under difficult circumstances." She walked over to my desk and hit a button on the phone. An intercom crackled into life. "Jarek, come into Judge Stone's office. It's time you met."

I heard the door open in the NOC and Dr. Jarek Carus walked in: weedy, white, and wearing jeans, t-shirt and a hoody. His silver hair had purple tips and black spacers stretched his earlobes. I restrained the urge for my jaw to go all Fargo with this nonsense.

He radiated wariness, but politely stuck out his hand. "Judge Stone, it's a pleasure." His accent was British, cultured.

He wilted slightly under my handshake but didn't squeak. That was better than I hoped.

"Dr Carus—"

"Please call me Jarek. I've a Ph.D. in Information Architecture, not a medical doctorate in psychiatry like Dr. Murray."

I inclined my head. "Right, Jarek it is. Where's your shirt and tie?"

He glanced over at Murray, expecting her to back him up, but she remained silent.

I got to the heart of the matter. "According to the rules, you must adhere to the dress code of 'business casual,' which is trousers—not jeans—a shirt, tie and blazer or jacket. And never shorts or sandals. Come to work tomorrow correctly attired or don't come back."

I noticed Murray's eyebrows rise and concern creep over her expression.

Jarek remained surprisingly sedate. "Well, thank goodness," he said.

It was a good job I'd kept my helmet on so he couldn't see me blink with surprise.

"I can finally dress like a gentleman rather than a ruffian. You have no idea how difficult it's been to fit in."

"Right," I said, trying to get back my equilibrium. "You're working for Judges now. Everything is by the book. We don't do grey areas or special circumstances."

"Understood," Jarek said, and he had the same gleam of enthusiasm in his eyes that the Judges had shown earlier. "Tonight, I'll iron my cravats."

Just when you think you've figured everything out, life continues to surprise you.

CHAPTER FIVE

20:02
04:00 hours to extraction

REED WAS PULLED back out of the world of long ago by a flickering at the edges of her vision. Her psi ability was ramping up. It was likely to result in her having immersive hallucinations of forthcoming events, but she hoped it would trigger her latent ability into a fully expressed talent.

For a moment she smelled the damp forest floor from her dream again, and it calmed her.

She straightened, and rapidly blinked her eyes in the darkened room.

Then she saw him: Judge Earl Stone himself—or a transparent version of him—standing by the doorway in full uniform, with a mug of coffee in one hand. He seemed to be observing the room beyond. There had been few archival images of him available, and most of them were from his time in college and on the bench. Here, in full uniform of the first Judges, he had an impressive presence.

She licked her lips; they felt parched. "Judge Stone," she whispered.

The image solidified, but the man didn't acknowledge her—

and why would he? Surely this was like a recording from the past, which had been imprinted onto this location. It would be impossible for her to affect it... if that's what was happening. Other, stranger theories began to blossom in her mind: time portals, quantum entanglement, a multiverse welt. What she did know is that she had unleashed a new, unpredictable variable into her disciplined mind.

She was both elated and freaked out by it.

Stone walked out of the room.

Reed punched her thigh again, and dust puffed off her uniform. Seen through the light of the glo-stickers, the mote patterns fascinated her. Their intricate Brownian motion stirred her pre-cog ability. A series of images bombarded her mind of particles moving from this point in time to become part of other people, structures, worlds, and universes.

That immense, widening ripple of probabilities nearly dropped her, but she inhaled from her diaphragm and reeled in her attention to this time and space. She narrowed her eyes and re-focused on the pages in front of her. She could read the words, but they made no sense.

Yoon's voice crackled over the comms. "Power on... not... working."

"Well, what can I do about it?" She thought she was slurring her words slightly, but perhaps she was being paranoid. That thought made the paranoia worse.

Reed looked up and had a terrifying vision of the structure collapsing in upon itself. Ceiling tiles cascaded from the roof, pillars shook, and snapped, the floor rippled sickeningly. But it was the deafening roar that spiked her heart rate. The building fell upon her with hungry eagerness bringing with it the blackness of death.

It passed. Reed crouched with her arms over her helmet, her breathing fast and panicked. Yoon was shaking her.

"Reed, you 'kay?"

Reed didn't reply, and Yoon repeated the question with growing concern.

Reed slowly uncoiled from her foetal position and mentally distanced herself from the images—it had been a hyper-real pre-cog vision. She rarely experienced one that vivid. Usually that indicated it was imminent and fixed. She just didn't know when it would happen.

"I'm fine, Yoon, just had a flash. But nothing useful."

No point scaring her.

It was always the difficulty with pre-cog—it wasn't easily directed to subjects you needed to know about. Sometimes the visions were downright obtuse.

Yoon fell back on reporting. "None of the computers will power on in the NOC, but I found discs." She held up a sturdy, heavy plastic carry case, and lifted the lid. About two dozen gleaming CDs, all neatly labelled, lay inside.

Her voice was awestruck. "They're like new."

"What's on them?"

Yoon wore thin anti-static silicon gloves. She picked up the first one almost tenderly. The label on it read *MISSIONS: September 2044—December 2044.*

A tunnel of zigzagging coloured light began to encroach on all sides of Reed's vision, like the worst visual migraine she ever experienced. The blizzard of flickering images began to consume her sight. Quickly, she thumbed open her med-pouch, and by touch nabbed her Anticonvulsant Meds.

She fumbled with her respirator with the pill in one hand, and tried to form the right words to let Yoon know what was happening. She knew her armour sensors would be picking up the changes in her blood pressure and respiration, but who could come and rescue them now?

She dropped the pill into her mouth and cracked its thin shell with her teeth. Her tongue numbed under the effect of the drug.

"I've taken a psi amplifier. I may be incapacitated for a while."

"*What?*" Yoon yelped. "You Psis are *crazy!* Who does that under these circumstances?"

There was very little rational thought left. It existed in the closing aperture of her vision. The whirlwind of light and noise was taking over.

Reed slumped on the floor by the cabinet.

"Taken anti-seizure meds." She swallowed. She could not feel her body any more. "Monitor vitals." She looked up, but only Yoon's chin was visible. "Leave me if I don't wake in time."

And Judge Pam Reed was swept up by the tornado.

PART TWO

PHOEBE WISE

CHAPTER SIX

Fairfax, Virginia
Tuesday, September 20th 2044
08:30

JUDGE STONE'S LAST words to us before the three of us climbed on our Lawrangers and hit the I-66 W were: "Do your job." He's not one for fancy talk.

At the morning briefing, he ordered us to head to Fairfax PD in Virginia, which he described as, "A hotbed of criminal activity. It runs the gamut: assault, drugs, prostitution and littering." Stone's got a weird thing about littering. We laughed 'cause we thought he was trying to loosen us up, but I'm catching on that Stone doesn't joke around much.

"First," he began with a serious case of the 'lecture voice,' "littering is a demonstration of a lack of regard for fellow citizens. Second, it's a blight on the environment. Third, it's filthy. Judges are here to remind citizens that a decent society is built upon adherence to law."

I didn't need to be a fortune teller to predict I'd be handing out misdemeanour fines in my future.

He said he'd assign us an active case once we arrived. Keeping us frosty, of course.

Stone's other quirk is that he doesn't swear, and he warned us he wouldn't tolerate it in his team. Priya and Maddox gave each other a little side-smirk at that, but I got it. Stone's all about keeping your actions and thoughts impeccable, and considering I'm fighting off head-noise all day long, I wish there were more like him in the world.

Stone and Jarek were following our team in the surveillance van, but we wouldn't know where they were. I knew it burned Stone to be riding shotgun with the nerd rather than roaring down the highway with the three of us, but he'd not fit, and he knows it. Stubborn, but not stupid.

The only benefit to being stationed in DC is people don't gawp at you—as much. Judges are as common as the homeless here, and most citizens gave us respect and distance. Not like in the boonies, where every gangbanger and junkie tries to put you down. Right now there's a killer in Minneapolis that specialises in picking off Judges with a sniper rifle. You never know when the coward is going to pop up. They're still an unsub—an unknown subject—but they've taken down five Judges so far. So helmets are essential. Plus, the bonus with mine is that it muffles the thoughts of people a little. I don't want to overhear all the boring and crappy thoughts people are ruminating over, but some of them project so loud it's a chore to block them out. I think of them like the tools cruising by with their car windows down, blasting their dope tracks at full whack. Thought pollution.

Stone-Face clearly sent us out of DC and into Fairfax to test us, since Fairfax is less hospitable to Judges. It also gave us the chance to taste a little freedom on the drive—including a few bugs in our teeth. I didn't mind. It was a gorgeous morning—blue skies, sunshine, and a gentler heat.

Murray's schedule over the past three months had been strict and mentally exhausting. Who knew exercising your brain-brawn was so hard? It felt like I could bench 300 kg with my thoughts alone... well, I wish I had *that* talent, if it exists. It would make arrests a helluva lot easier.

I've always liked structure and refining my skills, but I never realised how flabby my telepathy was. I can make my head an iron fortress to shut everything out, but I'd never invested in fine-tuning my ability to follow thought pathways and slip in and out of memories. First off, it never really felt *right* to do that. Like rifling through the contents of someone's diary or underwear drawer.

After my first day in Murray's lab, I had mental jelly-legs. That morning she'd told the three of us: "If you want to contribute to the Judges programme in a unique and useful fashion, then your ability needs to be as agile and honed as your body."

But the questions no one has raised yet were: what happens if our team fails Stone's appraisal? Will Psyche get shut down? And will we return to our previous posts, or will we be decommissioned? Or incarcerated—or worse? My guess is that Fargo and his advisors won't condone us wandering around in the world knowing we're packing these extra talents...

So I'm committed to this working out. I don't care that no one knows our extra agenda. Most Americans view Judges as an affront, but not as freaks. Fargo had written a special set of amendments to the Judicial Code for Psyche, and when in pursuit of criminals we had full discretion to use our abilities to capture perpetrators. But at the same time, we had to be tactful. No outrageous public demonstrations of abilities.

We all spotted traffic violations on our ride, but Stone instructed us to call them in and stay on mission. Some folks driving vehicles with busted tail lights lucked out, but the street cams will catch them. We passed one group of Hell's Angels, all big beards and leather gear, and they actually saluted us. My Lawranger captured their details just to be sure. Might just be trying to throw us off.

Sure enough, there was a BOLO out on one of them, but Stone handed it off to the state cops to pick him up. It went against what we wanted to do, but we complied with his orders.

After all, it could be another test.

Just as we peeled off onto the Old Lee Highway, Stone contacted us over the speakers in our helmets. The new noise-cancellation tech worked a treat. It was like he was riding pillion. Which was also kinda unnerving.

"Active shooter in the Huge and Healthy Hamburger on Lex and Ninth. Location has been sent to your bike navs." In my ear a soothing lady's voice instructed me to take the next exit.

Maddox, positioned at my six, spoke into his mic. "Oh, man, I love Triple H. Their Supreme Soy was my favourite."

"No chatter," said Stone instantly.

I grimaced. It made me realise that the three of us had become too comfortable in the lab. It was good to be back on the streets.

Ahead of me, Priya indicated and manoeuvred slickly around a big-ass SUV. The driver rolled down her tinted window to scream at Priya, and I enjoyed rolling past and seeing her belligerent pale face wilt as she realised who she'd been swearing at. I pointed at a traffic cam on the overpass, gave her a tight-lipped smile, and left her eating my fumes.

At the scene, local law enforcement had established a six-block lockdown. They waved us through their yellow cordons. There were no other Judges nearby, so it was up to us to resolve the problem quickly. The cops were setting up a command post two blocks from the restaurant, and no doubt SWAT was scrambling.

All of the cops had faces like they'd been chugging lemonade when they spotted us.

We parked and dismounted our bikes.

The lead officer, Sergeant Pérez, an older, trim man, walked up to us wearing a resigned expression. "Good morning, Judges," he began with a civil tone. "Do you want me to catch you up with the situation?"

Maddox nodded. "That would be appreciated, Sergeant Pérez." He introduced the three of us. A little courtesy goes a long way.

Some of our brethren don't believe in any chit chat with local police, but earlier Stone had reminded us to show them respect.

"No need to rub their noses in the fact they're going to be replaced. Some of them are able officers and might become Judge recruits if you offer a strong example. You are representatives of a new regime: remember that, and enforce it."

Pérez called up a map of the area on a tablet, and zoomed into the six-block radius of Triple H. It was a medium-sized square building with a drive-thru, playground and car park, so there was a lot of space around the building.

Pérez switched to the map's street view and we saw the giant triple H on top of the building, and the friendly Bernie the Bean mascot waving under their joists. He pointed at the glass double doors at the front.

"At 08:45 a white unsub carrying a black duffel bag entered the premises. He ordered breakfast and coffee and took a booth." He looked back up at us and continued. "We know this because one Brigette Zegrino, who had been in the Triple H, had forgotten a scarf and was returning to retrieve it just as he started shouting demands. She'd noticed him before she left because she thought he was acting jumpy. Guess she had good people antenna."

"That's helpful," Priya noted, but we waited for Pérez to continue. We leaned in because ambulances were showing up with sirens blasting, and a chopper was approaching—the media was on its way.

Pérez paused for a moment and heaved a big sigh. "He took out cams before he opened fire, so we have no eyes, but we estimate there are between twenty to thirty people in there, if you count customers and staff. Brigette witnessed him murder the cashier and the manager before she hightailed it. She was the last person to get out. There's been reports of another five-to-ten shots since then."

"Brigette also told us he put on a helmet." He nodded at us. "Apparently looks kinda like a makeshift version of yours."

I imagined Stone speed dialling Marisa Pellegrino's number.

A young white officer, Hutton, interrupted and addressed his superior. "We IDed the shooter. Zackery Meyer, 27, unemployed, used to work up in Boston as a police officer."

A slow smile spread across Hutton's face, like he was going to deliver news he found enjoyable. He nodded at us. "He quit to join the Judges programme. They bounced him after a week. He didn't take it well."

Maddox responded calmly. "Clearly they made the correct decision. He probably should never have worked in law enforcement in the first place."

Both policemen were frowning slightly, as if perplexed. I figured Maddox was evening out their mood to stop them escalating into belligerence.

Priya pointed to the map and asked, "Where are SWAT going to position their snipers?" I watched as Pérez pointed to the logical rooftop locations situated around the building. Normally I'd volunteer to unpack my trusty Remington Model 700 sniper—or Remme, as I called him—and take out the shooter myself, but we didn't have time. Unfortunately, all the windows and doors remained intact, and with solar reflection it was going to be hard to get a bead on the target. Plus, if he had a helmet, he probably had body armour. This was going to require a more up-close and personal approach.

Meyer was an ex-police officer with some Judges training. He was going to keep executing people until we came in and stopped him. He *wanted* us to come in. He wanted revenge on Judges.

"Thank you for your cooperation, Sergeant Pérez," I said. "Our team will go in to subdue Meyer as soon possible."

Pérez and Hutton had the expressions of people who had misplaced something and didn't know where to find it. Maddox had practised on me and Priya during our training, so I knew how strange it felt to have my emotions refuse to engage. But that was preferable to him reaching into you and sparking you into a berserker rage, or leaving you doubled over sobbing with grief.

Pérez objected calmly. "But the hostages—"

I put my hand on his shoulder in a friendly manner; it made it easier to assess his mind. Pérez was surprised at his lack of anger and frustration. He didn't care for us interfering, but he had worked with Judges before and had a grudging respect for our abilities.

Among the thought-cluster tagged with his past experiences with Judges, I added the thoughts: *They're trained for this. They're in charge. Help them do their job.*

He accepted it as his own idea, and then added, *And let them get shot to shit instead of my people.*

I restrained a smile and took my hand off his shoulder.

"You're in charge," Pérez said, and when Hutton made a noise as if to object, he raised his hand. "That's the way it is, Charlie. Let them do their job."

The chopper had arrived overhead and a news truck was screeching to a halt nearby.

He smiled at the three of us. "Everyone will be watching."

What Pérez couldn't know was I was far more concerned about Stone's silent observation of our efforts. Our team's existence was on the line.

I looked at Priya and Maddox. "Let's take this reject down."

CHAPTER SEVEN

THE STREET WAS eerily quiet in front of the Triple H. Everyone had been evacuated. I got to use my beloved Remme to shoot out the two exterior cameras on the building when we arrived, just in case Meyer was monitoring the external security. I used the gun's scope to examine the windows, but the reinforced, tinted glass hide everything.

"He'll expect us to hit the front and the back at the same time," Priya said.

We were hunkered down behind a row of parked cars on the far side of the street. The chopper hovered off to the right—the Justice Department had ordered it to remain at a suitable distance to ensure that Meyer wouldn't get the drop on our location by watching the newsfeeds. No doubt he was already famous online, and they were speculating endlessly on his motives. Why he was doing it didn't matter to us. Stopping him did.

"Do you think he'll booby trap the back door?" Maddox asked.

Priya nodded. "It's what I'd do."

They both looked at me, expectant.

I sighed. "I need to get closer, and I'll have to take off my helmet."

Priya winced. "Try to keep your brains on the inside, Fee."

I nodded and took off at a running crouch, going wide to the left to avoid being sighted through a window. I sped to the back of the building where there were no windows, but a row of dumpsters and the rushing sound of air conditioning vents. A grey metal door was the only entrance. My stomach rumbled at a waft of deep-fried fat, but it cut out its yodel once I got a whiff of rotting food. The sun had risen in a clear blue sky and with it, the temperature.

I slid along the back wall until I was close to the door. I removed my helmet and laid it on the ground.

I evened out my breathing and unfurled my thought-mesh, seeking other minds.

Below in the basement, a porter—Rodrigo Olave—had locked himself into a storage unit. He was repeating a Hail Mary over and over in his mind. He remembered his *abuela* Rosa clicking prayers off on her rosary beads and telling him it would invoke the Great Virgin's mercy. I tried not to get sucked into his panicked surface thoughts and slipped into his short-term memory. Everything was vivid, in sharp detail, like shards of glass.

The man in the Judge's helmet had shot Marcy, who had been on the register, and Lucas the day manager, at point blank range with a shotgun. Rodrigo had been on his way up from the kitchen and had seen it happen. Droplets of blood had hit him from two metres away. The customers began screaming.

Rodrigo dropped to the ground. He heard the kitchen staff running and the back door slamming a couple of times as they bolted.

"Don't nobody move," shouted the man. "I'm here to judge you all."

More shots, screams, and people moaning in pain. The man was commanding everyone to tie each other up. For what seemed like hours Rodrigo lay on the tiled floor, paralysed, expecting to be killed. He heard boots approaching the front counter.

It galvanised him. He ran half-crouched along the aisle of stainless-steel fryers, bubbling and crackling, and slipped behind a racking trolley full of trays. He was terrified, trying to contain his breathing, acutely aware of the man banging open the door to the drive-thru booth, kicking open the bathrooms in the rec room, and finally, checking the back door. He imagined himself smaller. Alarms and beeps were going off as food was left unattended. The smell of fries burning and charred bread filled the kitchen. A smoke alarm began to shriek. He hoped it would distract the shooter.

Finally, the man stormed past, around the counter, and back into the seating area. He began shouting at the people still alive. A child wailed non-stop and her mother desperately tried to shush her.

A short burst of gunfire, different from the first shots, fast and deadly. The baby no longer cried. Then a terrible, despairing howl—which ended after another rapid-fire blast of bullets.

"You have been judged!" the man roared.

People whimpered and cried.

A voice pleaded, "Please, please don't kill me. I have a family."

Rodrigo moved slowly, carefully, his hands trembling, and made it to the back door: but it was chained and locked. He'd played enough video games to also recognise the slab of C-4 stuck on the door with a detonator inserted. From the front another gunshot echoed, followed by a scream of agony.

Rodrigo dashed to the basement door and opened it enough so he could slip inside and down the stairs. There was a large storage cabinet down there, where he could hide, he hoped...

Phoebe rose out of Rodrigo's memories, quickly ran through an exercise to shake off any residual fear and anxiety. She'd seen and felt everything the young man had experienced, and it was a jolt to be back outside in the shadow of the building on a sunny day. She could still smell barbecue sauce.

She lifted her helmet and whispered into the comms. "Back

door is chained and armed with C-4. There's one hostage, Rodrigo Olave, in the basement. The rest are in the front seating area, tied up. Meyer is executing them based on some warped agenda."

Priya's voice. "I'll head to the back door. I can detonate the charge and absorb the energy. That'll distract him to the back. Maddox can come in front."

Something happened to my vision, the edges blurred, and suddenly I could see a ball of flame erupting from the front of the building. The heat seared my cheeks.

"The front door's armed too," I heard myself say. I didn't know how I knew, but if Maddox went in that way he was going to die, along with everyone in the room. I blinked rapidly and the image disappeared. There was something odd and dislocated about that image. As if it didn't belong to me. Kind of like borrowing a piece of clothing from a friend.

Stone's voice broke in. "SWAT are planning their move. You have fifteen minutes before they try it their way."

A muffled burst of fire from inside the building. "He's got a semi-automatic rifle, a shotgun, and no doubt a handgun or two. Plus those explosives. He might have rigged up a suicide vest."

Stone: "Find out for sure, Wise."

"Roger that." I picked up my helmet, and back in a crouch, moved along the left-hand side of the building, hugging the wall.

Priya sped by me and nodded as she passed. A couple of moments later she reported, "In position at the back door."

As I moved, I kept pinging the room inside, trying to pick through the inferno of distressed minds to locate the shooter.

Meyer's mind was the eye of the hurricane—a void at the centre of a whirlwind of minds oscillating with terror and dread. Getting through the surrounding noise was the hard part, and it took all my control to avoid being sucked into their living nightmares. I managed a quick headcount—eight left alive, and one bleeding out. I gritted my teeth and soldiered through the barrage. I was worried I'd have an issue with Meyer's helmet, but it didn't hinder my probe.

His mental sphere was oddly shaped. Huge sections of it were hollowed out, empty. His mission to *judge the people in the Triple H* was running in a loop in his mind, and it was attached to a memory of his rage and humiliation when he was expelled from the Academy of Law. It was like watching a clockwork toy that was running on a timer. Every few minutes the memory of his failure during Advanced Combat Training replayed, along with the question *Who are they to judge me?* This triggered a fury that could only be stopped by hurting a hostage.

This had been done to him—he had been programmed. I flicked rapidly through his mind, trying to find some way to interrupt the programme, but everything was smooth and rounded off, allowing no purchase. I moved up into his higher brain functions, which would alert him to something foreign in his head. But finesse was impossible now. This was a broken mind with one purpose: maximum pain and destruction.

I focused on gaining control of the cognitive command pathways to his hands. He was holding a Ruger AR-556, and had a Glock tucked in the back of his belt. He was wearing a simple suicide vest, which consisted of several pipe bombs packed between steel balls, screws, and nails for the worst possible shrapnel effect. The trigger faced out on his chest so he just had to hit it, or fall face-forward onto the ground, to detonate it.

I shifted about until I sat with my back against the wall and placed my helmet between my body and my knees so I could hear and speak into comms. I maintained and narrowed my focus.

"He's got a vest. I can control him for a short time once we begin."

Maddox spoke. "I'm at the back with Priya."

"Can you calm a group that size, Maddox?"

"I'll cope," he said, with typical understatement. I dread the day he ever indicates a situation is beyond his control.

Priya gave the countdown. "Three. Two. One."

There was a muffled *WHUMPH!* But I couldn't pay attention to anything else but controlling Meyer. I closed my eyes to block everything else out. He desperately tried to move, but I restrained him with an iron will. He was frozen in place, not even able to blink.

Around him, the hostages cried in fear. I could smell blood, piss, and shit in the room. A thick sludge coated the floor.

A voice roared in his head: *JUDGE THEM!*

I felt Maddox's influence enter the room before he did: a rolling wave of calm washing over the occupants. Even Meyer was affected. The orders in his mind were drained of their emotional power, like a cable yanked from a battery.

Priya's actions were energised, she zipped around the room, pulling people to their feet and ushering them to the counter and out the back door.

I managed to whisper, "Don't forget Rodrigo in the basement."

"Copy that," said Priya.

Maddox was kneeling by the elderly black man bleeding from a terrible stomach wound. I felt a flicker of instability in the ocean of calm. Maddox cared deeply for people, and he hated innocent civilians dying on his watch.

Meyer began to strongly resist my control. I could hear a voice in his head. *Zack, you are a worthy candidate. Bring Judgement to the world. If you are not worthy, none are worthy. Especially not Judges.*

A memory floated to the surface. Meyer sitting at the counter of a gloomy dive bar, seething with anger, peeling the labels off every bottle of beer. A man sat beside him on a stool, wearing a cowboy hat and looking remarkably like John Wayne. His eyes were ice blue, and he smiled the way a father did to a child.

"Can I buy you a drink, son?" he said. It was the warmest voice Meyer had ever heard. In it was contained security and forgiveness. Meyer needed that desperately.

"Thanks buddy, I could use it today."

The man clapped his hand on Meyer's back. Meyer thought of his father, long dead, and how he wished he was still alive.

"Call me Ramuz," the stranger said.

That word triggered a detonation in Meyer's mind.

A blinding pain hit me and I nearly barfed.

My connection was severed instantly.

"Get out, get out," I gasped, and began to crawl away from the front of the building. The heat of the sun beat down on my head, warming the scalp on both sides of my skull.

I experienced a peculiar doubling effect: as I crawled across the warm asphalt, I was also sitting in a darkened room thick with dust.

I stumbled and nearly nosedived into the ground.

:: Keep moving, Fee! ::

The voice from the forest, I thought. *Pam.*

And then the building exploded.

CHAPTER EIGHT

13:20

PELLEGRINO AND STONE debriefed me while I was sitting on a gurney at the back of an ambulance under the hard glare of its lights. Pellegrino had kicked out the EMT who had been checking me for concussion, with a causal, "Judges' skulls are harder than granite."

"That's not a fact, ma'am," the EMT had said to Pellegrino, but wilted under the force of her personality, and departed.

My ears were still ringing a little, but I risked protocol and gave her mind a tiny prod to see if there was a reaction. Pellegrino's charm was kind of uncanny, and I was curious if that's all there was to it. She gave nothing away, and I couldn't risk a stronger probe.

Today she was wearing a shirt and blazer over jeans, with a large *PRESS ID* card pinned to her lapel. She sat beside me and Stone stood, his helmet just brushing the roof. The ambulance did not feel big enough for the three of us, especially those two.

I described what happened, but made no mention of Pam. I wasn't sure how to understand that yet. I wasn't going to give them any call to doubt me or take me off duty. I didn't fancy becoming a lab rat in a government facility for the rest of my life.

Pellegrino had her tablet out and was tapping in a search on Ramuz.

She shrugged. “Nothing jumps out. It’s a surname—best known for a Swiss poet.”

“You say he looked like John Wayne?” Stone asked.

“Maybe,” I said. “Meyer saw a person that made him susceptible. Maybe his Dad liked John Wayne. He might have seen Morgan Freeman if that worked better.”

Pellegrino looked thoughtful. “So, this is another person with gifts.”

“Probably. He did a number on Meyer. There wasn’t much left of him.” I shivered involuntarily at the memory of the emptiness in Meyer’s mind.

Stone scratched his chin. “He’s out to discredit Judges.”

Pellegrino jumped up. “Speaking of which, I’m on spin control. Time to work *my* magic and ensure this is reported as a victory for the team.” She paused and pointed at me. “Which it is, of course. Nicely done!”

She moved to the back doors, beyond which emergency services and forensics were working to contain the scene now the fires were out. She was framed against the square of light and noise. “Don’t you think it’s funny that your team’s first case leads you to a Psyke crime?”

This lady had a love of the dramatic.

“There are no coincidences,” I said, “only synchronicities you haven’t figured out yet.”

“I like that. Your team should make it your motto.” And she left.

Stone remained looking down at me. “I’ll tell you what I told Madden and Dhar: good work. You saved lives and stopped a criminal. And your extra skills proved useful.” He pointed at my head. “That’s valuable, Wise. Keep it covered. Plus, it’s regulation.” His mouth tightened into a no-nonsense line. “Everything you do has to be by the book. You’re not special.”

"We're Judges with benefits," I said, deadpan.

I couldn't see his eyes through his visor, but he stared at me long enough to let the moment drag out into 'agonisingly uncomfortable.' I held my own.

"You're in the van with me and Jarek," he said, finally. He raised his hand pre-emptively. "I don't want to hear it, Wise. Your Lawranger will be picked up and delivered back to base. Madden and Dhar are driving back."

"Yes, sir," I said, trying not to be sullen.

Jarek parked the van—large and black, with no distinctive markings—near the ambulance so we only had a couple of metres to walk. My helmet was back on. The press was being kept away, but a drone or two buzzed overhead. The Justice Department had a policy of rarely giving credit to individual Judges for resolving incidents. We were part of a team, and no one was more important than another; but the media loved a hero, so they always pried and poked, trying to discover our badge name to drop it into the news cycle. I kept my head down and angled my shoulder away from the drones, but the uniform was hard to miss. I heard some shouted questions before I hopped into the back of the van.

"Good afternoon, Phoebe," Jarek called out from the driver's seat.

Stone climbed in awkwardly after me, working hard not to draw attention to his injured leg, and slid the door shut.

We pulled down the two jump seats and clicked on our safety belts. We were surrounded by an array of cupboards, a locked heavy armaments cabinet, and monitors that showed crime incidents, newsfeeds and tracked the whereabouts of Judges in the area. There was a little cubby space with a desk and stool where Jarek sat during active surveillance. A reinforced screen partition separated us from Jarek, but we could see each other. He had another two monitors by his dashboard, which looked like something out of a movie—all touchscreens and pretty lights.

Jarek was wearing a three-piece suit in a soothing grey, with a classy tie.

"Expecting to go to a funeral, Jarek?" I asked.

"Oh, no." He laughed. "I've every confidence in your abilities. Judge Stone pointed out I should be wearing business attire, and I agree with him heartily. I'm delighted to dress like a gentleman again."

Stone shook his head slightly as if exasperated, but said nothing.

Jarek added cheerily, "Clothes make the man, you know."

I looked down at my uniform. "True."

We lapsed into silence. The EMT had given me a light painkiller and I could feel it dulling my headache. I closed my eyes, hoping for a quick nap.

The city was immense, futuristic, surrounded by massive walls. Beyond it lay blasted, irradiated lands, home to mutated life. Inside the maze of city blocks millions of people teemed: fought, loved, played, and killed. It was chaos only held in check by one force: Judges, and the Law.

The van bumped and I snapped out of it.

A crazy dream. That explosion had really knocked me around.

My head dipped again and I fell into a vision.

Judge Felix had been given his instructions. The children in St. Anne's Orphanage were the offspring of degenerates and would grow into worse criminals. By cleansing them from the world, he would prevent future crimes. It was not enough to enforce the Law. Judges had to take measures to reduce criminal numbers and protect decent citizens—and there were few enough of them.

I woke up with a hammering heart and a wrenching urgency.

"Judge Anthony Felix!" I shouted.

Stone started at my outburst. "What?"

I unsnapped my belt and lurched over to the seat with the keyboard and monitor. I typed in my codes and accessed the Judges Database.

Judge Anthony Felix was stationed in Pennsylvania. He'd been reported missing a week ago while investigating a hit by a suspected Russian gang. They had found his bike and nothing else.

I angled the monitor so Stone could see it, and I pointed to Felix's file and his long, rugged face.

"He's next. He's been... programmed. He's going to attack an orphanage. St. Anne's. He'll kill everyone!"

"How do you know this, Wise?"

"I saw it. Just now."

Stone regarded me for a moment. "You had a dream?"

It was going to be hard to convey to them the realness of the vision, and in the van, surrounded by familiar, everyday objects, the original adrenaline-pumping alarm diminished.

"Yes, and no. It had a different quality." I tried to think of a good way to describe it. "It felt *true*," I said, lamely.

"All right, Wise. It can't hurt to call Pellegrino and enquire."

BOOM!

A massive explosion hit the rear of the van—it lifted into the air and dropped. I was flung up and slammed into the roof, before dropping onto the keyboard. Lights exploded across my vision and all the air was knocked out of my lungs. I fell to the floor and lay for a moment like a fish gasping for air. The van was skidding wildly to the right. Brakes shrieked. We were in danger of tipping over. I heaved a sip of air into my chest, which felt on fire, and got up on a knee.

"Hold on!" yelled Jarek from the front.

I grabbed the mesh in the van wall.

Stone was braced in his seat.

:: Roll! ::

I tucked and rolled for the back.

The vehicle connected with something. A sickening screech of protesting metal and the van slammed to the left, before spinning in a circle and stopping. Outside, other vehicles crashed. Horns blared.

Gunfire.

I uncurled. There was a huge indent at the spot where I had been sitting seconds before. Stone was already on his feet, unlocking the heavy armaments cabinet. He radiated a gleeful fury. I pitied whoever he encountered.

"You alive, Wise?"

"Yes, sir!"

"Jarek?"

"I'm just dandy."

"Where are our assailants?"

Stone grabbed an M4 and tossed it at me. I grabbed it neatly, yanked open the ammunition drawer, and grabbed armour piercing. I ignored the pain radiating throughout my chest. I didn't think I'd broken anything, but had certainly bruised my ribs. Painful, but not fatal. Stone seemed to consider the grenade launcher, and instead picked up a MP5 submachine gun and reached over to select incendiary ammo.

"I've turned on the outside cameras," Jarek yelled. I heard him chamber his weapon, one of the new Thurgood nine-millimetres with twin magazines and identilock. A Judge-issue gun.

One of the monitors was cracked, but two others were working. We could see a pickup truck crashed into a Camry behind us. Traffic was already backing up. There were two sleek black and chrome motorbikes weaving in and out of traffic; their riders wore all-black slim-fitting riding clothes and black helmets. Right out of a spy movie.

I heard Jarek contacting dispatch to relay our situation. I wondered how far ahead Maddox and Priya were. The van had spun around completely, so it was almost back in the correct position again.

Stone barked out orders. "Wise, take a knee in front of the back door."

I got into position, the gun aimed, waiting for him to release the door. Stone was watching the screen and judging an opportunity.

"Now!"

The door sprung open, and directly in front of me was one of the motorcycles slowly creeping up the aisle between the stalled cars on the highway. I inhaled and squeezed the trigger, hitting him square in the chest. He was knocked back, the bike skidded a little, but he regained control.

"Body armour," I stated. "Don't think the round made it through."

The rider stopped and reached for his weapon.

"Above you," stated Stone coldly, alerting me to his position, standing at my six. I remained steady, my gun trained on the target.

Stone shot a short burst at the helmet, scoring direct hits. They burst into fire and scorched the visor. The rider went down, his hands flailing at his face, the bike sliding along the ground. Passengers in the nearby cars screamed and ducked.

Stone stepped back to check the monitor.

"The other one is driving past on my right. Your left, Jarek. Wise, make sure that first perp is dead."

I jumped out, crouched, and checked right for the motorcycle in case he doubled back. I moved quickly between the cars, ignoring the moans of citizens involved in the crashes.

Our perp lay on the ground, dead. His helmet had shattered and melted onto his face. I'd seen a lot, but that was new. I squashed a spasm of revulsion; I didn't have time for it.

I knelt, removed my glove quickly, and checked for a pulse. Nothing.

But I got a burst of images from the dead man.

I jerked back, surprised. I didn't know that was possible.

But I didn't have time to investigate, I had to check on Stone and Jarek.

I shouldn't have worried. The second perp had attempted to speed off, but had encountered Priya and Maddox returning. They'd taken him out at long range. With no other traffic, it had been an easy shot.

Sirens wailed in the distance. People began to get out of their cars and hold up their screens to take footage. A couple of them launched camera drones. I didn't pay it any heed; the Department would track down any footage, erase it, and fine any service that hosted it. No doubt the algorithms were already blocking any live-streams.

I walked over to Stone, who was standing at the back of the van, inspecting the damage.

"He's dead," I reported.

Stone nodded and pointed at the scoring and burns on the back of the van. "We were lucky: it wasn't a direct hit. I think they missed us by a metre at least."

"There's something else," I said.

He waited, but I wasn't sure how to describe it.

"I think I can read the dead guy's mind."

Stone hooked his thumbs on the belt on his hips and looked up at the blue sky as if contemplating the beautiful day.

"It's never boring around this team."

He cracked a smile as wide as the Grand Canyon.

CHAPTER NINE

16:50

For the second time in a day I was in an ambulance. The two dead bodies lay side by side on gurneys, and I was positioned at the top, looking down at the ruined faces.

Stone was squeezed in on the right, and Priya and Maddox stood at the foot of the beds, with Jarek behind them. Everyone had removed their helmets except Stone. I was beginning to wonder if he slept with it on. I only knew what his entire face looked like because I'd peeked at the photograph on his file. I suppose he was embodying the Judge philosophy: it was a vocation, not a job. You were never off-duty.

A small drone camera, a slim black disc controlled by Jarek, hovered over the dead bodies. He had patched in Dr Murray, who was on speaker.

Priya had used her sniper rifle to pop the second rider through his right eye. Tears of blood streaked his face from a wet mushy hole, which led to a massive exit wound at the back of the head. The second rider's face was a scarlet bubbling mess, with most of the features missing. Neither of them had any ID, so their fingerprints were being searched through all the databases, official *and* unofficial.

The ambulance crew had left the air conditioning and lights running, but they had been ejected while we conducted our 'preliminary forensics examination.' We'd release the bodies to our technicians when they show up.

Helen spoke first, over the link. "Maddox, do you sense anything?"

He shook his head instantly. "No, doc, they're not generating emotion. I'm only picking up revulsion, horror and"—he inhaled sharply—"curiosity from the living." He glanced back at Jarek. "Man, you're weird."

"What? This is a completely unknown phenomenon. I'm *fascinated.*"

Priya tilted her head to one side and regarded the dead men with a wistful expression. "This is what happens when you field-test new weapons in live situations. You discover unique ways to use them."

She was right. I'd never considered reading a dead person, and the opportunity had never arisen before. It repulsed me.

Helen interrupted. "I'm speculating that results might diminish the longer they're dead. Go ahead, Phoebe."

"Lucky me," I said, and gritted my jaw, bracing for what came next.

Bare skin on skin always intensifies the connection, so I placed my fingertips gingerly on each side of the forehead of the man shot through the eye.

It was like walking into an empty house with all the furniture removed. Utterly silent.

I withdrew my hands, and a sudden profound sadness swept over me. A life had been wiped out from the world. It had not been a good one, but it was also unique and irreplaceable. I shook my head and happened to lock gazes with Maddox. He gave me the tiniest of sympathetic smiles: he knew what I was feeling.

"Nothing," I said.

Helen's voice was brisk. "Perhaps due to the extent of the brain trauma. I'll analyse the autopsy and map the areas damaged. Try the next cadaver, Phoebe."

Cadaver. A simple way to depersonalise the man.

I shifted to the right and regarded the remains of the other rider's face: a mess of scarlet burned skin fused with black plastic pieces of helmet. The eyes and nose were missing, the lips pulled back in a broiled rictus, and the front teeth were shattered. Forensics were going to give our team hell for removing the helmet, but Helen had given us the okay.

The smell of burned flesh rose from him, reminding me of the deep fat fryers from the Triple H earlier.

"Knock, knock," I said, and touched my fingers against the puckered flesh.

Immediately, I was tossed about in a maelstrom of fragmented memories. His name was Leo Salko, and Matthew Falen, and Hugo Johnston... his aliases and attached biographies swirled and dissolved around me.

I saw a lonely, hungry boy scrounging for food and money on the grey streets of an ice-bound, foreign city...

I witnessed him kill a man for the first time: a mugging in a park gone wrong. After his friends ran away, he hung back and watched the man bleed out and felt nothing, except a new purpose...

There were many, many beatings, stabbings, shootings and murders. They did nothing to fill the numb null space at his core...

The squall of slaughters blew through my mind and for too long I was adrift in their pain and awful senselessness.

I gained my centre again and slogged through the disordered, dying mind. I sensed it slowing down. Soon the ashes of his decayed life would fall around me and he would become an empty chamber.

"Kill the Judges," said the artificial voice on the phone, generated from a self-deleting message relayed via a secure app. "Wise is the prime target."

Ramuz.

"They're threatening the programme."

RAMUZ.

The memories fragmented under an explosion like a grenade.

I was hit with energy shrapnel, shredding my defences and laying bare my vulnerable consciousness.

Another barrier slammed up, deflecting the damage.

:: It's a mind bomb. GET OUT! ::

I staggered back, clutching my head. For the first time since I began training my mind, I had an awful realisation that there were vast new threats I could encounter. I might risk my entire personality and... soul.

I banged into a monitor, and Stone reached out a steadying hand.

"Are you okay, Wise—?"

"*Don't touch me!*" I shouted.

For several moments there was only the sound of my fast, panicked breaths in the small space. I stared at my hands, clenching and unclenching them, *feeling* my nails bite into my palms, and grounding myself back in my body.

I looked up and saw the pity in Maddox and Priya's eyes. They guessed, but they'd never truly know. Everyone watched me carefully, the way you did around a wounded animal lashing out at bystanders.

For the first time I considered quitting. But that was followed by the realisation that I wouldn't be allowed to quit.

A burst of familiar rage blossomed in my chest—nothing trigged my anger like feeling trapped.

Maddox spoke, "Do you want me to help calm you?"

His offer, given with kind grace, helped: I had support if I needed it. But I wanted to do this on my own.

"No," I whispered, and placed my hands on the sides of my head, dragging them along the stubble a couple of times. I knew it was a self-soothing gesture that might worry my spectators, but that rough sensation brought me fully back to myself.

Helen said the familiar words: "Ground and centre, Wise."

I ran through that mental exercise, and I appreciated the

usefulness of doing something thousands of times so it works like an automatic muscle even under difficult circumstances.

I exhaled a long shuddering breath, and grimaced.

"Now that's a talent I wish I didn't know about."

Stone had crossed his arms over his chest. His visor reflected my face. I didn't need to read his mind to know he was reassessing my capability.

I rotated my shoulders and stretched my neck to ease the tension.

"We have a problem," I began, trying to piece the information together. "Whoever hired these goons knows about our talents and considers us a threat. Me, particularly. But before I describe what it's like to watch a man die from the inside, did any of you check for any update on Judge Felix?"

CHAPTER TEN

Washington, DC
Tuesday, September 20th 2044
18:00

JAREK MADE A beeline for his NOC as soon as we pushed through the doors of the PSYCHE lab, intent on scraping for intel on Judge Felix. Stone pointed us at the briefing room, peeled off, and strode towards Helen's office. We filed into the room and all grinned at what waited: a selection of hot food, salad, bread, and a fresh pot of coffee.

Maddox hardly had his helmet and gloves off before he began layering salad and cheese on slabs of bread, while Priya poured out coffee into a mug first. She cupped it with both hands and inhaled deeply.

"That's what I'm talkin' about," she said, her New Jersey accent twanging. "Real coffee. Helen, you angel!"

I dug a wedge of lasagne out of a tray and slid it onto a plate, my mouth salivating and my stomach growling urgent demands. For a few moments the only sounds in the office were various appreciative noises and a lot of chewing.

Maddox pointed at me with a fork. "You remind me of Garfield. The orange cat? My grandma used to cut it out of the newspapers, when they were a thing."

I shrugged, and dug into a second slice. "Don't know it. Remember"—I jerked my thumb at myself—"I was home-schooled. If it didn't make my parents' list of allowed texts, I didn't see it. I know *nada* about pop culture."

Priya, slurping noodles like a fiend, paused, her eyes round like those anime characters she adored. "No cartoons, at all? No *She-Ra*, no *Steven Universe*? What kinda evil monsters were your parents?"

I felt a stab of guilt and a strange loyalty for my estranged parents rose. "They weren't evil... they thought they were protecting me."

Priya snorted, "Yeah, those heartfelt messages about friendship are *the worst*."

I swallowed another mouthful of cheesy deliciousness and thought about it for a moment. "Maybe their rules and restrictions saved me. I learned to shoot and hunt in the woods. I got time on my own. When this got intense"—I made a circular gesture at my head—"I could sneak away."

I omitted the part about my folks being part of a charismatic cult led by Sister Sophia Star—the real reason I kept escaping to the woods. And the lack of food was a real incentive to hone my shooting skills. I reckoned Helen and Judge Stone knew my background, but I hadn't talked about it with my fellow Judges before. I ran away when I was seventeen.

It felt like a lifetime ago.

Maddox sipped on water and placed the glass on the table. "I lucked out. My parents had money and influence. But I spent my childhood in therapy. It was a long time before I realised other people couldn't feel each other's emotions. That's why I got into gymnastics. Training my body helped keep me focused, and contained."

Priya reached for a chocolate-cream-filled cupcake. They were contraband for us. Jarek brought them because Priya liked them so much. "It helped that my moms owned a scrapyard. Lots of opportunities to practise setting shit on fire and putting it out again." She bit into the cake, and munched with a big smile on her face. She sighed, contemplated the remaining half, and her expression turned pensive. "I won't lie. There were some bad moments."

We nodded at that and glanced around in solidarity.

There were some bad moments. What an understatement.

It had been a long process to get to where we were okay at sharing this stuff: the wreckage in our past. These extra gifts made growing up a lot harder. We'd downright resented Helen's forced intrusion in our lives, scooping us up, putting us into this programme. All of us had busted our humps to be accepted and graduate as Judges. Then we were being separated out again. Our difference was highlighted.

But today, something had changed. We were quiet as we finished our meal, but I knew we all sensed it. Having this talent could be an asset. We could make a difference in a special way. And in this small group we could be fully open about ourselves.

A new potential yawned in front of me: it was exciting and frightening at the same time.

Maddox, as usual, knew what to say. "It's cool. We've got each other's backs."

Stone entered the room with Helen and Jarek close behind. We sat bolt upright. Priya hurriedly brushed crumbs off her uniform, and crunched up the wrapper in her hand to hide it.

"Chow time's over. Jarek, you're up."

Jarek touched the tablet he was holding. The screen in the room blinked on, and a map of DC appeared. "There are two St. Anne's Orphanages in the greater DC area, and unfortunately for our purposes they are north and south of the metropolitan area." Two red dots lit up.

Helen spoke with her usual clipped, efficient delivery. "We made a discreet enquiry and sent local police to investigate—there is nothing out of place."

Priya waved at the screen, "Leave a unit to watch them. Or better yet, one of the local Judges."

Stone crossed his arms. His mouth was a disgruntled line. "Based on what intel? A dream? PD might leak the story to the liberal press. They'd roast us in the feeds. And our people will query an alert. We're not lying to our own."

Helen looked at me. "You've never described something like this before, Phoebe, a ..." She paused as if casting about for how to describe it.

"A pre-cog flash," I filled in for her.

She frowned slightly. "That's a specific term."

"Just popped into my head," I said, "seemed right."

"Has something changed recently? Maybe that explosion..." Helen shook her head. "I don't like this. You need a proper examination and blood workup. I need to understand what's caused this new talent to express itself."

Stone's visor reflected the strip lighting as he turned towards me. "If this is new, why should we trust it?"

I knew what he was really saying. *Why should we trust you?*

When I thought about the vision, I felt again the bone-sure conviction of its likelihood, and echoes of pain and fear radiating down time to brush against my consciousness. I needed to do everything possible to avoid this terrible event. The death of those children. The obliteration of the Judges' good name.

The more I contemplated that potential, the more I could sense a great fork in the road ahead of us. In one future, the Judges programme perished and a dreadful future awaited me. My skull hurt, and my teeth ached. And beyond that more terrible horrors waited...

I closed my eyes involuntarily and under the table I clenched my fists, digging my fingernails into my palms.

Reflexively, I engaged my oldest mantra, created when I was a kid trying to make distinguish between my thoughts and other people's: *My mind is stone, I wall out the noise.*

"We should trust her," Maddox said. I opened my eyes and fell into his deep, assessing regard. "She's convinced she's right. And she's terrified what will happen if we do nothing." He took a deep breath. "It's bad."

"How soon?" Stone snapped.

"I don't know..." I tried to settle back into that image in my mind and get a sense of its imminence.

:: For this strength, less than six hours ::

"Within six hours."

Nobody spoke for an extended moment.

Stone radiated irritation. "We'll need two teams. One at each location."

Jarek spoke up. "I can requisition another van."

Helen pulled back her shoulders. "It's been a long time since I've been in the field."

Stone snorted. "Dr. Murray, the only thing you're doing is driving. Stay in the vehicle and don't get in the way. Jarek, you accompany and monitor Madden and Dahr in Van Alpha. Doctor Murray will drive me and Wise in Van Beta."

He paused for a moment and looked around the room as if assessing our capabilities anew. "No, scratch that. Jarek will go with Madden and Wise. I'll be with Murray and Dahr."

"That makes sense," Jarek said.

We all agreed.

:: This isn't a smart play, Phoebe. Something's wrong. ::

Before I could argue with her, Stone spoke. "Any update on Felix?"

Jarek shook his head. "Nothing. He remains missing."

My head had been too messed up to read any files on the ride back so I asked, "What was his mission before he disappeared?"

Jarek cast Felix's file up on the light screen in the room so we could all see it. Images of Felix rotated through his young beaming smile as he graduated High School, to his serious graduation picture from Philly PD, and a media still of him receiving a commendation from the Mayor.

"Anthony Felix was born in the Philly Badlands to a Puerto Rican mother and an Irish-Russian father. He lost several family members to gang-related activity during his childhood. He believed he'd make a difference in Philly PD, and worked undercover in the organised crime division. After five years, he helped take down an important Russian gang leader, a *Vor* known as Dimitri Jikia, who headed up an organisation known as The Sovs."

Jarek flicked a series of images that showed a tall, well-dressed white man with an intense stare, and tattoos creeping out of the edges of his shirt cuffs and collar, on the courthouse steps being ushered into a variety of cars surrounded by dead-eyed security men and with a narrow-faced blonde, dressed like a fashion model who'd recently been widowed, on his arm.

He projected a series of headlines about the murders and mysterious disappearances of witnesses that plagued the case. Some of the killings had been brutal. A heavy silence settled on the room as we considered the body count. This was what we hated: the subversion of justice through violence and manipulation.

"Felix saved the day with a witness he personally safeguarded and escorted so he could deliver his testimony. Jikia was sentenced to two consecutive life sentences on racketeering and murder charges. He's still caught up in a lengthy appeals process, and it's rumoured he runs the organisation from behind bars with the aid of his wife, Nika. Six months after the trial finished, the star witness disappeared, and a week later the man's tongue was mailed to Felix. He quit Philly PD the next day to join the Judges programme."

The Judges all nodded, as if we all identified with Felix and his reason to join our ranks.

"Since he graduated, he's been spearheading a push to shut down organised crime in the Badlands in Philly. No one knows the major players on the streets better than him. He was investigating a lead when he vanished. It is suspected that he was lured into a trap by a false informant. But no one's talking, not even under advanced interrogation."

Stone's voice sounded as if fury had been compressed and forged into an iron bell. "So they're going to use the Judge that took their boss down to subvert our programme. That's their twisted version of justice."

Somehow his posture got even more ramrod straight. "Not on our watch. We're not letting criminals murder children and destroy our reputation."

He paused and surveyed me again. "If your hunch is correct."

:: Don't waver, Phoebe. ::

I stared him straight in the visor. "I'll quit the programme if I'm wrong."

Everyone in the room froze. Helen opened her mouth as if to say something, but thought better of it. Priya and Maddox watched me with wide, surprised eyes. Jarek had the intent expression of someone watching a high-stakes poker game.

He nodded curtly. "I'll make the call to Fargo personally. And you better hope you're right, Wise. For you *and* this division."

"I understand," I said, trying my best to look confident. I could deal with consequences for myself: but what about the rest of my team?

As Stone began snapping off orders, I directed my attention inside.

You! Pam, right? We need to chat.

:: Yes, we do. ::

Well, I have a drive coming up. It's time we got acquainted.

CHAPTER ELEVEN

Spotsylvania County, Virginia
Tuesday, September 20th 2044
19:30

HELEN WOULDN'T CLEAR me to drive my Lawranger, so I rode shotgun beside Jarek in the van while Maddox rode his bike out front. It was twilight, and the commuter rush was settling down, so Jarek was able to weave through the loosening traffic. I watched the vehicles as we whizzed by, filled with ordinary folk hurrying home to their families, or setting out to have a good time in a bar or dancing. I felt a pang, a desire for that normal life of easy pleasures.

I brushed it off. I had more than that. The Judges had accepted me. Better than any of my kin. And I trusted them with my life every day.

We sailed through a dark river spotted with red tail lights and white beams, winding down the I-95 to our destination in Spotsylvania County. A quiet town, once affluent, but in the changing economic climate it had gone to seed. It was far from where Judge Felix last checked in from an abandoned steel works in Nicetown, Philly.

I suspected Stone bet on the St. Anne's in the northerly

Jefferson County to be the more likely candidate for trouble—if any trouble was coming. We kept in contact with the other team at fifteen-minute intervals. Stone had been on a couple of calls with Pellegrino and Fargo. They were keenly interested in the results of our little jaunt, and were prepared to mobilise other Judges if my insight proved correct.

My team was putting their faith in me. I couldn't let them down.

Jarek was upbeat and chatty as he monitored the navigation of the van. He'd always been relaxed around us Judges, despite knowing what we could do. I appreciated that; his trust in our ability to regulate ourselves, to not snoop or set things on fire. He was constantly enthusiastic about our abilities.

"You're real-life superheroes!" he said one time over lunch when Helen was out of the room. She always quashed Jarek's informality. As much as I liked Helen, I always felt that I was a test subject that constantly churned out data for her. Everything she did was to protect her project and extend—and expand—its remit. I was sure she had other candidates on file, waiting to be tested if we messed up.

But sometimes people's thoughts just *leaked* out, and I can't be held responsible when I trip over their mind mess. Over time I heard enough stray thoughts to know Helen saw tremendous potential in the Judges system. She was hitching her cart to a new horse that she thought could deliver subjects with a range of talents she'd never encountered before. I could tell how much Priya riveted her; that kind of ability was just so rare. Helen believed that most pyros died in fires as babies and were chalked up as accidental deaths; and the rest rarely made it to their teens.

Her experience made her cynical about the other federal agencies, which she determined were hidebound and cautious when it came to truly innovative work. Since her department was the residual stub of the discredited Project MKUltra, no one took it seriously, despite her innovations in the analysis of genetic information. Once everyone began putting their

DNA tests online, she had been splashing in a warm bath of information, but with no resources to do anything except float a couple of rubber duckies on it. The only reason PSYCHE had survived at all was the bureaucratic beast determined it was better to retain one specialist rather than risk missing a potential breakthrough. Yet it never gave Helen the support she needed to prove her theories on mutation and environmental stressors.

Judge Fargo had paid attention when Pellegrino discovered Helen and asked her to make a presentation. Helen found him receptive to the idea, and he cut through her persuasive sales pitch to knuckle down about the numbers of potential psykes, dealing with rogue talents, and possible infiltration by other agents. No one had ever given Helen the opportunity to offer a plausible case for increased funding and to establish a test group. For years, her colleagues laughed about her obsession in their private chat-groups and thought she was wasting her talents in a dead-end job.

I often wondered at her determination. She never explained why she toughed it out for so long in an underfunded department. Jarek only got assigned to her when Fargo gave the green light to set up a test group.

But what me and my fellow guinea pigs didn't like to admit was that the other reason Helen got her hands on us is that we didn't have a choice. When we were accepted for the Judges programme, we'd signed over our genetic information; it was in the fine print that most of us didn't read. The Judges initiative presented her with a golden opportunity to sift through the data of a large group of people, and the authority to commandeer them for her research. She could study psykes and become the leading expert on a new area of human study. If it panned out, then she could be moulding the future for a cutting-edge division of Judges—if none of us screwed it up for her.

"Penny for them," Jarek chirped, glancing at me briefly. It was fully dark, and the van's HUD and screens washed a kaleidoscope of coloured lights over his features.

I adjusted my elbow pad on my right arm. It tended to dig in badly. "Just hoping I'm proved right. Don't want to let anyone down."

He smiled and reached over to pat my arm. I flinched. He noticed and pulled back.

"My apologies, Fee," he said, his expression mournful. "I should know better."

"'Salright. It's a natural instinct."

He smiled. "I'm positive this will be a stonking success. You've always been reliable." He raised a clenched fist. "We'll vanquish the threat and save those kiddies."

I restrained the urge to squirm although I appreciated his impulse to lighten the mood. I thought the praise was unearned. "We'll see," I said, quietly.

"Why don't you have a quick kip? Sorry, 'nap.' I can wake you when we're ten minutes out or if an urgent situation arises."

As soon as he suggested it, I could feel the need to sleep dragging on my bones. My head and chest took that opportunity to complain about my earlier bouts. Helen had jabbed me with a painkiller before we'd left, but it wasn't strong; didn't want to interfere with my abilities or slow my reactions.

Besides, I needed a cover for figuring out why I had a stranger in my head called Pam.

"You're right," I said. "I could use a recharge."

I closed my eyes. The thrum of the engine and the whoosh of the other vehicles on the road soothed me. I inhaled the smell of stale coffee and the mint car freshener. It reminded me how much I enjoyed long drives at night on the interstate. I associated them with peace: moving in the dark in my own bubble, too fast to get embroiled in strangers' mind noise, and playing music so loud it kept me pumped and distracted from my own thoughts.

Pam?

:: Hello Phoebe.::

Her presence had a distinct quality. A warm resonance with a sharp intellect. Focusing on it, I could almost see her…

:: Let me. ::

I was in the woods, just like that time when I first heard her in my mind. It was the day I'd found out I'd been accepted into the Judges programme. I decided to spend time in my favourite spot since I didn't know if I'd ever see it again. I was wearing my comfortable hunting gear and that beat-up cap with the sun blocker flap at the back. Birds sang, the beech leaves rushed in a wind, and a shower of water pattered across the brim of my hat. My hunting rifle was propped against a tree.

The woman, Pam, stood in front of me in a Judge's uniform—but different from mine. It looked, well, cooler. Better designed, and with green pads. She didn't have a helmet or gloves on, and I could see she was African-American, maybe in her late 30s or early 40s. But her face: I *knew* that face. How?

"I'm Pam Reed," she said, and held out her hand.

I ignored the hand. "Why're you in my head?"

She smiled and withdrew her hand. "Good question, Phoebe. The short answer is I'm not sure."

"What kind of Judge are you? I mean, you *are* a Judge?"

She nodded. "Yes. I'm like you. A psi."

"Psi," I said, rolling that around. "I always thought 'psyke' was a stupid name. Only a scientist could come up with it." I looked around. "Where are you?'

She raised her hand to slide it across the side of her head. I recognised that gesture. "Well, that's complicated."

"Are you involved in these attacks? Are you trying to infect my mind or something?" The landscape responded to my mood: a distant thunder rumbled, and whips of thorns grew out of the forest floor and raised up, curled as if ready to strike.

She raised her palms and the thorns fell off the stems, which sprouted lush flowers of all kinds. Their perfume was rich and soothing.

"I'm not here to hurt you. If anything, I'm here to help. I think."

There was something around her. A light mist. No, a dust cloud. I squinted at it. And it zoomed out. Behind her, I could see our office, but it was dark and busted-up. It looked abandoned.

A bolt of fear shot through me. "That's our lab! Has there been an attack?"

"Not quite, not yet," she said.

She blipped, and was standing by my left side with her hand on my arm.

There was no barrage of thoughts and memories. Just the warm, comforting sensation of a friend's hand on my skin.

"We call this place a psi sanctuary. You build it in your mind. It's where you go when you need a safe space. You control it."

I really wanted to brush her hand off my arm, but I also revelled in that quiet contact.

"A psianctuary," I said, and grinned.

She laughed, a warm, genuine sound. She hugged me in a spontaneous, delighted fashion, and I tightened up.

Pam stepped back. "I forget about telepaths sometimes. Despite all my training. It's a tough burden. Especially where I come from." The lines on her face suddenly became more pronounced. I upped my estimate of her age.

"I'm a pre-cog," she said. "From... the future. When the world is different."

"How far in the future? What's different?" As soon as I asked, I realised I believed her. Here, it was impossible for her to lie to me. We could only be honest with each other.

"It's better I don't say. I'm unsure why we're connected."

"It must be about this case. You're the reason I got the flash about Felix."

She nodded. "That was my talent, yes."

There was a strange sensation, like a pressure change. We both looked around.

"That's odd," I said. "It doesn't feel like me."

Her eyes narrowed and I felt a strengthening and a seeking. "You're strong, Phoebe, but from where I come you're like a child. You're so under-trained. That makes you vulnerable. But there aren't many psis in your time."

"But there *are* others. There must be."

"Clearly. This person you're dealing with, who has mind-wiped the people he or she has programmed—that's an advanced technique. Your team is in danger. But I should be able to bolster you." She regarded me with a searching look. "If I wasn't here..." She trailed off.

There was a terrible wrenching moment.

I was sitting on a carpeted floor, my back against the wall. Everything was shaking, like an earthquake. A roaring and awful grinding noise battered my ears. I felt a stream of dirt and rocks bouncing off my helmet and sliding onto my legs. Very far away, like a song playing through the walls of several rooms, I could hear a woman's voice. "Judge Reed. You 'kay? Drokk it!"

I staggered a little. I was back in the woods. Pam was bent slightly as if someone had punched her in the stomach. Around us the branches hissed in a sudden wind. There was a storm coming. I could smell the harbinger of rain.

I reached out and held her. A sense of urgency galvanised me.

"You have to go back!"

Her stability returned, and with it her strength, like a twisted steel cable: flexible but resolute.

"No, Fee. I'm here for a reason. If I leave... I'm afraid of what will happen in your future."

The sky darkened and the wind rose. Leaves blurred the space between us.

A hand gripped my arm, shaking it gently.

Jarek's voice, so close to my ear it felt like it was in my head: "Phoebe. It's time."

CHAPTER TWELVE

22:05

I STARTED AWAKE and jerked away from Jarek's touch.

He raised his hand in a calming fashion. "That was quite the dream you were having."

I blinked my eyes. It was night. We were parked in some suburban street. Even in the poor light cast by the few working street lights, I could see it had an air of neglect: bad paintjobs and overgrown lawns, a couple of American flags hung from porches in a dispirited fashion. I'd have pegged this for a neighbourhood for people in transit or in low-paying jobs.

My head and chest pulsed a low painful beat. I groaned and rubbed my neck, and then my mouth. Ugh, a drool trail. Hardly a good look.

"Where's Maddox?" I asked.

Jarek touched one of his screens and a close-up map of the area appeared. St. Anne's Orphanage was a large L-shape with ample space around it. It stuck out, in a neighbourhood comprising mostly nondescript, regular houses.

"Maddox is positioned two blocks over." He pointed at a red dot on the screen. "He's rather conspicuous on his bike, so it was considered wiser to have him stationed on the main thoroughfare, and to do the occasional patrol. It will appear as if he's a Judge on a crime suppressant circuit."

There were no Judges stationed in Spotsylvania County yet, and definitely not in this half-horse hamlet. But Judges were making their presence felt in the smaller burgs by taking these long-range rounds. It was another initiative to acclimatise the populace to a future in which Judges would be the only law-enforcement presence on the streets.

Maddox was going to attract a lot of attention, but that should pull focus from us. Theoretically. But my gut told me that an unmarked black van in sketchy area would be just as visible. All the natives would be twitching their curtains and stashing their guns by the door. And if any of them were conspiracy nuts with an active online forum, then we could have company.

"It's a strange spot for an orphanage," I noted.

"The original patron, Mrs Veronica Holland, built it in 1888, and chose this location because she believed that clean air, regular church and hard work—in the orphanage's fields—were the best ingredients to forge better citizens. Orphans from bigger cities who'd fallen into bad habits were sent here to 'reform' their characters."

I snorted. "Sounds like an easy way to turn a profit."

Jarek turned from his screen to regard me. "Judge Fargo would probably approve of such a system. After all, it's taking unwanted children and giving them a home and a structured regime, with the aim of producing decent American citizens."

I didn't comment. Coming from a home with lots of kids and a fixed doctrine, I was less taken with the idea. But then, where had I run to? A stint in the Army and then the Judges programme. And I'd turned out... okay.

"Are there many occupants?"

"Since the defunding of many welfare programmes in the 2020s, there's been a sharp intake of children to St. Anne's. It's run by a small religious group, The New Sisters of St. Anne, who have a non-hierarchical nondenominational Christian ethos. Currently, they have eighty-six children registered, from as young as one to seventeen years old, but there are far more teens. The babies are easier to place."

"And there's no connection between Judge Felix and this orphanage?"

Jarek shook his head. "I've cross-referenced every database. He never had so much as a vacation or a school trip to this area. It is the 'Crossroads of the Civil War,' after all, and a popular tourist destination. There were four major civil war battles fought in this county alone."

"Great, a Yankee Judge—part of a new Deep State organisation planning on supressing American rights—comes to a site of Southern battlegrounds to wage a new war—on children." I raised my hands in despair. "The conspiracy nuts will lap it up."

"Yes, Ms Pellegrino imagined a similar scenario. She referred to it as a potential 'political shitstorm.' Judge Stone didn't appreciate the vulgarity."

He paused for a moment. "Have you had any more..."—he waved his hands in the air—"insights?"

I resisted the urge to roll my eyes. "Not really." But as soon as I began to recall the first flash, I could feel it like a residual imprint in my mind. And there was an urgency to it. A sense of imminence.

:: It's close now. ::

In my mind I could sense Pam engaging her talent. She approached it differently. It was like she held herself open for a much wider range of influences. An urgent thread thrummed, and she pulled on it until it began to vibrate wildly and a surge of energy walloped down the line towards us. I wanted to recoil from it instinctively, but Pam remained relaxed and receptive. It was like watching a person deliberately walk in front of a high-speed train.

It hit her (us).

It's night-time. I'm in the big schoolyard at the back. The basketball hoops look well-used. Ahead of me is a row of classroom windows in a two-storey red-brick building. It has that nineteenth-century, fake Gothic style. A pointy tower on top. Judge Felix walks through the space with a leaden step, and as he moves, there are slow-motion trails—other potential movements. Sometimes he doubles into two Judges. In the vision, his head is scribbled over like a cartoon, with wires popping out and crackling electricity arcing between them.

I understand now that these warnings are not always clear and contain layers of information in flux. I admire Pam's ability to observe, sort, and remember details. Behind all this, I get an inkling of the rigorous training she has undergone since she was a child.

He enters a short alley, and ahead of him is a security box.

The vision jumps forward and he is moving through a darkened, echoing hallway. Behind him is the gurgling, gasping sound of someone dying. I can't see it, but I know it's one of the Sisters. Ahead of him is a row of doors, all closed. Behind each one is an innocent, asleep and dreaming of a better future.

Felix carries an AK-74M. It will shred those vulnerable bodies.

"They must be judged," Felix says. "Offspring of criminals become criminals."

I pull myself out of the vision because I'm already reeling from the deluge of violence and pain. The sound of bullets, children's screams and shattered lives. The stench of blood and piss.

My throat constricts and I have a sudden urge to vomit. I open my eyes and can't prevent myself from making a gagging noise.

"He's here, close by!"

I reach for the car door, about to kick it open, but Jarek grabs my arm.

I turn to yell at him, but his expression is intent.

"Tell me what you know!"

That stalls me. I understand he needs to report to Stone's team, and I can't run off in a wild panic. He needs to understand what I experienced.

I drag in deep painful breaths.

"I saw Judge Felix disable the security system and enter St. Anne's. He's going to murder everyone he finds. It'll be a bloodbath."

He releases his grip on my arm and pats my shoulder instead, but I don't mind, on this occasion. Jarek isn't like the others. He's a considerate person. His thoughts don't pollute mine.

Jarek watches my face carefully. "You've seen the future?"

"A very strong potential. That means it's likely to happen unless we take action."

A suspicion grows in my mind that Stone has tasked Jarek with keeping a close watch on me. I take a very sly peek in his mind and there's a clear picture: Stone doesn't trust me, thinks I'm unstable. I slip out again, feeling guilty at taking liberties with Jarek.

Stone and Helen won't believe some crazy vision by a backwoods grunt with strange abilities. I need to convince Jarek, and explain why I knew what was happening.

:: Don't tell him about me, Fee! ::

Why would they believe me? But once they know that it's another psi—

:: An alien voice in your mind! Feeding you visions of the future. ::

Jarek was watching me intently. "Where did you go there?"

"I was doing mental exercises that Helen taught me. For when I'm overwhelmed."

But I was wondering now... could I trust Pam?

That complete and utter sense of her honesty that I experienced in my psianctuary had faded, and now it had fuzziness, like a fever dream. Perhaps she had been tricking me all along. Maybe she was going to subtly turn me against my friends. She could be the person who was hijacking people's minds. She'd thrown me an outlandish story to sway me to her side so she could manipulate me. And I'd bought it, like a sucker.

My mind seemed clear and crisp now, like I'd had a dash of cold water thrown over my thoughts.

I'd been a fool!

:: For Grud's sake, you know *I'm showing you the truth. ::*

Shut up, Pam.

I threw a shield up between the two of us, and behind it I could sense her hammering on it.

"I think I've been experiencing some kind of breakdown," I said, calmly.

Jarek's face was that of a kind, familiar friend. "Tell me everything," he said.

I suppressed the sense of dread. My instincts told me to sprint to the orphanage and stop the impending rampage. But I did not know if it was real or manufactured. I could only depend on what I knew to be true: my friends, procedure, and the law.

I told Jarek everything.

Afterwards, he sat for a few moments staring out of the windscreen, as if lost in thought. Outside, a burly man walking a German shepherd dog sneakily glanced at the van. He couldn't see us through the tinted glass. I suspected he took a picture of the vehicle with his bodycam. Another report logged for his neighbourhood watch group. Or his gang.

The sense of threat had not left me. I dug my fingers into my palm, to restrain the impulse to jump out of the car. It was all a ruse. I'd been lied to.

Jarek rubbed the bridge of his nose at the temple, as if he had a headache. "This is unfortunate, but we'll be able to course-correct."

He smiled at me with great warmth, and I knew I'd made the right decision.

"This will only hurt for an instant."

A blinding white bolt of energy hit my mind, shorting out everything.

CHAPTER THIRTEEN

Slowly, as if my mind was mired in mud, I began to regain consciousness. I couldn't open my eyes. I had no control of my body, but I had a distant awareness of it. Jarek was speaking to me. I could hear the tone but not the words. But some part of me was listening to his instructions.

I tried to push out with my talent, but it was like turning the key in a dead engine. Nothing.

I tried to remember my first cell phone number... but it was like sliding against an invisible wall. Much of my daily information was out of reach. I knew I knew it, but I couldn't gain access to the substance of it. A terrible niggling absence caused me to continually knock against the wall, trying to understand my boundaries.

Because I was so disconnected from my body, I couldn't rely on any of the breathing techniques I'd been trained to employ when panicked, but I didn't feel upset. That battery was also flat.

Eventually I discovered the boundaries of my cell. And my mind raced around it constantly, like... like something. An animal. Small. With a nose and a tail that swished. I knew its parts but not its whole or its name. I sniffed at the edges, hoping for a way out.

This creature was canny and always escaped. There must be a way.

Many mice never escape the trap, the voice told me. *When you know their weakness, you can lead them in easily enough. Once they are set in the maze, their purpose is to run it for the scientist.*

"Who are you?" I asked.

I'm the scientist. You are the mouse. You're going to run exactly how I programme you.

"I'll get out."

Soon you will be released—into that last darkness. Before that, you will do something important. You will expose Judges as trained brutes with no self-control and little oversight. After your act of violent judgement, everyone will rally to eradicate your kind. Even the President will abandon his pet project. Judge Fargo will be humiliated and his legacy gutted. And the other psis will be tracked down and weaponised for our purposes.

After all, Dr Murray's work will need a new patron.

While America destroys itself from the inside, we will continue to infiltrate and influence. We will whisper slurs against false enemies and praise tyrants. We will tarnish your heroes and subvert your political system. We'll place suspicions in your mind and you'll clap as we burn your icons. One day you will wake up in a country where you serve the trends and scorn justice, and you will believe it is the best future for your grand nation.

"People will resist."

We'll hijack their minds and sell them on servitude. It has already begun.

So thank you, mouse. You will die for a purpose, though not the one you signed up for.

The voice withdrew and I ran around my cell looking for some weakness, but whoever had constructed it had known their craft well.

I felt the tiniest of tremors.

A smell… decaying leaves and rain.

It reminded me of someplace safe. I concentrated on that feeling.

I heard a rushing sound: a breeze rattling leaves on trees.

Drops of water splashed on my face.

My ass was numb from sitting on a rock.

I stood and enjoyed the lithe action of trained muscles moving easily. My body appeared. I stretched tall, arms above my head, spreading my fingers wide, and revelling in the sensation.

Around me the forest grew into being, from gnarled roots, thick knotted trunks, and swaying crown of leaves. I laid my cheek upon rough bark and relaxed into the tree's stately presence. I inhaled the scent of mulch and moss.

Far away, a distant rumble of thunder provoked a trickle of emotion. I followed it and it led to a faded urgency, and—more useful—a snap of fury.

I was trapped. Tricked. Being made into someone's pawn to hurt others.

The anger sparked again.

They were going to kill children. They were going to make *me* murder children.

That got the rage simmering, and with that, the psianctuary burst into full life around me.

I raised my head to see pieces of blue sky visible through the green.

I shouted, "*Pam!*"

Birds chirped. A squirrel raced along a nearby branch.

My head still felt like it was stuffed with cotton balls, but in here I knew I had a chance.

The ground trembled a little. I could taste thick dust.

To my right, I spotted Pam, her fancy future uniform coated in dirt, sitting with her back to a tree, and her head hanging down as if asleep.

I squatted in front of her. Her hands lay on her lap.

I removed a glove and placed both my hands around her limp limbs.

I leaned close to her filthy helmet.

"Pam," I said, "you've got to help me."

There was a violent wrench, followed by a dizzying dislocation. Like that trick where the magician pulls the cloth from under the cups and plates, but in this case it felt like I was also rotated through time and space.

"Pam, you've got to help me!"

Yoon was shaking me, trying to pull me up and encourage me to stand. My drone's light beam was hazy with flying dust. My tongue felt thick and immobile in my dry mouth.

"Wake up! The drokking building is breaking up."

With infinite effort I raised my head. Yoon was scared, but determined.

"We're not gonna end up buried here!" She snuck her shoulder under my armpit. "I always heard psis were pampered. Could your ladyship get your legs working?"

I planted my feet—admiring the support and fit of the boots—and staggered upright.

"Sssorry," I slurred. It felt like I was a coma victim waking up with a hangover.

"I hope the amplifier was worth it."

"Ampli-what?"

"The pill! It knocked you out for hours."

"Rright."

"Can you stand?" She took her shoulder from under me, and tilted me so that I leaned against the wall.

She stepped back slowly hands up and ready to catch me if I slumped. I gave her a thumb's up signal.

"I gotta get my kit out of the NOC and haul it to the platform. You sober up and I'll be back in a jiffy."

Hardwick bellowed into the comms. "What are you two numbskulls playing at? You've thirty minutes to get out. If the block doesn't fall on your drokking heads first."

"On our way, boss," Yoon shouted over another crash. In the room outside, a section of the ceiling collapsed.

She dashed out of the room.

I reached down to my belt and flicked open the pill case. The lone pill waited. We had a term for a second dose of psi-flyers: the Event Horizon. Only to be approached when all else fails, because it can suck you into the void. Shenker would be furious—on the record—but he hated dead Psi-Judges more than protocol. As long as I wasn't mind-fried, I'd take the dressing down and the reprimand. I was their top pre-cog... well, Pam was.

"Bottom's up!" I whispered.

I unclipped my mask, slipped the pill into my mouth, and crunched down on it.

My tongue numbed immediately.

I collapsed to the ground.

CHAPTER FOURTEEN

Wednesday, September 20th 2044
01:01

I RETURNED TO my body with a jolt, my eyes opening wide as if from an adrenaline punch, but my body was inert and quiet. My mind was a slowly ramping battery that came with a euphoric elation and a belief that soon I'd be able to KO Godzilla with my thoughts.

No wonder this stuff is restricted!

A tiny rational impulse in my mind, muffled but observant, understood that there were costs to everything, and a massive injection of mind-mana had to come with a downer.

Otherwise all the juves would be doing it.

I was sitting in the back of the van on a jump-seat, with Judge Felix nearby. He had his helmet on, and sat facing forward, with his hands folded on his lap. He looked unharmed, if underfed.

I sensed the confines of the prison in my mind that Jarek had created.

I was high on my faith in my talent. A well-dressed Limey spy wasn't going to get away with brain-jacking me.

This is my *head and I make the rules.*

A pulse of power pushed through me and I simply entered the mental holding cell's barrier, became part of it, and separated from it again.

My sense of self came rushing back like a long gulp of my favourite drink on a hot day. Slowly, carefully I took inventory, delicately searching for signs of tampering. A paranoid thought about how I'd recognise any tinkering with my sense of self suddenly morphed into an overwhelming sense of dread.

Zero to anxious in one nanosecond. This effect increases paranoia, wonderful!

I fell back upon the grounding and centring exercises that Helen had taught me, and once the Fear got distracted and wandered off, I returned to figuring out if Jarek had done any lasting damage.

I sensed that he'd been in a hurry and didn't have the time to do a full reprogramming like he'd done on Felix. I spotted an unplugged connection between my emotions and my body: it would remain calm and biddable, so I left that alone. He'd be monitoring my armour sensors and any sudden change in my vitals would alert him. I wasn't sure how I'd cloak my escape from his cell if he checked in on me… but immediately a solution occurred, along with the knowledge of how to do it.

I quickly cloned a mirror image of myself and cast it into the cage. The ghost looked forlorn, which I hoped would boost Jarek's ego. I guessed he had to have a massive superiority complex: he'd hidden his abilities from fellow psis and had been watching us for months since he was assigned.

Infiltrate and influence, he'd said, with an aim to discredit the Judges programme. It had to be on behalf of another country, but the British were allies to our government… I left that problem alone, since I didn't have much time. Instead, I focused on trying to contact Pam.

Since Jarek zapped me, she'd been entirely absent.

I refocused, accessing the well of power pooling beneath me, and searched for Pam's signature: a steady, courageous spark.

She'd stashed herself in a hated memory, one I had sectioned off to keep it away from my everyday consciousness. That survival instinct had made it invisible to Jarek during his quick fumble through my memories. Pam had been lurking in my mind for longer and had spotted the secluded hiding place—I'd only noticed myself because the tenor of the memory had seemed different as I brushed past it. *Crafty*, I thought, as I made a note of the tactic.

I accessed the memory and walked into that familiar temple space I'd occupied so often as a child, and escaped as much as possible when I was older.

It was Sister Sophia Star's Sharing Space, the grand circular room in her temple, with nine stained glass windows casting fragmented, coloured light—except in the central spot where Sister Star normally stood: under a domed skylight which shone 'the pure light of the creative source' upon her long grey locks.

She had a wide, tall frame, so I always recalled her as looming over me, but she seemed older and frailer than I remembered. She had a cane, with a carved lotus flower on top, which she used to bang on the mosaic floor for our attention, but which I now realised she needed more for support.

In this moment I was a skinny eight-year-old, wearing a white shift. Sister Star's large, tanned hand was clamped on my shoulder. I remember her sickly rose perfume as she held me close to her side. To this day the stench of roses makes me gag.

"This child," she exclaimed, in her hypnotic chanting style, "is an oracle of truth. You cannot lie in her presence." Rows of believers were arranged around us, including my grandmother, mother, father and siblings, who had earned the prized front bench because of my gift.

"Rosalie," Sister Star crooned, and inclined her forehead at my grandmother, one of her earliest converts and longest supporters, "do you have anything to share?"

My grandmother's lined face hardened. She stood, her plain, black dress rustling. She was a tough, dedicated woman, who was unrelentingly strict and formal with everyone… except me. We'd always shared a bond. Such as the words we could whisper to each other in our minds.

"No, Radiant Star. I am restful."

I remained at the back, watching the scene replay, and grateful that my emotions were not registering in my body or otherwise I'd already be flushed from shame and embarrassment, and trembling from the confusing combination of dread and pride I always felt at being centre stage.

My family had little except their ardent faith in their leader, and my ascension to Sister Star's Truth Teller had given us respect and fear in our small community, which was more valuable than any currency.

But Sister Star had a way of pinpointing people's weaknesses and reminding them it was only through her connection to Universal Love that our eternal spirit could ever be forgiven for the inherent sinfulness of our temporary occupation of a human shell.

Sister Star's fingers clamped harder on my shoulder. Her thoughts trammelled down into my body, until I became a vessel of her intention. To everyone else she was a stern but smiling teacher, capable of turning on a wattage of warmth to those she favoured, but I saw underneath it to her canny manipulation. It was confusing, but she was the most important person in our world, and I learned to explain away the contradictions I knew between her sermons and her inner life. But we had many private instructions, during which she spoke to me in her singsong style, and afterwards I would have a hazy memory of our conversations. What was most important, I had been taught, was that she could not be wrong, and her access to the conduit of Universal Love could be weakened by disbelief.

"What say you, child?" Sister Star speared me with her focus. "Is your grandmother restful? Or does she hide truth from our congregation?"

I gazed across at my grandmother, who clasped her hands in

front of her body in a tranquil fashion. Gran had always been so controlled, but that was necessary for a telepath.

"Speak *her* truth, Phoebe, if she won't."

Watching the memory repeat, I could feel the points of Sister Star's fingers digging into my muscle, and my grandmother's resigned expression.

I forgive you, child, was all Gran said to me.

"She's been hiding her talent from you, Sister," I said, haltingly. "She can... tell truth, like me."

"So, she's been spying on us from the beginning?"

As one the congregation shifted to regard my grandmother with a range of expressions, worry and anger chief among them. "What lies could she have heard over the years? Silently she has judged us, and never warned us that she could see into our inner thoughts."

"Only the judgement of death is irrevocable," Gran replied, speaking one of our tenants of faith. "All people lie. It is not my place to judge a habit of the mind."

"But you admit you withheld this truth for decades?" Sister Star swept her arm dramatically around at our community. "In this sacred space of sharing, among your friends and beloved family, you have never fully been honest with us." At the last words she pushed me forward so I staggered a little, but I was directly in front of Gran.

Her shoulders softened as if a burden had been lifted from them.

"Yes," she said.

I could tell she would offer no defence or explanation. That was not her way.

Behind me I could hear the roiling thoughts of Sister Star, a raw, chaotic churn of fear and betrayal. They radiated so strongly I expected Gran could hear them too, but I guessed that might be the point.

"You are *removed!*" Sister Star roared. The congregation gasped in shock, but I could tell how many of them revelled in the excitement. My mother dropped her head into her hands and moaned. She would not stand up for Gran—they were always at odds, and this would be her way to break away from her permanently. And my father… he was utterly devoted to Sister Star.

I fell to my knees and grabbed the hem of Sister Star's dress.

Watching this, I felt sickened. I had wanted the love of my family so badly that I did everything they said was important to them. This was the moment when it all changed.

"No," I sobbed. "Please, no."

Phoebe, Gran said in my mind, *don't make a spectacle of yourself! You are a Wise! We do not beg.*

"As you wish, Sister Star," Gran said out loud.

She turned and moved past the sunned expressions of the congregation towards the aisle.

"You could apologise and seek forgiveness," Star said, and her voice cracked. Her anguish battled her fury at this deception, but always underneath it was the gnawing worry of what Gran had heard from Sister Star during their many years together. Sister Star had secrets she wanted kept. "Become my Truth Teller and I will release Phoebe from that service."

I wiped my eyes and stood up, hopeful.

"Please, Gran," I said out loud.

Gran's mouth flattened into a contemptuous line.

"The Wises do not beg."

I saw the hardness in her then. The rigidity that had kept her loyal to the community for so long but would not allow her to bend to remain. Not even for her vulnerable granddaughter.

She turned her back on the congregation and walked out of our lives.

I never saw my Grandmother again.

I spotted Pam, seated among the congregation, head downcast. I allowed the memory to continue. People stood in clusters and spoke together of their shock and outrage, while others consoled my family.

My younger self stood beside Sister Star, tears streaming down my face.

I could hear the echo of my thoughts: *My mind is stone, I wall out the noise.* And the first hatching of my plan to begin to pretend that my talent was waning, and upon puberty I would insist it had disappeared. I swore I would never allow someone to manipulate me again.

I sat down beside Pam. She was dressed in the plain clothing of Sister Star's acolytes, with her fingers laced together and on her lap.

I touched her arm and searched for her consciousness. Deep within, Pam had hidden herself quietly, under layers of protection. It was enough to evade a quick scan of my mind, and Jarek had relied on imprisoning me and executing his plan quickly.

As I held her arm, I sensed a mirrored pain in Pam upon witnessing this moment. A similar loss of a loved one at a young age. A great crack in her childhood that had been filled up with dedication, training, and a love for order and the law.

"We're running out of time," I whispered to her. "Jarek will make his move soon, and your building is collapsing."

Her eyes opened at that, and she turned her head to regard me.

"Time is not a straight line, Phoebe," she replied, her voice clear but hushed. "It is all moments, concurrently."

"So, it'll be a cinch to stop Jarek, save the kids and figure out how to get you back to your time before a city block flattens you?"

At that moment I felt a shift, both outside and in my inner world. A wave of power was surging, and I needed to ride it or drown.

Around us the surroundings and people faded into pale shadows against an increasing radiance. A giddiness gripped me. I needed to direct this energy before it turned on me.

Pam's voice rose with a hint of panic. "What did you do, Phoebe?"

"It's better if I show you."

I grabbed her hand, and we *merged*.

PART THREE

PHOEBE WISE AND PAM REED

CHAPTER FIFTEEN

Spotsylvania County, Virginia
Tuesday, September 20th 2044
01:42

WE FLOATED UP, dandelion-soft and entwined together, through layers of consciousness to passively observe the situation in the van. Any overt action could alert Jarek to our awareness. Even with our combined strength, we were unsure of the extent of his abilities.

Jarek had demonstrated careful strategy, restraint and immense talent. It would be an easy—and potentially fatal—mistake to succumb to overconfidence thanks to our buoying power. Despite damping the full force of our ability, and with our helmet on, we could perceive the undercurrent of Judge Felix's core self, constrained by a complex series of programmed instructions.

Gonna kill him! was interspersed with bursts of fear at the mission he was being forced to commit: *Not kids!*

We appreciated his fury, but he had no ability to break Jarek's hold.

The van moved at a sedate pace, stopped, and in our helmet, Jarek spoke cheerily to Felix and us.

"Rightio, lady and gent, last stop: St. Anne's Orphanage! Home to bastards and guttersnipes, dependent upon charity and society's handouts. The odious offspring of criminals and ne'er-do-wells. Time to disembark."

He released the back doors of the van—the cool night breeze rushed in, bringing the smell of rain after a warm day. We were parked in a trench of shadows, thanks to the broken street lights and an alley of trees. No doubt all the surveillance in the area had been hacked—Jarek had the access and know-how to remove or alter vehicles and people in all recordings. He could rewrite any files later to bolster his narrative.

"Smile for the cameras! They'll catch every grisly detail. I've choreographed your carnage along the route for the most flattering angles."

He paused, and speaking in a 'Hollywood movie trailer voiceover' voice, intoned: "Execute Operation Heracles."

The simple commands Jarek had hastily programmed into Phoebe's mind began to run: Enter the Orphanage. Kill everyone in the building. Kill anyone who attempts to stop you.

And Jarek could employ the mind-wipe RAMUZ command on Felix any point via comms. There had been no time to bed that into my mind.

Felix's internal screaming protests grew louder, but his body rose and stomped to the open van doors. His movements were wooden, but with no evidence of struggle.

Our body followed Felix's lead, and hopped off the van onto the street.

We walked around the side of the van and towards the front. The window was down, Jarek leaned his elbow on the opening, his expression smug and devious, a combination that made us want to slap it into the next state. We cloaked our presence as we stood in front of him, and we could feel him scrutinising our thoughts as he did our bodies. It was a cursory scan; Jarek was confident and arrogant, which we hoped we could exploit... somehow.

He chuckled like a vaudevillian villain. "I dub thee Judges Stalwart and True. Your quest awaits. Those kiddies won't slaughter themselves."

For a moment our control flickered and we almost head-butted him.

He frowned, his attention sharpened to a fine probe, and he checked on the prison he had constructed in our mind. Inside it, false Phoebe stood pathetically. It appeared to satisfy him and he slipped out of our thoughts again.

He pointed at the darkened building a short stroll down the street. "Get on with it. Once the blood's flying, I'll commence the live feed."

Felix and us turned sharply and walked down the street. We emerged from the shadows and into the glare of functional street lights, past the darkened houses and their slumbering occupants. We had to break Felix's programming before we entered the orphanage.

Thankfully, we were out of range of Jarek's psi abilities and could engage both our talents to their fully amplified state. We almost stumbled in our march when we uncapped that well.

A barrage of images assaulted us from Felix—we were treated to the highlights of his capture and torture. He'd been dragged before Nika Jikia herself—the Sovs' temporary leader and Dimitri's trophy wife... so everyone thought. But during his investigation, Felix had discovered that Nika was the true mastermind of the organisation. She was running scams and cons all along the Eastern Coast, with the goal of feeding information back to the SVR—the foreign intelligence agency in Russia.

Her people specialised in compromising politicians in all levels of government, but the Judges were proving to be the biggest threat to their covert plans, so the conversations turned towards finding a way to cripple the programme before it grew unassailable. A specialist was assigned to sniff out the Judges' secrets from within their most clandestine project.

Nosy Felix would have his reputation destroyed and become the very instrument to bring an end to the Judges programme.

Jarek's a Russian agent?

We had no time to ponder this longer. Felix arrived at the tall gate in the perimeter fence, topped with razor wire—it was hard to tell if it was to keep the kids in or safeguard them. He looked up directly at the camera pointed at the gate. Trying not to grind our teeth, we stood behind him and raised our helmet to the cheap plastic cube and its glinting lens.

In our ears, Jarek spoke affectionately. "Perfect. You're going to be stars. Use the gate code I gave you, Felix."

The keypad beeped as he plugged in the numbers. We desperately considered what we were going to do. It was essential that Jarek was captured alive and his talent incapacitated so he could be interrogated.

We sensed a titanic shift in the potentials around us: it was like being at the receiving ends of billions of conduits, each one leading to a different outcome. Some lines were indistinct and attenuated, while others were thick and magnetic. Along these lines bleak scenarios rushed at us, and in so many of them devastation resulted. Sometimes at the hands of our own people, but often due to other nations. We saw the Judges programme fail and the horrendous, spiralling effects of that, especially for psis.

As we experienced the annihilation of our country in an endless storm of visions, we barely kept our body functional. Felix pushed the gate open.

We breathe. We return to the body, to the now.

Our mind is stone, we wall out the noise.

We concentrated on every inhalation and exhalation, every movement of our muscles, as we followed Felix around the building into the yard with its battered basketball hoops. We knew where he was going. This was our opportunity.

We entered the blocky shadow cast by the building and what appeared to be a no-camera zone. We knew he would enter the small alley to access the security box: we allowed those moments to speed up and play out before us so we could choose an option. We had less than a minute.

We summoned all the power of our juiced-up talent in a moment of exhilarating liberation and delivered a stunning punch at Felix's mind, designed to paralyse him temporarily.

He halted. His mouth opened slightly, but we prevented him from gasping. We darted closer and planted the fingers of our left hand on his neck to increase our connection, and catch him if he collapsed.

The inside of Felix's mind was a mess of instructions, fail-safes, and countermeasures to prevent any interruption of the programme. Psi-Division mastered these techniques long ago, but it was troubling to witness Jarek's advanced ability way back in the 'forties. He had trained hard and been instructed well. The fledging Psi-Division in America was significantly behind in mental warfare.

Yet, Jarek didn't know all the tricks yet.

We dove fast and hard into the old brain. Deeply buried was the equivalent of a psychic reset lobe, a strange residual artefact of ancient ancestors who had developed an ability to shake off a mind parasite. A well-delivered psi-jab at that lobe would result in a type of psychic electromagnetic pulse and short out the programming long enough for Felix to regain control. Psis were trained to guard this part of the mind carefully, but for ordinary people it was a redundant faculty. It would be useful to us in this case—if it worked. The results were variable, but we were encouraged by the quality of Felix's mind. We suspected he was a latent psi, and that boded well for this plan.

Brace yourself, buddy, we said to him. *This will be weird, but you'll be free from Jarek's control. Don't make any noise, or fall over, if you can help it.*

Mere moments had passed in real time when we zapped Felix for a second time, and scampered fast from his brainpan to remove our presence when the self-defence effect triggered.

He trembled violently, but we held on to him.

We quickly assessed his mind: most of the constraints on

him had been broken, and his functioning mind was rapidly reasserting. Out of some cruel need to torture Felix as much as possible, Jarek had not hollowed out his consciousness. Jarek and his masters wanted him to be fully aware as he violated his deepest held beliefs and brought about the destruction of the Judges.

Felix, you must act as if you are still under his control. Carry out the plan until you gain access to the building. Then come up with some delaying tactic for as long as you can manage. We're going to double back and get Jarek. Take off your helmet as soon as you can—Jarek has planted a trigger word in you that is harmful.

More potential outcomes poured into our mind and we saw the best path to navigate back to the van. We had to be fast and unswerving.

"Are you at the security control unit?" Jarek said in our ears.

Felix spoke carefully, like a drunk pretending to be sober. "There's not enough light. I can't see it."

"Well, use your flashlight—your torch, man! I know I've curtailed your thinking, but perhaps you're just thick. But Fargo doesn't want smart Judges, does he? Just willing brutes. Except for this merry psi band he's assembled." Jarek paused for a moment as if he was mulling something over. "But we'll ensure they are gainfully employed after this catastrophe."

We pursed our lips against the anger.

"It's a shame you'll die tonight, Phoebe. How I would have enjoyed examining your memories and reshaping you for better purposes. I never tracked down that intriguing passenger in your head. Still, I'll have plenty of time with Priya and Maddox. We have no one with their abilities. Perhaps we'll spirit them back home for better study."

Revulsion prompted an involuntary shudder.

Jarek chuckled again. "When I'm through with them, they will happily burn and incapacitate their fellow Judges."

We raised our hand and pantomimed an L-sign over our forehead. Felix cracked a wan smile.

Good luck.

He gave me the 'okay' signal to indicate he understood.

We let the potential trails blaze into life around us and moved quickly, making minute adjustments of our footing and posture. Running crouched to the gate, we slipped through, and rolled into the shadows drenching the street around the van. Working on the fly required quicksilver instinct, and we were thankful for our experience. There was no time to overthink, we had to inhabit each moment fully and press forward into the best future we could sense.

"Have you overridden the alarms yet?" Jarek sounded edgy but excited. He clearly got off on being the puppet master of trained Judges, but he was eager for the big finale now.

As we crept towards the van, we could hear the edges of his thought-mesh. We had removed all restraint on our amped-up abilities. What was coming was going to be difficult, and perhaps futile. In many future realities, we would die and the children be murdered.

But in a few, we would prevail.

We took a wide course around the van and unholstered our Judge-issue sidearm as we moved behind the van and moved fast to the window—it remained rolled down.

At this close range, it felt as if we were moving *inside* his mental landscape, and we had to tread as carefully there as we did on our feet so not to alert him. We popped up with our gun raised.

The driver's seat was empty.

A wrenching tear occurred in our mind, as if someone gripped our fabric of reality and whipped it from under us.

We predicted the massive psi bolt walloping into us a second before it happened, and threw up a shield in time.

We spun, keeping low with a forearm up and ready to block a punch.

Jarek stood with his hands on his hips. He was angry, but also thrilled.

"A worthy opponent. At last." He placed a capsule in his mouth and crunched down on it. "But I don't like to lose."

Around us the potentials exploded into new activity, and for the first time, Jarek dropped all pretence and revealed the true extent of his ability.

In our heightened psi sensitive state, he appeared to grow several sizes taller.

It was going to be a monster brawl...

CHAPTER SIXTEEN

As we raised our gun, we glimpsed a future in which we discovered—too late—that Jarek had hacked our gun's identilock.

Drokk!

We threw it at his face instead.

This was not expected. It was momentarily satisfying to see the fleeting surprise flit across his features as he raised his arm to knock it aside. It whacked him right between his eyes with a *crack* and his eyes closed instinctively.

We leaped after the distraction. There was only one way to put him on a different footing and that was to rip Jarek out of his body and into an astral level. There, we would have a chance.

We landed a very satisfying punch to his jaw and followed it with a left jab at his larynx.

He immediately bent over in agony, and we slipped behind him to engage a headlock around his neck. But mostly importantly, we had physical contact.

He recovered fast, even as his face reddened.

A powerful mental punch, designed to paralyse us instantly, walloped into our shield. We held, barely. We gritted our teeth and bolstered our defences, while we tightened our grip around his neck. Strategies and future possibilities whizzed through our head, but we focused on getting him down on his knees.

He bucked and scrabbled at our hold and tried to dig an elbow into our solar plexus, but it skidded off our chest armour.

We sensed his mind maintaining its steely control even as his physical body went into shutdown.

As he refocused on removing our grip under all circumstances, we *reached* inside him, grabbed his energetic essence and *ripped* it out.

He collapsed immediately on top of us. Expertly, we rolled him, grabbed our cuffs and retrained his hands behind his back.

We sat cross-legged on the wet asphalt, and inhaled a deep breath.

He'd get back to his body eventually, so we'd have to disable him before that was possible. He was too strong, he'd turn people against us, against other Judges and innocent people. And all that valuable information about who employed him and what they'd been doing would be lost.

We switched comms to an all-team broadcast. "Wise needs assist. By the van near the orphanage. Felix, get over here. Jarek is compromised."

We pulled our helmet off and sat it beside us. Above us, the trees moved and creaked and cast a light mist of water over our head. It felt like a blessing from this time and place.

We removed our gloves, sucked in another deep breath, laid our hand upon his cheek and ejected our consciousnesses from our body to follow his trail.

CHAPTER SEVENTEEN

The Astral Plane
Out of Time

THE FIRST TIME Sergei had an inkling that his mother Irina had betrayed his father was when they landed at JFK in New York, and a trio of people in suits asked them politely but firmly to 'come with us.'

He noticed she didn't appear surprised, but quietly complied with the order. This from a woman who could verbally flay a waiter for handing her the wrong fork.

Despite flying first class, it had been a tiring journey from London. He and his twin sister Zosia had played *Glittering Scimitars X* in VR to alleviate the boredom. Now they were escorted to a small bland room with a table, two hard chairs and no devices. Half a wall was made of mirrored glass. He was the son of Dr Dmitry Dudayev. He knew what this meant.

Zosia and he gathered the chairs so they could sit side by side. They held hands, as that always intensified their connection.

Together, they could perceive the thoughts of the guard outside.

Witness Protection. Relocation. New identity.

They were not going back to London. Mama had lied to

them. This astonished them most of all. Their mother had never been able to keep a secret from them before.

Zosia rarely spoke out loud. Doctors declared she had a learning disability due to the trauma of her parents' divorce. She just preferred to use her mind and only liked to converse with Sergei. As a result, she had a better talent for it.

Zosia sighed. *Mama's learned to hide her thoughts.*

Not from both of us, together.

She shrugged lightly. *Perhaps. But do you wish to know everything she has seen?*

Sergei frowned. He didn't understand.

Oh, Sergei, she said, and gently squeezed his hand. *Papa was horrible to her.*

She provokes him! He said so.

Zosia swung her legs, but her thoughts fell still.

He didn't like it when she did this. She had a way of being remote sometimes. Of creating distance between them. That scared him more than anything else.

He gripped her hand, hard. He knew it hurt, but she didn't indicate any discomfort. *Don't do that, don't go away!*

Zosia swung her legs and sang a lullaby their nanny in London used to sing to them when she put them to bed. Afterwards, they would torture her with nightmares. She didn't last long. None of the staff stayed in their house, except for the cook; his head was like granite.

Let's make the guard see giant spiders.

Sergei and Zosia smiled and entered the mind of the man in the hall.

His screams couldn't penetrate their holding room, but they witnessed his panic attack anyway, swung their legs and laughed.

In the spirit realm of the astral, where mental and spiritual control could create anything, we had fashioned a hall of memory mirrors around Jarek—or Sergei—and hung above it in a shining realm of potential, watching what played out for him. Despite his skill, he seemed unfamiliar with working on an astral level. Being yanked into an unknown territory had thrown him into an old memory of having his life destabilised.

Still, he was a fast learner, and was on drugs too.

The father. That's the important link.

We keyed the construct for a memory of his father.

Immediately, the scene shifted.

IT HAD BEEN a long time since he'd thought of himself as Sergei. It was only in his dreams, and when Zosia visited him. She was long gone, killed by a botched hit on his mother. Poisoned by a box of Ptichye Moloko delivered to their second home in Florida. Jarek had found her, lying on the tiled kitchen floor, with the sweets scattered across the counter. He'd cradled her in his arms, but her essential self had vanished. Nothing remained but a shell.

He never forgave his mother for upending their life and forcing them to scratch for a living in America, but he hated her most for not dying instead of Zosia.

When she committed suicide just after Jarek Carus graduated from high school and was accepted into Cambridge, it was after several years of a fragmenting mental state. She harboured delusions that her son was torturing her in her dreams. Everyone praised Jarek for his stoic nature, and his mature reaction, especially after the tragic death of his twin sister years earlier. But Jarek easily found mentors and advocates. People liked him immediately. His handlers in the government saw his potential and groomed him for active service in one of their many agencies. He spoke several languages and people opened up to him. Anyone who met him came away convinced of his potential.

It was on his first summer vacation after a year of studies in England that he met his father for the first time in twelve years. Jarek had travelled via Interrail, a very normal activity for a first-year student, and ended up at the ancient city of Polotsk in Belarus.

Their reunion occurred on a park bench, where they silently fed pigeons side by side and Jarek spoke to his father in his mind.

Dr Dudayev had been studying people with psionic gifts since the fall of the old Soviet regime. He did not possess any abilities himself, but he was convinced there was a genetic component. After years of study, he selected his wife based on her family history of sensitive people and had designed her supplement regime during her pregnancies. She'd miscarried four times before giving birth to twins. Some years later, Irina had discovered his research and removed herself and their children to London, where she had family.

More than anything, Dr Dudayev wanted to be able to speak with his son via the same means. He'd been developing a drug that he hoped would allow those with non-existent or latent abilities to advance their faculties, but results had been disastrous. People died of aneurysms, seizures, strokes, but occasionally, when used in micro-doses, it increased the chances of conceiving a child with psi gifts. More useful: when used by people with talents, even with the weakest ability, it boosted their capabilities enormously.

It had risks, however: paranoia and migraines were the least debilitating side effects, but complete talent burnout and significant personality disorders could result from overuse.

Dr Dudayev gifted his son with samples, and after Jarek returned to college, they continued their communication via the Dark Web.

Once he completed his PhD, Jarek was recruited by the FBI—the agency believed *they* had been grooming *him* for years—and returned to the USA to begin siphoning secrets back to his father. Over time, he became acquainted with the network of operatives in the country working to subvert and infiltrate all levels of government. Jarek felt only contempt for his adopted homeland, and the simple minds he bent to his will. Back in

Russia, Dr Dudayev had over two decades of research into the circumstances that produced people with psionic abilities, and the methods to increase their gifts.

None were as impressive as Jarek, but there were others.

...others...

—errs—

The construct exploded and Jarek emerged from the disintegrating shards. He was gigantic, pure swollen ego and rage, driven to prove himself as the best talent in the room... or in this pocket of the astral, at least.

—You— he roared. *—You cheater! You have help! —*

And you've had years of training and a constant supply of drugs, we responded.

We grew in size, too, but we kept our form relatively simple, while he appeared to be experimenting with adding spiked, elaborate armour to his bloated shape.

Let's get ready to ruuummmmbbbblllleeee! he shouted, and stampeded towards us, stretching and growing a thousand legs as he ran. He was a giant armoured centipede bristling with axes by the time he barrelled into us. I merely allowed him passage and didn't engage.

All of this was burning off energy in this body, and we suspected that as a regular user of the drug, Jarek would have developed a tolerance to its effects. Certainly he was exhibiting a degraded mental state... or he had always been a psychopath and being allowed free reign with his talent had inflated his narcissism.

The centipede turned and reared, and its many limbs whipped out fast at us. At the end of every antenna was a taloned hand slicing at us. We dodged the snarl of grasping claws, but backed into a waiting vault he had conjured behind us. The door slammed shut and locked us into darkness.

Dimly from outside we heard bellowing laughter, and then a rushing noise: the chamber was filling with water. We transformed into a microscopic tardigrade and slipped easily out of the vault, too tiny to see.

This would be *easy*. We would wear him out here, bind him, and ensure he was no threat before we pulled him back into his body.

An excruciating pain buzzsawed through our essence.

An ugly tear appeared, and like a spiritual Band-Aid ripped from sensitive flesh, we were separated back to our individual selves...

I witnessed Pam cartwheeling away from me through the white space, her body returned to its last remembered shape dressed in her Judges uniform, now prone and unconscious. I glanced down, and I had also reverted to my waking form.

Jarek responded, replicating himself into a multitude of Jareks, dressed in a mocking parody of my uniform, with exaggerated pads and guns.

I dived for Pam, grabbed her and threw up a protective shell around us—just in time to repel the barrage of ammunition firing at us from the teeming Judge Jareks surrounding us on all sides of our egg-shaped space.

—I'll crack you!— they chorused, blasting at us.

It was like driving through a storm of stinging insects, and watching the glass begin to crack from their relentless onslaught.

Pam opened her eyes suddenly, her expression stricken, and grabbed my glove.

"I have to return!"

A force snatched Pam, and me with it.

We were sucked down a scintillating vortex of splintered light and slammed into Judge Stone's room at the PSYCHE lab. I remained floating over Pam.

She was being manhandled out of the room by Judge Yoon, who was panting hard.

It was dark and the air was so thick with dust the drones could barely illuminate a path.

"We're getting out, Reed," Yoon huffed. "I cut off comms. Couldn't listen to Hardwick's screams. I mean, I'm the one who should be freaking out!" A rumble shook the room again, and her helmet glanced up at the ceiling. "Please don't fall, please don't fall." Then she looked down at the floor. "Stay in place, a few minutes more."

I quickly moved ahead of them, checking their way out. Their route was clear, despite sections of wall that had collapsed. I returned to see Yoon moving slowly and steadily through the main room.

Yoon kept up a constant narrative. "Gonna kick this chair outta the way." She knocked aside the scraps of an ancient chair with her boot. Pam slipped a notch from her grip. "Pam, come back to me, woman. Could use a bit of help here."

I shouted at Pam, at Yoon, but no sound emerged.

Behind them the ceiling in Judge Stone's room collapsed with a frightening roar and a cloud surged out of the doorway.

"Not looking back, no siree," Yoon said, her voice cracking. "Eyes forward, Yoon."

I slipped closer until I was hanging in front of Pam, her helmeted head downcast and bobbing as Yoon dragged her along.

I attempted to move into her body, but couldn't.

I remembered what it felt like to blast a... psi bolt, and let that energy shift into my hands. A sparkle dusted my fingers. I thought about Jarek, laying on the ground beside my body, and what could happen if I didn't return in time to explain. He could make anyone believe anything. The Judges programme would be in jeopardy again. My friends could be subverted, and perhaps abducted.

The energy burned up through my arms and lit up my palms like torches.

I slammed them on either side of Pam's helmet, zapped her energetic body, and hollered, *WAKE UP, PAM!*

Her helmet snapped up and Pam shot upright as if she'd been injected with five shots of adrenaline. She staggered, her arms spread out and trying to steady herself.

"What the drokk?"

Yoon stepped back, but held her hands out in case she needed to grab Pam again. "We gotta go, Pam. Demo's going to blow it in ten minutes... if the block don't collapse before that."

Pam spun a slow circle, wheezing. "Where's Phoebe?"

"Who?"

I tried to yell at her again, but no sound emerged.

"Nothing. Psi stuff. We need to bounce." She took a shaking step forward.

Yoon grabbed her elbow to support and steer her out. "That's more 'zombie walk' than 'bounce,' Reed. Pick up the pace!"

As they lurched out of the room and into the hallway, Pam kept looking around. Trying to perceive me, I knew. I kept close to her, but she didn't seem to know where I was.

She mumbled, "Phoebe, follow the tether, follow the tether. Don't let Jarek wake up."

"Can't hear you, Reed," Yoon shouted.

Above them a crack zigzagged, as if pointing the way towards the suspended crane platform that waited for them.

Pam's body jerked as if zapped. She stopped, and then bellowed, "*RUN!*"

The two Judges spurted into a jog. Yoon jumped first onto the platform and Pam barely made her leap onto the swaying metal cage. Yoon clutched at her and pulled her on.

"We're secure!" shouted Yoon, accessing her helmet controls. "Go, go!"

Their helmets looked up into the shaft of light puncturing the darkness.

The crane wince groaned and whirred into life, spooling them back out of the hole. I floated up in tandem.

Above them, half a jutting floor broke off and whooshed past them to collide with the section of the hallway from which they had just emerged.

Hardwick's voice screeched. "Yoon! You finally saw sense and left that psi behind."

With remarkable timing, the pair emerged from the hole. Hardwick stood by the crane booth and scowled.

Reed leaned on the guard rail and nodded at Hardwick. "Good to see you too, Judge Hardwick."

A force began to pull me upwards. Below, I saw Yoon and Reed's cage land on solid ground. Other Teks helped them out. The crane unclamped and levitated away from the hole. Looking like toy figures now, the Judges waved and moved back from the building.

I was far above the broken building, and the vastness of the city began to be revealed to me, but I rotated around so I could only see the blue sky and the blazing light.

I noticed a thin shining tether that snaked from me and into that light.

I focused on the line. A force pulled me with a quickening pace into the shocking radiance, and I dissolved into it.

CHAPTER EIGHTEEN

02:14

I AWOKE IN stages, as if different parts of my brain software was booting up out of order. I could raise my neck, but couldn't speak.

I sat, slumped. My legs and ass were completely numb from the hard, cold surface.

Maddox was squatting beside me, his hand on my arm. I looked at his understanding face and felt completely safe.

"She's awake," he said, a troubled note in his voice.

Jarek stood in front of me, his hands still secured behind his back, his hair tousled and his face pale and distressed.

"She went mad," he said.

My disoriented, weakened mind could still sense him pushing on Maddox's thoughts, but it was clumsy.

Maddox frowned and shook his head as if bothered by a buzzing insect. He stood and offered me a hand.

I stared at Jarek with as much loathing as I could muster.

"Wire," I mumbled as if through a mouthful of marbles. I tried to slap my hand into Maddox's glove and missed, badly.

Maddox grabbed me under my armpit and hauled me onto

my dead feet. A massive rush of pins and needles assailed me and my legs refused their job.

Maddow allowed me to lean into him. He glanced between the two of us.

"So now you hate each other?"

Jarek's next shove at Maddox's mind was harder, but even sloppier.

"Phoebe, what the hell?"

He removed his support and I dropped to my knees, grateful for the pads.

Maddox had his hand on his helmet. "Are you influencing my mind?"

"'Snot me," I protested.

Jarek went for the Oscar with his performance. "She did the same thing to me, Maddox! After accusing me of being a spy, she incapacitated me with her mind."

I clamped down on the stream of protests, and instead focused on my love and trust of Maddox. That was his way of truth telling. He told me once he could see the complexities of emotion like a woven tapestry. And when people lied, it had a certain hue.

I spoke slowly and carefully. "He is a psi too."

"A what?" Maddox asked.

I projected a wisp of a shield around Maddox just before Jarek's next attack. It shredded, but kept the creep out.

Fury glinted in his eye, but Jarek's voice remained steady, persuasive. "She's delusional. She told me in the van earlier that she thought she had a breakdown. I have a recording."

Fear choked me for a moment, but I nodded. "I said that. But Jarek was provoking it."

I raised one knee and levered up into a shaky standing position and while doing that, gathered back my scattered force. This could get ugly.

"He is a spy. He's—"

BLAM!

The shot knocked Jarek sideways. A hole appeared in his

shoulder. Blood poured out immediately. He screamed.

Judge Felix emerged from the shadows, helmet off, arm raised, gun pointed unwavering at Jarek, who was doubled over, but standing.

Felix didn't come any closer. "She's telling the truth."

Jarek raised his face and it was blotched purple with rage and effort. "*RAMUZ!*" he shrieked. A lash of power flicked out and just caught the edges of Felix's mind.

Felix dropped as if a string had been cut.

I ran, wobbly, to him. "No no, no," I gasped. I threw myself into a slide to skid to a halt by his head. I laid my hands on his forehead and dove into his mind.

It felt like I was wrapped in wet paper, but it helped I'd been in Felix's mental landscape before. With Pam's expertise, we'd been able to short-circuit the mind programming Jarek had laid in, but the self-destruct was set deeper and half-firing.

I set about preventing Felix's mind from caving in on itself, fervently hoping that Jarek was no longer a threat. I wasn't sure what to do, so moved on instinct, thinking of Pam and how she simultaneously flowed with and directed her ability. I removed the link between overloading the impulses in the mind and the command word, and examined his mind for any further tampering.

I felt sweat dripping off my face and onto Felix. A wave of nausea rose in my body. I was pushing my mind beyond tolerable limits. I could smell rose perfume.

Had someone laid their hand upon my shoulder?

I opened my eyes, my vision blurring. Felix's face was peaceful despite the bruising and the signs of exhaustion.

Maddox was standing with his gun pointed at Jarek, who was on his knees, his head bent, his shoulders heaving. He was moaning in pain.

I managed to push onto my feet and shuffle next to Maddox.

He looked at me and said, "He's a liar."

I nodded.

Jarek was babbling, crying, and laughing. "It's gone, gone,

gone, baby, all gone. Sorry Daddy. I've no thoughts left." He raised his head. His skin was ghostly, and his eyes were open wide, badly bloodshot with pupils hugely dilated. Blood streamed from his nose.

He spluttered and spat red phlegm.

He peered into the shadows behind us and an expression of beatific love spread over his features.

"Zosia."

He sighed, and faceplanted.

Maddox and I heard the whirr of a van engine approaching.

Jarek's mind was silent.

I looked up at Maddox and punched his arm lightly.

"What do you predict: thumbs up or thumbs down from Stone-Face?"

The second van, with Helen at the wheel, pulled up sharply and parked behind our vehicle. The side-door slid open and Judge Stone hopped out with his cane, and a murderous set to his mouth.

A short distance away, Felix was getting on his feet with the speed of a sloth.

Maddox regarded Stone's approach. "He *loves* missing out on the action."

The older judge hobbled over to us. Dr Murray, wearing a black trench coat, walked by his side.

Both of them regarded Jarek's prone body. It's a credit to Helen that she remained collected.

Stone growled. "Never liked him." He glanced over at Felix, who was finally upright. "You located Judge Felix. Good. And no one's sleep has been disturbed at the orphanage?"

I nodded.

He was quiet for a short period as Felix staggered over to our small circle. Dr Murray knelt and took Jarek's pulse. She stood and shook her head at all of us.

Priya pulled up neatly on her Lawranger and joined us.

"What happened to Jarek?" she exclaimed.

Everyone turned to look at me.

I opted for the *Cliff's Notes* version. "He betrayed us and broke lots of laws."

Judge Stone twisted his cane into the ground so it made a disgruntled noise. He angled his head to Helen. "Your Judges tend towards flippancy."

She shrugged. "But they get results."

The three of us grinned.

Stone regarded us impassively for a beat. "Quit clapping yourselves on the backs." He turned and pointed his cane at the van. "Wise, Felix, you're with me on the drive back to base. I want a detailed verbal report. We'll start the paperwork when we're back in the lab."

Dr Murray was fishing a phone out of her pocket. "I'll request discreet transport for the body."

Stone continued, "I want a tight, clear report for Chief Judge Fargo. We need to set a gold standard for future missions."

I looked around at my fellow Judges and my heart warmed. *Future missions*.

I saluted Stone. "Yes, sir. We're Psi-Division. We get results."

"Division?" Stone snorted. "Don't get fanciful, Wise. We don't officially exist."

I smiled. "Not yet."

Dr Murray paused her call, looking dismayed. "What's wrong with Psyke?"

None of us said anything, but Priya was snickering.

A wave of fatigue crested through me, and my body's aches and pains reasserted themselves with renewed fervour. My head felt like it was an inflatable balloon.

But as I walked to the van with my team, I never felt so drokking good.

CHAPTER NINETEEN

Psi-Division, Mega-City One
Wednesday, September 21st 2141
03:38

Judge Pam Reed dreamed.

It was not a prescient vision, but her mind organising and categorising the day's events. The normal activity of a brain as it employs its nightly self-cleaning.

It glossed over much of her weary conversation with Judge Hardwick and his threats about what he'd put in his report to the Chief Judge. Yoon, grud bless her, made a blithe comment about how it was smart she hadn't followed Hardwick's order to leave Judge Reed behind—since they both survived fine and brought back valuable intel.

She'd hugged Yoon after Hardwick stomped off to categorise their find, and invited her to visit Reed at Psi-Div anytime.

Shenker had ordered her to take the H-Wagon for her return journey, and that memory did have a nightmarish quality. Shortly after they lifted off, Demo's controlled explosion of the Hildegard of Bingen block dropped the remains of the building, issuing a massive cloud of dust and fragments. Her dreaming mind placed her back in the dirty, deserted PSYCHE lab, by that black filing cabinet of secrets. From it voices began to whisper to her of joys and horrors, of past lives changed and futures twisted, until they became a howling tornado of accusations that shook the walls and collapsed the ceiling on her.

Her debrief with Shenker was long and tedious in a mind-proofed room, with a telepath sitting in to observe the conversation and ensure Judge Reed had returned mentally intact—well, as intact as any Psi-Judge after a mission.

The Psi-Div pre-cogs had settled down upon her return, other than the usual reports about smatterings of riots and small-scale carnage.

"The drug—" Reed began.

"Oh, yes," Shenker waved it off, "we'll overlook the breach in protocol this time. But if it happens again..."

"I mean, we didn't develop it. We obtained it."

Shenker raised an eyebrow and glanced over at the observing psi. "Above your grade, Reed," was all he said.

When they finished, he added, "Alert us to any further contact with Wise."

Reed stood, weary and dusty. "Hardly probable, don't you think, sir?"

Shenker watched her and drummed his fingers on the table. "You have your orders, Reed."

She'd been excused from active duties for a week, so her usual evening routine had been different from when she prepared her mind to scan the probability currents. But pre-cogs were always on—there was no way to block her talent without medical intervention.

After processing the day's events, her mind drifted through more restful places.

She heard the wind swaying branches laden with fresh rain.

Rough bark under her fingertips.

Grass crushed under her boots.

And blurred in the distance, a friend waved cheerily.

Judge Reed smiled and crossed through the intervening space to meet her.

ACKNOWLEDGEMENTS

I GREW UP in a small town in the West of Ireland, and for a nerdy girl in the pre-Internet era that meant I haunted my local library and was forever on the hunt for material that hinted at fantasy, science fiction or horror stories. *2000 AD* was a weekly dose of thrill-power delivered directly to my newsagent's, and I loved reading it.

So, a big thank you to the early influencers such as Kelvin Gosnell, Pat Mills, John Wagner, and Alan Grant for kickstarting my favourite dystopian universe, with an important acknowledgement to artists such as Carlos Ezquerra, Mike McMahon, Ian Gibson, and Brian Bolland (among the many talented art droids employed by Tharg) for shaping the look of the world. Everything I do here is based upon these early pioneers.

In particular I must credit John Wagner and Carlos Ezquerra for their masterful Origins series (2006-2007) that established the timeline for the pre-apocalypse era. I read the collected graphic novel several times while writing this novella and it was always inspiring.

Most of all I need to utter a powerful "Florix grabundae!" to my friend and superb writer, Michael Carroll, who continually encouraged me over the years, and has been hugely helpful with fine-tuning this novella. His knowledge, and love, of the *2000 AD* universe is immense. I benefited greatly from our discussions in person and over IM, and I treasured his picky notations.

I've dedicated this novella to Mike since he is as mighty as Tharg—and his puns are splendid too!

Cheers to David Thomas Moore for his patience, support and keen editorial eye, and for the input from Kate Coe. I'm ever grateful for those who help improve my work. I love the cover for this volume, so thanks to Neil Roberts for his fine artwork. This 'background' labour may be invisible to some, but I see it and am heartily glad for it!

My husband Martin is there for the good and the hard moments. His love, kindness and humour get me through many a stressful day when I'm dazed by imagined worlds. Thank you, darling.

I hit a sticky spot while writing this novella and my dear friend, and fellow horror writer, Tracy Fahey, sat down with me one morning and we talked through the various timelines. That conversation over coffee while I scribbled in my notebook got the gears moving again. I appreciate your generosity, my Goth Queen!

ABOUT THE AUTHOR

Maura McHugh lives in Galway, Ireland and has written three collections: *Twisted Fairy Tales* and *Twisted Myths*—published in the USA—and *The Boughs Withered (When I Told Them My Dreams)* from NewCon Press in England. In 2019 her short story 'Bone Mother' was adapted into a stop-motion animated short film, and her science fiction rom-com radio play, *The Love of Small Appliances*, was broadcast in June 2019. She's written comics for Dark Horse, Atomic Diner Comics, and *2000 AD*, and her monograph about David Lynch's iconic film, *Twin Peaks: Fire Walk With Me*, was nominated for a British Fantasy Award for Best Non Fiction.

http://splinister.com
@splinister

THE PATRIOTS

JOSEPH ELLIOTT-COLEMAN

Dedicated to my beloved late father
who was my most fierce and enthusiastic supporter.
Ebenezer Kweku Coleman (Nana Tono)
(1947–2018)
Daddy, you are *terribly* missed…

Terrorism is a psychological warfare. Terrorists try to manipulate us and change our behaviour by creating fear, uncertainty, and division in society.

—Patrick J. Kennedy

The tree of liberty must be refreshed from time to time with the blood of patriots and tyrants.

—Thomas Jefferson

Nothing is an absolute reality; all is permitted.

—Vladimir Bartol, *Alamut*

PROLOGUE

"AND FINALLY," A young woman said hesitantly. "I must know... I *need* to know that this is all... well... necessary."

The woman with heavily-tattooed arms began to speak. There was no irritation in her voice, although she'd lost count of how often she'd articulated this argument. It wasn't even the first time she'd articulated it to the girl. Or the rest of the choir. But many of them needed their faith reassured. Much was being asked of them, and of herself. So, like a priest reading a sermon, she spoke.

"The horror of violence," she said, as if reciting a mantra, "has historically been the only thing to shake a population out of its apathy and into action. It is the weapon of the revolutionary. People's fear and anger, when properly motivated and directed, can transform the world. Has not history taught us as much?" She sat closer to the girl, took her small, scarred, callused hands in her own, and squeezed them gently, to reassure her, as if she were a parishioner wrestling with her doubts.

In way, she was.

"This country is wilfully sleepwalking into an endless nightmare," the older woman continued. "The sour diet of totalitarianism is being fed to us like baby food, and we're gleefully swallowing it without chewing. The monuments upon which this country were founded are threatened by the rise of the fascist Justice department and their Nazi Frankenstein Judges. Justice is being taken away from the courts and placed in the hands of leather-clad, Nazi-jackbooted murderers, sporting gold badges that celebrate their licence to kill with impunity. The Republic is *bleeding*. Lawlessness is rife, corruption is almost... *rewarded*, and like Rome of old, its citizens act like sheep, kneeling, praying to a mute God for deliverance that will never come. They're dopes, fed a diet of ultra-violence, sex, reality TV, soap opera, religious salvation and soulless entertainment. They're desensitised to living in hell. The poor sheep don't even know the difference.

"*We*"—she struck her chest—"we must act. We are the vanguard of the republic. We are the flame, the light, the fire that burns away the sickness at the heart of this country. And from its ashes, something new... and beautiful... will take its place. They will hate us. They will demonise us. But when the new American republic rises, when that shining monument to truth, justice and freedom is raised aloft on wings of hope and citizenry, on that day, they will call us patriots. But first, we have to do the dirty work. First, we become sheepdogs, in order to save the souls of the sheep."

The younger woman sighed as she saw a long night ahead, with no sunrise to follow. Only blood and death.

"We're not sheepdogs," she said. "We're sin eaters. And they'll never call us patriots. Terrorists at best, traitors at worst. And make no mistake; we're weaponising hate. And that hate will be directed towards us."

"And do you have a problem with that?" asked the tattooed woman. "Sister?"

The girl leant forward and kissed the older woman on her cheeks and ran her fingers through her hair. Looking at her dead in the eyes, she answered grimly: "No. Do you?"

CHAPTER ONE
FORTRESS

Manhattan, New York
Monday, May 20th 2047
14:57

JUDGE CHARLOTTE CLARKSON wove through the Manhattan traffic on her Lawranger—she gathered the remains of the NYPD called them 'Death Machines'—like a leaf on the wind. Through her tinted one-way visor, she scanned the eyes of drivers reflected in the wing and rear-view mirrors of vehicles she passed.

They feared her, and rightly so. She was the grim reaper, death on wheels. A lawyer, police officer and executioner in one armour-clad body. And secretly, she loved the power their fear gave her. Sometimes, she swore she could almost feel their fear.

She arrived at the 84th precinct, nicknamed 'The Frontline'—more of a fort than a police precinct, four times the size of a traditional precinct and obtrusively armoured, with peepholes, power doors, smart cameras and A.I.-controlled gun sentries. It was built to withstand a coordinated assault, and if necessary to act a staging ground for an assault on The Pit.

Queens, or 'The Pit' as it was now called, was a hellhole, a hellhole that the Judges would one day have to descend into, to wash away all the filth like the biblical Great Flood. And how Clarkson yearned for that day. A New Yorker herself, resident of Harlem, she took personal umbrage at the state of her city—not to mention her country. *This* was *America*, not the post-Brexit starving nation of Great Britain, cutting its nose off to spite its face; nor the militarist Soviet Empire reborn. America, Land of the Free and Home of the Brave. Or of the broke and decadent, now; not since the last days of pre-revolutionary France had the divide between the hideously rich and the utterly destitute been so glaringly wide.

Once the heavy blasts doors opened, she drove down the ramp to the underground parking lot, parking at the end of a long row of Lawrangers belonging to the growing army of Judges based here. She looked about and saw new vehicles: the latest armoured response vehicles, mobile hospital units, shielded riot tanks, the new shielded three-wheeled Lawranger with stun variant and flechette missile launchers, and more...

This was not a police precinct, but an army barracks.

The war was coming, and soon. Judge Clarkson felt a flash of excitement as she dismounted and walked the steps into the station house, ignoring the dirty looks from some of the waiting police. She didn't hate them, because she understood their contempt.

Judges were still outnumbered by cops by a factor of five to one, and were resented and admired in equal measure. She'd seen Judges who threw their weight around and immediately gained the contempt of their police cousins, as well as cops who were actively combative and difficult with the new order. On the other hand, she'd also worked with Judges who showed enormous patience for the outgoing police force, recognising that their sacrifices, knowledge and wisdom were things to be respected; and she'd seen and worked with cops who appreciated and admired the expediency the Judges enjoyed, cutting through the legal red tape to give law enforcement agencies a fighting chance in the war.

And it *was* a war.

A war they were *losing*.

And like any war, the best way to ensure your survival was to listen and learn from the veterans. Being a Judge meant that death was a high probability, so it would be churlish in the extreme not to attribute her survival to the street smarts she'd learned from veteran cops, some of whom had died in the line of duty.

Cops bled the same blood as Judges.

The main concourse of the station house was a loud, ugly mess of bodies, a harsh contrast to the rancid smell of bleach and disinfectant that burned the nose and made the eyes water. It was still better than the lingering smell of blood and the stench of sweat and piss from uncooperative or violent perps in the throes of drug-induced hyper-mania. *Berzerk* was the latest development of the drug TranceTrance, and it turned its users into destructively violent, mindless zombies for anything up to three hours before a painfully debilitating comedown. Cops and Judges alike dreaded dealing with Berzerkers.

Just another Monday, then.

"Judge Clarkson!" The voice cut through the circus of noise like a gunshot. Clarkson turned and saw a tall, muscular, dark-skinned woman wearing a Sector Chief uniform walk towards her through the crowd like Moses parting the Red Sea. Though Sector Chief Agnes's helmet obscured her eyes, her mouth was curled with displeasure. Clarkson found herself instinctively tugging down the bottom of her armoured jacket, to look more professional.

"Sir," Clarkson said.

"Walk with me, Judge," said Agnes.

They walked back through the crowd. Unfortunately, unlike Moses, neither of them were headed to the promised land.

JUDGE CLARKSON SAT in a dimmed room which stank of sweat mixed with body lotion, a combination that turned her stomach and made her nose itch. An aura of conspiracy hung in the room. She guessed she wasn't going to like what she was about to be told.

Also present were Sector Chief Joan Agnes, who looked permanently pissed-off; Police Captain Mabel Attwell, a thin white woman with freckles and short blonde hair who couldn't hide her contempt for either of the Judges; and a large, round Latino police sergeant named Jorge Risso who had a pock-marked face and jet-black hair. Sergeant Risso looked as lost as Clarkson felt. Lastly, next to Clarkson sat her partner, Judge Niamh Douglas, a tall woman with short ginger hair.

Douglas slumped in her chair like a schoolgirl dragged to the headmistress's office, looking around with an annoying smirk. Clarkson liked her; they'd been on the street together for two years—the longest either of them had managed to hold down a partner—and had an easy familiarity she'd never found with anyone else. Even so, that smirk still managed to annoy Clarkson.

She met Douglas's eyes, and her partner's posture said, *Relax, it's okay*, as clearly as if she'd spoken.

"Judges, are you aware of the terrorist organisation calling themselves The Patriots?" asked Agnes grimly.

"We are, Chief," Clarkson answered as she leant forward in her chair. "We're also aware of their manifesto and body count. They believe they're trying to save America from—and I quote—'A nightmare of Neo-Fascism from which the American republic might never recover.'" Captain Attwell squirmed slightly in her chair as Clarkson spoke, and Agnes sneered. Sergeant Risso just stared blankly, like a war veteran who'd seen it all.

"They're simply terrorists," said Douglas. "Only thugs with delusions of grandeur who've read some Marx and Chomsky, watched a few history videos, and decided they can terrify citizens into rising up to save the country. It didn't work in Afghanistan or Algeria or Northern Ireland, and it certainly won't work here. There'll be no Second American Revolution, no American Spring. The Golden Eagle wants security, a full belly, reality TV and money in its pocket; not blood on the street. We'll find them, we'll judge them, and *no one* will remember them ten years from now."

Agnes nodded in silent agreement. Sergeant Risso sighed.

"The confidence and scepticism of youth," said Captain Attwell, scoffing.

"Sir?" said Clarkson.

Sector Chief Agnes turned her head slowly to face the captain and glared at her. Captain Attwell met her gaze undaunted. This was still her station house and she wasn't quite out the door.

Yet.

"Are you aware of their latest 'commando action,' Judges?" Captain Attwell asked.

"'Commando... action,' sir?" Douglas asked.

The captain paused briefly and scowled, then continued. "Yes. They've resurrected the old tradition of commemorating the fallen by christening their terrorist acts, in the manner of last century's Baader-Meinhof Gang."

"Who?" Douglas asked, and this time the Sector Chief groaned.

Clarkson sighed. "Jesus. Don't you read?" she asked under her breath.

"The Baader-Meinhof Gang, or Red Army Faction, were a group of hellions, spoilt liberal brats from West Germany, who terrorised Europe in the nineteen-seventies and eighties," said Agnes. "They believed they were saving Europe from the return of fascism and they fancied themselves as firebrands of the anti-capitalist movement."

"So, *educated*, *nostalgic* thugs, then," Douglas said dismissively. Attwell and Agnes traded looks with Clarkson. *Why is your partner not getting this?*

"And there it is," said Sergeant Risso. He spoke with a hard, gravelly Latino accent, like a man who had smoked twenty cigarettes a day for years and had only recently quit. Or who had screamed at walls of silence and bureaucracy that had prevented him from doing his job and allowed the scum to escape justice. He was one of the ones who actively welcomed the Judges.

"*That* is going to get you killed, Judge. Because you've just committed the mortal sin of underestimating your enemy."

"Sir, I don't see how—" Douglas started to say before the Sergeant cut her off.

As he leant forward in his chair, his cold eyes burning, Clarkson wanted to scream at her partner to shut up and listen because she might learn something.

"Over the course of twenty years, the Red Army Faction cut a wide, bloody swath across Europe. Most of them were never caught. They merely disbanded in 'ninety-eight and promptly vanished into thin air. But not before sending an eight-page letter to Reuters announcing they had dissolved. They had the gall to tell the world that their little terror tantrum wasn't fun any more and they were all going to go home and become... whatever. They all just walked away from the blood and mayhem as if it never happened.

"And that, Judge, *that* is what happens when education meets patriotism and extremism. Their actions are entirely justifiable in their minds. You sit one of them down and they'll quote and argue and defend their actions until you want to put their head through the wall. And they'll dare you to do it. And nothing, nothing on this earth deters them from the righteousness of their cause. So please, on pain of death, *do not underestimate them*, Judges. Because the most dangerous terrorists are the ones who are prepared to kill themselves and others in the name of God and/or Country. Because in their minds, the cause will never betray them; because the dream is always, *always* worth dying for."

The room fell quiet after the sergeant spoke, the words hanging around their necks like a millstone.

Then Douglas suddenly woke up, as if only now noticing that three heads of department were in the room with them at the same time.

"You believe they're going to launch an attack in New York," said Douglas.

"Well, I'm glad *someone* has their brain switched on," said Attwell.

Sector Chief Agnes smiled. "It's still early, captain," she said. "The engine's running a bit cold." She turned to Douglas. "Yes, Judge. We have evidence that leads us to believe this station house will be subject to such an attack within the next month. Possibly sooner. Chief Judge Fargo's office has taken a direct interest in the case."

"Your mission is to find The Patriots before they make their move," said the captain. "And prevent their next attack, if possible. Use any and all means at your disposal. You have been given carte blanche to accomplish your goal."

Clarkson let the order sit with her for a moment while a web of actions formed in her mind. There had to be a catch.

"Why us?" she asked.

"Because of your track records," said Agnes. "Your relentless pursuit of justice."

"You should also consider every closed door to be open," Sergeant Risso said.

Clarkson smiled and Douglas cracked her knuckles.

"Find them and terminate them, Judges," said Attwell. "By any and all means necessary. Do you understand, Clarkson? Douglas? By *any* and *all* means necessary."

CHAPTER TWO
REBEL WITHOUT A CAUSE

When Professor Jessie Smith opened the door to her office, the Judge saw her immediately clothe herself in contempt, as if she had opened the door to two Neo-Nazis. Clarkson imagined her spitting on the floor and cursing them. Indeed, both had endured worse.

"Oh, good evening, officers. I mean... *Judges*," the professor said, making the last word sound like she was swearing.

Clarkson expected contempt from an intellectual. She almost expected her to scream, "Heil Hitler!" The Professor was a tall woman, middle-aged, face thin and lined from years of poring over books and essays. Her skin was light brown, her accent vaguely Hispanic.

This educated relic, this woman of letters, had spent her life shielded behind walls of intellectualism and middle-class protectionism. The hell of the streets was a thing she saw only on TV. They were a thought experiment, an essay or an article, but never the ugly reality of a city tearing itself apart. There would always be a buffer between her and the world.

Which is why, when the two of them stood in the professor's place of power, surrounded by bookshelves reaching to the ceiling filled with material Clarkson was sure Smith had read, the Judge knew that nothing this learned woman said or thought mattered. She was a ghost of thought and rhetoric with no foothold in reality.

"I'm so, so sorry... I forgot we were living in a police state. Shall I produce my identity papers?" Professor Smith asked.

Behind her, Clarkson heard Douglas snort.

"We're here to ask you about one of your students, professor," Clarkson asked.

"Why? Are they to get sent off to re-education? Or simply thrown in the Gulag?" the professor said, with a smile as cold as it was acidic.

What a paper tiger you are, Clarkson thought. "The student's name is Ernesto Fukuyama."

The professor's mask fell away, leaving only disgust. She folded her arms and looked sternly at the two, like a queen before a court. Clarkson was going to enjoy this.

"Ernesto is *dead*," said Professor Smith, trying and failing to hide her pain. "He died of pneumonia three years ago."

"Yes, we know," said Clarkson. "In Burkina Faso in Africa. He was doing missionary work, yes?"

"Spare me the preamble, Judge. Where is this leading?"

"While he was a student here at Columbia University, he wrote an essay; actually, more like a manifesto."

"Yes, 'The Excesses of a Police State.' He wrote it over the summer break as a personal project and I suggested he publish it. It caused quite a stink." Smith beamed proudly at her student's achievement.

"Yes, as I assume it was *meant* to," Clarkson said. "Its timing was quite... *strategic*, wasn't it? Just as the Justice Bill was being argued on the Senate floor. One could almost believe that—"

"What is your point, *Judge?*" the professor asked. Again, she said it like a curse word. Clarkson had rattled her.

Behind them both, Douglas had taken a book down from a shelf and was sitting on one of many tables reading. And listening. Clarkson saw the professor's eyes dart to her partner and back, registering horror. It was only a moment, but it was definitely something. She pressed her attack.

"What was your *opinion* of the... *boy?* Of young Master Fukuyama?" She stressed the words, making each a stick to prod the professor with.

Turn up the heat.

"He. Was. Not. A. *Boy*," said the professor through gritted teeth. She took a step towards the Judge, who raised one hand and placed the other on her gun. Douglas had stood and did the same.

"Do you really mean to shoot a tenured professor on the grounds of her university?" Smith asked. "My God! Has this country *really* slipped that far into fascism?"

Neither Clarkson nor Douglas answered. After a moment, the professor took a step back, awkwardly sat on the edge of one of her many tables and knocked several piles of books onto the floor. Clarkson and Douglas stood down and took their hands off their pistols. A long moment passed.

Got you, thought Clarkson.

"Tell us about Mr Fukuyama," said Douglas finally. "Please."

"He was brilliant," the Professor said, her voice drained of anger. "Articulate. Erudite. Curious. Passionate. *Hungry*."

Clarkson noted the emphasis, but chose not to pursue it. The Professor had said everything without saying anything. No need to pile shame upon loss.

"Ernesto... Ernesto was a man who looked at the world and saw not missed opportunities but infinite possibilities. He once said that the world was an eternally shifting Rubik's cube, where anything was possible. He believed that it wasn't enough to step into the world with rhetoric and a string of letters after your name; that you had to be prepared to plunge your hands into the dirt the same as everyone else, lead by example."

"Because 'rhetoric ain't worth nothing without empathy,'" said Clarkson, quoting the late Fukuyama's essay.

"Did he ever communicate with you or anyone else while he was in Burkina Faso, professor?"

Professor Smith nodded. "But... those emails... they're personal. A dialogue between two thinkers. You'll find nothing... I mean, there's nothing incriminating in... oh, God... oh, God damn you."

The fight in her evaporated. She sighed, walked over to a terminal, used her fingerprint scanner to unlock it and with a few voice commands brought up the emails. "You'll be wanting copies, no doubt," said the professor wearily.

"If you wouldn't mind," Clarkson said softly, pulling out a tiny, high-volume memory chip.

"Of course," Smith said, standing aside while the Judge copied the data.

"I think we're done here," said Clarkson. "Thank you for your cooperation."

The Judges left the office, wishing the professor good night. Just before they closed the door behind them, Professor Smith, more aggrieved than beaten, said, "Judges. Tell me: Do you believe that those who write in good faith are responsible for those who use violence and mayhem to achieve goals meant for the ballot box?"

The question gave the two pause. "No," said Douglas. "People need to start taking personal responsibility for their own actions. Blaming a book or an idea is a coward's way out. You had a choice. So did Mr Fukuyama. So did The Patriots."

"Then, please. If not for my sake, then for his memory: don't blame Ernesto's writing for the actions of those... those *thugs*. Please," she pleaded.

"We don't, Professor," said Clarkson. "We won't. Good night, ma'am."

She closed the door behind them. The two waited for a moment and heard her weep.

The Judges left Columbia University, driving their Lawrangers through a crowd of angry, vocal students who soon became a mob, trailing them to the gates of the University, hurling a torrent of abuse at them. *Fascists! Nazi! Jack boots! Brownshirts! Dreadnoughts! Executors! Pigs!*

But none dared lay a hand on them.

"Rebels without a cause," Clarkson said with contempt.

CHAPTER THREE
THE MESSAGE

"*My Dearest Jessie,*" the letter began.

They both listened to a reading of the late Ernesto Fukuyama's emails to Professor Smith via a transcript played into their helmets as they sped through the New York streets, cutting through traffic and down alleyways. They were the lords of the streets.

The playback continued with a strange, synthetic approximation of the young man's voice.

"*I hope this message finds you well, I would be remiss if I did not enquire after your well-being. The stuffy, sweaty lecture theatres of Columbia University are a far cry from the arid heat and sand of Burkina Faso.*

"*You questioned my motivations for travelling here, saying that the problems that plague our society are on our doorstep. That is both true and untrue. Also, and I hope you'll forgive me, but I lied as to my true reasons for visiting this country.*

"*The entire planet owes a debt to Africa, Jessie. There lies not one single corner of the globe untouched by her forced contributions. Always taken under duress, never given freely, her children never reaping the benefit. Our American Republic, caretakers of the gift given us by patriots, owes its accelerated colonisation to the sweat and toil of African's stolen identity and erased culture. Not to mention the machinery of mass expansion being oiled by the blood of our Native American brothers and sisters. These debts have neither been acknowledged nor atoned for.*

"*(Note, I did not mention forgiveness as it would be inconceivable—dare I say impossible—for America to even begin to ask for forgiveness for the pain caused during its violent birth.)*

"*In order for our nation to begin the process of healing, a genuine acceptance of our nation's crime against its people must be attempted in a manner that is at once honest and bold. A new form of patriotism must be engineered at a grass-roots level that seeks both enfranchisement and reconciliation.*

"*Though you may believe I'm being overly naive to think that such a thing might ever come to pass, I'm reminded of a quote attributed to the late Ursula K. Le Guin, which gave fuel to the slow-growing seeds germinating inside of me:*

"'*We live in capitalism. Its power seems inescapable. So did the divine right of kings. Any human power can be resisted and changed by human beings. Resistance and change often begin in art, and very often in our art, the art of words.'*

"*There is not a thing is this world that was not first thought impossible, Jessie. Nothing that did not need proving possible by those who refused to be afraid of failure. Failure is a thing to learn from; growth and maturation come only ever from failure.*

"*We have reached a crossroads, Jessie. On one road lies the death of freedom and birth of totalitarianism. On the other lies a rebirth.*

"*It's late and I've drunk too much. We'll talk again soon.*

"*Watashi no ai o yoku nemuru.*"

The two pulled into a side street on the Upper West Side, a place of clean streets, smart cameras, armed rentacops and body scanners. Ahead sat a gated community, opening out among the brownstones as if the hand of God had just reached down and flattened a whole block of buildings over a hundred years old, clawing up the earth to make a safe space for the super-wealthy.

A God with money.

Corruption. It reeked of corruption and bribery. Clarkson pushed her growing anger down into her stomach and reflexively checked her sidearm, a standard issue Thurgood AS 9mm—the Judges had started calling it the 'Lawkeeper.' She reholstered it and dismounted. Douglas stopped her outside the next suspect's home.

"What?" she asked, half impatient to continue their investigation, and half smouldering with anger.

"That letter," said Douglas.

"What about it?" Clarkson asked.

"Aren't we going to talk about it before we go in?"

"I don't see what there is to talk about."

"While we were riding, I listened to the rest of the correspondence between the Professor and Fukuyama. There's nothing of importance there save for some heavily implied—"

"Wait a sec. You read them *all?*"

"I did. I also took this," said Douglas, tilting her wrist screen forward to show a photo of the humanities graduating class. Professor Smith sat surrounded by sixteen of her students, including Ernesto Fukuyama.

"You took this from the book you were..." Clarkson stopped when she remembered the look the Professor gave when she saw Douglas leafing through the book. "How did you know where to find this?"

Douglas smiled. "I made sure she saw me looking at her library. Then I watched to what she was most anxious of me looking at. When I touched the book, I found this photo in, she almost screamed in horror. Had one of my flashes."

"You gonna submit your gut feelings as evidence?" said Clarkson, raising her eyebrows, and Douglas grinned. "You're a very naughty girl. You know that, right?"

"Any and all means necessary," Douglas said. "You heard the bosses."

"So, what did the letters tell you?"

"That Fukuyama never lost hope," said Douglas. "That he tried to convince others not to do the same."

"But they didn't listen," said Clarkson.

"No. And the tone of his letters tells me that both he and the professor were scared."

"And who are the others?"

"Well, here's the tricky thing: there were only three email addresses on the list—Fukuyama's, the professor's and someone else. The others were ghosted, blind-copied, redacted."

"Why would they...? They were already... They both tried to stop them, didn't they? Fukuyama and the Professor."

"Correct. But they were too far gone by that point. Whoever they were, they'd been radicalised to the point of no return," said Douglas. "The people in this photo," she said, pointing to her screen, "they're all out of country and all check out."

"All except one," said Clarkson, thumbing the gated community behind her.

"Correct," said Douglas.

"I have a feeling," said Clarkson grimly, "that this is where things become difficult. The people who live here aren't poor."

"Well, the beautiful thing about being Judges is that we're equal opportunity ass-kickers," Douglas said.

CHAPTER FOUR
LITTLE PEOPLE

THE WOMAN WHO opened the door looked at the two with a mix of contempt and amusement. She was black, thin and athletic, skin clinging to her skeleton like silk, and wore a garish golden necklace and sheer, white clothes that left nothing to the imagination. Her hair was platinum white and looked as if it had been sculpted out of marble.

The woman's hands were covered with rings of silver, and her short nails seemed to glow in the porch light. She silently looked Clarkson and Douglas up down, then without turning called: "*Percy! Percy!* There's someone at the door for you."

"Who is it?" a male voice responded.

"Judges," the woman replied.

Clarkson and Douglas exchanged looks. *This is going to be interesting,* Douglas seemed to say.

A tall well-groomed man with jet-black hair strode confidently towards them. His knuckles were pronounced and callused. *This one's a fighter*, thought Clarkson. She looked again at the woman and saw neither bruising nor makeup heavy applied in any area. Nor did she bear scars. *He doesn't enjoy hitting woman, then,* thought Clarkson. *One point for him. Martial arts, perhaps?*

Douglas nodded and looked significantly at the woman's

trimmed fingernails. Maybe a fighter too?

Interesting, thought Clarkson. *Good observation.*

"Good evening, Judges," the man said. "I'm Percival St. George. This my wife Judith. Welcome to our home. What seems to be the problem?"

"We're here about Ernesto Fukuyama," said Clarkson. "Specifically, his connections with anyone involved with the terror attacks made by a group calling themselves—"

"The Patriots," Judith finished. She muttered a curse in a language that was not English.

St. George sighed. "Ernesto," he said, shaking his head. "Ernesto, Ernesto, Ernesto..."

"Think you had better come in," Judith said.

"ERNESTO. HE... HE was the best of us," said St. George. "He was like a flame we were all drawn to. He saw the world only as possibilities. He could see light in utter darkness. He cared deeply about the political process, and how it was the only genuine route by which change could be affected. He believed in a revolution—"

Clarkson and Douglas looked at one another.

"—Not one of bullets and mayhem, but of the mind. Of the soul. Believed in a transhumanist metamorphosis. The elevation of our species into something greater, kinder. More thoughtful. I remember once in class, he took out a five-dollar bill and held it up in front of all of us, there must have been about forty of us there, maybe more, I can't remember. Anyway, he held it up like this, and said: 'In a capitalist society we are all slaves to this. We prostitute ourselves daily for this. But what we've never realised is that this, this is a gun held to the head of every banker, every hedge fund operator, every CEO, every lawyer, every executive, every president. If every man, woman and child in America decided to withdraw every single cent, every single dollar, sell every single share they owned and refused to turn up to work on Monday morning, the country would grind to a halt by Wednesday and America would buckle to the demands of an angry public by Friday. It is only our fear of sacrifice and hardship and our love of ease that enables the corrupt to go unpunished. 'This is a weapon. And we seldom use it.'"

"So, he was a bit of a firebrand, then?" said Douglas.

Judith laughed dryly, lounging on a chaise longue like a Roman matriarch, a glass of whiskey in hand. The contempt came off her like the smell of turned milk.

"Do you have something to add? *Citizen?*" asked Clarkson.

Judith opened her mouth to reply, no doubt to spit venom, but not before St. George intervened. "What my wife means to say is that... these were the words and dreams of children. Life almost always grinds you down and wears you out." He rubbed his smooth chin, then continued. "The... idealisms of youth are always replaced by the responsibilities of adulthood. Money is not only a weapon, but an enabler."

Judith rolled her eyes and scoffed. "And that's the problem with you people. With your generation," she said as she took a large mouthful of whiskey. She didn't see Clarkson catch Douglas's eye and nod at Judith; and even if she had, she'd have no idea what was about to happen. Nor would she be able to do anything about it.

Clarkson smirked. This part of the job she loved. "What do you mean *you people*, citizen?"

Judith roared with laughter, seemingly amused at a joke that gone unspoken. She rolled off her chaise longue like a spider descending from her web and bared her teeth like a lioness, as St. George looked on in horror. "You people spent all your lives fighting and arguing over pettiness and minutiae: censorship, gender pronouns, religiosity, sovereignty. You small, little people. You small, petty little people who separate yourselves by class, and faith, and race and everything in between and—"

"Judith, please," St. George pleaded.

"—you're utterly oblivious to the truth of matter: that you've *always* done the work of the rich for them. *Always*."

"What's that?" Douglas said.

"Divide and conquer," said Clarkson.

"Yes. Your freedoms were bought by ruthless capitalists while you squabbled. You were herded like livestock into pens barely large enough to squat and take a shit, while the rich bought houses they never inhabit; bought only for investment. You've been indoctrinated to hear the word 'theft' whenever anyone utters the word 'socialism' and your people so resent socialised healthcare that it's become easier to die in this country than live. Even the water you drink is taxed.

"Your world and your future were bought and sold before you were born. And you've been brought up to believe living on scraps is what you deserve."

St. George rubbed his large smooth chin and nodded, a grim look on his face.

"I fear my wife is right," he said.

"She is," Clarkson said. "And the worst thing is..."

"We were all warned," said Douglas. "We were told what they were doing as they were doing it. But we didn't pay attention."

"No," said Judith. "No. You were consciously and deliberately distracted. They say... that you get the world you deserve, if you don't actively participate in it. The West realised that lesson too late to make a difference."

"I won't believe we fought... that we *fight* for nothing," Clarkson said. "I won't accept that."

"Then don't," St. George said wearily. "But how can you enjoy your freedoms if you can't afford to live or eat?"

"Indeed," said Judith. "But maybe—maybe the Judges Initiative is the answer. Maybe you'll turn it all around. Maybe you're the defence mechanism for our sick immune system. Maybe."

The four sat in the living room, with that ugly realisation permeating the air like the stink of rotten meat. Then Judith stood and quietly left the room.

"So that's why The Patriots fight, huh?" said Douglas. "They realise the game's rigged and the only way to effect change is to burn the house down. Hmm."

"I... I have something to show you two," St. George said, composing himself in the ringing silence.

"What?" Douglas asked.

St. George stood, and the Judges did likewise. He answered with a mischievous smile and led the two down a corridor, touching the wall at an unmarked point which glowed, revealing a hidden fingerprint scanner. The wall became a door that opened seamlessly. The lights inside brightened automatically. Inside was what could only be called a womb of technology.

"Oh, wow," said Douglas.

"Very impressive," said Clarkson.

Suspended from the ceiling via a web of cables was a cradle. Screens around the room, floating at eye height, flashed into life. The walls of the room morphed from sky blue to rolling footage from the home smart cameras.

Before either could speak, the man sat in the cradle and plugged in a small green gadget, no larger than a pea, behind his right ear. Almost immediately both the walls and the computer screens became alive with streams of data and imagery.

"Cybernetic synchronisation," said Clarkson. "He's connected himself to the computer system."

Douglas looked stunned. "This technology... it shouldn't exist."

"Judges," St. George said, "I have something to show you."

His voice did not come from his lips, but from speakers secreted in the wall. It gave him a detached and eerie quality.

A screen blinked to life in front of them, showing the emails between the professor, Ernesto Fukuyama and the as-yet-unrevealed third party. "See here, the names of the redacted senders, their identities blanked. They used something called a 'tumbler' or a 'revolver.'"

"A tumbler?" Douglas asked.

Clarkson scanned all the screens, trying to soak in every detail.

"Like a lottery tumbler full of numbered balls," said St. George. "You send an email to a tumbler and it rolls it around until all trace of the original is smoothed away. Then it assigns it a random keychain and spits it out to its destination. This is pure hacker tech. Dark Web stuff."

"Terrorists?" Clarkson suggested.

"No," St. George replied immediately, speaking over her. "The DW is self-policing. Certain keywords are flagged and matched to real-world events, and FBI or Homeland Security are contacted anonymously and alerted to potential threats. The people who operate on the Dark Web don't want trouble. *Big sister is watching you; behave yourself*. That sort of thing."

"So, an A.I. monitors these groups?" Douglas asked.

"Yes. Though it's more a set of algorithms. Barely a dumb A.I. Its name is Patriot."

St. George looked at them both, then cursed under his breath. "I never encountered anyone, anywhere, *ever* that would..."

They said nothing as he trailed off. He started again.

"Look... I'm a tech provider and weapons supplier to agencies the world over. Every component in your Lawkeepers and Lawrangers was designed and conceived of by Thurgood Industries, a subsidiary of Ashton Thurgood plc. *My* subsidiary. I've got military and civilian contracts in the trillions. Do you really think I would jeopardise all of that by associating myself with known terrorists?" He was almost pleading.

"Knowingly? No," said Clarkson. "But unknowingly... well, can you provide us with evidence to eliminate you as a suspect?"

It wasn't a request.

St. George's eyes shifted between the two. "Certainly," he said. "But first, as a token of goodwill, may I reveal the third party on these emails?"

"If you would be so kind," said Douglas. "Oh, and who built the A.I.? The one who monitors the DW?"

"The NSA, Judge," St. George said. "Under oversight by Homeland Security."

"I see," said Douglas. The Judges traded a look.

Clarkson saw the silent alert on her wrist screen a few seconds after Douglas.

"Wait a minute," said St. George. "Compound security's been deactivated."

The live video streams failed, leaving the walls painted with static.

"And I can't reinitialise it," he said. "The security systems have been put into stand-alone mode. No external connections. I only have access to what's in the house."

"Call it in, partner," said Clarkson, reaching for her Lawkeeper. As Douglas called for backup, Clarkson tapped her wrist screen and brought out a schematic of the house and a map of the immediate area. "Can you put the house into lockdown?" she asked St. George.

His eye lids flickered briefly. "Done."

"Incoming in twenty minutes," said Douglas. "Message is: 'Hold tight. The cavalry's on the way.'"

"Erm, Judges. What are we going to do?" St. George asked.

The two looked at him as if he'd suddenly appeared in the room.

"You got a panic room?" Clarkson asked.

"Yes." The fear was obvious in his voice.

"Good. Then call your wife and get her to—"

He shook his head. "She's a veteran."

"She's a what?" the two Judges said in unison.

"Yes," said St. George. "Judith's a combat veteran of the African Wars. She'll want to fight. She'll want to defend her home. And I won't be able to convince her otherwise."

"Maybe I can," Douglas said. "Are you prepared to let me try?"

Clarkson gave her a look. *I hope you know what you're doing.*

Before St. George could answer, and as if summoned, the door opened and Judith walked in, whiskey glass in hand, half-empty. "Have you turned off the security?" she asked her husband.

"No," he mouthed, shaking his head.

Clarkson watched as the woman straightened, icy resolve forming on her face.

"Percy," she said with authority, "wait here. I'll be just a minute. Pack up your kit. Backup your data. I'll be back to fetch you."

The two Judges watched as wife kissed husband, passed the glass over to him, then vanished out of the room without even acknowledging their existence.

"I'll help her pack," Douglas said, following quickly. The door closed behind her.

The screens flashed with code as St. George's computer system silently began the process of backing itself up and shutting down. "Your partner," he said, swallowing a mouthful of whiskey. "Do you trust her?"

Clarkson glared at the man. "I'll have that data now," she said, her hand outstretched. "If you don't mind."

"Of course," he said.

DOUGLAS FOLLOWED JUDITH into a bedroom and found her gently touching more hidden controls along the walls of the room, which slid apart to reveal drawers filled with pistols, rifles, ammunition, grenades. Enough to defend a home from an army. Her wardrobe swivelled round, hiding her haute couture garments and revealing military-grade body armour. Judith quickly stripped, peeling off her clothes and jewellery, and dressed in the waiting body armour. Douglas felt a single-minded determination flow from her like a wave.

She loved it. It was intoxicating. The utter certainty of will. The focus of action. The—

"Hey! Are you planning to stare at my ass all night, or are you going to zip me up?" said Judith, tearing Douglas out of her reverie. Douglas took a step forward...

...then was hit by a red haze of danger. It screamed at her, warned her, like a memory from her ancestors, to defend herself.

And she'd been trained to respond accordingly.

She immediately drew her Lawkeeper and pointed it at Judith.

"What are you doing?" Judith asked, still half-dressed.

"Step away from the guns," said Douglas. "I'll not repeat myself." She watched as Judith seemed to recognise the precariousness of her situation, and very, very slowly raised her hands.

"I'm not the one who disabled the security," she said. "Nor do I have anything to do with what's about to happen. All I want to do is protect my husband."

"And your plan was what exactly?" Douglas asked.

"Knock you out. Gas your friend and Percy, then carry him to our panic room. Leave you two to fend for yourselves," Judith said, bluntly. "I've seen too many people die because they wanted to be heroes, or because they were told blind patriotism was worth spilling blood for. I saw their lifeless eyes, frozen at the moment of their realisation that they'd died for arguments between foolish old men." She shook her head. "Not me, and certainly not him. All I want is to live a long life with my brilliant husband. All I want is our own square mile of peace. I can't save the world and neither can he, but we can save each other. Is that too much to ask?"

The haze faded from Douglas's mind, and in its place came compassion and honesty. She should arrest her. It was the sensible thing to do. It was the *law*.

But...

She holstered her Lawkeeper.

"No," she said. "No, it's not."

St. George handed the data module over to Clarkson without hesitation.

"And the identities on the email list?" she asked.

"All there. I give you my word. Please. All I want is to make the world safer. That's why my company bankrolled development of next generation law enforcement equipment. You Judges... you're the only ones who can turn this city around. Maybe... maybe the country, too. All I want is for everyone to share the safety and security my wife and I take for granted."

"So, no qualms about the death of due process, then?"

St. George considered for a moment, then: "If due process was a viable solution and truly workable, then we wouldn't have arrived at this nightmare. The game is rigged, Judge. Rigged in favour of the rich and connected. No, sometimes if a system is broken beyond fixing, it has to be scorched clean and purged. Then, build something new on its ashes. Civilisation is a work in progress, after all. And sometimes you have to reset the clock."

"Maybe someone should have told that to The Patriots."

He sighed and emptied the last of the whiskey into his mouth. His shoulders sagged. "Nostalgia's a hell of a drug, Judge. Go ask the British."

"Apparently, one worth killing for."

"The fools," he lamented. "The misguided fools."

The computer system had completed its shutdown process. The screens blinked and evaporated. Then the cradle disassembled and lowered itself into the floor, vanishing beneath their feet.

The door opened and Judith and Douglas walked back in. Judith wore body armour and sported an assault rifle. Around her waist were several magazines of ammunition. On her hip sat a pistol similar in design to those used by the Judges.

She tossed a carry-all to the floor with a heavy metallic thud and opened it, revealing a bouquet of guns, ammo and grenades.

"Use these to defend this house," she said. "I'll use this"—she pointed to her rifle—"to protect my husband. I'll signal you over the PA when we're in the panic room. We'll work on getting the security feeds back online."

She took her husband's arm and led him out of the room. "Good luck," she said as the door closed behind her.

"What did you say to her?" Clarkson asked once she'd recovered the power of speech.

"Nothing," Douglas replied. "All she wanted to do was protect her husband."

"Fair enough," Clarkson said. "Good job. He gave me the data, by the way. I'm already uploading it to the secure network. We'll work on it afterwards."

"I admire your ambition," said Douglas.

"Why wouldn't you, partner?" said Clarkson. "My ambition is for us to live."

CHAPTER FIVE
SIEGE!

When the security network failed, it affected every house on the compound. And not surprisingly, every resident evacuated to their panic rooms and waited for the all-clear.

If it ever came.

Clarkson linked her wrist screen to the house's network, enabling her to communicate with the owners, still working feverishly to get their security back online.

"What have we got?" she asked.

"Well, at present all I've been able to do is lock down the house," St. George said over the PA. "Internal security screens are online, but external ones are down, not to mention others around the community. I can't access the external compound's network until someone physically switches back to online mode. The best I can do is get external feeds online. How long until your people arrive?"

Douglas flashed the time to her partner. "Ten minutes," said Clarkson.

Douglas pressed a button on her wrist-screen which brought the video feed from their Lawrangers online.

Nothing.

Then, in the far distance, an inhuman roar cut through the silence of the compound. Like some wild beast, mad and frenzied. Hungry for blood.

"Wait," said Clarkson. "Did you hear that?"

"What was that?" Douglas asked.

"Did you two hear that?" Clarkson asked her wrist-screen.

"Hear what?" Judith asked.

Again, the roar came, bloodthirsty and savage. This time it was joined by another, then another. Now it was clearly audible.

"Erm... Yes. We both heard that," said Judith. "Best hurry, husband, huh?"

"It's coming from the front of the house," said Douglas.

The two Judges moved swiftly back through the corridors of the house, luxurious as it was, its walls adorned with modern art, display cases holding garish sculptures. Soon, all would be so much dust and rubble.

They arrived at the landing that they had passed on their way in with its stairs leading down to the lobby, fronted with a long wall of glazed doors, covered with thick, quilted curtains.

"Charges," Clarkson said. "Chemical explosives. I saw them in the bag."

"Wired to the doors?" Douglas said.

"Go," said Clarkson.

"On it," said Douglas, leaving the balcony and running back through the house.

Another roar came, now a choir of blood-curdling inhumanity. They were close.

"Judge Clarkson," said St. George, via her wrist-screen. "I've gotten the feed to the external cameras back online. Stand by."

Her screen flashed with static and white noise as the feed started streaming. Douglas walked in behind her carrying the weapon bag and began to dig out the explosive charges.

"We got enough?" Clarkson asked.

"Oh, we do indeed," Douglas replied.

Clarkson smiled.

"Oh, shit!" the other woman cried, taking a step back from Clarkson in horror.

"What? What is it?" said Clarkson. She looked at her screen. "Oh, my good God."

Outside, in the lavish garden, stood a mixed group of men and women. They looked gaunt and pathetic, veins visible along their arms and bulging on their necks and faces.

And their eyes...

The horde stared directly at the doors and howled in unison, like a pack of rabid wolves.

"Judges," Judith asked over the PA. "What *are* they?"

"They're addicts, ma'am," said Clarkson. "Doped up on a powerful, strength-enhancing, pain-reducing drug called Berzerk."

"Berzerk?" St. George asked.

"Derived from TranceTrance. Those people will rush into the house with no regard to their safety or lives."

"That's not possible. Berzerk can't do that," said St. George. "It can't make them mob like that."

"Say what?" said Douglas.

"It's the result of a failed Ashton project. We found TranceTrance on the street, reverse-engineered it. Tried to tap into the side effects, the 'bad trip.' The idea was to suppress fear response. It might send a loner over the top, but it won't do"—he waved at the glass—"that. *This* is something else."

"How do you know this?" Clarkson said.

"Because we're been trying to get Berzerk off the streets since the moment the formula was leaked from us."

Clarkson watched the feed on her wrist-viewer as more Berzerkers emerged from the garden and howled in the night. Their eyes were blank and completely absent of consciousness. They utterly horrified her.

Douglas took a rifle from the bag, loaded it, cocked it, and handed to Clarkson. Then she took the explosives, the wire and trigger in her hands. "I'm going to lay the charges," she said. "Cover me."

"You sure you know what you're doing with that stuff?" Clarkson asked.

"Certainly I do!" Douglas answered. She hurried down the stairs.

Clarkson took her position and aimed at the door. She double-checked her rifle and selected explosive rounds, then set it to semi-automatic.

"Headshots or centre-mass," she said to herself. "Headshots or centre-mass."

"WHY ARE THEY waiting?" Judith asked over the PA.

"I've no idea," Clarkson replied. She turned to her partner. "Your husband is right. I've never seen such a large group of Berzerkers before. Much less so... seemingly organised."

"Yes. That's… utterly unusual," said Douglas. "Yeah, they're definitely not Berzerkers."

They were an army now. Forty deep and holding. Roaring in unison, their blood-curdling screams a cacophony of horror.

Douglas had taken up position at the top of the stairs while Clarkson stood on the landing, her rifle aimed directly at the doors. Should the Berzerkers rush the door, the explosives were planted in such a way that the force of the explosion would be directed outwards, becoming a wall of fire and hot debris. They had enough firepower to take care of what was left.

Clarkson checked her wrist-screen: five minutes before reinforcements arrived.

They were going to see the sunrise.

"You getting any of your 'hunches' from them, partner?" Clarkson asked, not taking her eyes from the doors.

"Yes..." Douglas said, almost unsure of herself. "But it's strange."

"Define *strange*. Please."

"It's like... like they've been seized by a force. One they've willingly given their individuality to. But they're not lessened by it. Almost as if the whole is greater than the sum of its parts." Douglas shook her head. "It doesn't make sense."

"Wait. You mean... what the hell *do* you mean?" said Clarkson.

"I think... I think they're... networked?" said Douglas.

"Networked?" Clarkson repeated. "Networked." She shook her head. "Okay. Right. So how do we take down the—"

"*I don't know, okay?*" Douglas snapped.

The two were silent for a time. Then, "I'm sorry," said Douglas.

"It's all good, partner," Clarkson replied. "We're both on edge."

"I just wish they would make their move and get it over with."

"Yeah." Clarkson grimaced.

The howling ceased, and an eerie silence gripped the house. The Berzerkers stood in tight formation, like a military unit on parade.

"This is it," Clarkson said. "Get ready to fall back. When the explosives detonate, we don't want to be in the room."

"Oh, so you don't trust me? Partner?" Douglas asked. Clarkson didn't need to look to know she was smiling.

"Explosives are like children. They don't always behave themselves."

"Hmm. Good analogy."

They watched a small group separate themselves from the whole, walk forward and form into a tight group, then divide again. Three walked forward, then squatted into a crouch like athletes on the starting block. The groups behind stepped back. And for a brief moment, the Judges both saw a tall hooded figure of stocky build. The figure's features were obscured, but...

"You see that?" Clarkson asked.

"Yes," Douglas replied.

The three grunted, then rushed forward.

"Fall back," said Douglas, and the Judges left their positions and withdrew into the corridor behind them. They watched on their wrist-screens as the attackers threw their bodies into the glass.

The glass held.

They rushed the doors again.

Again.

Once more.

The glass cracked.

The horde behind roared with encouragement. The three Berzerkers rushed the doors again.

Again.

One layer of glazing began to buckle. A few centimetres more and they'd trip the sensor and trigger the explosives.

The Berzerkers roared, their bodies bloodied and glittering with fragments of glass. They were painful to look at.

They rushed the doors once more...

Detonation.

The screens went white with noise—

THE WHOLE HOUSE shook as the shockwave reverberated through flesh, bone, concrete and steel. Douglas felt the ecstatic fulfilment the three suicides felt at the moment of death.

And the wonder that came immediately after.

She pulled her mind away from the euphoric death of individuality and slammed herself back into the present.

"Thermal sight," Clarkson ordered, and their visors polarised and dimmed immediately, transforming the world into a vivid, though limited, coloured world. They crept around the corner, rifles raised, waiting for contact. Douglas felt the sweat run down her face, her helmet turning into a sauna. Through the dust and debris she saw the landing's banister had shattered, and the foot of the stairs was covered in shards of glass and metal that glowed with heat from the explosion.

"Make ready," Clarkson said.

Douglas crouched and aimed her rifle. "Ready."

AS SOON AS the words left Douglas's mouth, the horde came rushing in.

In chilling silence, they stampeded through the shattered doors and into the Judges' onslaught of gunfire. They fell like rag dolls against the wave of explosive rounds that obliterated their heads and torsos like so much pulverised meat. They fell backwards into the attackers behind them, knocking them back onto the wave behind, who clawed their way forward only to meet doom in the same way, leaving a growing mountain of gore. There was madness in their eyes as they ran towards death.

But Clarkson was numb, focused only on her task. She watched the ammunition count falling, ready to switch magazines. It all came down to training. She'd stopped thinking and muscle memory took over. She ignored everything.

Select target. Aim. Fire.

Select target. Aim. Fire.

She changed magazines without taking her eyes off the horde who grew closer and closer, their animalistic screams running straight through her. She began aiming every shot at the centre-masses, not bothering to aim for their heads, as the ammunition blew holes large enough for her to spit through. She saw Douglas doing the same. She barely felt the weight of the rifle, much less the recoil as it discharged.

Select target. Aim. Fire.

Select target. Aim. Fire.

Their number dwindled as the successive wave fell backwards on the ones who came after them, but still they scrambled over the piles of the dead, and still the Judges fired.

Eventually, no more came.

The Judges, both high on adrenaline, scoured the battlefield for their next targets, assuming it was a feint and that a second wave was forthcoming—or worse, that there were some still alive under the pile waiting for a fatal lapse of attention. Clarkson tossed several grenades down the abattoir-mountain of flesh and into the courtyard, where they exploded, tearing through the eerie post-battle silence.

Nothing.

All that stood before them, all that was left, was a pool of torn, burning things that moments before had been living humans.

And the smell, that sweet smell... like slow-cooked meat. It made Clarkson's mouth water. She retreated to a corner and threw up.

Douglas sunk to the floor as the horror of the violent death flooded her from the newly slain.

"Partner!" Clarkson said through bile and spit. "Douglas! Are you good?"

She scooted over, lifted Douglas up and took her in the corridor behind. Douglas was panting, trying not to hyperventilate.

"Douglas. Please," Clarkson said. She took her partner's gloved hands in hers. "Tell me what to do. How can I help you?"

"Just. Hold. Me," said Douglas through her teeth. Her hands shook. Tears rolled down her face. "*Please.*"

Without hesitation, Clarkson wrapped her arms around her partner as she began to cry.

CHAPTER SIX
AFTERMATH

THEIR BACKUP ARRIVED late.

The streets of New York had become gridlocked at multiple junctions, forcing the coming Judges and their police backup to mount the pavement, swerving through terrified pedestrians as they raced to relieve their sisters in black.

At that moment, they were more like a street gang than law enforcement: loaded for bear, furious angels, hell on wheels.

And woe betide those who crossed their path.

When they finally arrived, they were met by a trail of the dead. None of them had ever seen carnage on such a scale. Bodies had been ripped apart by high explosive rounds, shapes that once resembled human beings now looked more like wet chunks of meat, gore abounded, unavoidable horror. A few of the officers even prayed.

Before the army of the law entered the house, Clarkson recommended that Judith disarm. Although it was her home, and she was well within her rights to defend it, it could be dangerous—especially as a black woman. Even in the second quarter of the 21st century, for some police officers merely being an armed African American in America was still an immediate death sentence, and the Judges would rather not have to gun down cops to defend a woman protecting her home and spouse. The path of least resistance was far preferable.

Douglas gradually recovered. "It—it was like an overdose," she explained. "Like a drug high, an orgasm. Like touching God. It was like being born. Like dying." She wiped her eyes and collected herself.

Clarkson didn't understand her partner's insights. She envied them sometimes—Douglas lived in a world beyond the usual four dimensions—but she didn't think she'd want to live with them.

They suggested it might be in the St. Georges' best interests to be taken into protective custody, lest another attempt be made on their lives. Someone was prepared to go to extreme lengths to silence them, and there was nothing to prevent them from doing so again.

They agreed and were quietly bundled away.

As Clarkson and Douglas went to leave the house, they saw for the first time the killing field that the once well-manicured front lawn had become. They stood for a moment, acknowledged the sight, then waded through the river of gore to their Lawrangers.

Sector Chief Agnes was waiting for them at the road. While police and Judges rushed to secure the area, the sector chief stood impatiently, her arms folded, waiting for answers.

"You two mind explaining this?" Agnes asked.

"Before or after we shower the blood off, sir?" Douglas answered.

The sector chief's mouth curled into a grin. They both knew what was coming next.

"Before, Judges."

Goddamn sadist, thought Clarkson as the morning sun rose overhead.

CHAPTER SEVEN
SHOOK ONES

THE POLICE AND Judges shared a dormitory at the 84th, allocated for on-duty staff; many officers didn't return home after their shifts until their days off, if at all. For the 'lifers,' being a cop or Judge was a vocation, akin to being a doctor or a priest. The streets were a war zone, and they were soldiers on tour and never off the clock.

The dormitory was known as 'Hotel Purgatory.'

The room stank of the same bleach and antiseptic that stung the nose, but it could have smelled of manure and they wouldn't have cared. Sleep was the priority.

When Clarkson first woke, she considered staying in her bunk, but as soon as she opened her eyes, her mind started to work the case, turning over what she'd seen. There were huge holes.

She sat on her bunk and rubbed her eyes, feet dangling over the edge. The previous night ran through her mind like a zoetrope, the violence unrelentingly vivid. She let it come, determined to confront it rather than hide from it. If she couldn't, she had no place wearing the uniform of a Judge.

She only threw up once.

Eventually, she recovered, showered, dressed and was ready to confront the city.

Or what was left of it.

* * *

"O PARTNER! MY partner!" said Douglas, after swallowing her porridge and wiping her face. The smell made Clarkson's mouth water and her stomach ache.

"You're not eating?" she asked.

"Huh?" Clarkson answered blankly.

Douglas stood and walked around the table to Clarkson and sat her down. "Sit here," she said. "I'll fix you up."

Clarkson could only nod, her mind elsewhere.

Slowly, she became aware that she was the centre of attention. Eyes peered at her over shoulders; a low rumble filled the room like an army of ants—

"Here. Eat," said Douglas, slamming the tray of food down in front of her. "What?" she said to Clarkson's expression. "Food. Eat. In the mouth."

Clarkson ate slowly, only now realising how hungry she was. Porridge with maple syrup, fried toast, bacon burnt to a crisp, eggs, mushrooms, orange juice...

"So," said Douglas, while Clarkson ate. "I thought you'd like to know about the developments relating to the case."

Clarkson nodded.

"Whiles we slept, a localised state of emergency has been declared, prompted by the attack on the household."

Clarkson looked up from her bowl of porridge, spoon hovering.

"Yeah. It gave Governor Bensoussan the excuse she needed to go into full 'War on Terror' mode. The weaponisation of TranceTrace terrified everyone, right up to the Executive Mansion. The President himself has demanded its total eradication. Guess where everyone in New York agreed the source of drug making was."

"The Pit," Clarkson said. "Which means that they've been given clearance to purge the place." *Finally*.

"Correct," said Douglas. "The Gods of Olympus are upstairs formulating plans of action as we speak. Next: Titanomachy."

She hesitated. "Unfortunately," she continued, "Berzerk isn't the problem."

Clarkson swallowed a mouthful of breakfast. "Go on."

"None of those perps were hooked up on the drug."

Clarkson looked up. "Excuse me?"

"They were all clean. Every single one," Douglas said. "Even the ones we wallpapered with those explosives. All clean."

"So St. George was right?"

"Seems so. Also, remember when I told you that I felt they were 'networked'?"

"Uh-huh."

"Well, look at this." Douglas moved her chair around the table and tapped on her wrist-screen, bringing up a video stream. On the screen, a top of jumble of violent images—public executions, bomb victims, police brutality, acid attacks, radiation burns, sexual violence—was set in bold red text: *WARNING! RESTRICTED NEURO SUBLIMINAL MATERIAL. DO NOT DISTRIBUTE. POLICE/JUDGE EYES ONLY.*

The barrage of violence continued until Clarkson reached her saturation point. "Yeah, I think I've had enough." She pushed the screen away. "What was I supposed to be looking for?"

Douglas clicked a button sequence into her wrist keypad. Again, the video played, but this time a dark light-sucking vortex took the place of violence. Clarkson's eyes fixed on it. Attention to everything and everyone evaporated until she realised what was happening and shook herself back to reality.

"Whoa!" she cried. "What the *fuck* was that?"

"Subliminal messaging. Brainwashing," said Douglas. "Don't worry, all the junk that would have turned you into one of those mindless saps was removed."

"Well, thanks for the heads-up," Clarkson said sarcastically.

"You're welcome!" Douglas replied cheerfully.

"So... that's what they watched? That's what they saw that turned them into... that?" Clarkson asked.

"Yeah," Douglas said softly. "Not the drug. This."

"'We know where it came from?"

"Well, here's the thing, it's been on the web for a year. And it's received millions of views."

"For *how long?*"

"Yeah. A whole year. Millions of views on multiple sites. And they've only just issued a takedown."

"So you mean..."

"Yeah."

The two Judges sat in silence for a moment.

"You mentioned that you felt they were 'networked'?"

"The video is a virus. Encoded with a subliminal trigger," said Douglas. "I think whoever did this is... like me."

"Your 'hunches'?"

"Yeah. The video primes your brain for subversion. Doesn't give the attacker a lot of fine control, but allows them to direct a whole group of people at once, as long as all they want is violence."

"That's the one we saw? The one wearing the hood?"

"Maybe. Truth be told, we don't know who or what that was. We *do* know we didn't find their body."

Clarkson nodded and continued to eat her breakfast. "So, we're not invited to the party in The Pit. We've got a terrorist to find. One that might also be some sort of mind reader."

Douglas nodded.

Clarkson cut her bacon, eggs and mushrooms and stabbed them with her fork.

"So," she said, chewing. "You checked out the data?"

"Of *course*," Douglas said, affecting a wounded look. "We found the redacted names. Very interesting development on that front."

"Oh?"

"Yes. Everyone on that mailing list save for three people are now dead."

Clarkson fell silent. She continued to eat, and poured herself a glass of orange juice. "I thought they all checked out."

"Oh, they did," Douglas said. "Three months ago, when The Patriots first started their reign of terror. They checked again last night. They're all gone, and no witnesses. Three people left on that list now: Professor Smith—who's been taken into protective custody, much to her chagrin—St. George, and one other name."

"Whom?"

"One Hector Volução. Last time they checked, in Staten Island North and still breathing. Now it appears that he's vanished. But he's not who we have to speak to first."

"Who, then?"

"St. George. Seems our Percy found something he wants to show us. But he's adamant that he can only tell us face to face."

"Okay." Clarkson drank a mouthful of orange juice and continued eating. "Finish your breakfast and we'll go pay him a visit. See what's what."

THE JUDGES EXCHANGED their Lawrangers for a discreet patrol car. Driving to a safe house on two death machines was unwise. The vehicle was a black SUV with tinted windows and utterly undistinctive.

"So let me see if I understand," said Clarkson as they took possession of the vehicle. "Your grandpa, until his dying day, *refused* to accept that Jesus and his apostles were all Jews?"

Douglas shrugged. "What can I say? He was a disgusting anti-Semite and a knucklehead."

"Well, okay, yeah. Anti-Semitism is its own whole realm of stupid. You almost need a qualification to be that dumb. But still don't understand. I mean, what did he think Apostles were celebrating at The Last Supper? Anyone who's read anything knows it was Pesach, and they were all Jews celebrating Passover. How can a Christian of all people not *know* that?"

"Okay. Brace yourself for some grade-A bullshit: his argument was that Jesus' baptism was the fulfilment of biblical prophecy, and at the instant of that revelation of His divinity

He became the first Christian. And he would not be swayed. Even had learned Priests—Jesuits, for Christ's sake—who tried to reason him out of his stupidity. The mean old shit wouldn't budge an inch."

"Jesus..."

"Yeah. My parents kept us away from him as much as possible, and my grandma left him after she had my mother. She said she'd had enough of his bullshit to last a lifetime. The things that would come out of his mouth. Christ! *Unbelievable* things. They don't bear repeating!"

"I'll bet."

Clarkson pressed a button on the dashboard and the car sprang to life with a near silent hum. The map function immediately plotted a route to their destination.

"Huh. Okay," Clarkson said. "Wanna take turns driving?"

"Sure."

"Okay." Clarkson revved the car and was about to lower the handbrake when the car began vibrating.

"What was *that?*" Douglas asked. Almost as soon as the words left her mouth, her mind was engulfed by a red haze. Her gift screamed at her: *Retreat! Withdraw! Hide! Defend yourself!* Her eyes watered and the bridge of her nose ached from the suddenness of it. "Christ!" she growled through the pain.

Clarkson's jaw was clenched shut, teeth chattering, her hands locked firmly around the steering wheel and door handle anchoring in place.

The vibrating ceased as suddenly as it had begun and every vehicle alarm in that carpool screamed at their violation. Clarkson threw open the door and threw up on concrete.

"*Warning! Warning!*" came the synthesised voice from the SUV dashboard. "*Earthquake in progress! Drivers are requested to immediately halt driving and seek shelter! Warning! Warning!*"

"That wasn't a *fucking* earthquake," Clarkson spat, the taste of vomit fresh in her mouth. "*That* was a car-bomb."

CHAPTER EIGHT
ASSAULT ON PRECINCT 84

The Judges arrived back at the station concourse and were met with a scene of unchained chaos. Newly arrested perps, handcuffed and immobile, looked on with horror as if the ceiling would collapse on their heads. Lawyers, public workers, clerks and others huddled together in groups looking this way and that for the direction the terror might come. Police and Judges ran this way and that, screaming contradictory orders at one another as both groups tried to take charge of the situation.

BOOM! BOOM! BOOM! BOOM!

More concussions. Closer now. The bars covering the windows rattled, almost moaning.

BOOM! BOOM! BOOM! BOOM!

Closer still. The windows cracked. People began to pray.

Then came the gunfire. The building shook under heavy artillery fire.

"*Officers! Judges! Listen to my voice!*" a voice cried over the hell. All heads turned to look. Station Captain Attwell was stood atop the reporting desk, a hastily worn flak jacket on her chest, over which was strung a bandolier of shotgun shells for the assault shotgun she held. In front of her stood Section Chief Agnes and Sergeant Risso. Both were armed.

"Okay, boys and girls, listen up! We are under attack. The terrorist group known as The Patriots has coordinated a full scale assault against this station house. Not only that, but they have also launched simultaneous attacks at every single station house in New York City. We are under siege. Do you understand what I am telling you? WE ARE AT WAR.

"The sentry guns are taking care of what's outside. But it's what may already be inside *that I'm worried about.*

"At this moment I don't care whether you're a cop or a Judge, whether you want us here or not. What I care about is the defence of this station house and every living soul inside of its walls.

"WE'RE ALL LAW ENFORCEMENT. *We've all taken an oath to protect the public and uphold the law. If this house falls, if* any *house falls, it'll be open season for every cop and Judge from coast to coast and we might as well all just bend over, spread our cheeks and prepare to get fucked, because that's* exactly *what will happen. Now I don't know about you, I don't like getting fucked unless there's at least a four-course meal and several bottles of champagne as part of the deal!"*

The hall erupted with laughter. Chief Agnes shook her head and giggled. Sergeant Risso sighed but couldn't hide his smile.

"*PEOPLE! This is some* really serious shit! *There are assholes outside these walls who want to kill us; and there may be assholes* inside *these walls who want to do the same. That's the bottom line. Now I find that deeply offensive, 'cause I plan to see retirement. I've got two kids at home and a wife who gives me dirty looks whenever I step through the door, and I sure as hell don't plan to make her a widow and a single parent in one night. That thought makes me very, very angry.*

"So, here's the deal: ain't none of you dying on my watch. Ain't none of you catching a bullet on my watch. We hold this station house and make those sons-of-bitches pay dearly for every—single—centimetre. Escort the civilians to a secure area and the perps to the cells. Everyone else: ARM YOURSELVES! WE'VE GOT A STATION HOUSE TO DEFEND!"

"*You heard the captain!*" Section Chief Agnes cried. "*Haul ass!*"

"And people!" Sergeant Risso cried. All turned to listen. "Watch each other's backs. Be safe out there."

Immediately, Judge and cop alike sprang into action. Uniforms didn't matter, they were defending their castle, and their queen had commanded them to war.

"You two," said the captain, pointing directly at Clarkson and Douglas. "Come with us. *Now.*"

CLARKSON STILL HAD the sour taste of vomit in her mouth, made bitter by adrenaline dryness. *Relax,* she thought as she closed and opened her hands.

"Yeah. Relax," echoed Douglas. "I'm going to let you know something: anxiety is palpable. It's like an infection that compounds itself and only ever leads to disaster. Relax..."

Captain Attwell's office shook with every round the A.I. sentries fired and all five of them—the captain, Sector Chief Agnes and Sergeant Risso, as well as Clarkson and Douglas—found themselves having to shout over the roar of gunfire.

The captain sat behind her desk and rested her shotgun down, then opened a small fridge to her right. She threw bottles of water to each person in the room, who caught them and drank as if they'd all just remembered they were thirsty.

"Want more?" she asked. They all nodded.

"Okay, you two, tell me what I need to know," she said. "Because this looks eerily similar to what happened at that compound last night. So talk to me, Judges. Tell me how I save lives."

"Whoever's orchestrating these attacks is using some sort of trigger to turn innocent people into reckless killers," Clarkson said.

"People who watched that video?" Sergeant Risso asked.

"Yes," said Douglas. "Which makes anybody who's watched the video a potential attacker."

"Including Judges and cops," Clarkson added.

"Any idea what trigger?" said Agnes. "A codeword? A flashing light?"

"We have a suspicion, sir," said Douglas.

"When we engaged the mob at the St. George residence, we briefly caught sight of someone," said Clarkson. She didn't look at Douglas; her partner didn't like talking about this stuff in front of brass. "We only saw them for a moment before they withdrew, but we suspect that they might be triggering them somehow. There were... there were parallels with the material in our Academy briefings on possible psychic phenomena, sir."

"*Psychics?*" asked the captain, disbelieving. "We're dealing with psychics? Is that what you're telling us, Judge?"

Clarkson nodded.

"Psychics... they *really* exist?" said Risso, leaning back in his chair with his assault rifle on his lap. "I mean... you hear rumours on the streets, but it's bullshit, right? Fakery and scam artists."

"Not all of it," said Agnes. She sighed. "Attwell, Risso, this is need-to-know. Doesn't leave this office. We don't know how it works or where they come from, but what we *do* know is they've been around for a while. How long, we don't know. But they're out there. And we've been instructing cadets on patterns of behaviour. Good work, Judges."

"All right. They're out there. How does that help us?" Captain Attwell asked, drawing a line under that revelation. "Are they some sort of controlling influence or mechanism or something? If we identify who they are, will eliminating them release these people from their thrall?"

"We can't say for certain, sir, but we have to try," said Douglas. "The alternate don't even bear thinking about."

"Well, I'd rather *take* a chance than have none," said the captain. "Let's get to work."

* * *

An eerie silence had seized the halls of the station house. Though the thick main blast doors held fast, some of the other entrances and exits hadn't been so lucky. Barricades were constructed and reinforced while cops and Judges patrolled the walls of Precinct 84, ready and alert for any violation of the territory.

In the basement of the station house, on the ramp down to the underground parking garage, an armoured police bus sat. Its occupants' weapons were trained eagerly in the direction of the blast doors and every thud and explosion made their fingers flinch from trigger guard to trigger.

Everyone waited for the inevitable.

CHAPTER NINE
THE WARMEST PLACE TO HIDE

Being a law enforcement officer demands a level of concentration and determination that most people are incapable of, not to mention an eye for detail and almost manic persistence. Thus, a small army of Judges and cops found themselves trawling frame-by-frame through CCTV footage, hunting for their hooded suspect.

"Hey partner, can I talk to you for a second?" Douglas asked.

Clarkson almost did a double take at the fear in her partner's eyes. She stopped her examination of the footage immediately.

"Not here," whispered Douglas. "Somewhere quiet."

She stood and they left.

The shower rooms were silent and deserted, though both checked first. Judge Rule One: Assume nothing. Assumptions led to a bullet in the head.

The gunfire and concussions droned up above like the memory of a half-forgotten nightmare. Or like the Western Front, that century-old meat grinder. Violence hidden from sight, but not from mind.

"What's wrong, Niamh?" asked Clarkson.

Her partner ran her hand through her hair and flicked off the sweat. Clarkson could almost see her head radiating heat as she sat on a bench and caught her breath.

"Hey," Clarkson said with concern. "Remember your training: breathe. Okay? Breathe."

Douglas nodded and controlled her breathing. After a few moments, she was fine.

"You good, partner?" asked Clarkson.

"Yeah," said Douglas. "I am now. Look: you know when we were in the captain's office and you were talking about—"

"*We*. We were talking about it."

"Well, that's it, though, isn't it? When you were all talking about psychics and the like... I... I was... was... Christ in heaven."

"*What?*"

"It scared me, man. It was as if I was waiting for someone to point at me and say, 'There! There's one of them. She's the one! Get her!' Shit man, I mean... I mean, I haven't been that scared since my mom told me what I was. I felt like one of the Salem girls. Ready to be led to the stake. Shit, man."

Clarkson let her words sit with her; that awful reality that her partner also had one foot in the psychic closet. It would not be a stretch to imagine her partner becoming a suspect. Fear makes people irrational and stupid.

She removed her pistol and racked the slide, a single bullet flying out of the barrel, which she caught. She handed the round over to her partner, placing it in her hands and closing her own hands around them.

"Niamh. Look at me," said Clarkson.

She looked up.

"This bullet is my solemn promise that if *anyone* tries to lay a hand on you, they'll catch one of these between the fucking eyes. Understand? *Anyone.*" She squeezed her partner's hands, the bullet pressing into her palm. "You're a Judge. Ain't no one going to victimise you. Not whiles I'm around, and not while there's rounds left in this pistol."

Douglas smiled and nodded. She breathed out, seeming to inflate as she did. "There's something else," she said.

"What?"

"The psychic. The one who's triggering the mobs. They're in this building."

An ice-cold terror stabbed Clarkson in the soul and her whole body went numb.

"I can feel them," Douglas added. "I can feel them."

Clarkson hit her comm and selected the override for the station house PA system. "People, this is Judge Clarkson. This is an emergency. We have reason to believe that one or more of the perps responsible for the current assault is in this building. They could be a civilian, a perp in lockup. Anyone. Be observant. Look for anyone behaving strangely. If you believe you've identified the suspect, do not engage. I repeat, *do not engage*. Any officer or Judge could have unknowingly been subjected to the neuro-subliminal message and be susceptible to triggering. Be vigilant. Clarkson out."

She hit the comm again and turned back to Douglas. "Well, there it is," she said. "Now we hunt."

"So... I guess now I'm your psychic bloodhound, huh?" Douglas said.

"No. Don't take any unnecessary risks. We locate them and we deal with them. No heroics."

Floor by floor, room by room, police and Judges searched the complex. But like any predator, they were cautious. The holding cells were the obvious first choice, but all they met when they arrived was abuse, threats and bravado. The arrestees were frightened—if the station were overrun, there'd be no escape—but none of them seemed like a fit. It would have been too easy.

Because the next place they would look would be... problematic.

"So we got a list of civilians in the building?" Sergeant Risso asked.

"Uh-huh. We're working through them now," the captain replied.

Sector Chief Agnes scratched her nose and found her hand resting on her pistol, anticipating the call to action. Attwell's office seemed small, as if the walls had drawn in tighter since they were last here.

"Wait a minute... you hear that?" she asked.

"Hear what... oh," said Risso. "Oh, no."

Where previously the A.I. gun turrets had roared with fury, now they were deathly silent.

"Captain, finish checking the list," said Risso.

"Quickly," Agnes added.

Douglas's head exploded with red light, the world becoming a haze of terror and fear. She fell to her knees and tossed her helmet to the floor, clutching her head as if it were swelling. *Danger! Danger!*

"Fuck!" she growled. Clarkson crouched down next to her. "They're here. They're close. Shit, man."

"Point me in a direction," said Clarkson, her hand falling to her pistol. She helped Douglas to her feet and passed over her helmet. Every step was pain. And with every step, her power screamed at her with more intensity.

Danger! Danger! Danger! Danger!

"Hurry..."

"All right. That team downstairs ran an algorithm and synced with all video footage inside and out," said Attwell. "Twenty-four hours of the stuff, checked against every registered entry. We've narrowed it down to one of two people."

"Or both," Agnes added.

"Don't let the devil hear you say that, Judge," said Risso. "It'll give her ideas."

They watched the monitor as the captain pressed play. No one breathed.

The video played in silence.

* * *

THEY MOVED AT a crawl. Clarkson held her partner and felt her shudder with every step taken as they walked towards the holding area. She bit her lip as if she could feel Douglas's pain. Tears were running down from underneath her helmet and onto her cheeks as they walked.

"Stop..." whispered Douglas. "Please, stop."

Clarkson let her down and she slumped to the floor, her back to the wall.

"Can't... can't get any closer," she managed. "Might feel me... coming."

"Can you tell me who they are?" Clarkson asked as she drew her Lawkeeper and set it to the second magazine, loaded with rubber bullets.

Douglas answered with a weak smile.

"WAIT... THAT'S NOT... that's not possible," said Risso.

"Data doesn't lie, sergeant," said Attwell.

"But he's... That's Councillor Monage. He's served this city for over thirty years! He's the trigger man?"

"Yeah." Attwell stood and slung her shotgun over her shoulder. Risso and Agnes followed her through the door.

"YOU'RE CERTAIN?" CLARKSON asked.

Douglas nodded. "Go get 'em, tiger."

Clarkson smiled. "Be here when I get back."

"You bet."

CHAPTER TEN
THE HOLLOW MEN AND THE HOLLOW WOMEN

CLARKSON FLEW THROUGH corridors and down stairwells, pistol clutched tightly in hand. She daren't use the lift and give an opportunity for an ambush.

Four flights of stairs. Every corner checked, no chances taken. Death waiting patiently for her to make a mistake.

Second floor.

First floor.

Basement.

Basement one.

She stopped at the top of the stairs and waited. A small window offered a glimpse of dirty brownish light, and her mind had no problem conjuring the horrors awaiting her.

A door opened several floors above her and an army of footsteps raced noisily downstairs. She flashed back to the attack on the St. Georges' house. That mindless horde racing towards a wall of bullets. She looked up the stairwell and raised her sidearm. "Who goes there?" she shouted.

"Stand down, Judge," Sector Chief Agnes shouted back. "We're your backup."

Clarkson saw Captain Attwell at the head of a mob that included Risso, the sector chief and twenty to thirty other cops and Judges. She lowered her weapon.

"We know who it is," said the captain once they were face to face.

Good. Trying to explain how Clarkson got there would have been awkward. "I left my partner upstairs," she said. "She had some sort of episode. It's possible that psychic was trying to activate her and she was fighting it."

"We found her. Unconscious," said the sector chief. "But how can that be the case, if she only watched a sanitised version of that video? So did I. Why did they choose her?"

"Unknown, sir," Clarkson replied blankly.

"It's not important now," Captain Attwell said. "We can ask questions later. All that matters is what's behind that door."

"Agreed," said Clarkson. She turned towards the door and raised her pistol and was about to walk down the steps when she felt a hand on her shoulder.

"I don't think so, Judge," said Attwell, who walked in front of her and down the steps, her shotgun at the ready. "My station, my responsibility. Now, cover me."

Clarkson did as she was told, falling in close step behind the captain.

The army of law dogs followed close behind them.

With their backs to the wall, Clarkson watched as Attwell inched forward, then used the barrel of her gun to slowly open the door...

The corridor was dimly lit; a wet heat rushed past them and up the stairwell. Through the crack, she saw lights flicker, and shattered glass on the floor. Placing her foot in the door, Attwell crouched down and forced the door slowly ajar.

Clarkson stood behind her, covering, her visor switched to infrared, her pistol pointed into the crack. Nothing. With a single gesture, the captain motioned everyone to follow her, and the army filed down the stairs. One of them, a cop in full body armour, rushed down the stairs and stood behind the door.

"Ready?" the captain whispered. All nodded.

"Ready," said Clarkson, waiting for even a hint of movement from the other side of the door. Her heartbeat pounded in her head and she tried not to blink. *Breathe,* she told herself. *Breathe.*

"Go," Attwell said; the cop behind the door grabbed the handle and yanked it back while the captain rushed through the open door and took up a defence position in an alcove opposite. Clarkson followed and turned right, crouched and pointed her pistol in the direction of the darkness. Nothing moved. Her visor showed no heat signatures. Behind her others filed in.

"Judge." It was the voice of Sector Chief Agnes. "Shadow the captain, Judge."

"Yes, sir."

She turned, rushed forward, and with pistol in hand took up position behind Captain Attwell. By now the corridor was full of bodies. Clarkson looked to her left and saw Sergeant Risso tucked into another alcove, three Judges behind him.

"Can you *see* anything through that visor?" the captain asked.

"Yes, sir," Clarkson said, "Our visors have an infrared function that allows us to see body heat, among other things. But nothing's ahead of us."

"The holding area's up ahead and around the corner."

"I should have brought a rifle."

"Ain't about the gun, Judge," Attwell said. "It's about the woman behind the gun. I've seen cops use pistols like scalpels, and I've seen 'em use rifles like water hoses. They're only tools. Training is everything; the rest is bullshit. Lead on."

"Yes, sir."

Clarkson walked into the murky darkness.

THE FIRST THING that assaulted them was the unmistakable smell of vacated bowels. The second thing was a chorus of hyperventilating. Both sound and stench came from the pitch darkness at the end of a long corridor that swallowed hope and shat out fear.

"Where's the junction box?" somebody whispered.

"Opposite the mouth of the next turning," someone replied.

"Quiet!" the sector chief said.

In her infrared world, Clarkson saw the junction box up ahead, doors open, fuses littering the floor. *So that explains that,* she thought. Whatever waited for them around the turning of that corner wouldn't be good. She turned back and crouched in front of the group.

"Okay. The fuse box has been... attacked. If we attempt to fix it, we're walking into a trap," she said. "The only way I see it is for us Judges to go forward and deal with whatever's there. Anything that gets past us will be up to you cops to deal with. What do you say, sir?"

"Do it," said Captain Attwell without hesitation. "You Judges watch yourself. Understand?"

"Understood," Agnes said.

The Judges present weaved out of from the police officers, receiving pats on the back, fist bumps and nods of approval as they formed two groups around the sector chief and Clarkson.

"So how's it going to be, sir?" asked Clarkson.

"There's going to be civilians and police around the corner," said Agnes. "Collateral damage will not be acceptable. Incapacitate where possible. Switch to non-lethal rounds."

A quick tap on their pistols and the whine of sliding magazines.

"Attach suppressors."

A soft clatter as they complied.

"Infrared."

But Clarkson's thoughts weren't in that corridor; she was worrying about Douglas. Then her training kicked in and she pushed it out of her mind. *Kill everything that isn't the here and now. Nothing else matters in a crisis. Anything else is death.*

"Clarkson, on me," said Agnes.

"Sir."

"The rest of you, two by two. Check your corners. Assume everything's going to kill you. If you manage to get yourself killed, I'll *personally* write you up. Now let's move."

The Judges vanished into the darkness and were swallowed whole by it.

THE HOLDING AREA was actually a disused armoury. During the nineteen-sixties, the station was used as the main armoury for every station house within a ten-kilometre radius. Its basement was deep and reinforced, and from the 'seventies through to the late 'nineties it also acted as the main weapons testing range.

That all changed after 9/11. In the months and years afterwards, billions of dollars were spent developing and modernising the NYC police force apparatus to prepare them for the realities of a war on terror. In many ways, the Judges were the end result of that process.

Bullet holes and scorch marks peppered the walls, left uncovered like badges of honour. Clarkson could still smell the gunpowder and cleaning oils.

Rather, you *would* have been able to, if not for the rancid smell that crept under the doors like a fog. The smell made the Judges gag.

"Knockout gas, sir?" Clarkson suggested. She watched as her superior silently weighed up her options.

"Do it," Agnes said.

The crew immediately snapped gas filters over the mouths while Clarkson readied the gas charges. "Explosives are like children. They rarely behave themselves," she said.

"What's that, Judge?" the sector chief asked.

"Nothing. Just something my partner said last night, sir."

"Huh. Well, she's right. Make ready."

Clarkson popped the caps off the grenades. Another Judge crept forward, crouched behind one of the doors, and raised her hand to the door handle. The sector chief waved the others back to ready themselves for whatever came pouring out of the room.

"Do it," she said.

The Judge holding the handle slowly opened the door, just enough to allow Clarkson to throw her two grenades inside. Clarkson watched as they vanished in the darkness of the room and—

RRRAAAGHHH!

A wall of enraged, mindless bodies rushed towards them from the end of the corridor. In the Stygian gloom of infrared, they looked like a wave of shrieking green and yellow demons, mad with fury and hungry for blood. It was happening again, Clarkson thought. Exactly the same as the night before.

Rage seized her. She crouched down and drew her pistol as gunfire buzzed around her. She didn't need to look to know that Sector Chief Agnes was shooting along with them. Like before, the mindless bodies fell and were trampled underfoot by the attackers pressing from behind them.

After a few short minutes of violence, it was over. A small mountain of bodies rose in the corridor before them, some of them still moaning and twitching. Clarkson stood first.

"Clarkson. With me," Agnes said, motioning to the doors. Clarkson fell in close step behind her. The sector chief's anger was palpable.

They tore open the doors, a wall of raised weapons behind them, and saw...

Sat among sea of unconscious, soiled and degraded civilians and police officers...

One immaculately dressed lawyer. Councillor Monage. Legend. Firebrand. Warrior of social justice and reform.

Traitor and terrorist.

He lay there, slumped on his side. A briefcase clutched firmly in his hands.

"That man has served this city as councillor for over thirty years," the sector chief said. "Thirty years. And in all that time, for *thirty goddamn years*, he was *what? A sleeper agent?*"

Clarkson didn't reply. Rather, she calmly walked over to the lawyer and kicked him firmly between the legs.

"*Clarkson!*" Agnes roared.

"Just making sure the perp wasn't faking, sir," Clarkson replied as she handcuffed him.

CHAPTER ELEVEN
AFTER THE SMOKE HAS CLEARED

It took another three days for New York City to completely resolve its Berzerker problem. And although it was now common knowledge that the victims were not in fact Berzerk users, the name stuck.

When the doors to the station were finally opened, the street outside more closely resembled the Crusader siege of Jerusalem than 21st-century New York. Wave after wave of the attackers had rushed its walls and been cut down by sentry fire, leaving a macabre sea of wet, putrid death.

In the heat of summer, the smell of fresh, succulent human meat was too attractive for vermin, strays and birds to ignore, who happily gorged themselves.

Not all police precincts were as fortunate as the 84th. Some had been completely overrun, the living torn limb from limb or worse. Some had been spared the slaughter only to be razed to the ground, their doors locked and the victims cooked like Sunday roasts inside.

When the guns fell silent, over nine thousand people were dead. It was the greatest loss of life in New York history since 9/11.

And the city was angry, and scared.

The drug was a convenient scapegoat for the catastrophe.

The public screamed for action. The Governor was mobilised into action. This time he was met with no opposition.

War had been declared.

THE DAY AFTER the guns fell silent, Judge Douglas woke up and found her partner asleep in a chair next to her bed in the hospital she'd been transferred to. A drip was connected to her arm and a TV played the news on a constant loop. Within an hour, she'd learnt everything she'd missed.

She felt... mushy. Groggy. Completely defenceless and vulnerable. And that pissed her off. She tried to speak, but her mouth felt like cotton. When she let loose a string of curses, what she heard sounded like gibberish: "Fuh. Shih. Fuh. Cruh."

She lay back in bed and stopped fighting the drugs. Sleep came like a tidal wave and she welcomed it.

When she woke again, it was two days later. The curtains were drawn around her bed and the chair next to her was empty. She still felt groggy, but now the sounds that came out of her mouth were less like the grunts of a beast and more human-like. Her bladder was full—at some point, her catheter must have been removed. Getting out of bed would be a struggle; walking, a mission.

When she arrived back at her bed, half dragging, half leaning on her drip stand, she found Sector Chief Agnes, Captain Attwell and Clarkson waiting for her.

"Sirs," she said. "Partner."

For moment, she thought she saw suspicion in their eyes. Probably just projecting.

"How you feeling, Judge?" asked the sector chief.

"Like someone ran me over with a steamroller, then used helium to inflate me, sir," she replied. The two senior officers laughed. But not Clarkson. On her face she saw only... guilt.

I told you to leave me, she thought. *I* told *you to. I'm alive and it's because of you.*

Clarkson must have heard; Douglas felt the relief in her. She smiled as if the sun shone from her face.

"So. You'll need to be briefed," said Agnes.

Douglas shook her head and pointed towards the TV screen.

"Huh," the sector chief said.

"How are you keeping, Judge?" asked Captain Attwell.

"I'm alive," Douglas said slowly. She caught Clarkson wiping a tear from her eye. "I want to finish the case, sirs. We *both* want to... find whoever's responsible."

"Oh, you'll get your chance, Douglas," said the sector chief. "You can take that to the bank." There was an edge of menace to her words, and Douglas didn't know whether she liked it or not.

"Whatever happened..." Her mouth was dry. She reached over to the bedside cabinet for a cup of water, only for Captain Attwell to pour her a glass, which she drank hungrily, holding it out to be refilled. After her third glass, she tried speaking again.

"Sorry," she said. "Mouth was dry. Whatever happened to the... whoever was doing this? Can we interrogate him?"

The captain and sector chief shared a look, and Douglas glanced over at Clarkson, who shook her head.

"He's been transferred to another department," Agnes said. "He'll be interrogated by suitable officers. This is a matter of delicacy."

"*Delicacy?*" Douglas said.

"Yes," Attwell said, in a way that said, *This conversation is over.*

Again, Douglas had that sense of dread. *If they knew about me...*

"His briefcase contained something that will be of interest to your case," said the captain. "Something very peculiar."

"Peculiar, sir?" Douglas asked after another glass of water.

"Yes. His briefcase was filled with sheets of paper, on which one word was written over and over again."

"What word, sir?"

"Midwich," Clarkson replied.

CHAPTER TWELVE
UP NORTH TRIP

Clarkson collected her partner from hospital in a discreet patrol car to avoid attracting attention. In the aftermath of the sieges, some TV pundits had laid the blame for the death toll firmly at the Judges' door. In the absence of believable facts, believable lies were readily accepted.

The car slowly weaved through the streets. Once in a while, they would encounter the aftermath of some Berzerker street battle. Scorched earth, burnt-out cars, bullet holes... the city had been through hell. The streets were empty, though faces peered from behind curtains, their eyes dimmed and jaded as if the horror they'd seen was replaying in their minds. Terror unending. Waiting for the next bout of hell. The Judges silently wrestled with the horrifying idea that the worst was yet to come.

But something else was bothering Clarkson. And eventually her curiosity got the better of her.

"So tell me..." she asked, treading carefully. "When did you first *know?* You know... about your hunches?"

Douglas smiled. "Well, that's a long and wide story, partner."

"Long and wide, huh?" said Clarkson.

"Uh-huh. You wanna hear it?"

"Wouldn't have asked if I didn't," said Clarkson. "And we've got time to kill."

"Well, for starters, my mom told me."

"When your *mom* told you. So, your mom, she's also a... what?"

"Similar but different. Not people, but places. She worked for the FBI."

"Right. So how does that work? If you don't mind me asking."

"Well, in my mother's case, she could enter a crime scene and feel—*see*—the scene. She talks about trauma being like a stain on a place. It leaves echoes. Once, Mom took me to the Deep South. To some of those old plantations' houses."

Douglas fell silent and looked out of the window.

"It's all still there, you know. All of it," she said after a time. "All that pain and horror and sorrow. It's in the soil, the trees, *everywhere*. It's soaked in every acre of that part of the world. And we felt it. *God!* Those poor, poor people. Like a sick, toxic treacle of bitterness and anger. I felt it, Clarkson. *I felt it.*" She struck her chest, as if words were not enough. "That's when my mother told me what I was feeling. Told me what I was. And my grandma, well... she nearly lost her mind to it."

"Your grandma was the same?" said Clarkson.

"Yeah. She was at ground zero at 9/11."

"...What? Oh, God. Oh, dear God..."

"Yeah. Said she felt all those people die in an instant. You saw what happened to me at the house?"

Clarkson nodded.

"Imagine that, multiplied by a *thousand*."

They drove in silence for a while. Both visualising that day. That terror. Then, "She was in a coma for two years. She woke up crying. It took another year for her to heal. She was never the same, though."

"My folks say no one was," Clarkson said. "Some less than others."

"Yeah, that's what Mom says," Douglas said.

Clarkson chewed her lip. "So... has your family *always* been... gifted?"

Douglas nodded. "Yeah. Always down the maternal line. Grandma used to tell me that even before we stepped off the boat, us girls had always attracted the weird. I tell you, the things I've seen..."

"Like what?"

"Look, okay: this world has layers. Like an onion, right? And for your entire life you've been living on the outermost skin. As soon as you met me, a layer was peeled back, revealing the naked weirdness that is our precarious existence on this rock hurtling through space. And it's weirdness all the way down, sister, so brace yourself. Don't envy us, partner. It's far more a burden than a gift."

Clarkson let the words sit with her for a while. The reality of the last few days hovered around her like bad odour. *This hell we've fought through,* she thought, *this is the tip of the iceberg? What next? The Four Horsemen of the Apocalypse?*

"Christ," she muttered.

"And the Councillor? Monage..." said Douglas. "The one they renditioned..."

"Man, I don't even want to *know* that they're doing to him," Clarkson said. "They've probably got the poor sumbitch on some table somewhere, going to work on him with sharp instruments and a cocktail of drugs."

"I hear you, man. But I'm saying..."

"Yeah, I know what you're saying. That ain't you. That won't *ever* be you. You understand? And if they come for *you*, they have to go through *me*."

"DOES THIS THING have a radio?" Douglas said eventually, looking at the buttons. "I'll be damned if we're going to sit here and listen to—"

"*Audio system initiated. Would you like me to randomise, or do you want to choose a specific stream?*"

"Go ahead, partner," said Clarkson.

"Okay. Erm... anything but talk radio or politics," said

Douglas. "Actually. Play classic rap music. Nothing past 1996."

"*Acknowledged. I'm building a playlist now.*"

The screen showed a timer for a few seconds, then:

"*Right about now, N.W.A. court is in full effect! Judge Dre presiding in the case of N.W.A. vs. the Police Department...*"

"'Fuck the Police'? Really?" Clarkson asked, eyebrows rising.

"Really," Douglas said firmly. "We've earned this."

"...Okay, then."

CHAPTER THIRTEEN
MIDWICH

DAYS LATER:

Vid-call initiated
Host/Client verified. ID verified. Ghost server backup disengaged.
Level 4 quantum encryption engaged. Contra Peeping Tom protocol engaged.
Lag time test running... Lag time 0.005 seconds.
Conversation running...

The St. Georges materialised on screen in a luxurious sitting room, with Frazetta, Rego, Mucha, Saville and Moebius paintings adorning the walls. Clarkson recognised Judith's earrings: each of them cost more than a typical worker's yearly salary. She didn't loathe her for it. Being a veteran of the African wars came with its own burdens.

Her husband, though....

"Good morning, Judges," said Judith. "Thank you for everything you've done for us. We're very happy to see you both survived the flood."

Douglas laughed. "If only. A little flooding would have been easy," she said.

"Could you tell us what you know about a project called Midwich?" Clarkson asked.

Percival St. George's face went white as bone, as if all blood had been drained from him. He rose and walked off screen. He came back with two glasses of whiskey in his hand, one of which he gave to his wife. Clarkson and Douglas waited for his response. Judith also.

"Have either of you ever heard of Operation Paperclip?" St. George asked.

"Yeah," Clarkson said. "Americans got the V2 rocket scientists out of Germany after the Second World War. Von Braun and his crew. Got them working for NASA."

"Yeah." St. George swallowed a mouthful of whiskey while Judith held hers in anticipation.

"Midwich is... It's a ghost project. Abandoned, disavowed. A Second World War intelligence project that evolved into a Cold War weapon."

"The weaponisation and use of people with psychic abilities. Right?" Douglas said.

"Yeah," St. George said. "When my mother bought Thurgood Industries and made me responsible for the weapons development programme, I spent nights trawling through paperwork, Thurgood's *and* Ashton's. I wanted to make sure I hadn't inherited a poisoned chalice. The past has an annoying tendency to—"

"Skip the preamble," Judith said.

"Yeah. So I found files on a programme that used psychics as spies and couriers. Mostly by the British. Some were American. Eventually, they both used them to fight the Russians."

"And after the fall of Russia?" Douglas asked.

Clarkson decided to keep quiet. Douglas had a personal stake in the case. She wondered whether some ancestor of Douglas had her name on a document linked to this project. She prayed it wasn't the case.

"It became the intelligence agencies' dirty little secret. Everyone involved with that project was sworn to secrecy on pain of imprisonment for treason. On both sides of the water. Which made no sense to me when I read it, because if you've got trained operatives with ESP abilities, why would you abandon them when a war's won?"

"You save them for the next war," prompted Douglas.

"Yes. But here's the thing: they all disappeared, back in the 'seventies. All of them. Overnight. Their handlers had completely forgotten who they were—like their minds had been wiped—and every trail went stone dead."

"So everyone pretended like it never happened and prayed for the best."

"After the heads rolled and the dust settled, that's exactly what they did. And they all waited."

"For what?"

"For their vulnerabilities to be exploited. For leaks. Compromises. Blackmail. Never happened, though. The official line was they'd never existed, that the project never found any real psychics, and it was all a weird stunt to try and spook enemy spies. But Mom and I have a different theory. Maybe, just maybe, they wanted what we all take for granted."

"A life," said Douglas, intently.

"Yeah."

"Then last week happened. When did you begin to suspect it was Midwich?"

"The night after we settled into protective custody. I did some checking, prompted by the report I read that none of the Berzerkers who attacked our house were, well, on Berzerk."

"It was via neuro-sublimal suggestion."

"Brainwashing," said Judith, cutting in. "How? What was the delivery mechanism?"

"An internet video," said Clarkson, clearing her throat. "Released into the wild over a year ago. It's had millions of views already."

St. George's eyes opened wide with fear. He knocked back his whiskey, disappeared off screen and reappeared with his glass full. "Which means that there could potentially be thousands, maybe millions of people out there, nationwide, who are potential... Christ!"

"So, what triggers them?" Judith asked.

Clarkson hesitated, looked at Douglas.

"Psychic suggestion," Douglas said. "It takes people with... abilities like you describe."

St. George nodded, unfazed, and Douglas and Clarkson exchanged a look. "Now you understand my urgency for wanting to contact you," he said. "Then when the station houses were attacked all at once..."

"You thought you were too late," Douglas said.

St. George nodded. Judith put down her glass and put her arm around her husband.

"You couldn't have done a thing, sir," Douglas said. She breathed out as if St. George's sense of guilt had cleansed her anger. Clarkson felt the temperature in the room drop a notch. "Midwiches or not, they were already in play. No harm, no foul."

"We've already issued a takedown notice," continued Clarkson, "so the original video should be gone by now. But—"

"But the damage is already done," said Percival. "You'll need to be on watch for triggers for the next... Christ... This could go on for *years!* Decades!"

"What can we do to help?" Judith asked.

"What did you do with the Midwich file? Does Ashton Thurgood have experience with psychics?" asked Douglas, narrowing her eyes.

Husband turned to wife, and some sort of silent exchange followed.

"Yes," St. George said, eventually. "I did some more digging. Near as I can tell, psychics started popping up again around the turn of the century and organisations started to recruit them. There's at least one team somewhere in the US government actively looking for them, though I can't get a lead on who. Some of the talents are the children and grandchildren of the runaways, others... maybe they're new, maybe they just never showed up on Midwich. One is in our employ. She checks out."

"Her name?"

"Kaoru Kurimoto. She's our liaison with the FBI."

"We'll check her out for ourselves. There's another name we want to look at first."

"Whom?"

"Hector Volução. From your old group at college."

"Hector?" St. George said with surprise. "Watch out for that one, Judges. He was the quietest of us. But sometimes... the things he said... they scared the shit out of us."

"How so?"

"He once joked that if he were God, he'd create the most virulent plague imaginable and purge the human race from the planet, then give the dinosaurs a second chance. Another time, he argued that Adolf Hitler had the right idea but chose the wrong targets. It's not the Jews he should have slaughtered, but the politicians, the rich and the aristocracy. Everyone who led Germany to war and devastation. Hitler should have done what the French did and enfranchised the poor, the immigrants, the dispossessed, the disabled. He argued that a thousand-year Reich should have been built on a foundation of inclusion, its borders flung open. Creepy stuff like that. So, yes... Hector had a *problematic* worldview, to say the least. But given where he came from—Shaolin Island—you could almost forgive his radical ideas. *Almost*."

"Good luck with him. If you need any help, we'll give you anything you require," Judith added.

"Tell me, why are you helping us?" Douglas asked.

"When your mom heads one of the large providers of military and war enforcement tech on earth, and she hands you responsibility for running one of the most critical sections of her business, you quickly learn how to cover your ass," said St. George. "Our secrets are no use to me dead, or in jail."

"Speaking of which, my partner and me have been doing

some digging ourselves. Judith was your bodyguard, wasn't she? She watched over your ass when you travelled to Zimbabwe to negotiate mineral rights and broker a peace deal. Now, in some corners, that looks a bit like war profiteering, and neither your mother nor your shareholders want that kind of heat; so, your bodyguard was an employee, not a contractor. You two saw some action in Zimbabwe, right?"

St. George nodded.

"Good. So, somewhere along the line things stopped being completely professional. You kept your relationship a secret for a bit, but you figured your mother wouldn't make a fuss, because..."

"Because it didn't interfere with my work."

"Not just that. She was happy to have a guard right there in your home. Correct?"

St. George looked at Judith again, then nodded.

"You knew something was coming, didn't you?" Clarkson said, cutting back in. "You didn't know what shape it would take, but you knew. The moment they used Ernesto's words, you knew."

"Your emails suggest that you and Ernesto were the most vocal anti-capitalists in your group," said Douglas. "But something changed. Something forced you to reassess your beliefs. What was that?"

A shadow fell over Percival's face, and Judith shuffled over to him and took him in her arms.

They're genuine, then. Clarkson sighed; thankful she hadn't uncovered some sort of sham marriage.

"His father was killed," said Judith. "Murdered by someone doped up on TranceTrance."

"Ah!" said Clarkson.

"He... he realised that the system was broken beyond fixing and needed replacing. And the rhetoric—the philosophies and beliefs—weren't enough. Action was necessary, and sharp change."

"Comfortable anarchy," Clarkson said, recalling a phrase

from Ernesto's writing. "Anarchy so tolerable that it fades into the background… until it bites you."

"Yes..." St. George whispered, wiping his eyes. "Money and power can build, and it can destroy." He blew his nose, then continued. "At the point of truth, you find yourself unable to hide from your true nature. It's revealed to you; undeniable, naked in its purity. Mine... mine was a need to make the world a safer place. But I couldn't do it under the current governmental framework. Change is always reliant on consensus, and far too many have utterly selfish motivations for maintaining a broken status quo." He gulped at his whiskey again. Judith took a sip of hers.

"I... *we* all decided that wholeheartedly supporting Fargo's Judges initiative was the answer. It was the only valid solution for purging a broken system. A Judge has no restrictions on their mandate to execute the law. With enough evidence, they could walk right into a Wall Street office and judge someone for fraud, for insider trading."

"Or the White House itself," Judith added. "Impeachment is too slow."

Okay, then. Clarkson hesitated before she asked her next question. "So, to summarise, we're potentially looking at the descendants of long-escaped psychics who served in government agencies, and who have somehow been able to organise themselves into a terrorist organisation bent on—what? Revenge? Revolution?"

"Try all of the above, Judge," said St. George. He turned the glass around in his hands. "Here's the thing. After Midwich crumbled, near as we can tell, most anyone who uncovered real talents assumed they were the only ones. Stargate, the Goat Lab; they had nothing, no one with real gifts went near them. They just worked away where they could, not attracting any attention. And none of them, on either side, ever received a medal. Their services were never acknowledged. And that was their choice: to hide from everyone, or be nothing more than a tool."

"We're sure they're going to do it again," said Douglas. "The last two attacks were tests, and they both worked. And they're going to do it again, and they've got who-knows-how-many ready candidates right in the streets of the city to activate at any time."

"I agree," said St. George.

"And the governor's given the NYPD and the Judges the go-ahead for their purge," said Judith, dryly.

"They'll turn the city into a war zone," said Douglas as she sat on the sofa next to Clarkson.

"Which serves The Patriots' ends," St. George said. "Damn, this is some messy shit."

End Call.

CHAPTER FOURTEEN
SHAOLIN

STATEN ISLAND WAS an oasis of calm in a state that was now for all intents and purposes on a war footing. It had one of the lowest crime rates in New York and was one of the few places the Judges had yet to establish a permanent presence. Here, they were unnecessary.

"How do they *keep* it like this? And why do they call it Shaolin Island?"

Clarkson and Douglas were cruising through clean streets, absent of detritus or the signs of violence: no boarded and abandoned homes, no bullet holes nor burnt-out buildings. Trees and bushes were trimmed. Seemingly, civic pride was the lifeblood of the community.

Both Judges had grown up among violence, had lost friends and family members to it. Both knew the things that protect you from it: money, power and violence itself. The police were a non-issue.

So, when presented with the unreality of the place...

"Devil worship," Clarkson said, after a few moments.

"Devil worship?" Douglas replied incredulously.

"Yep," Clarkson said. "Devil worship. Shaolin's the name of an old satanic cult. *Sha-olin* being the name of one of Lucifer's chief lieutenants. They kidnapped investment bankers and hedge fund managers and mob lawyers at the dead of night and sacrificed them to honour her in an orgy of violence which keeps the place... like this."

"...You're not serious, are you?" Douglas asked.

"Oh, yeah; Satanic, new age, post-racial, post-feminist, inclusionary devil worship. Which is fact another wing of the New World Order, funded by the lizard people of the Neo-Illuminati."

Clarkson burst out laughing.

"...Aaand, you can *straight* go to Hell," said Douglas as Clarkson giggled. "Do not pass Go. Do not collect $200. Straight to Hell you go."

"It's an old nickname," said Clarkson, wiping her eyes. "The Wu-Tang Clan came up with it. Before either of our time. I guess it stuck."

They turned a corner and were met with a checkpoint, and the warm glow of the moment vanished. This was how Shaolin maintained their false ideal.

Huge steel gates punctuated a vast wall of concrete that had been painted an appealing lilac; armed guards walked its length. At either side of the gate sat a watchtower with blacked-out windows. A.I.-controlled gun sentries trained on them the moment they brought the car to a halt. The car reported that they were being scanned and targeted.

"These evil streets iz rough. Ain't no one we can trust..." quoted Clarkson to herself.

"*Bzzz! Attention, Judges. You are cleared for exit to Staten Island North. Have a nice day.*"

The great gate creaked opened and Douglas muttered a string of curses as they drove through.

It WAS AS if they had driven backwards in time. Because what lay on the other side of the wall felt more like the nineteen-seventies than the twenty-forties.

The first thing was the smell. Toxic, nauseous and visceral;

like the combined sweat of a quarter million souls had congealed and formed a fog of putrescent sickness.

The pavement was a patchwork of broken concrete slabs, poorly maintained and shoddy repaired, with a strange mixture of tar and concrete filling the holes. Videophone kiosks had been ransacked for their tech and turned into shelters for drug dealers peddling their wares, which they did without fear. The people looked lean, their eyes scanning for prey or predators. They eyed the Judges with vicious fear as they drove along the street, at once threatening violence and betraying hopelessness. Some reached to their waists or behind their backs as the Judges drove past. Their clothes were worn and patched.

The gutters were filled with garbage and the road was potholed, slowing them to a crawl. The high-rise towers of the housing projects rose on either side of the street, stretching along the road far into the distance. They were rain-streaked and dirty and poorly maintained, and would have been condemned as death traps if anyone cared for the occupants. The residents hung out of broken—or absent—windows. And everywhere were the signs of violence and neglect.

Along the street, in the shadows of the tower blocks and in what once were areas of greenery were tents. Endless tents, like a city within a city.

This was Staten Island North.

This was hell.

This was what The Patriots were fighting for. This was the fuel that had prompted revolutions in Russia and France and had toppled indifferent aristocracies. This is what had sent millions across a turbulent sea, fleeing a rigid, dogmatic, class-based world.

And here it was again, on the streets of their city. This was London in the nineteenth century; it was Mumbai in the twentieth.

This was why they had both become Judges; to force the scales back into balance. The awful indifference to abject poverty and suffering were but a few of the injustices that had motivated Fargo to create his Judges initiative. Due process and the slow grinding of the justice system had become a sieve that allowed crime to go unpunished and criminals to avoid incarceration.

And allowed the creation of horrors such as Staten Island.

A social-economic apartheid state, right here on American soil. The horror of psychically triggered Berzerkers faded and was replaced by the disgust and anger at the utter degradation and indignity they were witnessing.

"Charlotte?" Douglas said through her teeth.

"Yeah, Niamh?"

"The people who do this... We're going to find them and judge them," she growled. "We're going to send them and their friends and family and anyone who profits from this misery to jail for so long, their parole officers haven't been born yet."

"Sister," said Clarkson, "get in line."

The Judges bumped fists.

They turned a corner.

CHAPTER FIFTEEN
YOU GOTS TO CHILL

"WE ARE CONCERNED, Helena," one man said, nervously. He'd been chosen by the rest to be the voice of their concern. "Your plan—"

"*Our* plan, brother," Helena said. She scratched her tattooed arms. They'd begun to itch.

"Forgive me, *our* plan," he said. "We worry that our continued strikes at the machinery of capitalism have been too..."

"Enthusiastic," a woman said. "We risk attracting attention before we're ready. And worse, one of our number has been captured? Should he talk and reveal our plans..."

"We have planned for this, have we not?" Helena said. "Everything we have anticipated has come to pass. Our strikes at the symbols of fascism and injustice have revealed their weakness. The horror we have unleashed will soon coalesce into hate, then anger, then *action*. The streets of New York will fill with the people we are fighting to save, and then we will show the entire world the ugliness at the rotten heart of the American dream. For once, we have the advantage. We're no longer tools, nor weapons. We cannot allow our fear to dull our ambition. And once sublimed, you will all have the greatest of burdens: to guide the rest of us."

The group fell silent. Helena understood their reticence, and didn't resent them for it. They had all asked much of each other over the long years, and soon they'd be making the greatest of sacrifices. "Our brother, by volunteering to name our oppressors— to lay his life on the altar of freedom—he knew the price he'd have to pay. He knew. We must honour his death. We have to finish what we started. The action he took has now become the flame that will burn the lies from every corner of this county. *Remember him.*"

Another came forth. She was the oldest of the group, she had been with them since the beginning. She had found Helena before her transformation and quietly guided her towards the light. Trained her; made her strong. Made her a leader.

"Forgive us, child," she said. "Unlike the rest of us, you must walk the most precarious of paths. On one side, agent of justice. On the other, voice of reason and authority. Lean too heavily in one direction and all will be lost."

Helena acknowledged the concern. "Mistress, I hear you. I know well how delicate the balance between two worlds is. We all know that this is the most crucial time, when a single misstep could spell disaster and end our great enterprise."

The older woman smiled and kissed Helena on her forehead. "Be careful, my child," she said. "Much rests on your shoulders."

Helena smiled reassuringly.

CHAPTER SIXTEEN
CAN IT BE SO SIMPLE?

THEY PARKED THEIR car on top of the flattened rubble of a demolished project building, that squatted in the middle of three overcrowded towers like a playing field of dead dreams. Hundreds of eyes watched them as they sat in the security of their vehicle.

"*Destination reached,*" the car announced. "*Warning: risk assessment confirms multiple armed targets in vicinity. Extreme caution is advisable.*"

"Okay, then," Clarkson said. "You ready?"

"Would it matter if I say no?" Douglas asked.

"Sure," Clarkson drawled.

"Then no. I'm not. Let's go home," said Douglas.

"Nah," Clarkson said.

"It was worth a try," Douglas said as she opened the door.

The smell assaulted them immediately as they stepped out into the air, a sickly, acidic cloud. Their hands stayed close to their Lawkeepers as they walked.

"Hey," Clarkson said. "Your mojo giving you hell yet?"

"Like you wouldn't believe," Douglas replied. "It's taking all my effort to not run to the hills."

"Appreciate you sticking with me, partner," said Clarkson.

They approached the entrance of one of the buildings, where

a crowd awaited. They looked at the two Judges with dead, unreadable eyes, their body language saying what their eyes wouldn't: *You ain't from around here and we don't want you here neither.*

Douglas and Clarkson stood their ground in front of them. If things got ugly...

"Righteous!" said Clarkson. "We ain't here for none of youse. We're here to check up on a body, see if he's still breathin'. If so, protect his neck from heads that wanna burn him. If he's six feet already, we aim to find the schlubs who took him from the world. Lock 'em up in a box 'til their clan forget their names."

"Justice?" A tall thin woman with blonde hair, her body covered with tattoos.

"Justice, fam," Douglas said. "Judges ain't them blue-pigs. New law, new world. Old lady, that mother's got eyes now. See everything. See how you's living in a grave. No better than rats. God children ain't supposed to live like rats. Due's paid. Sins forgiven. All God's children equal now. Born and die equal. Sister Judge and I... aims to do something about it too. Word is bond. No 'ish."

"No 'ish?" said another. Looked to be East Asian. She was short, her lips and ears covered in piercings. She, like the blonde, was heavily tattooed.

"No 'ish," said Clarkson. She tapped her Judge badge with two fingers, the street sign for a promise made. "Word is bond."

"Who be you looking for?" asked a stocky African American man wearing a dashiki, trousers and sandals. He looked to be the oldest of the group. Probably a respect figure.

"A body named Hector Volução," said Douglas.

"*Dead-named*," said the blonde woman.

"Say what?" Clarkson asked.

"*Dead-named*, I said," the woman repeated. "Ain't he, *she* now. Him is her. Became her true self. Reborn. *Sister now*."

"What her name be now, righteous? She be here?" Clarkson asked.

"Name be *Helena* now," said the African American man. "María Santa Helena Volução. And she gone. She grown wings and flew almost two years back."

Clarkson stepped forward and stood in front of the man, took off her helmet and bowed slightly. "Your name be, papa?"

"Be born Alexander Tobias O'Grady. Name I give myself be Kwame Sankara Kenyatta," he said. "You Judges be welcome. Come on in now."

"KNOW YOU WHAT revolution be?" said the man named Papa Kenyatta. "Not what you readin' in a book. But true, true revolution?"

The two Judges remained silent.

"You be listenin'. Good," said Papa Kenyatta. "Revolution be an idea. An idea becomes like a bug. A mosquito. It infects, spreads. Patient zero could be a speech, a book, an act. But once the idea infects enough heads... well, then it like a disease. Revolutions are what happens when enough head become infected with an idea. But like any disease..."

"It mutates," said Douglas.

"*Right*. Damn. Judges be smart!" said Papa Kenyatta. "Not like blue-pig at all. Damn! Yeah: idea, infection, gestation, spread, multiplication, revolution. Epidemic."

"Papa, you missed a step," said Clarkson. "We were talking mutation."

Papa Kenyatta smiled. "Real smart," he said. "Yeah, mutation. Only when an idea is locked inside a head is it safe. Speak it into the breeze for others to hear... Infection. Speak it enough, enough people hear it? Multiplication *and* mutation."

"And Ernesto Fukuyama. His essay: 'The Excesses of a Police State.' You hear 'bout that?" Clarkson asked. "That was a virus that mutated?"

"Right, right. Mutated and infected near everyone. But a virus is just a virus. Not need to hate it 'less it be spreading hate. Then you have to create a new idea. An anti-virus. But that Fukuyama kid? Nah, he be young and pure. No more guilty than a cold that killed an elder. Couldn't have known people would have used his ideas for war." The man sighed, took a mouthful of the drink he was holding, and held the glass in his hands, locked in deep thought.

"You met him, didn't you, papa?" Douglas asked.

Papa Kenyatta nodded. "Yeah, sister Judge. I did. Kid was wise. Love for the whole world. Be horrified to see what was done in his name. Tell me, sister Judge: your people, where they from?"

"Originally? Be from Ireland, papa," said Douglas.

"Ah. Celtic folk. Proud people. Right, so you know like me and your sister Judge that freedom is a virus, we're all of us infected at conception."

Douglas smiled and nodded. "But how you get that freedom... well, the means differ, don't they?" she said.

"Right, right. Some use words, others use guns. Some use one as justification for the other," Papa Kenyatta said.

"Papa," Douglas said as she leant forward. "I've gotta ask. Helena, when you knew her... did she... was she able to do things with her mind? Like mind reading and such? Tell when a fella was a fool or true?"

Papa Kenyatta sighed and took another mouthful of his drink. Finally, he looked up.

"Yeah," he said. "Yeah, she did. Used to joke that she was the Mexican Bene Gesserit. Used to say that her gift was from God. Said she was like Superwoman. Needed to go out into the world and make it better for all bodies. Use that gift to make a difference." He wiped his eyes. "Girl broke bad. Girl broke *real* bad. History knows you can't change the world with bombs. History knows. But she joined those fools? That what you dancing around? Damn..."

"Did she say where she was headed when she left, papa?" Clarkson asked.

"Yeah," Papa Kenyatta said. "Said she was heading to the

heart of the beast. Great Satan himself. King of lies. Father of megadeath."

"She be in Washington," Douglas said.

"Figure so," said Papa Kenyatta. "Girl had a gift. Could have used it to make the world shine. 'Stead, she used it for violence? Damn." The man's face twisted with disappointment and grief. "Goddamn, man. It's a shame the way a body can go messing around with your heart."

"Papa," said Clarkson. The man looked up. "Way it be, world heating up. Hearts are growing cold."

"Way it's always been, sister Judge," said Papa Kenyatta, his voice full of pain. "Way it's always been. Some hearts, cold as stone. Others, world *makes* cold."

CHAPTER SEVENTEEN
CAREFUL (CLICK, CLICK)

THEY DROVE THROUGH two checkpoints to get to Washington, D.C.

The capital refused to allow itself to be wounded as grievously as New York had. Police and Judges alike patrolled the streets; vidcams had been installed at every junction. Sophisticated search algorithms scanned every second of footage in real time. The eternal digital sentry: indiscriminate, tireless.

Fear was palpable. It lurked in everyone's eyes now. No one trusted anyone.

"'And the moment a population loses hope, at that instant they become fuel for eternal fascism,'" quoted Clarkson.

"You know... the moment Fukushima died, a light went out in the world," Douglas said. "He deserved to see his words put to good use. Not as lazy justifications for murder."

Clarkson laughed laconically. "You don't need justifications for that. Just an excuse."

Ms Kaoru Kurimoto lived in an expensive apartment building belonging to Ashton Thurgood plc. The cost of an apartment here was more than a four-bedroom house in many parts of the country. One of the many perks of working for a powerful multinational weapons manufacturer. She lived on the fourth floor; each floor could only be reached via an electronic key confirmed by the user's DNA. No key, no entry.

The Judges' wrist-screens automatically overrode them.

"Is that lavender?" Clarkson asked as the lift doors closed behind them.

Douglas sniffed tentatively. "Yeah," she said. "Suppose dealing death weapons affords a pampered life."

"Cynical much?"

"Don't tell me you don't care."

"All too much," Clarkson sighed as the lift doors opened.

As soon as they crossed the lift's threshold, Clarkson felt a pressure at the bridge of her nose, which made her close her eyes and wince. It felt like a sinus cold coming on. But behind that discomfort lay sickness, fear, anger, frustration. She groaned, the strength of the emotions rushing through her like a tornado. "Christ," she muttered. "It's her. She's projecting. Isn't she?"

"She is," Douglas said. "She's fighting something—*someone*. We have to help her."

Kurimoto's flat was at the end of the corridor. The wall were painted in bland, neutral colours, but still managed to look and smell luxurious. Every step Clarkson took felt like wading through mud; her stomach threatened to empty its contents. Douglas, however, almost strode through it, sheer determination on her face. She slung an arm around Clarkson and dragged her forward.

"She's angry," Douglas said. "I can feel... her rage."

They were almost there, the rush of emotions pulsing from the door. Clarkson's eyes watered from the pain. One step, two steps, three steps. She put her hand over her mouth to catch her vomit, but only spit came. Douglas touched the door...

...and it opened. The room seemed to vibrate, she felt dizzy, up was down, down was up, her head playing tricks—the pain, the pain, *oh, God, I'm going to throw up*—

"Bedroom," Douglas managed.

Clarkson began to falter, she lost her balance and fell. "Go!" she said. "I'm right behind you."

Douglas limped forward, swaying like a reed in the wind.

"Bedroom," grunted Clarkson. She caught her breath and crawled forward, fighting the urge to vomit with every—

She couldn't do it.

She had to do it.

The door was ajar. Light was pouring out of the crack...

Douglas crouched beside a bed. She looked like she was praying. Holding someone's hand in hers. Kurimoto?

She dreamt she heard her name being called, but ignored it.

"Clarkson," it came again.

Douglas's voice.

"Clarkson."

"...Yeah?" Clarkson replied.

"It's done. Wake up."

Clarkson opened her eyes and looked up at her partner. "How long was I out?" she asked in a near-whisper. Douglas offered her hand and Clarkson took it.

"An hour."

She looked through the door to the bedroom and saw a large woman sitting on the edge of her bed, head in her hands, growling to herself. She knew what that sound meant: not grief, but fury. "So what did I miss?" she asked.

"We've got... Our problem is bigger than we thought," said Douglas. "The psychics we're tracking... one of them tried to activate Kurimoto. She'd seen the video." She frowned. "Dammit, are you listening to me?"

Clarkson turned slowly. "Psychics... are susceptible to triggering?"

Douglas coughed, nodded. "Touch and go, but looks like. God knows what they could have gotten her to do."

"All right. Good," Clarkson said numbly.

She was done. Her sympathy for the psychics, hiding from their exploiters for generations, had evaporated. That one person could rob others of their will, turn them into those... horrors... enraged her.

She had only temporarily been affected by Kurimoto's power,

if accidentally. Who else had been a victim of her attempt to defend herself? *No*, she thought. This was unreasonable. May as well give members of the public nukes.

Her sympathy had gone, and in its place a plan began to take shape.

"Step outside with me, partner," she said. "There's something we need to discuss."

CHAPTER EIGHTEEN
THE SUPER SHINOBI

KAORU KURIMOTO WAS a second-generation Japanese immigrant. She'd worked for the FBI for almost ten years and she was murderously angry and completely cooperative. The three of them sat in her kitchen around an oak table polished to a high shine.

Kurimoto drank hot chocolate from a large mug, her arms casting long shadows over the table. She looked over the brim of the mug, her bloodshot eyes revealing fury. A good weapon, if directed and focused.

Douglas leant forward in her chair, arms resting on the table, fingers interlocked, almost in prayer, and spoke. "For my partner's benefit, I'd like you to tell us what you told me. In there." She tapped her head. "I guarantee you that nothing you say will ever leave this room."

Clarkson placed a small black humming cube on the table. A gift from the St. Georges, courtesy of Thurgood Industries.

"This is a scrambler," she said. "We initialised it the moment we entered this room. It's impossible for anyone to make either a visual or audio recording."

The big woman set the mug down slowly onto a waiting coaster and stared at the open palms of her hands, opening and closing them for an age.

"*You* know what it's like," she said slowly. "When you're... like *us*. At first, you think you're mad. That you're going insane. Then you work out you're not. That the voices in your head are real, are other people's thoughts." She wiped a tear from her eye. "Then you learn control. Because you have to. You start to think maybe it's a gift. But you also learn to keep it to yourself."

She slowly cracked her knuckles and grunted.

Clarkson watched her carefully. Silence was the key now; just let the woman talk.

"You learn how to hide. To make yourself invisible. You're always on the outside. But... it's your secret pride. Something you hold close, that makes you... special. Your shield against the world."

"And your gun," Douglas added.

Kurimoto looked up and nodded.

"So, what happened?" asked Clarkson gently.

Kurimoto rubbed her eyes. "Self-defence. I panicked. I could feel someone trying to trigger me, because they knew who I was and that I'd watched the video. God knows how they found me. Maybe they knew where I worked, I don't know. What I know is that they tried... and I was barely able to hold them at bay."

"Nah," Douglas said. "You're wrong. I was in there too. They weren't fighting to get in. They were fighting to keep you *out*."

The big woman wiped a tear from her eye and grinned viciously.

Clarkson felt like a spectator, stuck outside a conversation she had no part in. She sighed.

"You shouldn't envy us, Judge," Kurimoto said. "Trust me."

"You can't do that," Douglas said softly. "Her thoughts are private."

"I'm sorry. I'm sorry," the big woman protested, her large hands raised in defence. "I'm... I'm still not myself yet. Those—" She rattled off a string of Japanese.

Clarkson smiled. She didn't need to be a psychic to know what Kurimoto needed. Not justice, but payback. Perfect. "You gonna tell us what happened?" she said. "Maybe we can find the people who did this to you. Maybe we can make them pay."

Kurimoto smiled viciously. "That sounds pretty good." She looked at her mug of hot chocolate, laughed, said, "I need something stronger," and swallowed it down.

"So," she said, leaning back in her chair and folding her large arms. "What do you want to know?"

CHAPTER NINETEEN
FAILURE?

"So... YOU FAILED." The young woman was rich, petulant, loyal but at times intolerable. "You failed *spectacularly!* Worse still, the fat Jap bitch has told that Judge—"

"Shut your filthy little mouth!" Helena snapped. She rubbed her tattooed arms and smiled. "It was a complete success, in fact. We learned more than we thought with that commando action. Now they'll be forced to act. They've been issued orders to find and destroy every shred of Berzerk in the city and detain every user they find, because they believe it turns them in tools we can control, blind to the real threat from the screens these fools cleave to. And these orders come from the office of the President himself."

"Wait a minute. You got all that from the Judge's mind?" the young woman said.

"From *both* of them," Helena said. "Anger is a door for some. A weapon or shield for others."

"And do you realise what this means?" said the old woman.

Helena nodded. "It means law enforcement agencies now have carte blanche to assault the city under the pretence of an emergency." She smiled, and whispered, "It's beautiful."

"Excuse me?" another woman asked, aghast. "Did you just say 'beautiful'? Did you actually describe this city's pending transformation into a war zone as *beautiful?*"

"I did," Helena said as she stood. "Now is the time. Now we'll reveal to America—to the entire world—how far we have fallen. We'll show the ugly face of American fascism to the world, and the people will rise. And we don't have to lift a finger. We only have to watch."

"Oh, God," said the other woman. "Do you realise... I mean... people are going to *die!* Hundreds, thousands of them! Judges, police, civilians..."

"Of course they will!" Helena replied. "Don't be so naive! Did you really believe that this revolution would be bloodless? That we would halt the rise of fascism with words, speeches and marches? We're not *children!* None of us can afford the luxury of innocence. You know—*all* of you know—that history is always made by actions, great and small. Words don't change the world; or if they do, it is only when they're backed up by action. When the people have had their eyes opened and their hearts filled."

Helena let her words sink in with the group, watching each of their faces for a reaction. The rich girl was cowed, but the woman she'd just admonished stared at her with ferocity that she found attractive and dangerous. She'd gone too far.

She knelt beside the woman and took her hands in her own. "Listen to me: things are always darkest before the dawn. Debate is worthless. People aren't *interested* in tackling their problems. They want to live in a cushioned world where nothing offends and nothing hurts. They're prepared to give away their freedoms for security. No, *horror*; horror and mortal terror are the only things that shake a desensitised civilisation out of its apathy. You know this is true."

The woman's mouth opened and closed several times, as she struggled to formulate an answer...

But none was forthcoming. She deflated, accepting the inevitability of what was to come. A calm descended over her that had not previously been there.

Helena didn't question it, but took it as the gift it was.

"So," the woman asked, "what do we do now?"

"We tie up loose ends," said Helena simply.

They all knew what she meant.

"Then we hide, and wait. Patience is now our greatest ally. We wait and prepare." Helena kissed the woman on the forehead; she smelled of lavender. "The end of the beginning is almost here. What come next will be biblical. And when we make our move, we'll make sure the entire world is watching."

CHAPTER TWENTY
EYE FOR AN EYE (YOUR BEEF IS MINES)

"Judges! You're still alive!" said St. George.

"Surprised?" Douglas asked with a smirk. Clarkson chuckled quietly in the background.

They were sat in their unmarked patrol car outside Ms Kurimoto's apartment complex. They had left the woman upstairs festering in a pit of anger. Eyes would need to be kept on her. She was a witness and a potential asset.

"Big man, we need a favour and a little intel. We think we can resolve this case, but we need your help."

"What's the favour, Judge?"

Clarkson leant forward making sure she was seen on the vidcam. "Okay. Hi, Percival," she said. "Thurgood Industries has a drone programme in development, right? Networked drones, talking to each other to scan large areas."

"I think I know the one you mean," St. George said as he stroked his chin. "Give me a moment." His eyes fluttered and his face became motionless and statuesque.

"He's not there, is he?" said Douglas. "It's a projection."

"That is correct," said St. George, though his lips didn't move. "I was swimming in the data stream. Ah! Got it." His face became animated and real once again. "Yes, we've got about two dozen machines, slaved and networked. They can scan for heat signals, sound samples, face recog, whatever. System's still a little buggy, but it's fit for purpose."

"Good. We're talking face recog," said Clarkson. "How reliable is it? How many faces can it look for at the same time?"

St. George smiled. "I take it you've run our psychic dossier through the Justice Department's CLEAR server."

The two Judges traded a look. "Think you can do it?" said Douglas.

St. George laughed. "My wife and I owe you our lives," he said. "Give me three hours."

"*Excuse* me?" Sector Chief Agnes said with horror. "But you want to do *what* exactly?"

"To temporarily deploy a fleet of drones in New York City airspace, while killing all air traffic and grounding all planes," Clarkson said.

The faces of the Sector Chief Agnes and the Police Captain Attwell were frozen in horrified silence. Captain Attwell herself hadn't uttered a word since the Judges made their request, though the look on her face said enough.

"We've already assessed the viability of our plan, sirs," Douglas said. "And if we do this right, it'll be a huge win for all involved. Judges, police, FBI, everyone, all the way up to the President himself. He'll be dining off this for years."

Sector Chief Agnes opened her mouth, then closed it again. Captain Attwell rubbed her eyes. The two Judges waited for the inevitable.

"Judges," said Attwell. "Understand, this will go one of two ways. One: You will fail utterly, creating enormous collateral damage and destruction of property. There will be a public outcry, and the President and Senate will come under huge pressure to reverse the powers given to the Justice Department. Don't think it can't happen, even now; every politician and essayist, pundit, virtue-signaller and keyboard-activist will jump on the bandwagon and you will be done.

"Two: This—whatever you're planning—will all be a resounding success; you will clean up the city's biggest headache and the necessity of your programme will be proven beyond a shadow of a doubt. And then..." Attwell trailed off and for the first time, Clarkson and Douglas noticed how tired she looked. She had seen too much, and had been soiled by her experiences. The streets could do that.

"Listen, the reason I say all that is... the future of your initiative—shit, probably the future of policing itself—could well rest on both of your shoulders. And if you mess this up, I will personally make sure everyone knows that. Trust me on this: every soul in this city; hell, in these United States. So, if you've gotta make this move, you've really, *really* gotta make it, you've gotta be *sure*. You can't have an ounce of doubt. You okay with that?"

The two Judges looked at one another. "Like God before the Great Flood, sir," said Clarkson.

"That... *does not* inspire us with confidence, Judges," said Agnes. "Do you know who Marisa Pellegrino is?"

Clarkson looked at Douglas, who shrugged. "No, sir."

"I should be so lucky. She's the person I have to make a phone call to right now and try and sign off on this stupid stunt." She sighed and rubbed her eyes. "Go on, start getting things in motion. I'll let you know when you have approval."

CHAPTER TWENTY-ONE
HAND ON THE PUMP

Nine days.

Nine days of grounded planes and diverted flights and no suspects.

Nine days of mounting political pressure to reopen the airports and allow air traffic over the city. Nine days of threats, promises and political intrigue. Millions of dollars lost every day the airplanes sat idle on the tarmac. Shareholders panicked as the market plummeted. Contracted airport staff found themselves being sent home. Air traffic control sat waiting, like the faithful awaiting the Second Coming.

Travel in and out of the city was restricted; schools, collages and libraries were closed.

And like night following day, people panic bought. Everyone made a run on their local convenience store and supermarkets, ransacking the shelves of every item.

Fights broke out.

Shots were fired.

People died.

People were Judged.

* * *

THE CITY'S HOSPITALS were pushed to breaking point as they became inundated with the elderly and the young. The power grid was put under enormous strain until rolling blackouts became a necessity.

The Judges brought food into the city and introduced rationing. It was quietly hoped that the queues in the streets would help the drones do their jobs.

The city newspapers and online sites were especially harsh in their condemnation of the Judges' no-fly-zone. The terror attacks of the previous week were already a dull memory; like a broken leg in a cast, the pain was almost forgotten. The dead police and Judges were irrelevant. The closures and blackouts, meanwhile, were happening right now.

But the Judges did not relent. They waited. They knew, like their police cousins, that they'd created a pressure cooker; and sooner or later The Patriots would be found. It would take only one face, one partial recognition. Someone would break cover eventually; an organisation was only as strong as its weakest link, and not all of the psychics on that list were hardened terrorists.

Meanwhile, the Judges and the police alike took full advantage of their emergency powers and swept through the roughest neighbourhoods of the city like a plague of locusts, heavily armed and emboldened, devouring everything in their path. Day and night, the sound of police sirens and the Rottweiler growl of Lawrangers assaulted citizens of the city.

Then came the bullets.

The blood.

The death.

The unavoidable cost of a war on crime. The graphic horror was captured hourly in high-res and broadcast across the globe. The death count climbed in real time, with odds offered on how high it would get before the city reached breaking point. The world watched from the comfort of their homes as New York City transformed into a grim coliseum of gunfire and gore, like a war zone; both sides utterly relentless and ruthless in their goal of annihilating the other. Quarter was neither asked nor given.

And the body count rose.

Garbage went uncollected. Streets went uncleared. Vermin fattened themselves on an all-you-can-eat buffet. People took to burning their trash, resulting in several house fires, and more death.

The city stank.

Something would have to give.

ON THE FOURTH day came the protests.

A million Americans descended on the city. A great cross-spectrum of souls, all disgusted at their great city being transformed into a battlefield, poured through its streets. A great army of citizens demanding the immediate cessation of violence. The price of security was too high.

Their demands fell on deaf ears.

So they stayed. Central Park and the surrounding area of seven square miles became the largest campsite in peace-time history, dwarfing the anti-Judge protests of 'thirty-six. A peaceful protest, an appeal to the whole world.

Shame was their only weapon.

ON THE SIXTH day, New York City lost its patience.

The Dow Jones had been bleeding all week and major manufacturers had started talking about permanent closures.

Money was a fickle God.

Mayor Rivera was given an ultimatum: *Get your city in order or someone who can, will.*

The National Guard was scrambled, martial law declared and a dawn-to-dusk curfew initiated. The protest camp was surrounded by a ring of tanks, and guardsmen in assault armour. The delicate process of removing the protesters began. The press was *strongly* encouraged not to cover the event.

The protesters were given a forty-eight-hour deadline to leave before extra-judicial assistance was implemented.

The protesters refused to move.

ON THE EIGHTH day, The Pit fell.

Police and Judge alike walked through the ruined streets, picking past bombed-out buildings and over dead bodies, their only reward for the week-long mania. The air hung heavy with the metallic smell of spent rounds and burning petrol. Despite discovering a major Berzerk manufacturing facility—suspected to be the main supplier for the entire Eastern Seaboard—their victory tasted like acid in their mouths; burning with guilt, horror and anger. It felt hollow and empty and pointless.

What had once been Queens now resembled the bombed-out shells of Second World War cities.

But... they had *won*.

A strange epiphany began to wash over the ageing remains of the NYPD. A blasphemous, but a painfully unavoidable truth: that it was all made possible only by the Judges. Their existence, their moral absolutism, their unflinching dedication to the law.

It had been years since the police academies stopped taking cadets. The time of New York's Finest was at an end.

What surprised many of the officers was how readily they accepted that reality.

That night a text-in poll was taken asking whether the actions taken by law enforcement were justified.

The result from New York voters came back 72% *Yes*.

The drones still circling tirelessly over the city had become useful in spotting known and potential troublemakers, allowing them to be quietly removed during the protests and the later crowd dispersals. Few questioned their disappearance.

But through all of the chaos and after tracking down too damn many false positives, The Patriots remained frustratingly elusive.

* * *

ON DAY NINTH, Clarkson was about ready to give up.

The protestors had less than a day to leave Central Park. The city held its breath as the world watched.

CHAPTER TWENTY-TWO
OLDER GODS

CLARKSON AND DOUGLAS watched as the CLEAR system filtered through hundreds of hours of footage. They'd existed in a tiny, insulated universe in a darkened room for days, protected from the goings-on in the city outside—though the news reports kept them informed. Their work was classed ultra-high priority, with footage farmed out to the FBI, the NSA, the CIA. So far there was nothing, and the two Judges' eyes ached with staring.

"Oh, Lord, what I wouldn't give for a cup of coffee," Clarkson said as she massaged her sore eyes.

"You mean, 'What I wouldn't have given for a hit of caffeine, before I became a Judge and accepted a prohibition against it,'" Douglas replied. "And I get it. The world's burning outside and we've been cooped up in this station house for so long that our eyes are bleeding." She reached for a bottle of sparkling water and drank.

Clarkson ate a cookie, and passed the pack to Douglas.

"You know, I just realised something?" said Douglas as she took a handful of cookies from the bag.

Clarkson scowled at the fistful of white chocolate cookies, her favourite. "What?"

"I haven't seen daylight in four days."

"Neither have the poor bastards The Patriots killed."

Douglas sighed. "I know. But this isn't getting us anywhere."

"Well, that attitude certainly won't."

"I'm serious, Charlotte. What's the plan? They hit the St. Georges, they hit the police stations, then... nothing? It's been a week—check that, nine days—and even when the shit in The Pit was at its worst, they didn't trigger any Berzerkers. What are they waiting for?"

Clarkson sighed and swung her chair around. "It's gotta be Central Park. Go for the big score. Just over one million people, all psychotic, all under The Patriots' control, killing cops, killing Judges, killing each other, with the whole world watching."

"Agreed. So why *haven't* they?"

"Because they want their actions to be vindicated by the people," came a gravelly voice from behind them. Sergeant Risso stepped out into the dim light of the room. "They want to be pure and righteous. Cleansed and justified in the new world they create. They want history to judge them kindly, so they can stand in the light. That's why they haven't triggered the protestors at Central Park. That's why they didn't trigger anyone at The Pit, and why they *won't* do it now unless they're threatened." Risso looked like some ghost of war, a mug of coffee in hand. He took a sip, then: "They haven't done it, Judges, because they don't want the blame. They tricked you into building the fire, and they figure the spark'll come by itself."

Clarkson slumped back in her seat. "...Shit."

Douglas bit her lip. "They've gone to ground. That's why this isn't working."

"How do we find them, then?"

Risso laughed. "You're kidding, right? Man, you Judges got all this fancy tech"—he waved at the screens—"but you ain't got the first idea how to be a cop. You use *dogs* to hunt dogs, not computers."

"We do," Clarkson said, brightening. "And not only do we have a tracker, but one who has a scent and who's hungry for blood."

"Kurimoto!" said Douglas.

"She's festered enough. Time to set her loose."

"So, LET ME get this straight," said Kurimoto. "You want me to be a psychic... tracker?"

They sat in her apartment in Washington, far from the pressure cooker that was New York. The skies above the capital were a foreboding grey. Again, they'd used the unmarked car.

"Essentially," said Clarkson. "Do you still have a... oh, Christ... what's the terminology?"

"A *connection* to them?" Kurimoto offered. "There's no such thing as psychic jargon, you know. We don't teach courses."

Douglas giggled.

"Okay, okay," said Clarkson. "Do you have still have a connection with them? Do you feel anything? Like... I don't know... Man, I don't even know what I'm asking."

"Yeah. Yeah, there is," Kurimoto said, swallowing a mouthful of whiskey from a large tumbler. There still was anger in her eyes, festering like a disease. Her anger permeated the room like a fog.

Clarkson found herself wanting to cough.

"But it's like a scab. And you're asking me to deliberately peel it back and gouge at the wound so that it bleeds. You know that, right?"

Clarkson hesitated. She couldn't imagine what Kurimoto had endured, nor begin to grasp the violation. She understood anger, though. She understood the need for revenge. "Yes," she said. "That's exactly what we want you to do."

Kurimoto looked at the two Judges. She swallowed another mouthful of whiskey. "What do you plan to do with the psychics once you find them?" she asked.

"Taking them in would be problematic," said Douglas. "How do we guard them? How can we be sure who has or hasn't seen that damn video?"

"So we're going to kill them," said Clarkson flatly. "*All of them*. They're weapons of mass destruction and they need to be decommissioned. There's millions of American lives—who knows, potentially *billions* worldwide—on the line. Those are the stakes."

Kurimoto said nothing. Clarkson met her gaze with the same fierceness she saw in hers. Then, the big woman swallowed the contents of the glass, stood and left the room without saying a word.

"Okay, what was *that?*" asked Douglas.

"Just wait a sec," Clarkson replied. "Trust me."

She returned moments later wearing a long coat and dark boots. She smelled as if she'd drunk a bottle of mouthwash. But her eyes... her eyes were ablaze with *fury*.

"Right," she said. "Let's go and kill 'em all, then."

"Excellent," said Clarkson.

CHAPTER TWENTY-THREE
THE INFAMOUS PRELUDE

ONCE MORE THE St. Georges provided facilities for the Judges to do their work; this time at a research facility, miles outside Washington, D.C.

"Okay," said Judith. "We're just about ready. The solution we've arrived at is pretty low-tech, but it'll work. You've got your hand on a rotary axis hanging over a three-dimensional map of New York State. Use the stick to track left, right, back and forth, and the dial to zoom. Turn the dial clockwise, the view magnifies. Anti-clockwise to zoom out. What we need is a rough idea of where The Patriots are and the drones will do the rest. Don't put yourself at risk. Get in, get out and let the Judges do the rest. Understand?"

"Understood," said Kurimoto.

The two Judges watched as the FBI agent scanned the darkened room, catching the eyes of the support staff, who shrank from her gaze. Clarkson liked her more and more.

"Okay," she said finally, as a tech strapped a heart rate monitor to her arm. "Can one of you guys keep an eye on my heart rate and blood pressure? If it looks like I'm going to have a heart attack or stroke out, inject me with that sedative. It'll be doing a hard reset. Though be warned, I'll be out for a couple of hours if you use it."

"Understood," said Judith. "So, are we ready? Good. Let's begin, then."

Again, Clarkson felt like a voyeur, a peeping tom in a world of the mind.

"Hey," Douglas said, almost whispering. "I see that look on your face. I don't need to read your mind to know what you're feeling. You can't control everything."

Clarkson sighed and nodded. "You going to be okay with this?" she asked.

"I don't know," Douglas answered. There was frustration in her voice. "I don't know what's going to happen. I've never met anyone like me who's as strong as her *or* The Patriots before. I just don't know."

"Hey. Chin up. We've got this. We're going to be okay. *Okay?*"

"Okay."

An almost cathedral silence fell in the room, as if the works of God and the angels were about to take place and the simple folk were there to bear witness.

The big woman locked eyes with the two Judges, grinned and spoke. "Watashinotomodachi o shinjite kudasai. Anzen e no yokkyū wa subete no idaide kōkina kigyō ni taikō shimasu."

Then she closed her eyes.

"Any idea what she just said?" asked Clarkson.

"'Have faith, my friends. The desire for safety stands against every great and noble enterprise,'" said Douglas.

"Ah. Tacitus. I didn't know you spoke Japanese."

"My ex-wife was from Osaka."

"Wait... you were *married?*"

"...Once."

Minutes passed, and the only sound was the hum of computers. Then, without warning, Kurimoto breathed in sharply as if cut, and began moving the axis. All watched as the map position moved on a large wall-mounted flexiscreen. Overlaid were Kurimoto's heartbeat and blood pressure. The position moved erratically, shifting all over the East Coast before coming back to New York State. Clarkson look back and saw Kurimoto was in pain, tears rolling down her face.

No, not pain. Anger. She wanted this. *Please don't kill yourself,* Clarkson thought. The view shifted and fell over Manhattan Island. And stopped.

"They're in Manhattan?" Judith said.

"Wait," said Douglas.

The view shifted to Queens. "The Pit?" said Clarkson. "Surely they'd have found them when they razed the place."

"Unless they hid themselves," said Douglas. "That is a possibility."

View shift. Zoom in: New Jersey. Kurimoto's heartbeat rose.

View shift: Philadelphia.

Pull out. View shift: New Jersey. Zoom in: Wharton State Forest.

View shift: Brendan T. Byrne State Forest. The view shifted between the two forests before arriving at a midpoint between. Zoom in. Zoom in. Zoom in.

Kurimoto cried out and let go of the control, pushing herself away from the map. She panted, her face and body covered with sweat.

"Hey, hey! You okay?" Clarkson asked.

Kurimoto grinned, showing her teeth. "They're there, Judge," she said between breaths. "They're trying really hard to hide themselves, but... oh, Christ... but they're divided. Oh, God. That was tough."

"Did they... *sense* you?" Douglas asked.

"No. At least... I don't think so. But regardless, we need to roll. I get the feeling they're about ready to scatter. If that happens... well, you'll never be able to catch them in a group like this again. *Hurry.*"

CHAPTER TWENTY-FOUR
STROKE OF DEATH

THEY FOUND THE farm exactly where Kurimoto had said it would be. Abandoned in 1999, it had been tactfully renovated some time in the last ten years so as not to draw too much attention to itself. Mind games did the rest. But mind games didn't work on drones with thermal imaging and facial recognition. And they were there: forty names on a long list of psychics.

The order was given, Judges and police fresh from the siege of The Pit mounted up and prepared to storm the farmhouse. Their orders were simple: it was a killing mission. No survivors, all bodies accounted for. Especially the woman named María Santa Helena Volução. She was the primary target.

Kurimoto was assigned the title of 'FBI liaison.' She was the shield to their sword. Her *abilities* weren't discussed, but she drew looks from the squad anyway. But none of them save for Clarkson or Douglas dared look her in the eye. Clarkson had no idea whether it was a deliberate psychic inducement of fear, or if she just gave off an air of intimidation. Whichever it was, she clearly enjoyed it.

The squad dismounted half a mile from the farm and walked the rest of the way in, eventually forming a tight perimeter around the building. Nothing was getting in or out without them seeing. The drones were flying high, and virtually undetectable to the naked eye.

They waited until dark and watched as the lights in the farm came on and the smell of food and the sound of laughter came from within. Thermals told the squads the suspects were all in a communal dining room, all forty of them. There were four exits to the dining room, and the teams split to cover them all. The game plan was to move fast and hit hard, not give the psychics time to trigger anyone. Far away, snipers wearing thermal scopes watched and waited.

Douglas, Clarkson and Kurimoto were not among those rushing into the kill zone.

Clarkson hated the silence, because it gave her time to think. She asked herself whether she really relished their imminent demise. Whether she'd derive any kind of pleasure or closure from it.

No, she thought. She looked over to her partner, who shrugged.

"Me either, partner," she said.

Kurimoto stood with her arms folded and waited for the inevitable.

"Hajimaru," she said. *It begins.*

Moments later, tear-gas grenades were shot through the windows of the dining room. Screams followed soon afterwards, then gunfire. The Patriots were fighting back. As anticipated, some of the psychics came pouring out of the exits running for the cover of the woods, and were cut down before they made it halfway to the treeline, their bodies exploding with gore. Others tried to sneak out under covering fire, crawling through waist-high grass, calling on their gifts to hide themselves from the waiting shooters. Their heads exploded in clouds of blood one by one as the drone-guided snipers calmly picked them off.

Eventually, one of the squads lost the patience and threw a belt of grenades into the dining room, and the wall exploded. Some... things... that were wet and barely human landed messily on the grass and were quickly put out of their misery. The four squads entered the building. Soon afterwards, bursts of gunfire erupted from inside. Then quiet.

Wood burned and cracked. Birds screamed. An ugly stillness hung over the arena where so much carnage and death had occurred. Clarkson almost felt their horror at their own deaths, their frustrated helplessness. She looked over to her partner and Kurimoto and saw their cheeks wet with tears.

"You felt them die, didn't you?" she asked. "Both of you did."

Kurimoto nodded, while Douglas wiped her eyes. "Yeah," said Douglas. "We did."

The signal came over the radio: all clear. They walked up to the remains of the smouldering farmhouse, guns drawn. Alert. Ready.

CHAPTER TWENTY-FIVE
MONSTER ZERO

IT WASN'T THE violence that froze her blood. Nor the gore that was splattered in almost every direction. It was the violation. Only a sick mind could have derived any pleasure from what they saw when they entered the farmhouse.

A shattered dinner table, handmade out of pieces of driftwood, showed patience and love. Clarkson ran her hand along one of the legs.

About her on the floor were the remains of supper, all trodden underfoot and spoilt, mingling with the broken remains of plates, bowls and glasses.

She began to walk through the house and in every room police and Judges were hunting for evidence, intelligence, anything that would provide them with clues as to the size of The Patriots' network.

Littered on the floor were photographs, some scorched and destroyed. The surviving shots showed love, joy, happiness. The rooms felt full of life; of lovemaking and joy. Peace clung to every wall and door, soaked into the very fabric of the building.

These people were family. A family of choice. They had all come here broken and in pain, and had found belonging. Where had they run from, Clarkson wondered as she ran her hands along the walls? How had they suffered, forever alone and isolated, until they discovered that they weren't? The bodies strewn across the grass and inside the house were of all ages and genders and ethnicities. The old had tried to shelter the young, using their bodies as shields but to no avail.

A great sadness fell over her. They were terrorists, mass-murderers. But they were also human.

She came across the open door to a room, inside which lay the body of a middle-aged Latinx woman, her hair long and grey and her back peppered with exit wounds. Under her was the body of a child, no more than sixteen. Asian. Male. Clarkson moved the woman off the child and saw no exit wounds, no sign of violence. She reached for her pistol...

...then stopped.

There was a small hole in the roof on the boy's mouth, and behind his head, a larger exit wound. She laid the boy carefully on the floor and stared at his body.

He looked like he was asleep.

Clarkson shut and locked the door, sat on the bed, took off her helmet and burst into tears. Judge or not, Charlotte Kwame Nkrumah Clarkson was still human.

"Clarkson," came a voice over wrist-video. "Where you at, partner?"

"I'm in the house. I'll be right out."

"Take your time; the dead ain't going nowhere. Okay?"

"Yeah. Roger that." Clarkson killed the connection.

She sat there in the dark, with the dead and her sadness as company, and looked at her hands. No blood, but her hands were plenty bloody.

Eventually, she roused herself. She pulled her gloves on and prepared to leave... but found herself staring at the two bodies. "No," she said. And she laid the two out side by side and put the woman's hand in the boy's. She looked at the two for a moment, nodded, then quietly left the room.

As she walked into the night, she felt lessened by what they had done here. *Dirty*. This was not how it was supposed to be. Was it?

It was quiet outside.

Too quiet.

"Where is everyone?" she said as she tapped her wrist screen. "Douglas? Where—?"

"Gone. Everyone's gone," came the reply.

She froze. "Where are you?" she asked.

"Far side of the house. Kurimoto's with me. We're tooled up and ready."

"I'm on my way." She drew her pistol and started running.

"WHAT HAPPENED?" CLARKSON asked.

"Suddenly couldn't raise a soul on the radio. Cops or Judges. Then felt something in here." Douglas touched her temple.

"I felt it too," said Kaoru. "Like someone trying to turn on a light in a room with no bulb."

"Oh, Christ. Someone got out, didn't they? They've all been activated," said Clarkson.

Douglas nodded. "Any that haven't were probably overwhelmed and killed."

"Who, though?"

"While you were gone, we did an ID check on all the bodies. Facial recognition. Finger prints. Spectral teeth scans. Thirty-nine confirmed in total. All names on the list."

"All save one."

"Monster Zero," Kurimoto spat. "Psychic bitch from hell."

"You called it in?" Clarkson asked.

"Yeah. Message was: 'Terminate suspect. All other considerations are secondary,'" said Douglas. "We're on our own."

"Of course we are. Can't risk sending more people in, can we?" Kurimoto said, following it with a long string of curses in Japanese to which Douglas replied in kind.

"We have an advantage, though," Kaoru said. "Two psychics against one. Two people who haven't watched the video. One who's been deprogramed."

"I think, between the two of us, we can... maybe... run interference?" said Douglas.

"All right. Here's the plan. We track down Helena. Take her out and she loses control of the horde, then we all go home," said Clarkson.

"And if any of the puppets try to stop us?" Kaoru asked.

"Then you defend yourself," Douglas replied. She checked her pistol for ammo, as did the other two. "Ready?" she said.

"Ready," said Clarkson.

"Ready," said Kurimoto.

The three women walked in a staggered line into the wood, knowing they might not walk out alive.

THE BRANCHES WHIPPED at them as they made their way through the dense foliage, their wrist screens telling them a massive crowd had assembled just short of a mile ahead of them. Approaching with stealth was impossible through the branches and leaf mould.

Douglas stopped when she saw a sniper rifle on the floor. "Loaded," she said.

"Any good with that?" Kurimoto asked.

Douglas replied with a smile. They moved on slowly, the wood conspired against them.

When the horde was within sight, they stopped. They stood like statues, unmoving, faces raised to the moon. They could not see Helena through the throng, but all three knew she was there.

"Okay," Clarkson said slowly. "You think if you climb up onto one of these trees you'll be able to get a clear shot?"

Douglas looked up. "Hmmm. Fifty-fifty, but you could make it easier for me."

"I plan to. Right. You two do what you can to—I don't

know—stop me from getting torn apart and I'll get you that shot."

"Wait!" Kurimoto said. "Where the hell are you...? Oh."

"Yeah," Clarkson said. "Time to meet the devil."

CHAPTER TWENTY-SIX
THE GREATEST TRICK THE DEVIL EVER PULLED

"HELLO," CLARKSON SAID to the horde as she approached. Not that she expected a reply.

They stood in the dim light, males and females, all grey, their faces flat and expressionless. Identities crushed by the ringleader using their bodies as a shield. Clarkson stopped dead when she saw that they had all wet themselves. The horror at not being in control of their bodies... the knowledge of what they might yet be willed to do....

Oh, you've got to go. she thought, not caring whether her thoughts were being read. *You've got to go.*

"I know you're in here, Helena. Show yourself. You owe me that much."

"And what did you expect, sister?" said a voice. It came from behind her. From somewhere in the crowd of police officers. *Is she using them as proxies?* "Tell me. I'm genuinely interested." *Is she here? Where?*

"A trap," she said.

"Nothing of the sort," came the voice, now to the side of her. "I think you should know I've been watching you for some time. Your almost evangelical embrace of the Judges' credo of state-sanctioned fascism is breathtaking. Tell me: when was it that you decided that the rule of law was more important than personal freedom and due process? At what point did you reason that security was more important than—?"

Clarkson laughed, suddenly, surprising even herself. She laughed at the self-righteousness of the terrorist, at her ridiculousness, at her earnestness, reciting talking points like a student activist.

"Yes, laugh, traitor to democracy," Helena said. "An executioner must be able to laugh as they do their work. They must have no conscience, or the cynicism to laugh at those with purpose."

"So tell me, *terrorist...*" Clarkson spat.

No response.

Okay, then, go *deeper.* "How are you able to reconcile your faith in democracy with your utter lack of faith in its execution? The people voted for us, and keep voting for us."

The whole horde swayed slightly, then, and Clarkson cringed at the power this woman held over them.

"We'll show them the reality of your existence," Helena hissed, "of what you will mean for this country if you're not stopped. The people are weak. They're scared; they trade freedom for safety. They'll see they've made a grievous error in abandoning their hard-fought-for—"

"Jesus H. Christ, woman, can you *hear* yourself?" Clarkson said, rolling her eyes. "You're waxing lyrical about the power of the people and their unalienable rights, yet you rob them of their will when it suits your purposes. You use your videos to turn them into puppets and throw them into a wall of bullets. You've even enslaved the officers here who—"

"Fascists and murderers," Helena said.

Clarkson didn't rise to the bait. "And you expect to be *absolved* somehow, of your mayhem and violence, because you did it to save *democracy?* How fucking *dare* you be so—?"

"*You know nothing!*" Helena roared, and Clarkson almost thought she could make her out in the crowd.

Got you, thought Clarkson. She restrained herself from smiling.

"I won't be lectured by a goose-stepping, brainwashed—"

"Goose-stepping? Mother of God, are you *blind?* Did you think we sprung spontaneously into existence? The creaking, choking inflexibility of the judicial system and the inability of the police to effect—"

"And what next, Judge? How long before being Mexican, being African American is reason enough—?"

"Woah! Let me stop you right there," said Clarkson.

Neither spoke for several moments. Clarkson was still scanning the crowd, looking for movement, trying to spot the woman hiding in their midst.

"'It is not only the slave or serf who is ameliorated in becoming free; the master himself did not gain less in every point of view, for absolute power corrupts the best natures,'" Helena finally said.

"Alphonse Marie Louis de Prat de Lamartine," Clarkson said with a sigh.

Again, that slight movement through the whole crowd, as though Helena's control slipped when she was surprised.

"Which is bullshit, of course," Clarkson continued.

"Oh, really? Give me one example of a benevolent dictator."

"Nerva, Trajan. Hadrian, Antoninus Pius. Marcus Aurelius."

A sigh. "What did the Roman Empire's expansion cost, in human lives? How many slaves died never knowing freedom? How many peoples vanished, their histories and cultures trodden into the dirt beneath Roman caligae? Really, Judge. The Roman Empire... *that's* your best example?"

"Theirs was no better or worse than American foreign policy."

"On this we can agree."

"But there is no justification for what you've done."

"Fascism intimidates the good into silence, and emboldens the corrupt. Terror is the only tool the downtrodden *have*. You sound like you're well read, Judge. Tell me I'm lying: is not history an endless ledger of slaughter and genocide?"

"Can't you understand that civilisation is a work in progress?" Clarkson said. "What would you replace it with? *Anarchy*?"

"Don't patronise me."

"That was not my intension. I apologise."

"Aren't you scared?" the psychic asked. "As to what this country will become, when the courts close and police are retired and justice lies entirely in your hands? Aren't you afraid to be God?"

The question gave Clarkson pause. "No," she said confidently. "I'd rather see justice dispensed immediately by trained, unbiased experts than the old broken system. The law was no longer blind, it belonged to the rich and connected. It was no longer an equaliser. But it can be once again. It *will* be. And if a few squandered freedoms are curtailed to bring that about, then... that's a price worth paying. There's always been a trade-off between safety and security. And people are always afraid to make that trade. And yet here we are. Manifest and clothed in terrible power. *Fear us*."

"*Sister*. You're wrong. Power in the hands of an elite always leads to corruption. You are the foundation; your descendants will wield power in its most brutal form. You will become the thing you hate." Helena trailed off and fell silent.

"As *you* have? Tell me, how many innocents have died in your thrall? Their wills confiscated by your power. Their lives thrown away, worthless, disposable. All because you're too much of a coward to martyr yourself? Because you hold your lives in higher regard than theirs? Is that the lesson you learnt on the streets of South Shaolin? Is that what you took from the words of Ernesto Fukuyama? Did his words motivate you to become a monster, or were you always a wolf in sheep's clothing, just looking for an excuse? Tell me, please tell, because I *really need to know* how *any* of this madness is *at all* justifiable? Please, explain to me how the mountains of dead, yours and mine, are in *any* way a price worth paying for democracy. What has it been for, but the petty, vicious revenge of the children of the Midwich project?"

No reply, though she saw Helena's shock as they stirred again. Helena had known, then. Known who and what she was, and where she came from.

"Yes, Helena. I've seen where you come from," said Clarkson. "Seen how you lived. Met your people. You grew up in a grave that you had to claw your way out of. Looking at you now, I wonder how much of yourself you left back there. And all those pieces of shit up there, the ones whose parents paid to have their asses wiped, all of them looking down their noses at you? Yeah, I understand your anger, and I sympathise. But you don't change the world with horror. You've become a *monster*."

Again silence. For a moment, Clarkson swore she had the woman doubting herself.

Only for a moment.

"No."

Clarkson drew her pistol and readied herself for the enviable.

"You think of us as monsters?" the voice asked.

One o'clock, Clarkson thought, narrowing her eyes.

"Is that why you slaughtered my family with such indifference?"

"With no more indifference than you showed the police and Judges—and civilians—who died in the slaughter houses you created. Consider it repayment in kind," Clarkson spat.

She heard a sound like a growl. Something raw and primal.

Then, like a buoy at sea, crashed upon by the relentless waves, Clarkson was being buffeted by the suddenly living crowd.

They weren't attacking, yet, but they were thrashing around, as though in pain. Hate, anger, grief, rage, despair, frustration... all showed raw and fresh on their faces. She tried to go back the way she came, pushing through the heaving bodies, but her legs were suddenly like jelly and her head spun. She tried to concentrate, and suddenly felt a hand on the back of her neck.

I see your thoughts, Judge, Helena screamed in her mind. *I see your petty admiration for this gift. Is this what you seek, Judge? Power without consequence?*

Clarkson screamed and fell to the floor.

Is this what you yearn for? This dark gift?

You think me a monster? You think us beastly? Very well. Evil shall become my good. I will make monsters out of you all, and when I am done you will never again be able to call yourselves women or men.

You have taken my family. I shall take yours.

Witness Hell!

Like a wave of human dominoes, the crowd collapsed, crumbling like puppets with their strings cut.

Clarkson opened her eyes. The pain and disorientation had vanished as quickly as it had arrived. She caught her breath and tore her helmet off, throwing it out the ground; she screamed with frustration. Screamed at her own weakness. By the time Douglas and Kurimoto arrived, all three of them knew the obvious.

Helena had already fled.

"Are they still alive?" Clarkson asked as she sat among a sea of unconscious bodies, the quiet carnage of an invisible battlefield. Then they caught the acrid smell of vacated bowels and emptied bladders, a final indignity for the woman's victims.

"They're not dead," said Kurimoto. "I mean... physically. I can't speak for their minds. God knows what the psycho bitch did to them."

"And I fear she's going to do a lot worse," said Douglas.

"I dread to ask but, define 'worse,'" said Clarkson, putting her helmet back on and collecting her pistol.

"Call everyone. Warn everyone. Helena's heading back to New York City. No one's safe."

"Oh, God. Please tell me she's not going to do what I think she's going to do." Kurimoto whispered with horror.

"She's gonna activate everyone she can," said Clarkson. "All she wants to do now is make everyone feel her pain. Any pretensions of political motivation have *evaporated*. She wants a bloodbath. We can't give that to her."

"She told you that?"

"Didn't have to. I've taken away her family, she said. She's gonna take away mine..."

CHAPTER TWENTY-SEVEN
THE PATH OF DESTRUCTION

SHE SPED THROUGH the darkness, a thing of hate and inconsolable rage. Her destination and end were fixed. She was going to die; she'd accepted it. She'd known it the moment she'd committed herself to this path.

Did she genuinely ever believe they'd win? That they'd be able to turn it all around and give back America to its people? That they would have even been *grateful?*

"Yes," she answered. The dream wasn't inconceivable. No more so than the freedoms fought for and won. Maybe it just wasn't their time. Maybe they weren't the ones who would light the fire. The torch would be passed to others; to a new generation. One for whom the words 'freedom' and 'democracy' were not empty words found in a book.

But not us, she lamented. *Not us.*

She remembered Ernesto's words. *There is no greater horror than when a generation is forced to fight and die, to protect the hard-fought-for freedoms their ancestors took for granted.*

A rage seized her. None of them—her fam back in Shaolin, fat and gross and sat in front of their TVs watching the world burn in 12k crystal definition; the Judges; the police, none of them, *no one*—was prepared to halt the coming of fascism. Indeed, they welcomed it. Either by deed or consent they'd willed the Judges into existence. Like a cancer returning from remission, the idea of fascism was always lurking, a genetic disease locked in every strand of DNA, waiting for an opportunity, a moment of weakness in the collective conscious. Weakness, indifference and intolerance were its allies.

And fear, most especially fear.

They didn't deserve their sacrifice. They themselves were unprepared to fight for what they'd given away freely. They were terrified to make the sacrifice for it, because they knew the price. All of them, locked in prisons of comfort and safe conformity, with the anonymity of the internet being the only safe place for them to dare show any form of courage. But courage without risk was nothing.

She imagined the city ablaze, its citizens seized by bloodlust. Its streets awash with blood and entrails, its sky blackened and filled with screams.

It did not give her satisfaction.

That was not justice.

Is this to be our legacy, then? she thought. *A bloodbath? Mass murder? Is this what we have become? Is this truly what we stood for?*

The fire that burned in her chest dulled and Helena pulled the motorcycle over to the side of the road, riding into the thick grass and into the woods. She took off her crash helmet and looked into the night sky, a thousand stars looking back at her with casual indifference. She realised that if the world were to spontaneously combust and every living thing were incinerated, no God would weep or mourn their passing.

Is this what we stood for? How I wish us to be remembered? Have the dead made a scaffold of their bodies just to burn Rome to the ground?

"Am I become Nero?" Helena asked the sea of stars. "Or worse, Frankenstein's hateful son? Shall I delight in pain and mayhem? Is that what they all died for?

"Am *I* a monster, Ernesto?"

No answer came. Only stillness. As if the world had gifted

her a brief pause, a moment to reconsider before continuing on the path of destruction.

If she were to race into the city and do as she planned—to turn it into the human abattoir—then everything she believed was false, and they had all died for nothing.

And no one would know the love they shared or the names of the dead. The kindness and safety they enjoyed. The small peace they enjoyed. Their memories would be lost. Swallowed by an orgy of violence which now served no purpose.

An emptiness filled her at that moment, and she felt as if she were the only woman—the only human being—alive in the world.

"No," she whispered as tears rolled down her face. "I *cannot* do this. I *must* not do this. I must bear witness to truth. Become the speaker for the dead. We weren't monsters. I am not a monster."

CHAPTER TWENTY-EIGHT
EL DIABLO ELLA DESAPARECIÓ

THEY FOUND THE motorcycle two days later. A crash helmet was hanging from its handlebars.

As a sea of drones danced overhead, a nationwide hunt begun. Every arena of intelligence and law enforcement was mobilised. Extra security was placed at all air and sea ports. The Coast Guard patrolled the shorelines, while the Air Force flew overhead. Not since 9/11 had America so viscerally felt the presence of its military might.

And New York City waited to be engulfed by a tidal wave of violence.

AND THEN THE city breathed again. The travel restrictions were lifted again, the schools opened again, the trash collectors returned to their jobs. Judges and community leaders met and talked about the future, and accords were struck. An unsteady truce returned to the streets, and all—without a shot fired—the protests in Central Park gradually evaporated as the emergency had passed.

New York had changed. The people hadn't surrendered, quite, and the Judges hadn't won, quite, but their reality was becoming accepted, in a way it hadn't been in fourteen years. It was a brave new world.

AND, FOR ALL the show of force, and much to the chagrin of all, after two months not a single shred of evidence as to the whereabouts of María Santa Helena Volução had been found.

The most dangerous woman on Earth had vanished.

Then, almost three months to that day after the terrorist group know as The Patriots had been neutralised, a letter was handed in at 84th Precinct.

It was addressed to Judge Clarkson.

Dearest Judge Charlotte Clarkson,

You've won. Congratulations. I'll not waste time lecturing you because... what is the point? You are as committed to your cause as I am to mine. I hope the world you seek to bring into being is as fair and equal as you imagine it. And that your initiative is truly as fair and impartial as it proclaims itself to be. The tendency towards corruption in systems where power resides in the hands of the few is a matter of historical fact, as you well know. Revolutionary action is the only tool that can cleanse society. I won't bother to preach to you about the morality of such actions, nor try to defend them, because history cares little for attempts, only results and change.

I've come to realise that we made a mistake. One that cost the lives of almost all my family. The People's indifference to the investiture of judicial power in your person—indeed, their enthusiasm for it—should have been a warning. They don't care. They're not interested. They wanted a result and you were it. They were never interested in freedom, only the illusion of it. True freedom is a terrifying thing. A dangerous thing.

Goodbye, Charlotte. Back in the closet goes your gun. Such a pity; you used it so well and subtly that I doubt you're even aware of it. But then sometimes a badge and gun make a good substitute for a closet. You've won. I hope you make the world a better and safer place.

For a time.

—The Patriots

CHAPTER TWENTY-NINE
IT AIN'T HARD TO TELL

THE FRONT DOOR opened immediately after she knocked, as if she already knew who stood there.

"Clarkson," said Douglas. Her partner wore a loose t-shirt and faded tracksuit bottoms. Her forehead was covered in beads of sweat and a towel was slung over her shoulder.

Douglas appreciated her loyalty, now more than ever. Her *friendship*, though... that was an honour.

"Partner," said Douglas. Clarkson smiled and invited her in.

Her apartment was Spartan: sofa, coffee table, wooden dining table, four chairs. A kitchenette entirely absent of utensils or cooking appliances. Her walls and floors were entirely bare, and smelled of antiseptic and bleach. On first inspection, you would be forgiven for believing that the flat held no tenant at all, but for one thing:

Books.

In every corner and along every corridor were bookcases, ceiling-high, filled with books. Novels of all genres; philosophy, science; history, autobiographies, politics; art, art theory, art history and criticism. Pride of place in her living room were three bookcases filled with books on law: huge, weighty tomes that looked worn and old, as if they'd been handed down and reread over and over.

"My father was a criminal lawyer," Clarkson said, answering the unasked question. "My mother, too. Grandparents on both sides. Both of my sisters and two brothers are all lawyers."

"So, what are you, the black sheep of the family?"

Clarkson smiled, but there was a nervousness behind it. "You could say that. Please, sit."

Douglas removed her helmet, showing a face awash with ginger freckles with short red hair and hazel eyes. She was about to place it on the coffee table—Clarkson's gleaming, polished coffee table—when she caught the look in her eye. "Ah," she said, and placed it instead on the sofa next to her. Clarkson nodded with approval.

"A drink?" Clarkson offered.

"Tea?" Douglas asked. "Herbal, of course."

Her partner smiled. "Sure."

Moments later, Clarkson returned with two cups of tea. She fussed with coasters before setting them down, which amused Douglas. She wanted everything to be right. No, she wanted to be in full control of her environment.

The two sat side by side and drank in silence. Douglas preferred it; the silence. Her gift, in such a loud city, could be taxing. Sitting here, with a person of such clear thoughts... she appreciated her more than words could express.

"They're scaling back the emergency," she said. "Three months with no leads. New York wants to heal."

Clarkson nodded. "I'm not surprised. It wants to forget. To rebuild. And the drones will be going too, right?"

"Yep. The entire fleet's gonna be recalled on Sunday morning. Clear skies from Monday morning onwards."

"Crime rates'll shoot back up."

"Yep. Honeymoon's over. Back to asskicking and gunslinging." Douglas brightened. "Oh, yeah, remember Kurimoto?"

"Oh, yeah. I was wondering about her. What about her?"

"She's been accepted into the Programme."

Clarkson blinked. "Oh, shit! *Really?*"

Douglas nodded with enthusiasm. "Oh, yeah. Fast-tracked application to the DC academy. On the recommendation of Fargo's office, apparently. Earmarked for some hush-hush team led by Judge Earl Stone."

"Stone? Old white guy? Wasn't he killed in, like, Wyoming, a few years ago?"

"Apparently not."

"So why hush-hush? Think they're looking to use her gift?"

Douglas placed the cup back on the table. "I figure," she said. "She's already asked for a copy of the Midwich list."

"A special team of secret psychic Judges is a pretty scary idea. Do you know what they've done with Councillor Monage? Does *anyone?*"

Douglas opened her mouth to respond, but words failed her.

"What about you? Do they know about you too?"

Douglas shrugged. "If they don't, Kuritomo's gonna tell 'em." She sighed and picked up her cup again. "I hear DC's nice, except for the bugs."

"She's still out there," Clarkson said.

"I know. We'll find her. Believe that," said Douglas.

Clarkson nodded and the two drank in silence, each waiting for the other to speak their piece. Outside, a motorcycle started up and drove into the night.

"Niamh," said Clarkson hesitantly. "I... I shouldn't have left you. Back at the station house. When we were looking for the trigger man. I shouldn't have left you in that corridor. I *still* feel guilty about it. I shouldn't have done it. I'd never have forgiven myself—"

"Hey!"

"—if something had happened to you—"

"Hey, hey, hey. Stop that!"

"And it would have been my fault if—"

"Stop it. Stop it *now,*" Douglas said, setting her cup down and taking Clarkson's hands in hers. "Charlotte. Look at me."

She did.

"I *asked* you to leave me there because I knew that I was

safe. Because I knew the danger was far away and the safety was close. It wasn't self-sacrifice, it was tactical. Understand?"

Clarkson nodded. "You sure it's okay?"

"Hey, would I lie to you, baby?" said Douglas.

"Hope not," Clarkson whispered.

"Nah. You'd see through my bullshit *immediately*. Wouldn't be worth the effort."

"Okay."

Douglas sensed there was more. Something else. Another, more pointed revelation. Her fear was still there. Clarkson *radiated* it. Which was unusual for her. Something had cut her deeply and she was terrified to give her fear a name.

"Partner, what the hell did that psychic bitch write in the letter that got you scared shitless? What did she say?" Douglas waited for Clarkson to find the right words, but nothing seemed to fit. Clarkson opened her mouth and stared at her for a moment before speaking.

"She said... what she said was... 'Back in the closet goes your gun. Such a pity; you use it so well.'"

"Charlotte...," Douglas said, smiling. "I mean, shit. That statement underlines her whole attitude to her *gift*. But—" She stopped when she saw Clarkson's look of confusion. "You can put your gun away, Charlotte. You're not a tool, you're a human being, a servant of justice."

Clarkson ran her hands through her short cut hair and looked up at the ceiling as if truth would descend from heaven, brought by angels.

Tears ran down her cheeks.

"What do you want to tell me?" said Douglas, almost pleading. "What do...? Oh. Oh, my God. Your gun is... you mean you're... you're like *me?*"

"I've... I've always been able to... I can *feel* your surprise," said Clarkson. "Your surprise, your joy, and... and..."

Douglas covered her mouth. "Empathy," she said.

"What?"

"Empathy! You can feel others' emotions. You're an *empath*.

Oh, my God! That explains a lot. Wow. *Wow!* I'm the stupidest woman on Earth. I should have seen it. Man, I'm dumb!"

"Well, you are *pretty* dumb, Niamh," Clarkson said through the tears.

Douglas laughed.

"I mean, shit, maybe I should have worn a sign."

"Well, that would have helped," said Douglas. She wrapped her arms around Clarkson and held her tight. Kissing her lightly on her head, she said in her mind, *Sister, you are not alone*. Over and over, like a mantra, her words were soothing and warm and wiping away her fear. Clarkson wept on Douglas's shoulder, their arms wrapped around one another, now more than partners and more than friends.

Her words became a hymn; glorious, uplifting, Godly.

Sister, you are not alone. Sister, you are not alone. Sister, you are not alone.

ABOUT THE AUTHOR

Joseph Elliott-Coleman has been writing and telling stories since he was a child, with science fiction being his wheelhouse. Enduring and overcoming countless barriers, his work first saw print in the *Not So Stories* anthology. He lives in Croydon, London.

THE FALL OF DEADWORLD
RED MOSQUITO
SPECIAL LIMITED EDITION
MATTHEW SMITH